Alexandra Potter was born and brought up in Yorkshire. She spent time in Los Angeles and Sydney after university but now lives in London with her boyfriend Pete. She freelanced for various women's magazines, until one day she decided to sit down and write that book she was always going on about. The film rights to her first novel, *What's New, Pussycat?* have been sold, and the follow-up, *Going La La* was published in 2001. *Calling Romeo* is her third novel.

CALLING ROMEO

Alexandra Potter

BLACK SWAN

CALLING ROMEO
A BLACK SWAN BOOK : 0 552 77003 5

First publication in Great Britain

PRINTING HISTORY
Black Swan edition published 2002

3 5 7 9 10 8 6 4

Set in 11/12pt Melior by
Kestrel Data, Exeter, Devon.

Black Swan Books are published by Transworld Publishers,
61–63 Uxbridge Road, London W5 5SA,
a division of The Random House Group Ltd,
in Australia by Random House Australia (Pty) Ltd,
20 Alfred Street, Milsons Point, Sydney, NSW 2061, Australia,
in New Zealand by Random House New Zealand Ltd,
18 Poland Road, Glenfield, Auckland 10, New Zealand
and in South Africa by Random House (Pty) Ltd,
Endulini, 5a Jubilee Road, Parktown 2193, South Africa.

Printed and bound in Great Britain by
Cox & Wyman Ltd, Reading, Berkshire

For my wonderful mum and dad
With lots of love on your ruby wedding anniversary

Acknowledgements

First of all I'd like to say a huge thank you to everyone at Transworld for making me feel so welcome, especially my fantastic editor Diana Beaumont who not only believed this was going to be a great novel, but by pushing and encouraging me, helped make it even better, and to my equally fantastic agent Stephanie Cabot for her constant support and enthusiasm (not to mention all those vodka tonics) when the going got tough – next time the drinks are on me.

As always, I also want to thank my parents for providing me with the perfect writers' retreat deep in the Yorkshire Dales (not to mention all those cups of tea and homemade meals), my sister Kelly for all those transatlantic phonecalls and my best friend and fellow scribe Kate Mulvey for our walks, conversations, and for always understanding. Thanks also to Georgie for letting me pick her brains about the world of advertising, Dave for lending me his flat to write in, and Katie, Melissa and Lynnette for all their help and advice.

Finally, there's one person I can't thank enough, and that's my beloved Pete. Thanks for whisking me off to Verona, disappearing to Zanzibar so I could finish this novel and, last but not least, for being my Romeo.

Chapter One

How would you feel if you were stood up? Embarrassed? Upset? Pissed off?

Juliet was all three. Sitting conspicuously by herself at a table for two in a fashionable bar-cum-restaurant in Soho, she glanced self-consciously at her watch – nearly 7.30 – and tried to ignore the pitying glances of the cosy couples around her. She was going to kill Will. Being stood up was bad enough, but *by her boyfriend*.

She'd been waiting for over half an hour, which didn't seem like a long time when she was curled up at home on the sofa watching *Sex and the City* – one minute it was the opening credits and Sarah Jessica Parker was stumbling around in a tutu, the next it was all over and the commercials were on – but it was a completely different storyline when she was marooned in the West End in a brand new pair of killer heels and a dress that should read 'do not wear unaccompanied' next to the dry-clean-only instructions. The outfit was meant to get Will's attention, not that of the minicab driver, the workmen on the corner with their hard hats and hard-ons, and the suited cityboys at the bar.

Draining the lukewarm dregs of her 'house speciality' cocktail she toyed with the idea of another round. She'd already finished off the complimentary olives – and she didn't even *like* olives, nasty bitter bloody things – read the *Evening Standard* from cover to cover, including the boring pink bit that came in the middle, and sent text messages to everyone she could think of on her mobile. Now it was make her mind up time. Should she order another drink and give Will ten more minutes? Or go home, put a bunny on the boil and lie in wait for him with a bread knife?

Juliet stabbed her last remaining ice cube with her straw. Feeling as she did right at that moment, she was sorely tempted to go for the bunny option. But instead she did what every female does in times of emotional crisis. She called her best friend.

The answering machine picked up immediately. 'Hi, you've reached Trudy Bernstein designs . . .' Email, fax and mobile numbers followed, plus an entire electronically piped verse of Chaka Khan's 'I'm Every Woman' that seemed to go on for ever. Finally there was the beep to record. 'It's me, pick up the phone,' hissed Juliet.

She knew Trudy was at home screening her calls. She'd been doing nothing else since she'd met her new fling, Fergus, three weeks ago. Not that she was trying to avoid him: on the contrary, she was desperate to see him. But she didn't want *him* to know that. A firm believer in playing hard to get, Trudy wanted Fergus to think she was a cool, independent woman with a hectic social life, not a mass of insecurities who stayed in every night, glued to the phone like an elastoplast waiting for his call.

Trying to hide from the inquisitive stares of the other diners, Juliet pressed her mobile to her mouth, hunched her shoulders and sank like the *Titanic* into the depths of her coat. And tried again: 'Trudy, this is really important . . .' Her pleading voice wavered as she locked eyes with the alarmingly hirsute waiter leaning against the bar. Juliet winced – she could smell his Kouros aftershave from where she was sitting – and dived back under her sheepskin collars. 'For Godsakes Trudy, I know you're there . . .'

'How do you know?' A sudden voice gasped indignantly. 'I could be at some wild party, taking shitloads of drugs, drinking endless supplies of champagne, being chatted up by dozens of fabulous men . . .'

Hearing Trudy's unmistakable New York accent – Woody Allen with a twist of *Rhoda*'s Brenda – Juliet felt her panic being swallowed up by immense relief. In fact she didn't think she'd ever been so relieved to listen to one of Trudy's neurotic monologues. 'But you're not at some party,' she interrupted.

She was cut down.

'Gee, thanks a lot. Is there really any need to hammer home the abysmal reality that I'm alone, I'm wearing sweatpants, and the only drugs in my possession are junior-fucking-aspirin?'

Trudy stopped, suddenly aware of silence on the other end of the line. 'Jules? Are you still there?'

'I'm not sure. Is it safe?'

There was a sigh. Trudy's temper evaporated as quickly as it had ignited. 'Oh gawd, I'm sorry, Jules. What's up? Don't tell me you've had another row with Will.'

'Not yet.'

'I thought he was taking you out for dinner.'

'So did I.'

A pause, and then a yelp as the penny dropped. '*You cannot be serious!*' Trudy could do a pretty good impersonation of McEnroe *circa* Wimbledon 1981 when she wanted to.

'Do you hear me laughing?'

'Where are you now?'

'At the restaurant.'

'*Ohmygawd*. You're there by *yourself*?'

Juliet didn't answer. She was beginning to regret the phone call. The idea was supposed to be that Trudy would make her feel better, not even worse.

'Where the hell is Will?'

'I don't know.'

There was another '*Ohmygawd*,' as oblivious to her discomfort, Trudy continued. 'What's the matter with him these days? He's acting like such an asshole. I thought tonight was supposed to be a big deal. For Christsakes you've been looking forward to it for weeks . . .'

'Months,' corrected Juliet. 'In fact, make that six months. Ever since Will started up his bloody landscape gardening business we haven't had a night out.' She fingered the hem of the dress she'd bought especially for tonight, a luscious raspberry red swathe of silk embroidered with tiny flowers that emphasized all the right bits, and tried not to think of the price tag. 'Unless of course you count the movies.'

'What? Sitting in the pitch black, not speaking for two hours,' scoffed Trudy. 'I'd hardly call that going out.'

'Will does.'

'Need I say more . . .'

Noticing the silence on the other end of the line it dawned on Trudy that no, she didn't need to say any more. In fact she'd said quite enough. As a dutiful friend she shouldn't be bitching about Will, however tempting it might be, knowing all the effort Juliet had gone to for tonight – maxing-out her credit card in Bond Street on an outfit to wear, spending her lunch hour freewheeling around Boots, a further two hours after work at the gym, *not to mention* the time spent in the changing room doing a makeover Laurence Llewelyn-Bowen would be proud of. No, she should be offering reassurance, comfort, *support in times of crisis* and ignoring the fact that she wanted nothing more than to kick Will's ass.

She made a swift U-turn. 'Look, I'm sure he'll be turning up any second now with his tail between those goddamn skinny legs of his,' She forced a laugh. Canned laughter would have been more realistic. 'What time are you supposed to be meeting?'

'Seven o'clock.'

'It's half past.'

'I know,' muttered Juliet miserably. Casting another hopeful glance at the door, she caught the eye of the hirsute waiter. Picking his teeth with a cocktail stick he was staring right at what little cleavage she'd managed to create with her bought-specially-for-tonight plunge bra from the Salon Rose range at M&S. Cursing Will for the hundredth time that evening she wrapped her coat protectively around her chest like a bullet-proof vest.

'Have you called him?' Trudy was doing her best at trying to be helpful – not one of her strongest points – and had resorted to asking the obvious.

'His phone's on voicemail.'

'Did you leave a message?'

'Does shouting "*you bastard*" down the phone count?'

Trudy laughed grimly. 'In that case he's definitely *got* the message. So what are you going to do?'

'I'm supposed to ask you that.'

Trudy knew what *she'd* do, but then that probably explained why all her relationships (note plural) had failed and Juliet's relationship (note singular) hadn't. Well, not yet. She tried to adopt a mature sitting-on-the-fence attitude. 'There's got to be a perfectly good reason why he's late . . .' She paused, trying to think of something feasible. A head-on collision? Pulmonary embolism? Her *ER* fuelled imagination went into overdrive, before she remembered that even though Juliet was pissed off with Will, suggesting that he could be on the critical list in A&E might not count as a good reason. 'I think you should give him another fifteen minutes . . .'

'And then what?'

'Come over to my place. I'll order takeout from Chopstix on the corner.' Comfort eating was Trudy's answer to everything. 'They do an awesome chow mein.'

'I can't wait.' Juliet knew she should at least sound more grateful, but she'd been looking forward to a romantic evening, eating deliciously expensive food from large white plates and getting slowly drunk on champagne. Sitting in Trudy's draughty Hampstead flat, picking at soggy spring rolls and sweet'n'sour pork from a tinfoil tray, while drinking a choice of flat Diet Coke or black 'cawfee' wasn't much of a consolation.

Promising to call Trudy back, she hung up and beckoned the waiter. Sinking into a pit of depression she ordered another drink. After all, it was supposed to be *happy hour*. She looked at her watch.

Will had fifteen minutes to go.

And counting . . .

Squashing a teabag against the side of his chipped mug, Will squeezed out the last few drops before dropping it, still stuck to the teaspoon, into the sink. It sank without a trace into the washing-up water that had gone cold, its bubbles long since dissolved by the greasy vindaloo ring that clung around the edges of the white porcelain butler sink. It was his turn to do the dishes, but as usual he'd left it until every utensil in the flat had been used – even the gravy boat that his mum gave him had found a use as a soup bowl – and now he couldn't face it. He'd just got in from work. He was knackered. He'd do it later.

Kicking off his mud-caked boots and sprinkling dried clods of dirt all over the kitchen floor he picked up his mug and padded into the living room, snagging his sock again on the nail that needed hammering down on one of the floorboards. Ignoring it, he flopped on the sofa and stretched out happily. Juliet was always nagging him to get changed out of his work gear, especially since they'd just splurged on a new velvet three-seater from Habitat, but what she didn't see she wouldn't know.

Will wasn't used to being home alone. Arriving back at the flat a few moments ago, he'd been surprised to discover it empty. Since setting up Dig It Designs he worked late most nights and Juliet was at home when he walked through the front door; there would be an aroma of cooking, the sound of the TV blaring from the living room. But tonight there was nothing but silent darkness. He must have forgotten she was working late, he thought, feeling around the edges of the cushions for the remote control. Or maybe she'd gone to Trudy's. Still, having the flat to himself for a bit wasn't such a bad thing, he mused, digging the remote out from underneath him.

Will flicked on the telly. Pretty boring as usual, just the usual soaps and a holiday programme. Oh hang on, what was that? *Top Gear*? Aside from architecture, Will's passion was cars, especially sportscars, and he could see Jeremy Clarkson filling the screen in his SwapShop jumper. Test-driving a canary yellow convertible, the presenter was blasting through the British countryside with the roof down, his droning voice barely audible above the roar of the 16-valve engine. Chuffed at his discovery, Will grinned to himself and, sipping his tea, lay back against the cushions.

He must have fallen asleep because the next thing he knew he'd woken up with a start.

What the?

Will wiped a gloop of spit that was trickling out of the side of his mouth. What time was it? Groggy with sleep he sat up, spilling the tea which had been balanced on his lap. *Shit.* Frantically rubbing the velvet cushions with the sleeve of his jumper, he tried to mop up the cold PG Tips before it stained for ever. *Shit, Shit, Shit.*

The flat was in darkness, apart from the glow from the telly, and switching on the light Will peered at his watch. Seven-thirty. He furrowed his brow – where was Juliet? She should be home by now. His eye fell on a stale, half-smoked roll-up loitering in the ashtray, and with no-one around to tell him he was being disgusting, he relit it and walked across to the window. Cupping his hand around his eyes, he peered out into the rainy darkness, half expecting to catch sight of her walking down the street. But there was no sign of her, just a few people sheltering from the drizzle at the bus stop and the obligatory traffic warden gleefully pouncing on the motorists who'd left their cars on double yellows, foolish enough to think flashing hazard lights would protect them while they nipped into Oddbins.

Frowning, he caught sight of his reflection in the double-glazing. Crumpled. Knackered. Hair all over the place. Bags under his eyes. Clothes like a tramp. Bloody hell, I look like shit. I need a shower, a haircut . . . he rubbed the bristles on his chin . . . a shave. Turning side-on he checked out his silhouette, sucking in his stomach and then letting it deflate like a soufflé over the waistband of his jeans. Christ, I look pregnant, no wonder Juliet's always messing around and saying she can feel it kicking.

Will rubbed his belly protectively. All it needed was a few more sessions down the gym, a few sit-ups and he'd give Beckham a run for his six-pack. In fact maybe he should go tonight, lift a few weights, do a session on the running machine . . . Yawning, he breathed out a cloud of smoke and ran his fingers through the strands of his dirty blond hair, still damp from the rain. Then again, maybe he'd go tomorrow, after all, it was getting pretty late, and Juliet would be home any time. Which reminded him . . .

Digging out his mobile from his back pocket, he began looking around for the charger. The battery had gone down at lunchtime and he hadn't been able to receive any calls. Maybe Juliet had left a message saying she was working late. His stomach rumbled. He hadn't eaten all day. And he was starving. Maybe he should ring her at the office and ask her to pick up a takeaway on the way home.

Perked up by the idea of chicken jalfrezi, he began searching for the charger, scouring the shelves jammed with dog-eared *Rough Guides*, his collection of CDs – long since separated from their cases – Juliet's stash of magazines which she insisted on hoarding, even though they dated back to the nineties – and a jumble of photo frames all vying for space. No, nothing there.

He crouched on the floor and began tracing the knotted cluster of wires behind the TV. It was full of crap there, but among the plugs, dust and long-forgotten Blockbuster videos, he finally found what he was looking for. Relieved, he was about to plug in his mobile when he noticed a piece of paper underneath the coffee table. Probably a flyer for some new pizza restaurant, or maybe one of those annoying book-club supplements that always fell out of the Sunday papers.

Under normal circumstances, Will would have left it there – tidying up wasn't one of his strong points – but curiosity got the better of him and he pulled it out. It was an envelope with his name on it. He stared at it. It must have fallen off the fireplace. It must have been put there by Juliet. To be opened when he got home from work. *Alone*.

For a crazy moment Will wondered what he'd do if it was a 'Dear John' letter but then dismissed the idea. *As if*, he thought. Juliet and I are rock solid. So what if we've had a few arguments recently, what couple doesn't? Grinning at the absurdity of the thought, he began ripping open the envelope.

The shrill ringing tone of his mobile interrupted him. He glanced at the screen as DIVERTED CALL flashed up, grabbed the phone and cradled it in the crook of his neck. The automated voicemail service told him he had one new message.

'You bastard,' Juliet's voice yelled into his ear.

What the hell . . . Will stopped as something clicked in his head like a 100-watt bulb being switched on.

And he remembered. *Don't say it's today. Don't say it's today I'm supposed to be taking her out for dinner . . .*

He glanced down at the card he'd just pulled from the envelope. The heart on the front made his own plummet to somewhere around his ankles as he read the three dreaded words.

Happy Valentine's Day.

Oh fuck.

Will groaned. He was in deep, deep shit.

Chapter Two

'Would madam care for another drink?' Hovering around her like a mosquito, the waiter buzzed loudly in her ear. '*While she waits?*' Juliet scowled, feeling as if she was under a huge spotlight. When she'd first arrived the restaurant had felt cosy and intimate; now it was small and claustrophobic. She knew what everyone must be thinking. Poor girl, all dressed up and by herself. Every female in the room feeling thankful they weren't in her shoes. Designer or not.

It was eight o'clock and the reality had finally sunk in. Will wasn't going to turn up. Wasn't going to rush through the revolving door like Superman, with an apology and a dozen red roses. *He'd forgotten*. Looking forlornly at her table, littered with ripped-up paper napkin and a plate of olive stones, she could feel the tears prickling behind her eyelashes, threatening to fall. She made herself blink them away. She couldn't cry, not here, not in the middle of this restaurant. Pulling her Visa card from her wallet, she waved it like a white flag in front of the waiter. 'No, just the bill.'

Juliet had been going out with Will for two and a half years, and living with him for eighteen months. Will was what they always called in magazines 'long term', a phrase which Juliet hated as it made him sound like an illness. But what should she call him? Her *boyfriend*? Will was thirty-three with his own business and a hairline that, although he didn't like to admit it, was beginning to recede. Somehow a boyfriend conjured up past images of *Just Seventeen*, O levels, and teenage boys with acne trying to get their hands into her double-A bra. Her *fiancé*? Very romantic, and a possibility if they were engaged – although it did have period-drama-slash-Barbara Cartland overtones – but seeing as they weren't getting married, and Will looked unlikely to propose in the near future, fiancé is out. Which left *partner*. Yuk.

But it wasn't not knowing what to call Will that was bothering Juliet. After all, it was a problem faced by a lot of women who'd moved on from angst-ridden Bridget Jones singledom into angst-ridden coupledom. In fact, on paper her life was perfect. She was thirty, an account manager for a top London advertising agency, and had a serious, monogamous, maybe-this-could-be-it relationship with Will.

So what *was* wrong?

Well, nothing she could put her finger on. As couples go, she and Will were a pretty average been-together-two-and-a-half-years couple. They ate, they slept, they argued, they had sex. Everything was ticking over quite nicely.

Which was the problem.

Whereas Will appeared to have settled happily into a contented familiarity, Juliet felt something was missing. Romance? Passion? Novelty? Excitement? Juliet wasn't exactly sure. She didn't expect their relationship to be the same as it was in those heady first months, when Will spent the whole time whisking her off for candlelit dinners and romantic weekends away, but that didn't stop her hankering after them. Now it was takeout and a video and, if they ever did have a weekend away, which lately was about as rare as a Jewish foreskin, she had to book it, organize it, and pay for it. Fluffy bathrobes or not, it just wasn't the same.

That's not to say there weren't things about her

relationship that Juliet adored. She and Will were the best of friends, they knew each other's secrets, good habits, and bad habits. They didn't hide anything from each other – she no longer walked out of the bedroom backwards, with the lights off, so he couldn't see the cellulite down the backs of her legs; he didn't wear a T-shirt tucked into his boxers to hide his hairy back. But she couldn't help thinking that maybe they'd become too comfortable, too honest with each other. Being close enough to share a bath with Will was one thing, but being so close that he sat on the loo reading *Auto Trader* while she was in the bath was quite another.

Putting it bluntly, Juliet felt in a rut. A rut so big it was verging on the Grand Canyon. Which is why tonight was so important. For once they were going to forget about bills and mortgages, whose turn it was to do the washing up and the argument about what to watch on the TV: golfing highlights from some rainy place in Scotland or *Celebrity Facelifts – A Female Exposé*. Tonight they were going to get drunk on champagne, remember how much they fancied each other and grope each other under the table. It was going to be special. Romantic. Just the two of them. Together. Laughing, teasing, flirting, kissing. *Just like they used to.*

Or that was the idea, thought Juliet, watching as the waiter sidled towards her, brandishing her payment slip. She cast her eye over the bill, trying not to baulk at the outrageous prices. Obviously unaware of the concept of personal space, the waiter was watching over her shoulder; Juliet could feel his breath on the back of her neck, smell his overpowering odour of aftershave and stale sweat. Purposely leaving the gratuity blank she signed her name. *Juliet Morris*.

'Where's Romeo tonight?' the waiter sneered loudly, annoyed at not being left a tip, causing the couple at the next table to stop eating their rocket and Parmesan salads and look up.

Juliet pretended not to hear. Fighting back tears she stood up, and with a fanfare of Whitney Houston's Zen-remix of 'I Will Always Love You' serenading her over the concealed speakers, walked self-consciously past the other diners and hit the revolving doors.

Outside it was raining. Not just the drizzly, spitting kind of rain, but the bucketing-down variety that sent people scattering like marbles, trying to shelter in shop doorways or making a dash for it with Safeway's carrier bags on their heads. Except for Juliet who, needing to hail a taxi, braved the downpour and began making her way up Wardour Street, trying to hurry as quickly as she could – no easy task while wearing a couple of pieces of leather and two knitting needles that the Fenwick's shop assistants had fooled her into thinking were a pair of shoes.

Feeling the rain bounce off the flagstones and up her bare St-Tropez-tanned legs, she scanned the road for the sight of an orange light. Unfortunately, everybody else seemed to have had the same idea before her. Sure, there were plenty of black cabs, a whole gridlocked street of them, but they were all full of warm, comfy happy people. Men and women. Boyfriends and girlfriends. Husbands and wives. *Couples*.

Watching them sharing some joke, smiling at each other, their silent laughter, Juliet felt robbed. That should be her and Will. They should be cuddling up together in the back of one of those cabs, her face snuggling into his neck, his hands around her waist. Was that too much to ask? One thing was for sure, she shouldn't be walking the streets of Soho, in the pouring rain, *by herself*.

Realizing the hope of finding a cab was akin to that of winning the lottery in a rollover week, she took a shortcut onto Oxford Street and began swerving in and out of umbrellas, heading towards the tube. Trying to catch up with her mind which raced ahead, veering between anger – *that's it, I've had it with Will. I'm going to tell him I'm leaving, I'm going to tell him it's over. I'm young, I'm attractive, I'm good at my job, if Will doesn't appreciate me I'll find someone who does*; and self-pity – *I'm thirty-one next year, I'm getting creases in the corner of my eyes, I'm going to turn into one of those sad, lonely career women who have designer flats and designer lives, but no-one to share them with. I love Will, I want us to work things out.*

Around and around, from every which way, Juliet stewed about Will, about their relationship, about what she was going to say to him when she got home. She rehearsed her side, then his, backwards and forwards, trying to work out what she wanted, what she didn't want, how she felt, how she wanted to feel. Immersed in her thoughts, she wasn't aware of what was going on around her. And so she didn't see a car approaching. An Aston Martin. Didn't see it overtaking a double-decker bus and pulling back to the inside lane. Didn't see its wheels catching the deep puddles that had swelled from the blocked gutters at the side of the road.

Until it was too late.

'What the fuck!' she gasped, as gallons of muddy rainwater drenched her new sheepskin coat, her new dress, her new slingbacks. She couldn't believe it.

For a moment she stood on the side of the pavement, mouth opening and closing like a fish, eyes blinking, hands held away from her sides, water dripping from her face, until looking up she caught sight of the offending vehicle. Her expression morphed from shock to anger. What an idiot, what a stupid fucking idiot. She glared at the car. Bloody typical. Trust it to be some flashy sod in a penis extension. Trust it to be a man.

She snatched a brief glimpse of his silhouette – male, dark, thirtysomething – through the rain-streaked glass, but he didn't see her. He was too preoccupied with negotiating the traffic ahead, one hand on the wheel, and talking to someone on his mobile.

Juliet was livid. 'Why don't you look where you're going?' she yelled, more out of frustration than anything else. She didn't expect him to hear her or see her. Well he won't, will he, she thought, furiously wiping away a splatter of dirt from her forehead. He's obviously too busy chatting in his nice, warm, dry car to notice me, an insignificant pedestrian.

And Juliet would have been right. And she would have gone home, taken a bath, made up with Will, and never given the driver a second thought. If, as he accelerated away, he hadn't glanced out of his side window.

And made eye contact.

For a split second they stared at each other. A fleeting, lasting moment. One person noticing another person out of a whole crowd of strangers. It happens a million times a day in London. Glances between commuters as they pass each other on the Underground escalators, pedestrians exchanging looks as they walk in opposite directions on a crowded street. Busy, absorbed, daydreaming men and women, going about their everyday lives, suddenly catching the eye of other busy, absorbed, daydreaming men or women.

But most people never acknowledge the other person. They probably don't even notice, or if they do they look away feeling slightly embarrassed or awkward and pretend they haven't, speeding up their journey to avoid further contact. Or maybe they'll smile briefly, before carrying on to the office, the pub, their homes, their lives. And most people will probably never ever take it any further, or give each other another thought.

Most. But not all.

There was a hissing skid of tyres and the glow of red brake lights. Crikey, he's going to stop, thought Juliet, shielding her eyes from the rain with the back of her hand and peering through the blurry watercolours of traffic lights, shop neon, car headlamps. Clouds of white smoke pumped from the car's exhaust as it slowed down, its engine rhythmically growling. Juliet realized her heart was thumping like a jackhammer. Anger? Fear? Anticipation? *Excitement?*

White lights lit up as the Aston Martin reversed with a whining screech. For a few moments she watched the driver, saw him turn to look over his shoulder, searching for a gap in the traffic.

There was an orchestra of horns. A whole brass section, loud and rowdy. Juliet saw the silver sportscar swerve and narrowly avoid a double-decker bus that had pulled in front, heard the conductor start shouting abuse. For a moment it seemed as if the driver was hesitating, then the car revved loudly and accelerated into the outside lane. Despite her determination not to give the driver the satisfaction of seeing her looking at him, she couldn't help staring. Which is when, through the swarms of people milling around her on the pavement, she saw him giving her a backwards glance before being swallowed back into the army of traffic. Swept along with the rain towards Marble Arch. Through the lights. Gone.

Wiping away a trickle of rain that was dripping from across her forehead, Juliet paused to watch the red tail-lights disappearing up Oxford Street. What a surprise. He didn't stop. Why did she think he would? What possessed her to think a handsome man in his expensive car with its leather interior and heated seats would bother to even buzz down his electric window to see if she was OK? Why should he care that he'd just ruined a £400 outfit, no actually, a £1,200 outfit if she included the sheepskin coat and the salon-applied St Tropez tan. He wasn't going to be her knight in shining armour. On the contrary, he was an arrogant, selfish, thoughtless prick who obviously only gave a shit about himself.

A shiver rippled through her body and Juliet became conscious of how cold she was. Cold, tired and pissed off. Pulling her sodden coat tightly around her she was about to rejoin the throng of pedestrians when she caught her reflection in a full-length mirror in the window display of New Look. It brought her up short. For Christsakes, what was going on? It was Valentine's Day and she was wet through, frozen and alone.

And it was at that moment, standing in the middle of Oxford Street, with people pushing roughly past her and the rain pummelling her face she realized the waiter was right.

If she was Juliet . . . Where the hell was Romeo?

Chapter Three

The windscreen wipers cut like scythes through the torrents of rain lashing down as the Aston Martin raced towards the lights. 'Look, I'm going to have to call you back in five minutes, something's just come up.' Cutting into the conversation mid-sentence, the driver flicked his small silver Nokia shut and tucked it into the breast pocket of his jacket. With Heart 106.2 blaring from the stereo and the heaters on full blast, he put both hands firmly on the steering wheel and looked in his rearview mirror.

She was still there.

He watched her figure growing smaller and smaller as he was carried along in the current of traffic on Oxford Street. Motionless on the pavement, she was soaking wet and covered in the mud thrown up from his tyres. He cursed himself under his breath. Why was it that five minutes earlier he hadn't even noticed her? Hadn't even seen her walking on the pavement when he'd overtaken that bus? And now he couldn't take his eyes off her?

It's not as if I didn't try to stop to see if she was OK, he thought to himself, slowing down behind a cab that had just stopped dead in the middle of the road to pick up a fare. Impatiently, he drummed his fingers against the leather steering wheel. So why was he feeling so guilty? He glanced at the clock on the walnut dash. Eight-fifteen. He'd arranged to meet up with a couple of old friends for a reunion at a bar in Chelsea and he was already running late. He checked his rearview mirror again. But he couldn't just leave her standing there and drive on. Could he?

He felt irritated. What was wrong with him? He was used to making firm, instant decisions. Seeing things in black and white. Being resolute. There was no choice to make. He was meeting his friends. He was already late. He didn't have time to go back. *But he was going to.*

Putting his foot down he made an illegal U-turn, blowing his horn to scatter a crowd of pedestrians playing chicken with the rainsoaked traffic, and roared through a series of lights. It was absolutely pouring down. He'd only been back in the country for 24 hours, and faced with the London weather, memories of Italian winter sunshine were dissolving fast. Braking sharply, he peered out of his side window. Running his fingers through his dark, curly hair in agitation, he scrutinized the pavements for any glimpse of her. She must be around here somewhere . . . maybe further along. He looked, and looked again, but he couldn't see her. Couldn't see a long-haired woman in a sheepskin coat, a flimsy dress and bare legs.

Briefly he continued the futile search, more out of hope than in the belief he would see her. Giving up, he flopped back against the cream leather seat and stared into the neon darkness, absent-mindedly watching the thousands of pedestrians jostling, rushing, pushing, swerving, running. He was too late. She'd gone, left, vanished. He was surprised at how disappointed he felt.

The shrill ringing of his mobile broke his thoughts. Pulling it out of his breast pocket he flicked open the mouthpiece.

'Hey, where the hell are you?' It was his friends calling from the bar.

'Oxford Street.'

'Christ man, what are you doing? Your beer's getting warm.'

He caught himself. This was crazy. *What was he doing?* He had old friends to meet. He hadn't seen them for months and here he was wasting vital drinking time searching the West End for a woman he'd never seen before and who he'd never see again. 'Sorry guys, I'll be there in ten minutes.' Indicating right, he pulled out into the traffic, turned up the stereo and put his foot down.

Chapter Four

It had almost stopped raining by the time Juliet reached Shepherd's Bush. After being drenched she'd decided to pass on Trudy's offer of sweet'n'sour'n'sympathy and catch the tube straight home. Unfortunately, just when she'd thought things couldn't get any worse, they had. The Central Line had been delayed, probably because some poor woman had thrown herself on the line because her boyfriend had stood her up, Juliet had thought bitterly as she'd waited, shivering on the platform for half an hour until an overcrowded train finally turned up.

Pushing through the ticket turnstiles, she walked out of the station and along the busy main road that was lined with taxi ranks, pubs and strip-lighted burger bars. On days like this, Juliet couldn't think of anything nice about living in London. It was cold, wet, grey and miserable. Rather like me, she thought, pulling her coat tighter to keep out the bitter wind that blew around her legs.

These were the kind of days when Juliet dreamed about charging into Thomas Cook and booking one of those last-minute all-inclusive deals to the Caribbean so that she could wear a luminous wristband and get sunburnt and pissed on free watersports and rum cocktails. Or packing in her job and moving to Tuscany to write one of those novels about living in a bougainvillaea-covered farmhouse and eating dinner outside on a vine-covered trestle table with locals who looked like Andy Garcia. And Will, if he could be bothered to show up, she thought grimly, dashing across the road in front of a juggernaut.

Taking the shortcut home, Juliet hurried past the shops, weaving her way through back streets of once-grand pillar-fronted, four-storey Victorian houses that had long since been cut up into bedsits and flats, their wrought iron railings chopped down during the war to leave amputated stumps, the icing-white smooth plasterwork left to grey and flake. But not for long. Trendy bars had started opening up around the corner, organic restaurants were appearing, junk shops were being turned into designer boutiques. The whole area was changing. Soon these big old houses would be covered in scaffolding and bought by some ex-Spice Girl.

Juliet had thought she'd be pleased – she liked drinking Cosmopolitans and spending ridiculous amounts on new clothes as much as the next girl – but she'd discovered she had a bit of a soft spot for the old greasy spoons and the pubs with swirly carpets and a dartboard in the corner. She liked the local market crammed with stalls selling Indian fabrics, Caribbean spices and Mexican hammocks. Enjoyed nothing more than hunting out a bargain to the loud, beating rhythms of the salsa and reggae tapes that a man sold from an old battered suitcase. Now they were disappearing, she was beginning to miss them. The estate agents said the area was undergoing a 'makeover'. To be honest, it felt more like a takeover.

Turning into a tree-lined street, she slowed down. As streets went it was much the same as any other anonymous road in West London: bay-windowed terraces, permit parking but no parking spaces, a couple of teenagers with nowhere to go hanging out under the lamppost on the corner sharing a half-litre of Woodpecker cider. But Juliet thought it was much nicer. Especially number 34.

She started digging around in her bag for her keys. Strictly speaking, the one-bedroom ground floor flat was Will's, but since moving in she'd removed all traces of bachelordom with her Indian throws, bright pink sheepskin rug and crates full of photograph frames. Now it was their home, and she loved it. Which was a lot more than she could say about Will right now, thought Juliet, wearily climbing the front steps and putting her key in the door. But then theirs had never exactly been love at first sight.

Juliet had met Will at a housewarming party in Putney, on 15 May 1998. As times and places go, it didn't sound a very romantic place for a first encounter. Juliet often wished she could say, 'We found each other at the stroke of midnight on New Year's Eve', or, 'We noticed each other across a crowded New York bar', but unfortunately she had to make do with 'We were introduced across the cheese'n'biscuits.'

The party had been thrown by a girl called Kate from the accounts department at Harris, Selwyn & Bennett Communications, an advertising agency where Juliet had been working. The party invite was in the form of an email – block sent – which said something about 'having a crazy wild time' followed by lots of exclamations. In hindsight they should have made Juliet suspicious. She always thought exclamation marks were the reserve of People! Trying! Too! Hard! But, not having anything better to do, and being new to the firm, she'd decided it wouldn't hurt to go along. After all, it couldn't be that bad. Could it? It could.

Coming face to face with a drunk Hooray Henry type in a rugby shirt (collars up) and feather boa who answered the door, Juliet knew she'd made a mistake. But it was too late to change her mind and she was ushered upstairs to the strains of Celine Dion's 'My Heart Will Go On', and into the living room where there were about a dozen people – all but one of whom were female – hovering around the mantelpiece drinking wine from two-litre cardboard boxes from Waitrose. So this was the party, she'd thought, accepting a glass of something warm and white, and wishing she'd stayed in to do her hand washing.

The next hour was spent making polite chitchat with 'my-name's Suzie and I'm getting married next month' on a wide variety of topics: finger buffets versus a sit-down do, the pros and cons of wearing white – 'ivory can be very draining but then it is so wonderfully traditional' – and honeymoon destinations, until finally she managed to excuse herself and escaped to the kitchen. Which is where, among the twiglets and taramasalata, she was trying to figure out how she could leave early when she heard Kate's drunken shriek: 'William, let me introduce you to Juliet, she's just started at Harris, Selwyn & Bennett.'

Oh-oh. Reluctantly dragging her attention away from the buffet – she used the term loosely – Juliet had turned round expecting to see a William Hague lookalike. But what she had got was a six-foot-something with scraggy blond hair and a lopsided smile that had stretched out the cleft in his chin to reveal the bit he'd missed shaving.

Nice, but not my type, Juliet had thought. He looked older than her, probably about thirty, and was wearing a blue linen shirt and jeans. The kind that style magazines always referred to as 'smart casual'. He also had a suntan so he'd obviously just been abroad. Holiday? Working? By himself? Doubtful. He was too attractive to be single, attractive that is if you went for slim, blond, blue-eyed Swedish types. But Juliet didn't. She preferred chunky, dark, brown-eyed Latin types. Swarthy, hairy kind of men who made her feel small and feminine. Though admittedly he did have a nice arse, she'd thought, checking out his Levi's. Juliet had a thing for nice arses and she'd clocked his immediately. In fact she'd clocked all this in the space of time it took for him to hold out his hand and say, 'Hi, I'm Will.'

He had a Yorkshire accent. It was Juliet's second surprise. Being a friend of Kate's she'd presumed he'd be more of the Home Counties type.

'Oh, hi.' Her voice was muffled. Despite chewing frantically her mouth was still crammed with Brie and crackers. What timing. One hand shielding her mouth, she held out her other. 'I'm Juliet.'

He shook her hand. His hand was firm, but friendly. Warm, strong and very confident. Juliet hadn't realized before how much could be read into a split-second handshake.

'So how are you enjoying the party?'

'Erm, yeah, it's great . . .' she lied enthusiastically, trying oh so delicately to pick the chewed-up, leftover bits of crackers and cheese out of her molars with her tongue. No doubt she'd have a huge bit wedged between her two front teeth. She gave up and used her finger. 'Well, no actually it's not so great . . . to be honest I was trying to think up an excuse so I could leave.' What was the use of pretending? The party was a disaster. *Well, it had been until now*.

Will grinned lazily. 'Me too. In fact I was just trying to get out of the door when Kate collared me.'

Juliet was suspicious. She hardly knew Kate, but everyone knew she was on a manhunt. Why hadn't Kate kept Will for herself? Juliet stared at him. Maybe he was married? Nope, no sign of a ring. Divorced? Nope, no sign of tan mark where the ring had been. Gay? No, not with that handshake. A misogynist? She hoped not.

'Well, don't let me stop you leaving.' To be on the safe side she feigned disinterest.

'Don't worry, you won't.' With a faint air of amusement lingering around his mouth, Will lit up a cigarette. He didn't offer her one. 'But seeing as I'm here, I might as well have one more drink.' He began refilling his wine glass.

Hmm, arrogant, thought Juliet watching him take a

swig of red wine. Blond and arrogant. Definitely not my type.

Three hours later and Juliet was to be found flirting with Will by the fat-free dips, all thoughts of going home firmly abandoned. By the time everyone was drunkenly trying to locate their coats, which lay in a pile underneath Suzie – who'd obviously had a rehearsal for her forthcoming hen night and had puked up and passed out on the bed – Juliet had discovered Will was single, he was rather nice and he wanted her telephone number.

She wrote it on the back of his cigarette packet with her eyeliner.

It probably smudged, she thought when he hadn't called the next day. He probably didn't fancy me, she thought after a week. Who cares? He wasn't my type anyway, she thought after ten days. So when Will finally did call her a fortnight later 'to say hi' she was clipped and cool. So cool that she'd waited a few days to return his call 'to say hi'. Another week for a no-strings-attached coffee and nearly three weeks before a testing-the-waters trip to the movies.

During which time Juliet learned all about Will. His ambitions: he was an architect and worked for a garden design company in Islington but was hoping to set up his own business one day. His hobbies: playing five-a-side in Holland Park, meeting up with friends and drinking too much red wine, reading the Sunday papers at his local greasy spoon. And most crucial of all – his love life: three serious girlfriends, a broken engagement, and most recently a 24-hour fling with a dental hygienist called Yvonne who, after one night of alcohol-induced sex, had scared him off by suggesting they spend a coupley afternoon together flying kites on Hampstead Heath.

Will always dropped the bit in about Yvonne as a word of warning to would-be girlfriends. But Juliet didn't need one. She wasn't about to scare him off with suggested trips to Tiffany's to look at rings. She knew the signs of a man who wasn't looking for a relationship. Because she was a woman who wasn't looking for one either. After a couple of serious relationships herself, beginning with her first love, a drippy nineteen-year-old geography student called Matt who she'd met at university, followed by half a dozen non-starters including Bob, the ex-heroin-addict who'd played bass in a pseudo-Irish band, she was currently single and loving it.

So their purely platonic relationship, bar a few *double-entendre*-infused conversations and a bit of flirting, trundled along until all their friends stopped asking when they were going to get it together, because they thought they already had. Everyone thought they were a couple, when in fact they were just good friends.

Of the *Harry Met Sally* type.

They might not have admitted it to each other, or even to themselves, but Juliet fancied Will and Will fancied Juliet. And they might have always remained just good friends. They might, but of course they didn't.

After three months, three days, and one too many tequila slammers in a tacky Tex-Mex in Fulham, alcohol had played Cupid, and they'd ended up in her single divan for more-than-just-friends sex. It could have been the kiss of death. In Juliet's experience, sex with a friend was either brilliant because you knew each other so well, or excruciatingly embarrassing because you knew each other *too* well. But when she woke up beside Will the next morning and, opening his eyes, he'd smiled at her, she knew it was the former.

'So what do you want to do now?' he asked, curling his long sinewy arms around her and pulling her towards him.

'I don't mind,' she murmured sleepily, feeling him

kiss the side of her face, her neck, along her collarbone, watching his blond head disappear under the duvet. 'Just as long it's not flying kites.' She'd heard muffled laughter as he pulled the covers over her head, dragging her into the depths of the bed where they'd dissolved into giggles and a whole bunch of other stuff which sure as hell beat any outdoor activity.

And so they began seeing each other. Well *Juliet* called it seeing, Will called it shagging, but then he never was much of a romantic. It was the summer of '98 and every night Will would pick her up from work in his beloved sportscar, a shiny red MG Midget he'd discovered rusting away in an old woman's garage and painstakingly restored. They'd head down to the river, to one of the pubs heaving with office workers – blokes with their ties loosened and jackets off, women liberated from their all-year-round opaque tights – and they'd sit outside at one of those wooden picnic tables, her legs draped across his, flirting like crazy and enjoying the novelty of British sunshine.

Juliet had never been out with someone like Will before. He was older than her, more successful than her, and he earned more in a week than she did in a month. She'd been used to going out with graduates who let her pay for her own drinks at the pub, popcorn at the cinema, night bus home. Not Armani-clad architects who bought her Seabreezes (which Juliet knew were now as naff as a DelBoy cocktail, but this *was* the nineties) and treated her to three-course dinners at Luigi's, his favourite Italian.

Looking back, she'd been so happy. Cruising back to his flat, roof down, stereo on, she used to snuggle up next to him, smoking cigarettes and grinning like the cat that had got the cream. At twenty-seven, the fear of heart disease, lung cancer and lips like pleated curtains was years away and, watching London fly past, she'd enjoyed the intoxicating headrush of lust and nicotine.

She was young, she was going out with Will, and she was in love. What more could a girl want?

A nice meal, a glass of champagne and some dry clothes would be nice, cursed Juliet, feeling her dress sticking to her inner thighs like a wet dishcloth. Opening the front door she stepped into the dry warmth of the hallway and flicked on the light.

Chapter Five

Cue the explosion of a huge row. Charged with emotional outbursts, angry words, pent-up frustration and sexual energy which had culminated in Will tearing off her wet clothes in the hallway and making mad, passionate love to her on the kilim rug they'd bought on a British Airways citybreak to Marrakesh.

Actually, that's what Juliet would *have liked* to happen. Unfortunately, this wasn't a carefully scripted movie scene starring Julia Roberts and William Baldwin, but unrehearsed real life starring Juliet Morris and Will Barraclough.

'Jules?' Will's voice wafted out to her as he heard the front door slam. 'Jules, is that you?' He appeared barefoot at the doorway of the living room, blinking at the harsh brightness of the bare lightbulb in the hallway. Shit, he really must remember to get a lampshade for that, he reminded himself, before catching sight of Juliet.

He whistled through his teeth. 'Blimey, you're wet through.'

Dripping like an old teabag onto the welcome mat, Juliet threw him the dirtiest look she could muster. '*Am I?* Ooh, silly me. I hadn't noticed.' Prising a clump of soggy hair that had welded itself to her left nostril, she bared a teeth-grinding grimace. 'Thanks for pointing that out.'

Holding her head high she attempted to stomp past him to the bathroom with at least some pride intact.

Unfortunately her new stilettos had other ideas and her heels skidded out from beneath her, making her look like a cartoon character on banana skins.

'Jules . . .'

Narrowly missing twisting her ankle she grabbed the bathroom door handle for support.

'What?' she glowered.

Will shrugged. 'I'm sorry.'

'Me too,' she snapped, flouncing into the bathroom and slamming the door behind her. She knew that refusing to speak to Will wouldn't get them anywhere and that as a mature adult she should try and sort things out. Except she didn't feel like being a mature adult. She felt like being a grumpy bitch.

She didn't care if she was being childish. As far as she was concerned after what she'd just gone through at the Soho Brasserie, she had every right to be a grumpy bitch. It was Valentine's Day, she was supposed to be sent Interflora bouquets *to the office* and taken for dinner, she wasn't supposed to be left sitting in the restaurant by herself feeling like she was back at school and the last to be picked for the rounders team. Will hadn't even got her a card, for Christsakes.

Bolting the lock, she peeled off her clothes and sulked under the shower until every last splatter of mud and smear of her forty-quid St Tropez tan had disappeared down the plughole. Will spent the whole time on the other side of the door, not knowing how he should be handling this situation, but giving it his best shot by continuing to apologize and trying to make amends by offering to 'cook us both some tea . . . how do you fancy a Spanish omelette?'

After ignoring him for a good forty minutes, Juliet emerged from the bathroom wrapped in towels to discover Will standing with his back to her in the kitchen, stirring pans on the hob. He was stark-bollock naked.

'What the hell are you doing?' She couldn't ignore him any longer.

'Cooking.'

'With no clothes on?'

Will knew it was now or never. Struggling hard to keep a straight face, he turned around, covering his crotch with a Jamie Oliver cookbook. 'I'm a naked chef.'

Juliet knew this was Will's way of waving the white flag. He was offering an olive branch – well, maybe not a branch, she thought as her eyes strayed to his unconventional choice of fig leaf – and in the past she would have accepted it. Except this time she wasn't going to. Naked or not, she wasn't going to laugh and put her arms around Will because this time it wasn't about him leaving wet towels on the bathroom floor, recording *The Big Match* over her *Sex and the City* tape, or rolling in pissed and stinking of chilli kebab at 2 a.m. when he'd told her he was having a quick drink after work. This time it was about a lot more than that.

'Are you hungry?' Deciding the silence meant he'd been forgiven, Will gave her a nudge-nudge-wink kind of smile.

She wiped it off his face. 'Nope,' she deadpanned, wishing her stomach would stop contradicting her by making those loud, desperate gurgling noises. Did Will really think all he had to do was take his clothes off and joke around and everything would be all right? It wasn't as if she hadn't seen it all before. She watched him lift the lid on the pan to check its contents, his pale backside lit up under the harsh halogen spotlights. That's what annoyed her so much about Will: he could never be serious, he had to try and make everything into a joke. Even tonight. She could feel her eyes prickling with tears. And there was nothing funny about tonight.

'I've made your favourite. Chicken jalfrezi and pilau rice,' he continued, as it began to dawn on him that perhaps Jules wasn't finding this as funny as he'd hoped.

'That's *your* favourite, Will,' she corrected sullenly. Even so, she was actually rather impressed. Until now spag bol, with the help of a bottle of readymade ragu sauce, had been the lofty heights of Will's culinary expertise.

'It's gonna be top pukka, luverly jubberly, you just wait . . .'

How pathetic. Unimpressed by Will's appalling impression of Mr Oliver she leaned against the Smeg fridge. She was determined to sulk. Being a Taurean she was nothing if not stubborn, and she was prepared to go to bed with an empty stomach to prove a point. Even if he does look bloody ridiculous, she thought, watching Will as he bent over to check the plates warming in the oven.

Which is when, out of the corner of her eye, she noticed a carrier bag brimming with takeout cartons that he'd obviously tried – and failed – to hide by stuffing it behind the microwave. She should have known. Since when had Will ever gone to the effort of actually cooking her a decent meal?

'What are these?' Leaning across she pulled out the bag and dangled the damning evidence in front of him.

'*Those?*' Will attempted astonishment. It was ham acting at its finest. 'Erm . . . ah, yeah, didn't you know? Curry tastes much better if you eat it from tinfoil trays. It adds to the flavour. A bit like chips in newspaper.'

Digging in the bag, Juliet produced a Visa receipt. 'Does it also help the flavour if it comes from the Bombay Express?'

Dropping his wooden spoon, Will held up his hands in defeat. 'I've been rumbled.' He put on his best hangdog expression. 'Guilty as charged. I throw myself on your mercy, ma'am.'

Despite being faced with his confession *and* a full-frontal Juliet didn't laugh. 'I'm going to get an early night.' She began walking out of the kitchen.

Will panicked. She was serious. *'Jules wait . . .'*

She paused by the doorway.

Sighing, he gave in and dropped the act. 'Oh c'mon, Jules. Don't make this into such a big deal. I know you're upset about tonight, but I didn't forget on purpose. You know I've had a lot on my mind.'

But not me, thought Juliet, although she didn't say it. She didn't say anything.

Her silence made Will gasp in frustration. 'OK, so I forgot it was Valentine's Day and we were going out to dinner. I've said I'm sorry, what more do you want me to do? Get down on my hands and knees and beg forgiveness?'

'It'll do for a start.'

Putting his hands on his hips he tutted, before realizing he was being stared at by Violet, the octogenarian pensioner who lived across the street. Streaking across the kitchen he hurriedly pulled down the blind. 'Since when have you been so bothered about some lousy Valentine's Day anyway? The whole thing's a marketing gimmick. You of all people know that, you're the one who works in advertising.'

'You just don't get it, do you?' Juliet shook her head. 'It's not *just* about Valentine's Day. That's not why I'm upset.'

'So what the hell is all this about?' Will was confused.

Biting her lip, Juliet watched him running his fingers through his hair in agitation. What was the point of trying to explain? That he'd had to ask said it all. She sighed as a wave of tiredness hit her. 'Look, I don't want to argue with you.'

Will felt relieved. 'Neither do I,' he paused, deciding whether or not to say something. He went for it. 'Look, you're probably going to hate this, but what the hell . . . when I went for the takeout I got you something.'

Juliet folded her arms and waited expectantly. What stunt was Will going to pull next?

'You've got to close your eyes for a minute.'

She was half tempted not to, but she obeyed, sighing.

There was a lot of rustling.

'OK, now you can open them.'

With the ta-daah of a magician, he produced his present from behind his back. It was a familiar blue box of Cadbury's chocolates. Giving them to Juliet, he grinned apologetically for the terrible pun he knew he was about to make in the name of grovelling. 'I bought you some roses . . .'

This time she had to smile, even though she tried not to. It was too crap a joke not to. Because that was the thing about Will. He could upset her, annoy the hell out of her and make her question their relationship, but somehow he always knew how to break her mood – even though it was him, more often than not, that put her in the mood in the first place – and make her smile, laugh, love him again.

She felt her anger ebb away. 'You idiot,' she grinned, putting her arms around him.

Will's face flooded with relief. Thank God, he'd been forgiven. Now he could stop doing the full monty and put some bloody clothes on. Well, maybe in a minute, he thought, hugging Juliet's body, which was naked but for a bath towel, tightly against his. Leaning back against the oven, he began kissing her. Mmmm, why didn't they do this more often?

'*Fuck!*' Jerking forwards, his hard-on was forgotten as he jumped away from Juliet, clutching his naked buttock, 'Fuck, I've just burnt my arse.'

Juliet took one look at his startled expression, and burst out laughing. 'You see, that's what happens when you stand me up.'

Jigging around in the kitchen, his face creased with pain, Will hitched himself up onto the edge of the sink, stuck his bum under the mixer tap and turned on the cold water. Feeling the icy jet on his bare buttocks, his face relaxed. 'What happens?'

Juliet smirked. Now it was her turn for the crap jokes. 'You get a hell of a lot more than your fingers burnt.'

Chapter Six

'So, when are you going to marry me?'

'When do you want to marry me?' smiled Juliet.

'Today.'

'*Today?* Oh, I don't know . . .' She paused to brush the hair away from her face with a woolly-gloved hand. 'Shouldn't you ask your wife first?'

The next morning, Juliet was in a tiny shoe-box of a café on the corner of a Soho back street, waiting for her usual breakfast order of a toasted cheese bagel and cappuccino from Mario, the stout white-haired owner. Regardless of how she looked first thing in the morning, Mario always insisted on calling her *bella* and demanding to know when she was going to marry him. He'd been asking her for the last three years.

'What do you think, Rosa?' asked Juliet mock seriously, winking at Mario's tiny wife who was standing behind the counter in her immaculately white apron, building a mountain of sandwiches.

'Aww, you can 'ave 'im.' Pausing from buttering ciabatta rolls, she shook her black, ringlety head and threw her gold-ringed hands in the air. 'I'll 'ave myself a toyboy.' She burst out chuckling as Mario darted across from the toaster and began squeezing his adored wife around the waist, a torrent of good-humoured Italian spilling between them as she slapped him good-naturedly on his hairy forearms with the butter knife.

Watching them giggling and cuddling like two

lovestruck teenagers, Juliet didn't want to interrupt. Leaving the money for her breakfast on the counter, she stepped out of the warm café and began walking to her office. Seeing Rosa and Mario only seemed to highlight what was wrong with her own relationship and, hugging the warm bagel to her chest, she sipped her scalding hot coffee and thought about her and Will.

Last night they'd kissed and made up. After slathering his blistered left buttock with Savlon, she'd spent the rest of the evening watching *Sleepless in Seattle* on Channel 4, eating curry and digging for fudge and Brazil nut caramels. Will had lain next to her on the sofa, without complaining once about his 'third degree burn' or being left with all the hazel whirls and caramel kegs. Neither had he made his usual disdainful enquiry, 'You're not crying, are you?' or snorted with mirth when Tom Hanks gave his wonderfully moving speech about his dead wife on the radio. Instead he'd remained remarkably quiet, which for Will was quite an achievement, considering that they were missing a 'classic' (his words not hers) Gene Hackman thriller on the other side.

She hadn't mentioned the restaurant again and neither had he. There was no point. Will seemed genuinely sorry and, even if he hadn't understood why she'd been so upset, she knew deep down he hadn't forgotten deliberately. He just hadn't thought. But that was just it. Will never did think, did he?

The cappuccino was burning her mouth. Pushing down the tab on the lid to stop the heat escaping, Juliet lifted her face to the faint rays of February sunshine and took deep lungfuls of cold inner-city air. What a difference from last night's driving rain and relentless wind, she thought, cutting across the small grassy square opposite her office. Remembering how she'd cuddled up next to Will on the sofa, the central heating on full, the lights dimmed low, she thought about her decision just to forget about everything that happened and let herself be unashamedly swept away by the movie.

Sleepless in Seattle was slushiness at its best. Perfect Valentine's night entertainment. Passing Will a Turkish delight – she didn't like those either – she'd watched the scene where Meg and Tom see each other for the first time, a brief glimpse across a busy main road. Juliet always loved that bit. She must have seen the movie half a dozen times but that part always got to her, even though she knew it was Hollywood bollocks. As if two people who've never clapped eyes on each other before, would stare at each other like that. Would fall in love at first sight. That kind of stuff just didn't happen. *Did it?*

She'd suddenly had a funny feeling. A flashback to earlier that night. Oxford Street. The guy who'd soaked her.

That's how they'd looked at each other.

Juliet's stomach had gone all jittery. Unnerved she'd hurriedly flicked over the channels, much to the delight of Will, who'd perked up at the sight of Gene Hackman.

But after a few seconds the feeling had passed as rapidly as it had appeared and she'd been left feeling faintly ridiculous. For Godsakes what was she thinking of? What had happened between her and some idiot who couldn't drive wasn't the same at all. He was a stranger, a man she was hopefully never going to lay eyes on again, and the only reason she'd stared at him was because he'd just sprayed her with gallons of muddy water. He was lucky that's all she had done. The way she'd been feeling right at that moment she could have killed him, never mind stare at him.

Closing her eyes, she'd buried her face in Will's T-shirted chest. She was supposed to be forgetting about tonight, putting it out of her memory *for ever*. Will wrapped his arms around her, and Juliet wriggled comfortably. As for *Sleepless in Seattle*, it was just a load of old sentimental claptrap anyway.

Pushing through the revolving glass doors, Juliet entered the glossy reception of her office, SGC. This was one of the most, if not *the* most, fiercely successful advertising agencies in Soho, renowned for creating some of the biggest, most popular and most lucrative campaigns of the last decade – and it wasn't ashamed to blow its own trumpet. Directly ahead was a huge plasma screen showcasing its TV and film commercials and to the right, behind the colossal front desk, was the trophy wall: SGC was named Agency of the Year by *Campaign* magazine, Worldwide Agency of the Year at the American Clio awards for two years running, and presented with two golds at the prestigious annual British TV awards.

'We don't follow trends, we set them,' was the quote from Alex Schmart, the agency's chief executive, on the home page of their website and, predictably in an industry obsessed with appearing cutting-edge, the offices were situated in prime media ground. Overlooking the lawned garden that was a mecca for office workers in summer, Soho Square was a cappuccino's throw away from film and music company headquarters, model agencies, its bars and members-only clubs.

Juliet had been making the daily commute there for less than three months. Fighting off stiff competition to win the job as an account manager, she'd been over the moon when she'd received the phone call telling her she'd got the job. After slogging away in the industry for the last six years, graduate training programmes, dogsbody, assistant, account executive, she'd finally found herself in a company and a position that she'd only ever dreamed of. Being an account manager meant she had a hell of a lot more responsibility – she had her own clients and their accounts to look after, her own assistant, her own expense account and her own ergonomically designed swivel chair. Not to mention her own rather fantastic pay rise.

'Hey Juliet, how was last night?' Annette the receptionist – 'that's two n's and two t's' – popped up from behind the front desk like a glove puppet. Of course it wasn't really a question at all. Annette didn't really want to know about Juliet's evening, she wanted to tell her about hers. Which she proceeded to do without waiting for an answer. 'Mine was amazing. Stevie took me to this really amazing restaurant and bought me champagne and a rose and . . .' she giggled, as if remembering some private joke. 'This.'

Expecting the boastful waggle of an engagement ring, Juliet was both relieved and dismayed to see not a solitaire, but a large soft toy being waved in her face. 'I've called him Big Ears. Isn't he adorable?'

Big Ears looked like something you'd win at the fair in a polythene bag. In comparison, her own lack of Valentine's gifts didn't seem so bad. In fact, faced with a furry fuchsia elephant, resplendent in an already-fraying synthetic tartan bow and a nametag that read I BELONG TO . . . her Cadbury's Roses seemed suddenly wonderful.

'Mmm, he's very . . . er . . . sweet,' nodded Juliet, trying to look as if she meant it. She didn't. She'd never been able to understand the mentality of women who liked soft toys. Malboro-Light-smoking females who had teddy bear collections in their bedroom. She could imagine Annette's, all lined up on her duvet. *All with names.*

'Oh, I know what I was going to ask you.' Disappointed by Juliet's less than enthusiastic response to Big Ears, Annette quickly switched topics. Being stuck by herself on reception she was always desperate for someone to talk to. There was only so far she could string out *Good Morning, Sanderson, Gregory &*

Capulet, can I help you? and she had recently taken to hijacking anyone who happened to be walking past the front desk and bombarding them with questions before they could think of an excuse to escape.

'*What* are you wearing on Saturday night?'

Juliet groaned. This had to be the most frequently asked question by females in the office. On Saturday night SGC were throwing a large charity ball and, because the date coincided with the Venice Carnival, some bright spark on the party committee had come up with the *groundbreaking* idea of having an eighteenth-century masked Venetian ball. The organization and speculation had been bubbling under the surface for months.

To be honest, Juliet couldn't see what all the fuss was about. It was a glorified office party. But to many of her colleagues, with a guest list that included boy-band members and *Big Brother* housemates as well as clients and people in the industry, it was the equivalent of the Oscars. In recent weeks she'd found it impossible to walk into the ladies' loos, stand by a vending machine, or read any internal email without being quizzed about what she was wearing, who she was bringing, and whether she thought Robbie Williams would be there.

'I've hired a couple of costumes from a shop on High Street Kensington.' Balancing her cappuccino, Juliet began loosening her scarf to cope with the stifling central heating. The thermostat in reception was always set to the high eighties so that Annette could show off her suntan, courtesy of the Electric Beach tanning salon on Acton High Street, even if it was minus five outside.

'You've hired costumes? But that's cheating.' Under her bronzer, Annette looked gutted.

'It's not a fancy dress competition. Nobody's giving out prizes . . .' Juliet's voice trailed off as she saw Annette's tearful expression. Obviously she'd been spending the last few weeks at home with her superglue and sequins.

'But I thought . . .' Annette began whining, but at that moment Danny and Seth came through the revolving doors looking as if they'd just rolled out of a club. A couple of Diesel-clad twentysomethings who worked in the Creative Department, these boys were Bill and Ted of the ad world.

'Hey how's it hanging?' croaked Danny, wearing his shades and drinking a can of Red Bull.

This was a man who prayed to the god of Keith Richards. Seth followed him, silent but for the sound made by the devouring of an Egg McMuffin and fries.

'How was last night?' chimed Annette cheerily. After Juliet's disappointing reaction, she was delighted to see more people.

'Awesome man, awesome.'

'Mine was amazing. Stevie took me to this really amazing restaurant and bought me champagne and a rose and . . .'

Seeing her opportunity, Juliet grabbed it. Leaving Danny and Seth staring bemusedly at Big Ears, she moved quickly off down the corridor.

She was early and the office was uncharacteristically quiet. It wouldn't stay like that for long. The place usually filled up around ten, Capital Radio would be flicked on, MTV would begin blaring out, gossip and banter would start up.

As it was an office that was based on appearances rather than practicality, the walls were made of clear Perspex. Admittedly, they *looked* absolutely fabulous, but they were absolutely useless. Installed to give the illusion of space, they didn't actually block out any noise and despite trying to soundproof hers with layers of Post-it notes, Juliet spent most of the day listening to Neesha her assistant, who sat at the next desk, yakking on the phone to her relatives in Delhi, and the Creative Department.

Situated at the opposite end of the office, the creatives were the people responsible for coming up with ideas for the new campaigns. In reality, they seemed to spend most of their time coming down from drug-fuelled nights, lusting over Angelina Jolie and playing with whatever new gismo was knocking around the office.

As an account manager, Juliet liaised between the different creative teams and their clients, but with so many delicate egos involved, she spent most of her time trying to be diplomatic. Only this week she'd had to break the news tactfully to Danny that the brand manager from Bodyform had described his idea for a 'Mutant Ninja Turtle surfboarding on a panty liner' campaign as 'the biggest load of shite he'd heard in his entire career', while sweet-talking the aforementioned brand manager into believing this was a mere creative teething problem. And not, as Danny had put it when he'd heard the news, that he and his company were 'a load of fucking philistines'.

Reaching her desk, she flicked on her iMac. Dean Martin began crooning 'Everybody Loves Somebody' out of the speakers – her regular morning wake-up call – and she was about to sit down when her phone rang. She glanced at her watch. It wasn't even nine o'clock yet. Sighing, she picked up.

'Hello, Juliet Morris speaking.'

'What's taking you so long? The crispy duck's getting cold.'

Juliet's face relaxed into a smile. It was Trudy, wanting to know where she'd got to last night.

'Sorry, I completely forgot. I meant to call you when I left the restaurant . . .'

Trudy didn't let her finish. Her curiosity superseded any hurt feelings. 'With Will?'

'Without,' said Juliet, pricking her hope-filled balloon.

'What *a shit*, what a *total shit*.'

Juliet bristled. Despite what had happened, she could feel herself rushing to Will's defence. It was a girlfriend's instinct. *She* could slag him off, but if anyone else did she couldn't help getting territorial and protective. Will might be a shit, but he was her shit. She interrupted Trudy's character assassination.

'I was going to come over to yours but it was pissing down and I couldn't find a cab, you know what it's like in Soho. And then I got completely soaked by some arsehole who . . .'

'*We need to talk*.'

The voice behind her made her jump. Coffee spilled down her white shirt. *Great*. Looking up she saw a figure striding past, wheeling a stack of matching Samsonite luggage behind her. It was Gabby, her account director, who'd been away on a skiing holiday to Val d'Isère and wasn't due back until Monday. Juliet groaned inwardly. She must have got an earlier flight and come straight from Heathrow. Great.

In her late thirties, with two kids, a husband, a nanny, and a four-bedroomed house in Chiswick, Gabby was one of those bionic 'I can have it all' career women who made normal women exhausted just reading about them in *Femail*. Blond, bronzed and big-hipped, she was immaculately groomed, wore Prada and Dries Van Noten and went to her exclusive gym at six every morning to ensure she fitted in an hour on the treadmill before her 12-hour day at the office. She was having it all, all right. Including a nervous breakdown.

'What arsehole?' yawned Trudy, still on the phone.

'Oh, it's a long story . . .'

'I like stories, they're a lot better than TV. Talking of which, have you seen what they face you with in a morning, what is this GMTV *crap*?' Juliet could hear her flicking over the channels. 'Christ, I've got to get cable.'

Juliet had never known Trudy wake up until noon. 'What are you doing awake so early anyway?'

'Couldn't sleep.'

'Why not?'

'Fergus didn't call . . .'

Putting her highlights-done-personally-by-Nicky-Clarke head around the door of her office, Gabby eyeballed Juliet. No mean feat considering she insisted on wearing her trademark Chanel sunglasses at all times. *'Right now?'* Stress seeped out of her very strangled syllables.

Forcing a ventriloquist's smile, Juliet squashed the receiver to her mouth and hissed, 'Sorry Trude, but I can't speak now.'

'What about a drink after work?'

'Juliet!' Gabby was hollering from inside her office.

'I've got to go. I'll call you later.'

'That's what they always say,' yawned Trudy as she hung up.

Chapter Seven

Wiggling further down on the dozens of velvet cushions and feather pillows swamping her antique French bed, Trudy grabbed the opened box of Coco Pops from her bedside table and zapped the TV with the remote control.

'Jeez, what is she wearing,' she muttered as she flicked onto GMTV and saw Geri Halliwell on the sofa being interviewed by a gushing Lorraine Kelly. 'Silver PVC hotpants? And flipflops? *In February?*'

Eating handfuls of dry cereal, she skipped channels . . . news, more news, cartoons, a commercial for diapers. A close-up of a baby's bottom came up on the screen as the voiceover cheerily declared: 'now able to absorb pee and soft poo.'

'Oh, *yeuch*,' she cringed, gagging on her mouthful of mushed-up chocolate goo. She hit the off button. As the screen of the small portable went blank there was a crackling sound of static electricity, loud in the sudden quietness of the flat.

Thirty-seven, mostly single and mostly Jewish, Trudy hailed from Manhattan, but had lived in London since she was twenty-one and a student at St Martin's School of Fashion. Since graduating, she hadn't exactly reached the dizzying heights of Stella McCartney, but then she was a daughter of a Jewish orthodontist not a world-famous Beatle, which didn't quite cut the same stir in celebrity circles. In order to pay her credit card bills she worked part time as a fashion stylist for the glossies, and the rest of the time she spent designing clothes from her flat in Hampstead. This was a large untidy fourth-floor studio, decorated with an eclectic mix of artefacts she'd collected from her travels, and cluttered with swathes of fabric, racks of clothes, and her ever-growing shoe collection.

Described by the *Evening Standard* as 'one to watch out for', Trudy had an outrageous sense of style that she incorporated into her clothes – zany, colourful creations made out of silks, velvets and leather and decorated with feathers, shells, diamanté and anything else she could lay her hands on. Gorgeous but impractical, her clothes weren't designed for bus-catching, tube-using, office-working women, but Mercedes-driving, kitten-heel-wearing women who spent their days shopping for seasons: not Spring/Summer, Autumn/Winter, but Swiss Alps/St Tropez, Bali/Barbados. Not to mention the opening-of-anything-vaguely-interesting-in-Notting-Hill season which, happily for Trudy's bank account, was all year round.

But while her career was firmly in place, her love life was slightly more erratic. Since breaking up with Sam, her one and only long-term boyfriend, Trudy had worked her way through a dozen one-night stands, endless four-week flings and a four-month affair with a married Parisian banker called Bernard (he'd pronounced it Ber-*naard* in a delectable French accent, which made his name slightly more acceptable). The affair had only ended three weeks ago when his wife had gatecrashed one of their clandestine dinners at the Ivy, poured piping hot lobster bisque all over her husband's crotch and, calling Trudy a 'Yankee beech', frogmarched her into a waiting black cab. Once she'd got over the shock, Trudy had been very impressed. So it was true what they said about French women being sophisticated.

Bernard's wife had even thought to pre-pay the taxi driver.

But Trudy wasn't the type to cry over spilt milk – or lobster bisque for that matter – and the next day she'd gone to a media hangout in Notting Hill that masqueraded as a restaurant, to have lunch with a fashion editor and a stylist from *Vogue*.

Unfortunately she was the first to arrive – Trudy had been aiming for fashionably late, not desperately early – so she'd sat by the window on lookout, pretending to be interested in the wine menu. Except her interest wasn't caught by the Chilean reds but by a man leaning against the blue Perspex bar. Beer in hand he was staring hypnotically at the thousands of fibre optics underneath the surface and telling anyone that would listen in a loud Irish accent, 'hey, come and take a dekko at this' as if it was an amazing new concept and not a twelve-year-old gimmick that everyone had got bored with back in '89.

Unsurprisingly he was being ignored. The restaurant was popular with men who looked like boy-band members, and size six females who draped themselves languidly across tables like week-old tulips hanging over the edge of a vase, inhaling Malboro Lights and Caprianas. This out-of-towner who'd stumbled in accidentally, stuck out like Gulliver in Lilliput.

Tall, clean-shaven and heavily built, he'd got the basic formula right – jeans, shirt, leather jacket – but he'd got it oh so wrong. His jeans were black (black jeans? Nobody wore black jeans, unless of course you counted the Bee Gees and Sir Cliff, which Trudy didn't), on the waist and *stretch*, his shirt, albeit white, had a grandad collar and a shiny pinstripe running through it; while his leather jacket was elasticated and had Michael Jackson-*so-this-is-Thriller*-type epaulettes.

If that wasn't bad enough, there was more.

It was also distressed.

Normally Trudy would have been too. A fashion fascist, she would have looked away in abject horror, but something kept her staring. Maybe it was the accent. Or it could have been that beneath the fairboy attire he was broodingly handsome. Trudy didn't know. But whatever it was, when he asked if the seat next to her was taken she said no without hesitation and was soon engrossed in finding out all about this Dublin-born bookie called Fergus, who'd wondered if she'd like to go and grab a bite to eat?

Indeed she'd been so preoccupied with swapping numbers she hadn't even seen Fenella and Mirabella clambering out of a black cab, until they were swooping upon her with a flurry of moaw-moaw air-kissing, Evian ordering, cigarette lighting. She didn't even have a chance to say goodbye before they were ushering her hurriedly away to their table with Fenella gasping in between cigarette puffs, 'Poor you darling, having to talk to that creepy man,' and Mirabella tutting, 'Did you see his jacket? Honestly, the management should really have him removed. He'll put customers off their food.'

But he hadn't put Trudy off. On the contrary, he'd whetted her appetite. So much so that 24 hours later she'd found herself cuddled up to that very same jacket. Adoringly stroking his leather sleeve as if it was Alexander McQueen she'd played with his straggly black ponytail. Or Titian mane, which is how she'd chosen to describe it when she'd called Juliet the next day to tell her all about her awesome date with Fergus and how they'd ended up spending the night together.

Unfortunately that was the only night they *had* spent together. Since their first date there'd been a trip to the movies, a pub-grub lunch at the Shakespeare Arms and a couple of blowjobs. Hardly an affair to remember, thought Trudy, eyeballing the phone which lay next to her on her rose-festooned bedspread. It stared back at her. Temptingly.

Picking it up, she passed it from one hand to another like a hot potato. She desperately wanted to see Fergus, but should she make the first move and call him?

Trudy pretended to give it some consideration but she already knew the answer. Of course she shouldn't call him. No sane woman should call a man she hadn't heard from since he'd stuck his dick in her mouth last Thursday and then zipped up his fly, jovially kissed her on the cheek and hastily left her flat waving, 'laters'.

But Trudy didn't feel sane. Fergus was playing it cool and so should she. But she couldn't. Fergus was sullen, sexist and about as intellectual as the Yellow Pages, but in a weird way that's what made him so fascinating. Not to mention that he was big, beefy and fabulous in bed. Trudy felt like Lady Chatterley, and Fergus was her gamekeeper. He was completely different from the kind of men she usually met – smooth middle-class professionals who had high-earning jobs, half-a-million-pound *pied-à-terres* and clean fingernails. Fergus was her bit of rough, a bad boy, and that's what made him so attractive. So challenging. And so *damn sexy*.

But she wasn't kidding herself. Trudy knew she and Fergus didn't have a future together, that it was probably going to all end in tears – hers, probably – but she didn't care. Long-term boyfriends bored Trudy to tears. Despite the regular question, 'What's wrong with you?' that accompanied the social stigma of being female, thirty-seven and single, she was no Bridget Jones. She wasn't looking for The One.

And why should she?

That was something Trudy could never understand. To her, Juliet's relationship with Will was a mystery, a hassle, a bore. Why, when there were so many men out there, was she supposed to *want* to limit herself to just one? It was like asking her to choose one pair of shoes that she'd have to wear for the rest of her life. Perish the thought: if that was the case she'd still be in brown lace-up polyfelts. Her concerned mother, Veronica, kept telling her she just hadn't met the right man yet.

But not to give up hope because one day she would and that would be it. She'd have a big Jewish wedding and a life of 2.4 kids, chicken soup and vacations in Long Island.

It was enough to make Trudy call Fergus immediately.

Defiantly dialling his number it crossed her mind that she should be slightly perturbed that she knew it off by heart, but she consoled herself with the thought that she had a photographic memory. *Kind of.*

His line began ringing. At precisely the same time as the buzzer sounded to her flat. She ignored it, it was probably the postman delivering her new credit card. She kept running up debts at Jimmy Choo, cutting up her cards, and reordering new ones 24 hours later. The buzzer went again.

'Go away,' she hissed, listening to the ringing tone and trying to compose her thoughts to decide what she was going to say when he answered.

This time the buzzer didn't just buzz, it buzzed and continued buzzing. Someone was leaning against it determinedly. They weren't going to go away.

'For fuck's sake.' Slamming down the handset, she vaulted naked out of bed. Maybe it was the TV licence people after their payment. She hoped so. She was in the mood to start bawling somobody out about the shite they put on the fucking thing. Dashing across her pigsty of a flat, her bare foot landed in the opened Domino's pizza box lying on the floor, her toes sticking to day-old, 12-inch, meat feast. 'Goddamnit,' she swore and half hopped, half leapt towards the intercom.

'Who the hell is this?' she yelled.

There was the unmistakable Irish lilt. 'Fergus.'

Chapter Eight

Oh my gawd. Trudy reeled as horror, panic and excitement hit like a juggernaut. 'Oh, hi Fergus.'

'Sorry, did I wake you up?'

She'd been awake for hours. 'Oh, I was only dozing.' She did a bit of yawning to add realism.

'Seein' as I didn't see you last night an' all, I thought I'd come round and give you a late Valentine's present . . .'

The word's belated, thought Trudy, biting her tongue.

'. . . I thought I'd give you breakfast in bed.'

'Breakfast in bed?' she squeaked.

'Aye, so are you gonna invite me up then like, or what? I'm freezing my knackers off out here.'

Trudy saw herself reflected in the large gilt-edged mirror that took up most of one wall. It was frightening. 'Sure, come on up,' she breezed, pressing the buzzer. Hearing the thud of the front door, her demeanour changed. *Fuck. Fuck. Fuck.* He was coming up to give her breakfast in bed and she looked like . . . she glanced in the mirror again, noting her old greying underwear, unshaven legs, puffy mascara-streaked eyes, hair all over the place . . . she looked like a fucking *yeti*.

Clutching the doorframe Trudy tried to calm down. OK, so he had five floors to climb. Even if he did two steps at a time she had roughly . . . she tried to work out the seconds it would take him to reach her flat, but arithmetic had never been Trudy's strong subject. She gave up. Oh fuck it, she didn't need to know the precise number of seconds to know that there weren't very many of them. She had to do a makeover in less than a minute. She glanced at her reflection for the third horrifying time. She was a stylist, not a miracle worker. It was a race against the clock. *On your marks, get set . . .*

First, underwear. Grabbing a pair of pathetically weeny and overtly lacy knickers from an overflowing drawer she yanked them on and tried to find the matching bra. Hmm, fat chance. She couldn't find a bra let alone one that matched. In desperation Trudy dived into her wicker laundry basket and began digging around. It was like a lucky dip, except she wasn't feeling lucky.

After a few attempts she managed to pull out a bra that wasn't either her big mama sports one or had bits of underwiring poking through greying stretch cotton. It didn't match but she'd never met a man yet that noticed such things. They were usually too interested in getting the things off to comment upon whether or not the Chantilly lace was the same design as the thong. She sniffed it. *Pheww.* It had been nestling next to her sweaty gym kit for God knows how long. Not to be deterred, she grabbed her Dolce & Gabbana perfume from the clutter of her nineteenth-century dressing table and gave it a good spray. This was much more effective than Febreze. And at £30 a bottle, about ten times more expensive.

Now hair. Trudy stared dolefully at it in the mirror. Pinging out all over her head it looked like a fibre optic lamp. No amount of serum was going to tame this motherfucker. It had a life of its own. It was a static bomb waiting to go off if she as much as flicked on a light or touched a door handle. Swooping on the spray bottle she used for ironing, she began to attack it with water, spritzing with one hand, while with the other she grabbed her make-up bag.

This was the biggest test. Usually she needed a good

forty minutes to layer on make-up to achieve a natural bare-faced look, but right now she had until she counted to ten. She shook the contents out all over the Nepalese rug. There wasn't enough time to indulge in the luxury of blending. Scooping up a big gloop of foundation that fell on the rug, dust, digestive crumbs and all, she began daubing it on. Blusher, concealer, lip gloss, mascara. Mascara? She peered at her piggy eyes in her compact. She needed more than mascara.

She needed her Ray-Bans.

Spotting them on the sofa she thankfully thrust them on and began bolting around the chaotic mess of her tiny studio spraying everything with perfume. It was going to smell like a tart's boudoir but she didn't care. Better that than Domino's pizza. Remembering the pizza she stopped dead. *She hadn't cleaned her teeth*. She heard a noise on the stairs. Shit, she didn't have time. There was nothing else for it. Opening her mouth, Trudy held her breath and gave a big squirt.

Nearly choking as she gargled Dolce & Gabbana, she clamped a hand over her mouth and listened. Now she could definitely hear his footsteps thundering up the stairs. Hastily kicking the offending pizza box, she sent it skidding across the room where it camouflaged itself underneath her triffidian cheese plant, and threw herself onto the bed. Only to leap back out again to leave the door off the latch, pull on the curtains and turn on her Mexican lamp. Flattering 40-watt prisms of coloured light shone against the amber-painted walls as she flung herself under her floral eiderdown.

Urgently, she began strategically positioning it around her rude bits in a suitably starlet pose. Lying on her side, stomach in, boobs out, one arm stretching up over her head, one leg across the other. It was probably easier with just a sheet, she thought, trying to drape a quilted, tasselled bedspread across her butt.

All done, she closed her eyes and waited.

* * *

There was a knock.

'It's open,' she purred. Christ, she'd always wanted to say that.

The door was pushed roughly open and Fergus bounded in, ruddy cheeked and windswept. He grinned when he saw her. 'Well, don't you jus' look gorgeous when you're sleeping.'

Trudy faked waking-up. Arching her back, she writhed under the bedspread as if she was stretching, let out a few suitably gaspy sighs and blinked rapidly as if the light was too bright – even despite Bono shades. 'Mmmm, what time is it?' *Like she didn't know.*

'Too early for you to bother your pretty little head about.'

Christ he was so sexist, thought Trudy, loving every un-PC minute of it.

Grinning, Fergus began to clomp towards her in huge buckled motorbike boots. 'Be Jesus, have you been having a party in here?' He looked at the mess. 'Without me?'

'Maybe,' she smirked, trying to look guilty. Let him think she was having a party last night. It was better than him knowing she'd stayed home with *Frasier*, a takeout pizza, and a silent telephone.

Covering the room in three strides, he wedged his bulky frame on the edge of the bed. He took off his motorbike boots and began stroking her arm, his rough hands and bitten fingernails running up and down her forearms like a woodplaner. 'I was on my way to the meet at the races but I had half an hour to kill.'

In the past such a statement would have caused Trudy to jump on her feminist high horse. Now she thought, *damn, we've only got half an hour, we'll have to get a move on.*

'An' I fancied breakfast in bed.'

Followed by a wave of disappointment. *He'd come round to eat?* She turned her head towards the glaring evidence of the empty cereal box on the Indian bedside table. In all the rush she'd forgotten to bin it. 'I think I might have some Pop Tarts somewhere.' She made a motion to get up.

Fergus gently pushed her down onto her broderie-anglaise pillow. 'Not that kind of breakfast,' he laughed, taking off his lumber jacket and revealing a black and burgundy checked cable-knit jumper. A spidery tuft of hairy chest poked out of the V-neck.

'Oh,' she gave a squeak.

Pulling the jumper over his head, the acrylic-nylon knit making a crackle of static electricity, he threw it to the floor. 'How do you like your coffee?'

Trudy didn't answer. She was too busy staring at his naked chest. Covered in a thick, dark pelt, it curled over his collarbone, across his rather impressive pectorals and into a thick rope of hair that ran all the way down to his belly button. She began stroking it. It reminded her of Juliet's sheepskin rug.

'What's that?' she murmured.

'Your coffee. Weak or strong.'

Fergus was looking at her intently, his face blotchy with excitement.

'Oh, strong,' she nodded vigorously, suddenly getting his drift. So Fergus was into talking dirty? And there was her thinking he was the strong silent type. She smiled wickedly, this was more like it. Throwing in a bit of heavy panting for good measure, she put on her best porno voice. 'I like my cawfee so . . . (gasp) . . . incredibly (. . . sharp intake of breath) . . . *strong*.'

'And the butter for your toast, hard or soft?' Never taking his eyes away from hers, Fergus began undoing his belt. Trudy tried not to notice it had a skull and crossbones buckle. Or that his Y-fronts were emblazoned with Ronan Keating's face. Albeit somewhat faded.

'Hard,' she squeaked.

'How hard?'

'Erm . . . as hard and as firm as . . . a . . .' (desperately trying to think of something suitably phallic, her eyes fell on his penis which was suddenly looming over her, engorged, throbbing, and shaped uncannily like a '. . . *doorknob*.'

The word came gasping out loud before she could stop herself. She kicked herself. *A doorknob?* Couldn't she have said something a little more, well, complimentary? She snuck a look at Fergus. He didn't seem offended. In fact, judging by the glazed look on his face, he was clearly enjoying himself. And, by the look of it, *so was his doorknob*.

'Tell me again, how hard is that doorknob?' With his stretch jeans now around his hairy calves, Fergus was clambering on all fours across the bed, the buckles on his boots catching on her paisley valance.

'Rock hard,' gasped Trudy, trying to think of more adjectives.

'This hard?'

With his Y-fronts stretched to breaking point between his hairy knees, Fergus pulled her thong to one side with a deft flick of his thumb.

'Oohh,' gasped Trudy, and this time she wasn't faking it. Grabbing his hairy tattooed buttocks with both hands, she pulled him deep inside her.

Now that's what she called a full Irish breakfast.

Chapter Nine

'*Finally*,' scowled Gabby.

Realizing that her account director was in an even shittier mood than her normal shitty one, Juliet hesitated by the open door of her office. A shrine to minimalism, with its Purves & Purves glass desk, Philippe Starck lamp and obligatory white-orchid-in-glass-vase, Gabby had recently had it Feng-shuied by some guy she'd met at an organic juice bar. Two grand and a water feature later it was now supposed to invoke a Zen-like calm.

She'd been ripped off.

'Well, don't just stand there. *Sit down*.'

Sitting regally in the original *Big Brother* Diary Room chair she'd bought at an internet auction, Gabby waved dismissively towards the chair opposite her desk. It was no coincidence that it was at least six inches lower than her own.

Forcing a smile, Juliet closed the door behind her and sat down. The last two weeks without her director had been hard work but blissful. But now she was back. And being a complete fucking bitch *as usual*.

'Obviously, being away for the past fortnight, I haven't been very hands-on, and no doubt things have begun to slide around here . . .' Gabby paused. She did a lot of that. She punctuated her speech with long pauses and heavy pronunciation in the belief that it made her sound serious and intelligent. Unfortunately, it made her sound like a teach-yourself-a-foreign-language tape.

'But now I'm back. *And just in time.*' She arched an overly-plucked eyebrow behind the shades. 'BMZ, the Japanese car company, are launching a thrilling new sportscar – the long-awaited MAXI – and they've approached three agencies to come up with a new campaign. This morning we received the news that we're one of them.'

'Wow, that's great.' Juliet didn't know much about cars, but even she'd heard about the MAXI. Will had been going on about it for months.

'You do realize how important it is for SGC to win this account, don't you?'

'Of course, I—'

Gabby interrupted. She always did, her motto being why let people finish their own sentences, when she could finish them better herself? 'This sexy two-seater soft-top is *the car* everyone will be killing to get their hands on.' Picking up a press photo of the sportscar, she skimmed it across the glass desk with a flick of her wrist.

'Would *you* kill for this car?' Like a voiceover for a movie trailer, she did another pause. Now wasn't the time for Juliet to confess she preferred using the tube to driving – in traffic-congested London it was much quicker.

'*Well?*'

Admittedly, the sportscar *was* gorgeous: red, dinky, with chrome wheels, a silver dash and tinted windows. Any driver would feel like a million dollars in it. Looking at the photograph, Juliet was reminded of when she used to zip around in Will's convertible. How it had felt escaping to the coast, roof down, wind in their hair, as if they'd been two fugitives. It had been so exciting. So exhilarating.

So unlike now.

She looked at her boss, who was waiting for a

suitably dramatic response. If there was one thing Juliet had learned about advertising, it was that she had to take everything very seriously. Even the most mundane household goods had to inspire life or death reactions.

'I'd murder for one.'

'Excellent.' Nodding her approval, Gabby stood up and began pacing around the room. 'As you know, there are other agencies pitching for this contract. One of them is our main rival, Montague & Murdoch, and this morning I heard they've flown back one of their best new creatives who was working in their Italian office.' She swivelled on her stiletto. It made a mark in her new wood flooring. 'The talented Mr Sykes.'

The name meant nothing to Juliet, but then she hardly ever read the trade magazines that her assistant kept putting in her in-tray and she kept putting, unopened, into the bin. She made a memo to herself to have a flick through a few when she had a moment, and not keep borrowing Annette's *heat*.

'Of course I know we're going to get this contract,' Gabby continued, her armour-plated confidence less steely than usual, 'but even without our Mr Sykes we've got some stiff competition – ' she rattled off a few other of the big London agencies – 'so it's not going to be without a fight.' Leaning across the desk, she put her face up close to Juliet's. She was so near, Juliet could smell the in-flight booze on her breath. 'Which is why I've decided to let you take the reins on this one. I'm giving you a chance to show what you can do.' Sitting back in her chair she kicked off her Manolos, looking very pleased with herself.

And no wonder, thought Juliet, experiencing a rush of foreboding. Gabby's motive for handing over control wasn't to let Juliet reap the rewards and make promotion when their pitch was successful. *It was so that she would have a scapegoat when it failed.*

Looking after number one was Gabby's golden rule.

When Juliet had first joined the company it hadn't taken her long to work out that despite her new boss's insistence on behaving like her best buddy – 'please, call me Gabby, Gabriella's far too formal' – her friendliness was as fake as her tits, and if the shit hit the fan her best buddy would suddenly decide she was working from home for the next few days, her mobile would be switched off, along with her email, and Juliet would be left to mop up the mess.

Alternatively, if there was the merest whiff of success Gabriella (she always reverted to using her full name when there was praise to be had) would be seen on every floor of the building putting in more appearances than the Beckhams in *OK!*, and her usually firmly closed office door would be flung wide open so that she could embrace the 'well dones', admiring backslaps and invites to Groucho's for a celebratory drink – 'mineral water, no ice'. Being constantly on some form of detox, Gabby professed to have cut alcohol out of her diet. Which was odd, considering that her Fendi bag was always so crammed with miniatures that it was known around the office as 'the mobile minibar'.

'Here at SGC we value success: *success* is what we're good at. We don't like failure, because we're not very good at it.' She stared at Juliet. 'If you know what I mean.'

Juliet knew all right. Sho could already hear her P45 being wafted underneath her nose. She managed to nod. 'Absolutely.'

'Splendid. I'm so glad we had this little chat.' The account director's top lip curled over her porcelain veneers. 'I know I can rely on you.' It was a veiled, *Godfather*-type statement.

Taking it as her cue to leave, Juliet stood up. She looked at her boss sitting in that *Big Brother* chair, elbows on her desk, fingertips lightly touching. All she needed was cottonwool balls in her cheeks and she'd be Brando in drag.

She turned to leave.

'Oh, there's just one more thing . . .'
'Yes?'
'Saturday night.'
Juliet braced herself for the inevitable question about what she was going to wear to the ball.
'We've invited a lot of important clients to this ball, including the team from BMZ, so it's important we put on a good show. Winning contracts isn't just about ideas, it's about selling an image. Our image.' She checked her French manicure. It was perfect as usual. 'You are going to be there, aren't you?'
Juliet was caught off guard. She should have known Gabby wouldn't be interested in her choice of clothes. This is a woman who had a personal shopper at Harvey Nics. Enough said.
'Of course I'm going to be there.'
'And your boyfriend? I can never remember his name.'
Her boss was the archetypal smug married. 'Will. Yeah, he's looking forward to it,' lied Juliet, blocking out of her mind his less than enthusiastic reaction when she'd shown him the invitation.
'Good. I'll look forward to meeting him.' Gabby dismissively flicked open her compact to check her lipstick. 'Let's hope he's an asset to you.'

'C'mon you shitty, fucking, stupid pile of crap. *Start, you bastard, start.*'
Huddling in his draughty Land Rover, listening to the depressing whine of his flat battery, Will swore loudly, flicking the ignition key backwards and forwards as he pumped the gas, trying to get the engine to cough into life. It didn't. It wheezed like an old man and then surrendered with a feeble simper.
'*Fuck.*' Slamming his hands down on the steering wheel, he took a deep breath and tried not to explode. Something told him it was going to be one of those days.

Conscious of his teeth chattering like a wind-up set of joke dentures, he pulled his fleece tightly around him and peered gloomily out of the icy windscreen. He'd accidentally fallen back to sleep after Juliet had left for work, and now he was late for an appointment. Not late as in his usual five or ten minutes – time-keeping had never been his strong point and he'd come to accept that his was always going to be an approximate life – but this time it was an inexcusable forty. He glanced at the clock on his mobile. Who was he kidding? More like an hour.

Will swore again, louder this time so that he saw his breath form white clouds, and then bounced back in his seat in agitation. He was supposed to be driving over to Kensington for a 'breakfast meeting' with a potential new client who'd called him up yesterday, demanding he 'come over immediately' as he wanted to turn his decked roof terrace into a Japanese garden complete with teahouse, footbridge and water-lily pond, 'because I've heard it's really in vogue'. 'Great idea,' he'd enthused, setting up the meeting. 'Japanese is really of the moment.' *Back in the late eighties, you pretentious arse*, he'd thought, hanging up the phone.

But now, instead of cutting a deal over cafetières and all-butter croissants in a plush pad in Kensington, he was freezing his arse off in a useless heap of rust that had only gone and died during the night. Will rested his elbows on the steering wheel and put his face in his hands. He wasn't going anywhere. Fast.

Staring miserably out through the gaps in his wide-spread fingers, Will noticed Violet, his neighbour, cheerily waving good morning from between her net curtains. Briskly adopting a less suicidal pose, he waved back, forcing a jovial smile. Christ this was ridiculous, he couldn't sit here all day. He was going to have to call the AA. That's if he was still a member. Opening the glove compartment Will fumbled around among piles of unopened mail. Since starting up the business he'd been so busy, he'd let a lot of things slide – and not just his AA membership. He couldn't remember the last time he'd gone up to Yorkshire to see his family, or had a decent night out with his mates. And then of course there was Juliet.

Will stopped himself. After last night's fiasco with the restaurant he didn't want to follow that train of thought. The ostrich option was much more attractive. In fact burying his head was something he'd become quite adept at since he'd set up Dig It Designs six months ago with his mate, Rolf.

Since he was an architect, the original plan had been for Will to take responsibility for the design side of things, while Rolf, a horticulturist, would take care of all the hands-on gardening. Will had liked this plan a lot. He'd liked the idea of spending most of his time drawing up plans and being creative from the cosy comfort of his bedroom-turned-office, listening to Moby and eating Choco Leibniz. In fact, apart from occasionally popping down to the site to liaise with clients and check that things were going according to his plans, he'd loved the idea that all the dirty work would be left to the builders, whose job was to dig, shovel, hammer and cement his neatly drawn designs into reality.

At best, this could have been called optimistic.

At worst, delusional.

For the past six months Will had been shovelling cement and laying patios in all-weather conditions. He hadn't seen his office once. As for Choco Leibniz and his CD collection, it had been flasks of tea and cheese and Branston sandwiches, listening to the whirring drone of the cement mixer, and Dwayne his casual labourer talking about how many piercings his girlfriend Leanne had.

Things were not going to plan at all.

Giving up his search for the number of the AA, Will pulled out a wallet of Drum and Rizlas. Being self-employed was harder than he'd thought. Even though he and Rolf had been putting their heart and soul into Dig It Designs, business had been pretty slow over Christmas and New Year and the bank manager was breathing down his neck for repayments on the start-up loan. He really couldn't afford to go missing appointments.

Feeling his stress levels rising, Will dug out his matches. Time for a fag break. Sliding down in his seat, he put his feet up on the dashboard and, closing his eyes, took his first drag of nicotine.

'What the hell . . .' Startled by the sound of bony knuckles rapping against the side window of the Land Rover, he snapped open his eyes. Steeling himself for an exchange of expletives with one of the uniformed parking attendants who patrolled the streets like some kind of militia, he was surprised to find himself staring through prescription lenses into watery blue irises.

'Would you like to come in for a nice cup of tea?' Wearing her pinny and a pair of fur-trimmed tartan slippers, Violet was standing on the pavement.

Hurriedly sitting upright, Will tried to wind down his window. It was jammed as usual and he had to bang it with his fist before the glass reluctantly slid halfway down.

'Jesus, you frightened the life out of me,' scolded Will affectionately. 'What are you doing out here?'

Eightysomething and still going strong, despite a spot of arthritis, failing eyesight and the death of her husband, Albert, Violet had taken it upon herself to be a surrogate grandmother to anyone in the street under fifty. Always sending out birthday cards every year, which she made from cutting up old Christmas cards with pinking scissors, she regularly gave presents of handknitted vests and frosted icing butterfly buns. Will, who was one of her favourites, had quite a collection of unworn knit-one-purl-two oatmeal vests in the back of his wardrobe.

She laughed. It was a hacking smoker's laugh. 'Oh, I am sorry, luv. I thought you might fancy a brew. To warm you up like.' Despite living in London for the best part of sixty years, Violet had still kept her thick Barnsley accent as a souvenir of her childhood. 'I've put the kettle on,' she added hopefully, patting her home perm in a parody of Mae West. Getting old hadn't stopped Violet being a flirt.

'Thanks, I could do with one, but I'm already late . . .'

'The teapot's big enough for three,' she added hopefully. 'If Julie wants to join us, like.' Violet could never get the hang of Juliet's name, despite the fact that she saw a lot more of her than she did her own grandchildren. It was difficult for Violet to read even large-print books and it was thanks to Juliet reading aloud a few chapters at a time of whatever she had on loan from the pensioners' mobile library, that she got her weekly fix of love, passion and romance. Violet was rather partial to her weekly dose of Barbara Cartland and Mills & Boon. And Jackie Collins if she could get her. But there was always a long waiting list.

' 'Fraid she's already left for work.' Will shrugged. He was still feeling a bit put out that he'd barely had the chance to say two words to Juliet, before she'd left for the office.

'Now, that is a shame.' Violet wouldn't have minded a chapter or two.

'. . . which is where I should be.' He glanced at the clock on his mobile again. As much as he could quite happily sit here all day, he had a business to run. At least for the moment. Reaching out he put his hand on hers. Underneath his palm he felt her skin, which had worn to a tracing-paper thinness.

'Maybe next time?'

She nodded brusquely in an attempt to hide her hurt feelings. 'Right you are.' Patting his hand she turned away and began walking slowly back to her gate, taking careful fairy steps in her tartan slippers.

'Do you want a hand?' he called out, unaware of her disappointment. But with her back turned, she didn't hear him. For a moment he watched as she paused to look at the brightly coloured flowers decorating her front step. Planted in a variety of junk, including old wellies and rusty watering cans, none of them were real. He smiled as she stooped down to rub the city grime from their plastic petals with the edge of her apron.

She might have the right idea, he thought. Perhaps he should suggest fake flowers to some of his less green-fingered clients. Talking of which . . .

Focusing his attentions on the Land Rover Will decided to have one more go at resuscitation before admitting defeat and calling Rolf, who was working on a garden in Islington. Closing his eyes, he turned the key in the ignition. And prayed. With a groan the engine spluttered into life.

'*Yesss, you beauty*.' Crunching the gears into first he put his hand on the horn as he blasted past his neighbour in a cloud of black exhaust fumes.

Left behind with her plastic flowers, Violet looked up to see the blurry outline of the Land Rover. She gave a little wave as she watched it disappearing into the thronging traffic. Everybody was so busy these days, she thought, contemplating the empty day which stretched ahead of her. A gust of wind blew around her American tan ankles and she pulled her woollen cardigan around her. It was chilly. Better get inside and have that cup of tea, she thought, putting her key in the latch. Afterwards she could do a bit of housework. In fact, thinking about it, that back bedroom could do with a good hoover.

Shuffling inside her flat, Violet let the door fall shut behind her.

Chapter Ten

'Two Jack Daniels with Coke,' yelled Trudy, relieved to have finally got the attention of the barman. 'Actually no . . .' Spotting Juliet at the entrance of The Bull, she took one look at her friend's harassed expression and changed her mind. 'Skip the Coke and make them large ones, on the rocks.'

Standing up and balancing on the rungs of her barstool, Trudy began waving exaggeratedly so that Juliet would notice her. It would have been impossible not to. Dressed in an outfit of her own design – a pea green velvet jacket trimmed with *faux* fur and a pair of tangerine satin flares – she stood out against the backdrop of blokes. Dressed head-to-Nike in denim and black, they looked as if they were trying to resemble something out of a Guy Ritchie film, which was a bit ridiculous, considering this was a well-heeled bar in Hampstead and not a gangland pub in the East End.

'Scotch OK?' she hollered, over a rowdy buzz of the early evening crowd that was flooding in after work.

'Whatever,' yelled back Juliet, squeezing past a group of men with pints of Guinness and wiggling out of her sheepskin coat. After a long day at work she was knackered. She needed a drink.

'So, break the suspense. What happened?' Skipping the pleasantries, Trudy dived straight in. It was the New York therapy streak coming out in her.

Juliet dropped her shoulder bag on the floor and collapsed against the bar. 'My boss called me in this morning and dumped the new MAXI sportscar account on my desk, which I know is a great opportunity and if I pull it off it'll look great on my CV, but I've only got a couple of weeks and there's other agencies pitching for it . . .'

Trudy managed to get a word in. 'No, I mean *last night*. Fill me in on all the gory details. Even the bit about chopping off Will's balls,' she grinned, pushing a drink across the bar towards Juliet.

'Christ, who do you think I am? Lorena Bobbitt?' Juliet admonished her, ignoring the fact that less than 24 hours ago the thought had been very tempting. Unrealistic, but tempting all the same.

'That was his dick. I'm talking balls,' corrected Trudy, not giving up easily.

Bundling her coat under the barstool, Juliet clinked her glass against Trudy's. She put on her *AbFab* voice. 'Don't you always, darling.'

Trudy was Juliet's closest friend. The kind of friend that held her hair when she'd overdone the margaritas and was saying hello to them a second time round in the toilet bowl, who listened patiently and interestedly while she repeated, analysed and painstakingly dissected every word uttered by Will during their last argument, and was the only person brave enough to tell her that the lace dress she'd spent her last hundred quid on at Karen Millen was more doily than diva.

They'd met through the small ads – a one-liner Trudy always used on men as it appealed to their lesbian fantasies – seven years ago when Juliet had first moved to London and, looking for somewhere to live, had answered an ad in *Loot* for a flatshare in Battersea. A mute, headbanging surfer had answered the door. Wearing an oversized striped jumper, baggy-past-his-knee skateboarding shorts and a pair of headphones, he'd waved her over the doorstep without saying a word and led her into what could only be described as a pigsty. Well, actually it had been a kitchen, but Juliet had only worked this out by the sight of a cooker ring, which was hiding underneath the kind of stuff you'd only touch with a pair of rubber gloves.

Around a table had been an oddball assortment of people – a skinny guy in a sarong eating muesli and yoghurt (it wouldn't have seemed strange had it been 6.30 a.m., not p.m.), a Swedish blonde applying liquid eyeliner, a good-looking older bloke in a tartan suit leaning backwards on his chair smoking a joint and a girl who was wearing some weird tie-dye ensemble and had thick mousy hair that fell around her head like a lampshade. This was obviously the (un)welcoming committee.

In her head Juliet had heard the sound of a wrong answer on *Family Fortunes*. *DuhDuuuhhh*. She'd made a mistake. This wasn't what she wanted. She wasn't what they wanted. These people were grungy, alternative, fashion types who had a distinct 'we read *The Face* and listen to Pearl Jam' look about them, whereas she had a nine-to-five job in an office and had a 'I look at the pictures in *Hello!* and watch *EastEnders*' look about her.

Regretting that she hadn't changed out of her polyester work suit into something that didn't have a British Home Stores label, she'd been about to mutter something about getting the wrong address, when the girl with the lampshade hair had stood up. Holding out a large hand covered in lots of chunky silver and turquoise rings she'd introduced herself, 'Hi, I'm Trudy,' and given her one of those Oscar-winning Julia Roberts smiles.

Juliet had moved in the same day.

'So Will just forgot?' Trying to recover from a ten-minute burst of laughter that had resulted from hearing about Will's burnt buttocks, Trudy wiped the tears from her eyes and tried to get serious. All this laughter was not good for her crow's-feet. 'He just forgot it was Valentine's Day and he was supposed to be taking you out for dinner?' Taking a swig of Jack Daniels she sloshed it around her teeth as if it was Oral B mouthwash. She always did it when she was concentrating. A throwback to years of indoctrination by her orthodontist father.

'It's not funny,' protested Juliet, laughing herself. She looked at Trudy who was sitting cross-legged on the leather sofa, making light work of the bowl of complimentary Kettle Chips. On their second large JD and ice, they'd moved to a comfy corner of the pub, next to the 'Authentic Irish Seafood Restaurant'. A rather euphemistic term, Juliet always thought, for a few shunted-together tables, a chalkboard menu of salmon fishcakes and a measly basket of stale soda bread.

'I know it's not, I'm sorry, honey,' grovelled Trudy, trying to put on a straight face. 'Didn't you remind him?'

'It was dinner in a restaurant not a dental appointment.'

'Ahh, yeah, good point.' She nodded, crunching loudly.

'I shouldn't have had to remind him. He should have been looking forward to it. *I was.*'

In commiseration, Trudy pushed the bowl of crisps nearer to Juliet. 'Did you buy that dress you'd seen in Whistles?'

'New dress, new shoes, new make-up, new underwear . . .'

'Lingerie? Wow, you were really going for it, weren't you?'

Juliet nodded, sipping her drink. 'I bought the full works . . . matching bra, G-string and this kind of floaty négligé thingy.'

'*Négligé?*'

'Well, I thought I should give my Gap pyjamas a miss.' She caught Trudy's uncertain expression. 'It's very Agent Provocateur with black see-through chiffon and these little pink rosebuds on the straps . . .' her voice trailed off at Trudy's lack of interest. 'Well, I thought it was sexy.'

'No, I'm sure it is.' Trudy tried to sound enthusiastic. Black chiffon and pink rosebuds was not her thing. She was more of a naked-under-the-sheets kind of gal. Or rather she had been that morning, she thought, thinking about her earlier shag-a-thon with Fergus.

'*Was,*' corrected Juliet. 'Anyway, I wish I'd saved my credit card the bother. Will probably wouldn't have noticed anyway.'

'Oh, c'mon, you know that's not true. Will loves you to bits, he thinks you're gorgeous . . .'

'Does he? I don't think so.' Juliet pulled a face. 'Not any more. He doesn't seem to notice I'm even there half the time. I remember when he used to leave Post-it notes with 'I love you' stuck to the bathroom mirror. Now the only things he leaves are his smelly socks and skidmarked boxer shorts stuck to the bathroom floor.'

'*Aww, please,*' laughed Trudy, wincing. 'A little less reality, please.'

Grinning, Juliet drained the last of her drink. Will would kill her if he knew she was telling Trudy his innermost habits, but what the hell, after last night he didn't deserve any girlfriend loyalty. 'Well I'm sorry, but nobody ever tells you what it's really going to be like when you move in with a bloke.'

'Why do you think I live alone?'

'What about Sam?'

Trudy rolled her eyes. 'Sam was anally retentive. His socks were kept in neat little balls in his wardrobe and his computer magazines in date order. He even used to make himself a packed lunch for the next day. I used to find his sandwiches in the fridge at night, all carefully wrapped up in clingfilm. They were always exactly the same. Cheese, tomato and salad, no mayo. I ate them once for a joke. He never forgave me.' Trudy started laughing. 'Sam was a guy who plumped cushions for a hobby. And believe me, that's far worse than being a messy son of a bitch.'

Shaking her head, Juliet sighed. 'It's not about Will being messy. It's about how he used to make me feel fantastic, like I was the best thing that ever happened to him. I couldn't imagine being without him . . .'

'And now you can?'

Juliet avoided her question. 'I really love Will, I really do . . .'

'But?'

'But nothing.' Shaking her head, Juliet lay back against the back of the sofa. She didn't like where the conversation was heading. 'Ignore me, I've just had a crap couple of days.' She was tempted to say months.

Trudy licked the flavouring from her fingers. 'Valentine's Day's just a load of commercial garbage anyway. Just because he forgot doesn't mean jack shit.' She purposely hadn't told Juliet about her own belated gift from Fergus. After whingeing about him being a bastard for not ringing for the past week, Trudy didn't think Juliet would approve somehow. 'He dropped in for a quickie' didn't have the same ring to it as 'He sent me a bouquet.' Which was a shame. Shagging was a lot more fun than twelve poxy red roses.

'Yeah I know,' nodded Juliet, 'but that wasn't why I was upset.' She began peeling a beer mat in half. 'Though it would have been nice to get a card.'

'What did you want? A padded satin one with a bunny on the front?'

'I'm sad, but not that sad,' quipped Juliet.

'No, you're just a romantic, honey.' Trudy looked sympathetic, as if she'd just diagnosed an illness.

'What's wrong with that?'

'It's outdated. If men were romantic women would say they were being sexist.'

'Of course we wouldn't,' argued Juliet. 'Anyway, whose side are you on?'

'Nobody's,' replied Trudy, shaking her head. 'I'm just saying that we've told men for so long that we're equal, we can open our own doors, carry our own bags, pay our own way, that now they're afraid to offer in case we accuse them of sex discrimination. If you were a man would you buy a woman underwear? I wouldn't dare. What if she throws it back in your face and calls you a sexist pig? What if she accuses you of loving her for her body not her brains?' Trudy swigged back the rest of her drink. She was on a roll.

'So they've tried to turn into new men, but that's no good either, because now we're telling them to be masculine. We don't just want them in a pair of Marigolds cleaning the oven, that's not good enough. We want them to take control, to whisk us off to hotels, buy us dinner, and make mad passionate love to us all night. We want it all ways. Women want to be feminists *and* romantics. We want them to be heroes *and* handy with the vacuum. No wonder the poor guys are confused.'

'So am I,' smiled Juliet wryly, waving her glass in defeat. 'Which is why I need another drink.' Easing herself off the sofa she stood up. 'Jack Daniels?'

Bringing her monologue to a swift end, Trudy siphoned off the last few drips of her drink and held out her empty glass. 'Now there's a guy that always gets it right.'

They left the pub a couple of hours later. Outside was bitterly cold after the stuffy warmth of The Bull, and pulling on scarves and jackets, Juliet and Trudy began walking towards the tube at the top of the high street. They'd only walked a few feet when Trudy gave a sharp intake of breath and clutched Juliet's shoulder.

'Ohmygawd, Jules, I've just noticed.'

'Noticed what?' Juliet stopped buttoning up her coat. '*What?*' Trudy was still staring at her, and now she was beginning to feel impatient. Trudy could be such a drama queen when she wanted to be. 'For Christsakes what's the matter, you look like you've seen a ghost.'

Trudy took her hand away from her mouth and pointed at Juliet's sheepskin coat. 'Your coat. That's not the same one you bought last week, is it?'

'Oh, yeah,' nodded Juliet, glumly. Fudge-coloured and floor-length, it had cost a small fortune, and in her excitement to wear it, she'd never got round to having it Scotchguarded.

'Unfortunately it is, yeah.'

'But it's . . .'

'. . . ruined?' finished Juliet. After leaving it in the airing cupboard overnight to dry to a cardboard stiffness, she'd thrown it on that morning as she'd dashed out of the door. It was only when she'd got to the office she'd realized how terrible it looked in the daylight. 'I know.'

'What happened?'

'It was that dickhead last night.'

'You mean Will wasn't the only one?'

Juliet smiled ruefully. 'No, this dickhead was on Oxford Street. I was trying to find a cab and he drove past and completely soaked me. Can you believe it?'

They were climbing uphill now and the wind was whipping around their faces. Putting her head down, she stuffed her hands in her pockets to try and keep them warm.

'Wow, just like in *That Touch of Mink*,' observed Trudy.

'What?' That wasn't the reaction Juliet had been hoping for.

'You know. The film with Doris Day and Cary Grant.'

Juliet looked blank. She was a Blockbusters, latest-Hollywood-releases person, unlike Trudy who was a member of an arty video shop and had watched every black and white, Technicolor, animated, world cinema, subtitled, dubbed, silent, MGM classic film ever made.

'Oh c'mon, you must have seen it,' continued Trudy,

gripped with a surge of enthusiasm. 'Cary Grant plays this rich, suave, handsome dude and one day he's in his chauffeur-driven car and it's raining, and he drives past Doris Day, who's all dressed up in this fabulous fifties suit, y'know the kind with the nipped-in waist and really great fur collar . . .' Trudy found it difficult not to get carried away when it came to fashion. 'Anyway his car gets really close and splashes her, not on purpose of course, but she's completely soaked. Obviously, she goes crazy, but he doesn't notice what's happened at first and doesn't stop. Which makes her even more furious. But then, right at the last moment he sees her, but it's too late. And when he tells his driver to turn the car around she's gone.'

'And then what?'

'He tries to find her.'

'Does he?' Puffed from walking uphill, Juliet stood still in the middle of the pavement to catch her breath.

'Of course he does,' tutted Trudy, as if it was obvious. 'And then he spends the rest of the movie wining and dining her, flying her to fancy hotels, trying to get her into bed.'

'And what does Doris do?' They set off walking again.

'She spends the whole time torn between fancying him like crazy and trying to resist.'

'And what happens in the end?'

'What do you think happens in the end?' said Trudy impatiently. 'They get married and live happily ever after. It's a movie, for Christsake.'

Juliet sighed. Sticking her hands deep inside her pockets she continued trudging up the high street, absent-mindedly looking in shop windows, glancing over faces in restaurants.

'So was this guy who soaked you the rich, suave, handsome Cary Grant type?' Trudy began tying the flaps of her bearskin hat under her chin to stave off the wind.

'How do I know? I only caught sight of him for a couple of seconds.'

'But . . .' Trudy raised her eyebrows.

Juliet relented. 'But yeah, I suppose he was handsome.' She grinned. 'Handsome, but still a dickhead.'

Trudy looked triumphant. 'You never know, he's probably still scouring the streets of London looking for you right now,' she teased.

'I doubt it,' retorted Juliet, laughing off the idea, but a tiny seed of thought had started to sprout. Well, actually it wasn't a seed of thought, more like a seed of hope. *Hope? Juliet, what are you doing?* She scolded herself. It was all the Jack Daniels, making her lust after strangers. Correction: *A stranger*.

Reaching the red-tiled entrance to the tube station perched on the steep corner of the hill, Juliet quickly said her goodbyes to Trudy before either of them froze solid to the pavement, and hurried inside to catch the lift. She just made it. Squashing up between woollen overcoats, backpacks and long hair, she watched as the doors slid closed.

With so many bodies, the lift was warm after the icy chill outside and leaning against a framed advert for a new West End show, and a teenager in a puffa jacket, Juliet experienced that soft-focus, woozy feeling that was the result of too much alcohol, warmth and cigarette smoke. Waiting as the lift slid down into the bowels of the ground, she slipped dreamily back into her thoughts. Maybe the driver wasn't a dickhead. Maybe he was actually a really nice bloke. The thought gave Juliet a twinge of guilt and, as the doors slid open, she dismissed it. Who cared *what* he was? Striding out of the tunnel, she made her way to the platform. She was never going to see him again anyway.

Chapter Eleven

Galloping towards her, he jumped down from his mighty steed and strode manfully towards her. She trembled, her heart fluttering like a trapped bird, as he swept her into his strong arms, pressing her against his chest.

'I adore you.'

She sighed as they gazed into each other's eyes. Until, unable to control his passion any longer, he pressed his lips against hers in a heady embrace.

Looking up from the well-thumbed page of Violet's latest bodice-ripper, Juliet glanced across at her neighbour who was settled in her Shackleton's armchair, sucking mint imperials and puffing away on her Lambert & Butler cigarette. Silent, except for the faint rattling of the mints against her dentures, she was gazing dreamily out of the window.

It was Saturday night and glammed up in a beaded evening dress with her hair swept up in a chignon, Juliet cut a surreal figure on the faded chintz sofa. She'd called in to quickly visit Violet, who'd been adamant about seeing her party outfit, but twenty minutes later she was still there, sitting in front of the three-bar gas fire reading *Bittersweet Dreams* and fending off offers of tea and bourbon biscuits, while she waited for Will to get ready for the SGC ball.

'Is it OK if I stop there? The taxi should be here any minute.' Juliet folded over the corner of the page to bookmark it.

Rousing herself from fantasizing that she was the busty damsel in distress being rescued by her dashing lord of the manor, Violet brought herself abruptly back to reality. Careful of her arthritic knees she shifted slowly around in her chair and, taking off her glasses, rubbed the red mark on the bridge of her nose made by the heavy inch-thick prescription lenses. 'Aye right you are, luv,' she nodded, repositioning them and bringing the real world back into focus. 'Bit of a shame though.'

Juliet felt a pang of guilt. She was being selfish. Who was she to deny an old lady her only bit of romance?

Washing down the mint imperial with the cold dregs of her cup of tea, Violet took a drag of her cigarette. 'I was hoping we were just about to get to a mucky bit.'

Juliet had been at Violet's for the past half an hour. She and Will were supposed to have already left but there'd been a hitch. At the last minute the fancy dress shop in Hammersmith had rung with the news that the costumes she'd hired had been double booked. In a panic, she'd had to throw on her old faithful number from two Christmas parties ago, while Will was making do with his DJ which had been screwed up in the back of his wardrobe for ever. Impatiently, Juliet checked her watch again. All dressed up and ready to go to the ball, she felt like Cinderella. Unfortunately this particular Prince Charming was running late. It was a wonder he was even going at all.

'I was thinking, maybe we could go see a film tonight,' he'd suggested to her that morning, pushing open the door of a small Portuguese café. They were at the unfashionable end of Portobello, where the fashion and antiques stalls deteriorated into broken junk and tatty jumble and the shops were an unpretentious mix of cash-only restaurants and mini-markets selling halal meat and brightly painted Moroccan tagines stacked into towering Pisa piles on the pavement. 'There's that one with Will Smith I wouldn't mind seeing.'

Rosy-cheeked, having walked all the way there from their flat, Juliet pulled a face. 'Oh, but you know I hate those big budget science-fiction flicks, and anyway tonight's . . .'

But Will wasn't listening. Actually, the cinema was a really great idea of his. He'd been wanting to see the film for ages, and he and Juliet hadn't had a night out together. What could be better? 'Apparently the special effects are amazing.'

Without managing to reply, Juliet found herself inside the café. Warm, noisy and familiar, it was cluttered with small white Formica tables, brown plastic chairs and a heaving mass of dedicated customers, who made the weekend pilgrimage for their renowned *nata*, small, caramelized egg custards, and tall glasses of milky white coffee. It was one of those places you always think is a real find, until you read about it in the *Time Out* guide and realize that half of London knows about it.

'And then if you want, afterwards we grab a takeaway. A Thai, maybe, or what about an Indian?' Will was brimming with enthusiasm as he looked around for somewhere to sit. As usual the place was full and they hung back in the doorway, waiting to see if anyone was about to leave. 'Or if you want we can eat first and go to the last showing, I think there's one about 10.30.'

Juliet finally got a word in edgeways. 'But tonight's SGC's ball.'

'What?' Will looked blank.

'I told you weeks ago.'

'You did?'

Juliet could feel herself getting annoyed. Will's memory loss was annoyingly selective. He never had a problem remembering five-a-side practice, what time the big match was on, or the number of the Indian takeaway, but seemed to suffer total amnesia when it came to remembering his relatives' birthdays, buying loo roll, or that they were supposed to be driving over to her parents' for Sunday lunch. 'It won't be that bad,' she argued. 'And anyway, it's to raise money for charity.'

'Not to mention your ad agency's profile,' he fired back.

Unzipping his fleece, he glanced sideways at Juliet who stood next to him, staring glumly at her trainers, hands dug deep into the pockets of her even sorrier looking sheepskin. She chose to ignore his cynicism. She didn't want to argue. Instead she decided to appeal to his better nature. He had one in there *somewhere*. 'Oh, c'mon Will. It's really important that I go tonight. You know what it's like at these work things. I've got to network, schmooze. Boss's orders.'

'So you won't be needing me there, will you? I'll just get in the way.' Spotting an empty table he threw down his bundle of newspapers to claim ownership. *Great.* Just *great.* The last thing he felt like doing tonight was hanging out with a load of wanky ad people. Apart from Juliet of course, he mused, digging around in his pockets for his wallet.

Juliet was eyeing the back of his mussed up hair suspiciously. Since when had Will ever bothered about being in the way at a party? He was always the life and soul. 'You're trying to get out of this, aren't you?'

Her accusation gave Will a change of heart. He didn't want another row. 'No, course I'm not trying to get out of it. You're right, it'll be great. I'm looking forward to it.' He leaned over, giving her disbelieving face a kiss. 'Now, what do you want? The usual?'

Leaving Juliet squashing herself into the corner seat, next to the Calor gas heater, Will went to join the queue that was winding around in front of the glass counter full of pastries and croissants. He didn't want to talk about it any more. Of course he wasn't looking forward to some shite ad party. To be honest, he'd forgotten all about it and, after the mess he'd made of Valentine's

Day, he'd thought he'd suggest going out together, just the two of them.

Sulkily he ordered a couple of milky white coffees, two cheese croissants and, what the hell, a couple of those *natas*. Now, instead, he was going to spend a boring evening making smalltalk with people he wasn't interested in, who certainly weren't interested in him, and who he'd never see again. He probably wouldn't even get to speak to Juliet all night. Yeah, he was *really* looking forward to it. In fact, he *couldn't wait*.

Paying the café's moustached matriarch he stuffed his change in his back pocket and grabbed a handful of sugar sachets.

'S'cuse me, s'cuse me.' Precariously balancing two plates on two glasses of milky coffee, he began weaving his way across the café towards Juliet.

'Will?' Looking up from the colour supplements, Juliet watched him negotiating the tables. His tongue was stuck out in concentration, as if he was eight years old and in an egg and spoon race. 'Do you really mean that?' She'd been mulling over what he'd said.

'What?' Will plonked the cups down on the table, the lattes splashing over the edge.

'About wanting to go tonight?'

Glancing up he saw Juliet's face. She looked worried.

Suddenly Will felt guilty. He was being a selfish git. OK, so the Will Smith movie was out, but there'd be other nights. This ball was obviously a big deal to her.

'Yeah, I really mean that.' Trying not to think about the poncy costume he was letting himself in for, he sat down and picked up the sport section. '*Promise*.'

'I bet you're right looking forward to having some fun with all your friends tonight, aren't you?' Easing herself up from her armchair, Violet reached for the cosy-covered teapot.

'They're not really my friends.' Juliet thought about Gabby. 'It's a work thing.'

'Work? Dressed up t'nines like that?' Violet tutted disbelievingly. 'In my day you'd be lucky to get a clean overall and a bucket.' As a cleaner for the gas board for most of her life, one of Violet's favourite gripes was how young people today didn't know they were born. 'Another cuppa?'

Juliet shook her head politely. She'd already had three.

Not to be put off that easily, Violet replaced the teapot on the nest of mahogany tables and reached for the tartan biscuit tin. Taking the lid off, she rattled it at her. 'Go on luv, dig in. There's some of them garibaldis right at t'bottom.'

'Not in this dress,' smiled Juliet. She breathed in. She hadn't remembered it being so snug at the Christmas party.

'Don't be daft. There's nothing of you.' Helping herself to a couple, Violet shuffled over to the french dresser which doubled as a drinks cabinet. 'I know . . .' she grinned happily, showing off both sets of acrylic dentures. 'I'll make us both a snowball.' Violet liked a tipple, and having guests round was the perfect excuse to indulge. 'Did I ever tell you I was drinking snowballs the night I met my Albert?'

About a dozen times, thought Juliet, smiling as she replied, 'No, were you?'

'Oh, aye,' she nodded, pouring huge glugs of advocaat into old-fashioned pint glasses with wobbly glass panes and handles. 'I'd gone to a big party at t'Labour Club with my fiancé Maurice Bennett. We'd been courting for two years and there'd been talk of us getting engaged that summer . . .' Unscrewing the bottle of lemonade, Violet let the bubbles fizz out of the neck before filling the glasses, '. . . and we probably would've if he hadn't had to leave early and left me by m'sen.' Holding out a frothing pint glass to Juliet, she gave a chesty laugh. Juliet could hear the result of sixty years of cigarettes rattling around in her lungs. 'My

Albert was a handsome devil in those days. When he asked me to dance, we could hardly keep our hands off each other.' She peered at Juliet through her thick prescription lenses. 'Don't look so shocked. You young 'uns didn't invent sex, you know.'

Juliet cringed. There was nothing worse than old people talking about sex. Well, actually there was. *Old people having sex.* Weren't they supposed to sit on park benches and hold hands? Sipping her drink she steered the conversation. 'So what happened to Maurice?'

'Last I heard he'd moved to Morecambe and opened a pawn shop.' Violet slurped the foam from her snowball. It left behind a white moustache. 'I was fond of him like, but we were never right for one another. He kept pigeons and he showed more lovin' to them birds than he ever did to me.' Licking the foam from her top lip with her tongue, she smiled as she reminisced. 'Besides, I could never have stood for all that bird shit. The poor bugger was always covered in it.'

Laughing, Juliet glanced at the gold carriage clock on the mantelpiece. She wouldn't have minded staying longer, listening to some more of her anecdotes – Violet had eighty years of them – but she didn't have time. 'I'm sorry, but I really should go and get Will, I don't want to be late.' Before her neighbour could argue, she stood up, bending low to give her a kiss on her powdery cheek. 'Thanks for my drink.'

'You only had a drop.' Grumbling, Violet dragged on her cigarette, which had an inch of ash ready to fall on the carpet, and blew out a chimney of smoke that wafted up through the wisps of her fringe. In contrast to the rest of her white-blond curls, it had been stained a nicotine yellow like her anaglypta walls.

'Are you sure you're going to be all right by yourself?' Despite Violet's feistiness. Juliet couldn't help worrying about her. She often wondered if either of her grandmothers would have been anything like her if they'd still been alive. Probably not, she thought, as she watched Violet flick the ash into the palm of her hand and surreptitiously tip it into the geranium on the porch windowsill.

'Don't worry about me, I'll be as right as rain.' She patted Juliet's bare arm. 'You go on and have a grand time with William. He's a grand lad, you know.'

'Yeah, I know he is,' smiled Juliet, experiencing a twinge of guilt as she remembered last night. Moaning to Trudy about Will and gushing about some idiot in a silver sportscar. Christ, when she'd had a few drinks she really did say the stupidest things.

'You'll live on memories of nights like tonight when you're an old bugger like me,' Violet tittered good-naturedly, 'so make sure it's a good 'un.'

Juliet squeezed her tiny hand. 'I'll try,' she said. Lifting the latch, she pulled open the front door and stepped outside onto the crazy-paving path. It was dark, except for the shaft of light pouring from the open door.

'And mind yourself. You'll have all the fellas after you in that frock.'

Juliet smiled at the compliment.

'You've not got a bra on, have you?'

Now she was grinning. Violet wasn't one for mincing her words. 'I'll pop over and read some more of *Bittersweet Dreams*.'

'I'll look forward to it, Julie.' Leaning against the doorframe for support, Violet chucked her cigarette stub on the front step, squashing it with the rubber sole of her slipper. 'I know those books are daft, but I do like a bit of romance. Even at my age.'

Putting her hands in the front pocket of her pinny, Violet watched Juliet negotiating her slippery path. It was like turning the clock back fifty years. That could have been her, all dressed up and going to a party. She used to go to a lot of parties in those days. Her and Albert. Not like now.

'But I'll tell you sommat . . .'

'What's that?' Shivering, Juliet paused by the gate, pulling her embroidered shawl tightly around her bare shoulders.

Popping another mint imperial into her mouth, Violet pushed her glasses up her nose.

'Nowt's a patch on the real thing.'

Chapter Twelve

Juliet knew something was wrong as soon as she walked into the living room. Expecting to find Will looking dashingly handsome in his DJ, she saw he was on the phone in the tropical fish boxers his mother had bought him last year for his birthday, his crumpled shirt lying abandoned on the ironing board. 'I'll call you back,' he hissed, hurriedly putting down the receiver. Turning to Juliet, he smiled.

He looked as guilty as hell.

'Something's come up . . .'

Juliet looked at him. Was this one of his jokes?

'At 7.30? On a Saturday night? What could have *come up*?' she tried to joke, mimicking his choice of casual phrase. 'Your lottery numbers?' She laughed nervously: this was probably him just fooling around. But she had an awful feeling he was serious.

Will ran his fingers through his shower-damp hair as he looked at the expression on Juliet's face. Bollocks. There was no easy way to say it, so he might as well just say it. 'It's Rolf, there's a problem at work . . .' Once he'd started the words began tumbling out. 'I need to go over to Kensington and sort out a wall that's collapsed. It's an emergency.'

He *was* serious. Juliet had a sudden desire to put her fingers in her ears and start humming loudly. 'But we're leaving. The taxi's here.'

There was the sound of a horn as a minicab pulled up outside. For once the cab was on time. Unlike Will.

He began trying to explain. 'Look, I know it's bad timing . . .'

'*Bad timing?*' Juliet looked at him incredulously. 'This is more than bad timing, Will.' Thoughts of going there by herself began sinking in like a stain. She imagined Gabby's reaction. And then immediately wished she hadn't. Hearing the cab's horn again, she rubbed her forehead in agitation. Tonight was fast turning into a nightmare. 'Everybody's with their partners. I can't turn up alone.'

'Maybe Trudy will go with you.'

'That's even worse, they'll think I'm a lesbian.'

'Perfect. You'll be every man's shecret fantashy.' He tried cheering her up by putting on his Sean Connery accent. Bond was one of his favourite, if not one of his best, impersonations. Raising one eyebrow he put both his arms around her waist and pulled her towards him. 'You'll definitely shwing the contract . . .' He was trying to lighten the mood, but Juliet wasn't laughing.

In fact she felt like crying. 'Can't you get out of it, can't Rolf manage himself?' She looked at Will. He looked apologetic, but resolved.

Juliet felt something snap. 'I can't believe you're letting me down like this. I can't believe you're going to leave me in the lurch.' Pushing him away, Juliet stood back and glared at him. She knew it was below the belt to bring Valentine's Day up, but what the hell, she was so pissed off. She threw the word like a dagger. '*Again*.'

Will didn't react. He was feeling bad enough about everything as it was. But not enough to back down. 'If there was anything I could do . . .'

'Don't give me that. You didn't want to go in the first place.'

'That's not true,' he protested, even though he knew it was. 'But you'll probably be better off without me being there anyway. I'd only get in the way when you were trying to network.'

'Stop making excuses, Will.'

'It's not an excuse.' Now he was the one beginning to lose it. He understood that Juliet might be a bit upset that he couldn't go, but there was no need to make such a big deal. He was the one going to have to stand outside in the freezing cold trying to fix some fuck-up Rolf had got them both into, while she was at a ball getting pissed on champagne and enjoying herself. 'Do you really think I wanted this to happen? That I've done this on purpose? It's just that this job is a big deal, I can't jeopardize it . . .'

But you'll jeopardize our relationship, thought Juliet, feeling hurt, disappointed, saddened, angry. She didn't say that though. She didn't say anything, until she made one last effort.

'You promised.'

There was a pause.

'I know.' Will shrugged. 'I'm sorry.'

For a moment they looked at each other, neither of them speaking, until finally the silence was broken by the cab driver honking his horn impatiently outside. Picking up her bag and house keys, Juliet walked out of the living room and out of the flat. A blast of wind slammed the front door shut behind her.

That was Will's last chance.

And he'd just blown it.

Chapter Thirteen

Sweeping up the gravel driveway, impressively lit by the flames of ten-foot-high burning torches, Juliet pressed her nose against the window of the minicab as Sommerville House came into view. Transformed for the evening into a Venetian palace, the stately home rose before her, its white pillared front illuminated by thousands of coloured lights like a gargantuan birthday cake.

Winding down the window she leaned out, her breath white in the frosty evening air. Above the minicab's stereo she could hear the familiar strains of Vivaldi's *Four Seasons* wafting out across the landscaped gardens, intermingled with the whooping laughter and excited chatter of the arriving guests. Wearing eighteenth-century costumes and Venetian masks, they were being greeted by dozens of masked footmen. After the row with Will, Juliet had been dreading the party, but seeing the spectacle unfolding before her now, she felt a flutter of anticipation.

It looked like being one hell of a party.

'Wow, I must say I'm impressed,' whistled Trudy, who was sitting in the front passenger seat, next to Eccles, the Rastafarian minicab driver. Fifteen minutes ago she'd been slobbing in front of the telly, halfway through *Blind Date* and a Chinese Chicken Pot Noodle, wearing her trackie bottoms, bumble-bee slippers and a self-heating face-pack, assuming she was staying in for the night.

After Fergus's early morning wake-up call, he'd left promising to phone. He hadn't. Gutted, she'd been locked in her flat ever since, hugging to her chest the unwashed pillowcase upon which he'd once laid his Brylcreemed head and steadfastly ignoring phone calls from family, friends and furious clients who'd been clogging up her answering machine with wailing, foot-stamping messages about how they were going to die if they didn't get their hands on one of her duchesse satin trouser suits with diamanté piping.

But by Saturday night she'd had enough. Pining was way too much effort. Trudy was bored. She was starving.

And the pillowcase stunk.

Which is why when Juliet had called, she'd immediately yelled yes to the party invite before sprinting into the bedroom as if she was Clark Kent, and sprinting back out minutes later in one of the aforementioned trouser suits and a pair of Jimmy Choos.

Fuck Fergus. She wasn't lovesick. She was ready to party.

'Thanks for coming, Trude.' Faced with the dire prospect of having to turn up alone, Juliet was grateful to her friend for agreeing to step in at the last minute. And for lending her a fabulous antique gold chiffon dress.

'What the hell is that you're wearing? Monsoon?' Trudy had shrieked as soon as Juliet had walked into her flat. 'And what's with the hair?' she'd continued, yanking out the kirby grips and dismantling all her hard work. 'Do you wanna look like a friggin' bridesmaid?'

'Lucky I had that free window in my hectic social life,' grinned Trudy, as she finished tying on her court jester mask that sported a huge beaky nose, and looked at her reflection in the minicab's sun visor. She could never understand the attraction of themed parties, they were just an excuse to make people look ridiculous.

Fortunately Juliet had allowed her to wear one of her own creations. Unfortunately she'd still had to wear a mask. Turning sideways, Trudy checked out her profile. Jesus Christ, it was like seeing herself pre-rhinoplasty.

Reflected in the vanity mirror she saw Juliet sitting on the back seat. Although the top half of her face was covered in a black and white harlequin mask, Trudy could see she was gazing broodily out of the side window. Juliet hadn't given her details, but it didn't take a psychologist to know all was not well in the Barraclough–Morris household.

'Don't let him ruin your evening, Jules. He's not worth it.'

'I know,' muttered Juliet. Now she knew why all the movies ended when the girl got the guy. It was so audiences could imagine them walking off into the sunset, hand in hand, confetti swirling around their heads like one of those plastic snowglobes. Now she was finding out what happened when the cameras stopped rolling. And it wasn't happy ever after. She forced a smile. 'What am I going to do?'

'Whatcha gonna do?' boomed Eccles, their Rastafarian minicab driver, who'd been earwigging on their conversation. A raucous belly laugh erupted at her startled expression. 'I'll tell you whatcha gonna do.' Pulling up behind a convoy of limos, he switched off the engine and leaned over the back of his furry seat cover. Fixing her with his dark brown eyes, he put his face close to hers as if he was about to let her in on a secret. 'You's gonna 'ave a fuckin' good time, sister.' Breaking into a broad gold-toothed smile, he held out his palms towards her.

Staring at his outstretched hands, the dark creases etched into the pale palms, Juliet felt suddenly self-conscious and faintly ridiculous. He'd misunderstood. She'd been referring to her relationship, not this evening. The last thing she felt like doing was high fives. She felt like . . . like what? Being miserable because of Will? Letting him ruin another evening?

Lifting her hands Juliet smacked her palms against his. Once. Twice. So hard she could feel her hands stinging. Her face broke into a smile and with delighted amusement she threw back her head and joined in Eccles's deep-throated laughter.

'Good evening, ladies.' Stepping out of the cab they were pounced on by one of the uniformed footmen. 'Welcome to Sommerville House.' Hired from a local amateur dramatics society, Malcolm, whose nine-to-five job was as a chartered accountant in Holborn, was taking his acting role very seriously. 'A night of intrigue, anonymity and excitement awaits you. Come join the party and leave your inhibitions behind.' He bowed so low his powdered wig looked in danger of overbalancing and falling onto the gravelled driveway.

Juliet felt a flutter of excitement. That's exactly what she felt like doing. And with a mask to hide behind, she could do anything. *Anything at all.*

They headed through the impressive marble entrance hall towards the sound of chatter and clinking champagne glasses. Over the years Juliet had been to a lot of advertising junkets and, regardless of the hype that surrounded them, they were always just bog-standard office Christmas party minus Slade and the mince pies. An empty dance floor with a few secretaries self-consciously braving the peripheries, the moustached DJ with his collection of ABBA and Fatboy Slim for the under-forties, not to mention the unnerving spectacle of seeing workmates dressed up in their 'Saturday-night-out' pulling garb of boob tubes and novelty waistcoats. So she was completely unprepared for the sight that met her eyes when she walked through the arched doorway.

Dripping with chandeliers, coloured streamers and lavish flower arrangements, the grand ballroom stretched out before them, buzzing with hundreds of guests. Frock-coated waiters flitted in and out dispensing champagne cocktails, stripy-jumpered gondoliers were handing out cornettos and bite-size pizzas, courtesy of the high street pizza chain that was sponsoring the whole bash, while a dreadlocked troop of fire-eaters, stilt-walkers, jugglers and acrobats, recommended by Danny and Seth from their last trip to Glastonbury, were creating a carnival atmosphere.

'Oh my lawd, it's Silicone Valley out there,' drawled Trudy, grabbing a glass of champagne and looking out across the sea of corseted cleavage.

The invite had requested eighteenth-century costume and most women appeared to have gone for the *Dangerous Liaisons* look, in the hope that a crinoline and a tightly laced corset would make them look like Uma Thurman or Michelle Pfeiffer. They did not. Thankfully, the men appeared to have fared much better, although there were a few who'd obviously left the costume hiring until the last minute and had been forced to wear whatever was left on the rails. With some unfortunate results.

'Jeez, take a dekko at Robin Hood,' howled Trudy as a bespectacled fortysomething wearing green tights, a leather jerkin and what looked suspiciously like a cowboy hat with a feather in it, slunk past self-consciously looking for his wife.

'Will you stop it, I work with these people,' hissed Juliet, who was feeling underdressed. Normally she was the first to join in a good piss-take, but tonight she had to put on her account manager head and was scanning the ballroom, trying to spot any of her clients. Boring, but necessary. Unfortunately, Trudy thought it was girls' night out. Watching her drain her glass in one go, it dawned on Juliet that she'd unwittingly saddled herself with a liability.

'Oh, c'mon Jules, this is hysterical, you've gotta laugh.'

'But not quite so loudly,' she pleaded, grabbing another drink from a passing tray and handing it to her. Maybe that would shut her up. Alcohol tended to make Trudy sleepy. Juliet was hoping for unconscious.

'Now that's more like it.'

'*Trud-ee.*'

'No, I mean it, really,' protested Trudy, lifting up her mask for a second to do *that look*. It involved making her eyes spookishly wide, flaring her nostrils and clenching her teeth and was usually used in conjunction with a nod towards a member of the male species. 'This one is *very cute*.'

Juliet caved in with curiosity. 'Who's too cute?'

'Ten o'clock. Man in red devil mask.' Trudy had watched *Charlie's Angels* on video too many times.

Juliet squinted across the ballroom. It was difficult to see because there were so many people milling around, and to be honest, she wasn't expecting much. Trudy's taste in men left a lot to be desired. But then a waiter moved and she saw him. It had to be him. Five-ten with broad shoulders, he was wearing a DJ and was standing with another man and two blondes in little black dresses. All wearing masks, the cheap plastic kind you get from the newsagents on Hallowe'en, they appeared to be listening to a story he was telling. It must have been a joke because at that moment, he made a gesture with his hands and they all burst out laughing.

'I see what you mean.' She couldn't stop staring. Trudy was right. Even though his face was hidden beneath moulded red plastic, there was definitely something about him.

She was still watching him when, all of a sudden, he seemed to sense he was being gazed at. Turning his head he looked directly at her.

'Oh, fuck he's just caught me staring.' Ducking her head down, she swivelled round to face Trudy. 'How embarrassing.'

Trudy laughed. She'd never been able to understand the English obsession with being embarrassed. What was there to be embarrassed about? 'I think you've just lucked out, the guy's still staring over at you.'

'How do you know it's me? It's probably you,' fired back Juliet. She was disconcerted to feel a spark of excitement.

'Bullshit,' dismissed Trudy. 'You've definitely got yourself an admirer there.' Totally oblivious to the effect her words were having on Juliet, she turned her attention to the tray of bite-size pizzas being waved under her nose. She'd barely eaten anything all day. 'Mmm, these look sensational. What d'ya fancy? Quattro Formaggio or Meat Feast?' She looked up from the tray. '*Jules?*'

But Juliet wasn't listening.

They spent the next half-hour shaking hands, spotting celebrities, eating canapés and drinking champagne. Juliet was actually beginning to enjoy herself, when she was pounced upon by a woman wearing a Marie Antoinette costume and an elaborate wig. Staring at the powdered curls, Juliet was reminded of the infamous paparazzi shots of Elton John, arriving shamefacedly at his birthday bash at Hammersmith Apollo in a removal van because his wig was four feet high. This wasn't far off. Even worse, it was baby blue.

'Well, lookee here, it's Marge Simpson,' whooped Trudy, snorting with tipsy hilarity into her third champagne flute.

Marie Antoinette didn't laugh. Neither did Juliet. Even beneath the diamanté-studded mask, she knew instantly, it was her account director.

'Juliet, you're looking wonderful.' Thrusting out her bony chest, her sunburnt skin stretched tightly across it like a rack of lamb, Gabby fanned herself affectedly. 'Although I see you decided not to wear costume as requested on the invitation . . .' Her lip curled as her eyes ran critically up and down Juliet's body, '. . . and *plumped* for vintage instead.'

'It's a Trudy Bernstein actually,' interrupted Trudy, before Juliet had managed to think of something less catty in return. 'This season.'

'I'm sorry,' said Gabby, not sounding sorry in the slightest. 'And you are?'

'Trudy Bernstein.'

Oh dear. Juliet could feel the conversation spiralling downwards into a slanging match. She had to take control. 'At the last minute, Will couldn't make it,' she ventured, hoping her explanation would get them both to back off. 'Trudy's an old friend.'

'That's a shame,' said Gabby.

What is? thought Juliet. Will's absence or her friendship with Trudy?

She didn't have to wait long to find out.

Trudy chose that particular, *perfect*, moment to let rip an unceremonious belch, remarkably similar to the kind of croak produced by giant Costa Rican frogs. 'S'cuse me, this stuff is so gassy,' she giggled, in a fake Southern drawl.

Juliet felt her toes curling like the witch in *Wizard of Oz*. Over the years she'd got used to Trudy's revolting habits of belching, farting and – worst of all – blowing her nose with her fingers in the street when she thought nobody was looking. Usually she just ignored her, but not tonight. Tonight Juliet could quite happily have killed her.

It was with relief that she saw Magnus, SGC's creative director, making a beeline for their happy threesome. Thundering towards them in a Henry VIII costume, he was pushing his way through a crowd of photographers who were taking pictures of a girl-band member and her latest accessory – a newborn sprog which she had strapped across her ample cleavage in the obligatory Bill Amberg sheepskin papoose – while her rockstar boyfriend was threatening to nut them.

'Good evening, Magnus,' queened Gabby, as he bore down upon them. Fresh off the dance floor, he was panting like a St Bernard and large sweat stains were spreading outwards from his velvet armpits.

'Hey, how did you know it was me?' He sounded disappointed.

'It was probably the fez that gave it away,' said Juliet kindly. 'Or was it the Birkenstocks?'

SGC's creative director had recently undergone a remarkable change of image. After a fortnight's holiday in Goa last year he'd 'found himself' and returned home to London, chucked out his Ozwald Boateng suits and Oliver Sweeney shoes, and taken to wearing Birkenstocks, a salwar kameez and an embroidered fez to the office. Unsurprisingly, this had set off a few alarm bells in senior management – fortysomething creative directors didn't have their nose pierced and have yin and yang henna tattoos – but they'd soon fallen silent when they'd realized that his sudden change of appearance and kooky behaviour were winning them contracts. Big contracts. Which meant half a million in bonuses for them last year, not to mention the brand new Mercedes company cars and expense accounts at The Ivy.

Pushing his mask onto his forehead, he began furiously wiping away the sweat that was running in rivulets down his goateed cheeks. 'Comfy as hell, you know,' he panted, lifting up his hairy foot to show off his sandals. 'Wonderful for dancing.' He sighed. 'Shame we never got their contract. Had some wicked ideas for a campaign . . .' Magnus's attempts to mix a Gordonstoun vocabulary with that of the street made him sound like Tony Blair. His voice trailed off as he noticed Trudy.

'I don't think I've had the pleasure of being introduced.' Fixing her with a smile, Magnus performed a mock-bow, twirling his hand in an over-the-top flourish.

Juliet winced. Professionally she had a lot of respect for Magnus, but when there was an unattached attractive woman around, he always acted like such a prick. She glanced at Trudy. She was going to crucify him.

But instead Trudy laughed. *Flirtily*. Cynical, foul-mouthed Yank she might be, but give her a little flattery and she was a giggling pushover.

'Would my fair lady care to dance?' Magnus continued. Now nothing would stop him, not even Gabby's icy presence.

'Why, siree, I don't mind if I do,' giggled Trudy in an even more shocking wench-like accent. Taking his hand, she gave Juliet a wink over her shoulder and began prancing off towards the dance floor. Juliet watched her in disbelief. Yep, there was no doubt about it. She was actually *prancing*.

Chapter Fourteen

Finding herself alone with Gabby gave Juliet an uncharacteristic urge to network. It was the lesser of two evils.

Or so she thought.

A couple of hours later she was having second thoughts. Trying to impress the Japanese suits from BMZ into giving them the MAXI account was hard work. Even harder was having to stand in five-inch heels, laughing politely at golfing anecdotes told by groups of middle-aged male clients, followed by smalltalk with their Range-Rover-driving, Cartier-watch-wearing wives who insisted on telling her about their charity work. Not even consuming the equivalent of two bottles of Moët made it any more bearable. She needed something stronger.

Like Rohypnol, she thought as Roger, the brand manager from Doc Martens, droned on about their oil-resistant rubber soles. Having collared her twenty minutes ago he hadn't yet paused for breath.

'Now what I think is even more fascinating is the lace-ups versus slip-on debate . . .'

Dear God no. In despair she drained the contents of her flute in one go. If only someone would rescue her. Nodding politely at Roger and making lots of 'mmm, yes, absolutely' noises, she let her eyes drift over his shoulder.

It was him again.

'Personally, I've always preferred slip-ons, much

easier to put on, less fiddly, more of a slip-on and go . . .'

Juliet tried not to look at him but it was impossible. She stared across the dance floor, past the strumming harpist and the ice-cream toting gondoliers. He was still talking to his friend, who had his arm around one of the blondes. Did she know him? No, they definitely hadn't met before. She would have remembered.

'. . . but on the other hand, or should I say foot . . .' Pausing, Roger began tittering at his side-splitting wit: 'there is a lot to be said for lace-ups . . .'

And you're going to say it, thought Juliet, reluctantly forcing her attention back to Roger who was dressed up like Dick Turpin. If she didn't escape soon there was a high risk of her entering persistent vegetative state. Thankfully, desperation and alcohol took charge and she heard herself yelping, 'I'm sorry, can you excuse me. I need to powder my nose.' As the words came out of her mouth she cringed. She sounded like something out of the 1950s. *Powder my nose.* Who the hell powdered their nose these days? *Whilst wearing a mask?*

She didn't give Roger time to ask questions. Excusing her way through the crowd of partygoers she grabbed another glass of champagne in true marathon-runner style, and practically jogged to the Ladies.

She was met with an inevitable queue. It snaked all the way down the corridor. Not even a certain surgically enhanced supermodel had managed to jump it and was having to stand obediently in line, mobile in one hand, yapping Shih Tzu in the other. Juliet suddenly felt she was bursting. This was her bladder's party trick. It was empty until it saw thirty women waiting for two cubicles and then – hey presto, as if by magic it was excruciatingly full.

Then Juliet saw the answer to her bladder's prayers. *The Gents.*

Chuffed at her initiative, she pushed open the door and scanned inside. Being in a stately home they weren't the usual kind of men's urinals; these toilets had carpet, gilt-edged mirrors and a pile of white linen hand towels. More importantly, they were empty. Juliet poked her nose around the door and sniffed. It smelt remarkably OK. Even air-freshener scented. She hesitated. Should she? She looked behind her. No-one. She looked at the queue for the Ladies. It hadn't moved.

Dashing inside she pushed open a cubicle door and locked it quickly behind her. Flicking down the seat with one finger, she was going to hover over it – the normal practice in public loos – but heels and alcohol played havoc with her balance, and instead she plonked herself down. Untying her mask, she loosened the straps of her stilettos, rested her flute of champagne on her bare knees and relaxed her muscles. Aaahh, the relief.

Against all Juliet's cynical expectations, tonight was actually turning out to be a great party. Trudy was having fun flirting with Magnus, Danny and Seth were getting stoned in one of the gondolas on the terrace, Annette was enjoying the attention her shepherdess costume was causing. Even Gabby, it had been rumoured, had been spotted doing Hey Macarena. Everyone was enjoying themselves.

Everyone except me, thought Juliet, suddenly aware that the 'fucking good time' she'd promised herself wasn't exactly emerging. What had happened to her enjoying herself? Flirting a little? Letting her hair down? She rested her cheek against the coolness of the wall. Instead she was sitting in the Gents, feeling woozy, and suddenly rather sorry for herself.

'Let's look at the evidence.' She spoke aloud, imitating Loyd Grossman. 'This week my so-called boyfriend has stood me up. *Twice*. I was soaked on Valentine's night, on Oxford Street, in my new six hundred quid sheepskin coat. *By a wanker*. Oh, sorry Trude. I mean Cary Grant. And now I'm at this fabulous party with free drinks and everything and I'm sitting on the sodding loo . . .' Juliet paused. She'd had a few too many drinks and in her alcohol-addled mind she'd lost all concept of time. Suddenly she realized she must have been sitting there for ages and reached for the loo paper. Her hand rattled the empty cardboard insert. 'And would you believe it, I'm wearing a G-string and *there's no sodding bog roll*.'

She heard the door swing open. There was the sound of footsteps walking across carpet and onto the tiled area near the latrines. Juliet froze. *Somebody was there*. She prayed it wasn't winner-of-personality-of-the-year Roger. Or the people from BMZ. Or even worse, Magnus. Unlike a lot of women in the office, she hadn't seen Magnus with his trousers down. And she didn't want to. Still, at least it would solve the problem of either having a soggy G-string wedged up her bum cheeks and drips trickling down her inner thighs, or ripping up the cardboard inner tube and trying to *blot*.

'Er . . . S'cuse me.'

There was no answer. She leaned forward, straining to hear.

'*Hello?*'

Blimey. Juliet jumped back, startled. The voice came from right outside her cubicle door. She looked down. She could see the shiny black tips of a man's shoes.

'Are you OK in there?'

The voice was posh. Very, very posh. Royal Family posh. Now she was regretting opening her big gob. This was a stately home after all, not Yates Wine Lodge. And she was supposed to be doing a PR job for the company, not behaving like some drunk old slapper. She mulled over the option of not saying anything, pretending she wasn't really there. Maybe he'd go away. Alternatively, worst case scenario, he could call the fire brigade.

The idea compelled Juliet to speak. 'Erm, yeah . . .' she began and then stopped. 'Actually no . . . I'm not . . . there was a queue in the Ladies, you know what they're always like. Well, no, you probably don't, but anyway, I really needed to pee and because there wasn't anyone in the Gents I thought . . .' she realized she was waffling. She was pissed and waffling. *In the Gents*. This was definitely not good PR.

'Have you locked yourself in?' He began rattling the door.

'Oh my God, no, no . . .' Images of him breaking the door down flashed through her mind. 'There's no loo roll.' She tried to make it sound more posh: 'I mean, toilet tissue.' She winced. Now she sounded like a voiceover from one of their ads. 'I wondered if you wouldn't mind passing a few sheets under the door.'

'Sure, no problem.'

A few seconds later a hand appeared with a whole bundle.

She grabbed it. 'Thanks.'

'Any time.'

If she wasn't mistaken, she could have sworn he was laughing.

When she had flushed the loo Juliet faffed around for ages, fastening her stilettos, tying on her mask, fluffing her hair, trying to sober up. When she finally emerged from the cubicle she was relieved to see the man had disappeared. The coast was clear.

Well not exactly.

With the door to the Gents swinging noisily shut behind her, she saw a man outside in the corridor. *He was wearing a devil's mask.* Juliet felt a jolt of recognition.

Leaning against the wall, he stood up straight when he saw her. 'I don't suppose I could tempt you with another glass of champagne?' He looked at the empty flute in her hand. 'Or are you a strictly Andrex-only woman?'

Juliet felt a hot flush of embarrassment. So this was the mystery loo-roll passer. She winced. Any chance of trying to play this cool had just gone right out of the window. She tried to salvage some threads of dignity.

'Thanks, but I think I've had enough champagne for one night.' Her mind raced. Was he chatting her up? Part of her hoped that he was. *Woah, easy, girl.* She took a lungful of air. What was going on here? Normally she didn't take much notice of men. Apart from the odd passing comment to Trudy about a bloke having a nice shirt, or the guy behind the bar being a dead-ringer for Johnny Vaughan, since meeting Will she'd been in a hermetically sealed bubble. A 'couple bubble' that made the rest of the male species invisible.

But now, in an instant, her bubble had burst. All she was conscious of was the presence of this man. His musky, lemony, clean kind of smell that reminded her of holidays in the Mediterranean. His voice: low, textured, confident. The way his hair was almost black against the tanned olive skin of his throat.

Juliet stopped herself. She'd had a row with her boyfriend and too much to drink. That was all. A stranger was flirting with her. Flattered, she was getting carried away. She was being ridiculous. For Godsakes, it wasn't as if they even knew what each other looked like. Juliet forced herself to start walking down the corridor.

'Oh c'mon, where's your party spirit?' he called after her.

Without turning around, she replied without missing a beat, 'It's taking the night off.'

Back in the ballroom the charity auction was under way. On a makeshift stage, Magnus was getting into the swing of things.

'Dinner for two at the Ivy. Do I hear one hundred

pounds? . . . a hundred and twenty? . . . forty . . . oh, two hundred from the lady in the court jester costume . . . going, going . . .' he whacked the lectern with his gavel. '*Gone*.'

There was a round of applause. The jester looked delighted, the bells on her hat jingling merrily, while Robin Hood, her husband, pulled out his American Express. He looked less so.

'And now we have two tickets for the London Eye, as modelled by our new account manager, Juliet Morris.'

There was a pause in the proceedings as Magnus waited for her to appear. Juliet groaned. She'd forgotten she'd been roped in to do her trolley dolly bit. She remembered to kill whoever's bright idea this had been when she got back to the office on Monday.

Rushing up to the stage, she grabbed the tickets from Magnus. Now what was she supposed to do? What did they do on telly? Juliet smiled awkwardly and thought *Wheel of Fortune*.

'We'll start the bidding at two hundred as these are wicked tickets. You've got a capsule all to yourself and we're even throwing in a couple of bottles of champagne. Share a romantic toast with the city of London at your feet . . .'

Now Juliet knew why Magnus was an ad man. Standing next to him, her jaw beginning to ache, she listened to the bidding going up. It was at £500 when she heard a voice from the audience.

'A thousand if Juliet agrees to accompany me.'

What? She tried desperately to see where the voice came from.

'Oh tremendous, that's the spirit,' hooted Magnus.

'No, hang on . . .' she began, but she couldn't make herself heard over the cheers and wolf whistles.

'Going, going . . .'

'*No, wait* . . .'

But it was too late.

'Gone!'

* * *

'OK, so it's cheating, but I figured it was one way of getting to talk to you again.'

Walking off stage a few moments later, Juliet was met by her mystery bidder. It came as no real surprise to discover it was the man in the devil mask.

'You paid a thousand pounds to talk to me?' She was flattered. It irked her to realize she wasn't annoyed by his tactics, but impressed. He had to win the prize for the best chat-up line.

'And drink champagne with you. *With the city of London at our feet,*' he mimicked Magnus. Juliet began shaking her head. 'Oh no, hang on. Look, there's no way I'm actually going to agree to this.'

'Why not?'

This is the point where I tell him I've got a boyfriend. Juliet hesitated. She'd suddenly lost her voice. She couldn't tell him. She didn't want to. Thankfully she didn't have to, she had a bona-fide excuse. 'I don't like heights.'

Standing in a small alcove by the French windows, she heard the orchestra start up again.

'Would you rather dance?' Not to be put off, he gestured to the dance floor. 'Oh, don't tell me, you don't like dancing either.'

Christ, this man was cocky. Juliet shook her head. 'I can't waltz.'

'I'm a good teacher.'

'I'm sure you are.' Cocky or not, she couldn't help herself. *Jesus, Juliet, what are you doing?* she thought. You're flirting. You're engaging in terrible *double-entendres*. You're acting like you're single. *And you're not.* You have a boyfriend. You live with him. You even wax his back for him – sometimes. And, shithead or not, that means you're taken. If you're not careful this man is going to get the wrong idea. He's going to think you're interested.

She was.

'Do you smoke?' He held out a packet of cigarettes. She didn't recognize the brand.

'No, given up.' *Move, Juliet. Start walking. Before you do something stupid.*

'Me too,' he laughed.

Rooted to the spot, Juliet watched as he took a cigarette out of the packet, the lighter out of his breast pocket. He was wearing cufflinks. She noticed he had nice hands. Tanned with a plain silver ring around his middle finger.

'Sorry, do you mind if I take this thing off?' He motioned to his mask. 'While I have a cigarette?'

'Why should I mind?' She tried to sound cool. And failed. She was desperate to see what he looked like.

As he pulled off his mask she was momentarily frustrated to see his hair falling over his forehead, the darkness of the corridor shadowing him. Until, running his fingers through his hair, he turned to her. Noticing his mouth, with the full lips and easy smile, the small lump across the bridge of his nose, the heavy-lidded brown eyes framed with lashes that were wasted on a man, she watched as he looked right at her. *Stared right at her.*

And that's when it hit her. It was him. The driver of the Aston Martin.

The dickhead who'd soaked her.

And he was abso-fucking-lutely gorgeous.

Chapter Fifteen

Juliet woke with a jolt as Hazell Dean's piercing warbling blasted into the bedroom. *What the fuck?* Rolling over, she flung her arm out of the duvet and groped for the plastic figurine of a dancing hula-hula girl that was the radio alarm clock. According to Will, who'd bought the clock at Camden market years ago, it was a fifties original and a collector's item. Right at this moment, Juliet couldn't give a monkeys if it was a priceless antique.

Finding the hula-hula girl face down under a discarded T-shirt, Juliet whacked her as hard as she could to turn off the radio. She stopped wiggling her hips. And Hazell Dean's high-pitched shriek fell silent. Thank God.

Propping herself up on her elbows, she prised her dried-on mascara eyelashes apart and peered at the time, hidden inside the moulded contours of the grass skirt – 7.30 a.m. For a split second she thought she had to get up for work, but then the clouds of sleep briefly parted and a ray of lucidity shone through. It was Sunday, and she didn't have to go anywhere.

The relief.

Obviously someone had been messing around with the alarm. That someone being Will. Juliet glanced across at the guilty suspect. He was fast asleep. Arms flung crucifixion-style across the blue gingham duvet cover, face buried deep in his pillow, he was emitting a faint porcine snuffling. A damp patch around his mouth was forming on the polyester-cotton pillowcase.

Feeling the murmurs of a hangover Juliet sank back onto the mattress, submerging herself in the feather duvet. Ignoring the stale smell of cigarette smoke clinging to her hair, the layers of make-up she'd reapplied throughout the evening and hadn't been arsed to take off, she tried to succumb to the waves of sleep. But she couldn't. It was impossible. Her mind didn't want to roll over and play dead, it wanted to pick over last night's events at the ball, like a vulture scavenging for juicy bits.

She'd finally left Sommerville House at two-ish that morning, when the ball had begun winding down into the usual surreptitious spliff smoking, disconcerting drunken groping, and 'guess who's copping off with who' gossiping that always signalled a party was nearly over; and, for anybody still sober enough to have any sense, that it was time to grab partners, coats, and a taxi before everyone else tried to.

Professionally, the evening had been hailed as a huge success, with their CEO Alex Schmart declaring it a 'spectacular achievement, media and charity coming together' in his speech, which, cutting the ad crap, meant clients had been arselicked, egos boosted, backs patted, *HELLO!* were going to feature it in their social pages, and of course a big photo-opportunity cardboard cheque was going to charity, always a good PR move.

But it was all the behind-the-scenes stuff that made last night one Juliet would remember. Spotting fancy dress fiascos and celebrity cellulite with Trudy; watching Magnus on the dance floor (she hadn't been able to work out whether he was being ironic or whether his Patrick Swayze *Dirty Dancing* style pirouettes were all part of the eighties revival); eavesdropping on Gabby drunkenly accusing her stockbroker husband Edgar of flirting with Annette – '*you bashtard, you've been ssshhtaring at her titsh all evening'* – a somewhat slurred accusation considering she didn't drink.

And then there'd been him.

At the memory, Juliet turned over, trying to find a cool part of her pillow. She still didn't know what to make of it all. After he'd taken his mask off and she'd discovered who her mystery bidder really was, she'd been surprised to find herself lost for words. She thought that was only a cliché, that it didn't really happen. But it had. For a few seconds anyway. Until she'd found some. In fact she'd found quite a few.

'So what do you do? Apart from hanging around in the Gents?' Taking a drag on his cigarette, he'd eyed her with amusement.

'I hang around on Oxford Street getting drenched by dickheads who drive around, not looking where they're going, in sportscars that are *so obviously* extensions for their very small penises, it's embarrassing.' *Phew, where did that all come from?* She'd smiled sweetly. It was immensely satisfying to see that for once he didn't have a witty answer.

'What?'

'I've been looking for you all over the joint.' An unmistakable East Coast voice behind them had made them both turn around. It had been Trudy looking a bit the worse for wear. Her white satin suit covered in a variety of red wine, vodka and champagne stains, she was minus her mask and one of her Jimmy Choos. Steadying herself against the french window, she'd grinned at Juliet. 'You're missing the fireworks.'

'Believe me, they haven't even started,' she muttered, before announcing loudly, 'Trudy, I want you to meet Cary Grant.'

'Cary Grant?' Trudy had looked nonplussed. Half a gram of coke, two heavily loaded spliffs and God knows how much free booze meant her brain was cloaked in a chemical fog. Like a fruit machine, it had whirred the information slowly around, until bit by bit, everything fell into place and began jangling out its jackpot. 'You mean . . . ?'

Both women had turned to look at the guilty party. Smoking a cigarette, he'd been listening to the conversation going on about him. Juliet had been irked to see that he appeared to be faintly amused.

'He's the guy? On Valentine's night?'

If Juliet had known what Trudy was going to do next, she would never have nodded. But she didn't. And neither, it appeared, did he. Otherwise he would have ducked as Trudy wrestled a soda siphon from a passing waiter, roaring, 'See how it feels, you limey bastard,' and began spraying him with a jet of soda water.

He'd looked shocked. So had Juliet, who'd watched with hypnotized horror as Trudy used the siphon like a semi-automatic weapon, whooping with delight as she squirted his jacket, his shirt, his face. Until, after what seemed like for ever, the soda had run dry.

Silence. Nobody had said anything. Then, like a slow handclap, Juliet had heard the sound of drips of water plopping onto the marble floor. He was completely drenched. His hair plastered to his face, his shirt clinging to his chest in wet ripples, his DJ stuck to his shoulders like a soggy wetsuit. He'd been the best-looking drowned rat Juliet had ever seen.

Preparing for the inevitable row, she'd untied her mask and taken it off. His reaction couldn't have surprised her more.

'It's you.' Recognizing her face, he'd broken out laughing. 'Well, I guess I deserved that.' Wiping the drips off his nose, he'd slicked back his hair and smiled at Juliet.

It would have melted glaciers. Any thoughts of a row, of telling him what she thought of him, melted away with it. And Juliet had realized she was smiling back at him.

'Ah, trading secrets with the enemy, I see?'

In the commotion nobody had noticed Gabby bearing down upon them with an entourage of bouncers, big pumped-up meatheads dressed like something from *The Slipper and the Rose*. Glaring at the driver of the Aston Martin who'd been starting to form a large puddle, she'd folded her arms authoritatively and barked, 'I don't believe you have an invitation,' before instructing her heavies to 'escort this gatecrasher out of the building. He can join his friends on the driveway where you threw them.'

A gatecrasher? Now it had been Juliet's turn to be surprised.

'Hey, I'll go quietly.'

She'd watched him laughing and holding up his hands in surrender. Turning to her he'd smiled apologetically. 'Look, I had no idea it was you. About the other night, I'm really sorry, I tried to stop but . . .'

'But you were just leaving,' Gabby had finished.

For a moment he'd hesitated. Then shrugging, he'd peeled off his jacket and begun walking towards the exit, shadowed on all sides by the bouncers.

'Well, I must say I'm rather surprised.' As he'd left Gabby started speaking to Juliet, but she wasn't listening. *He'd recognized her.* She'd watched his retreating figure through the ballroom, wishing he'd turn around. She'd thought he wasn't going to, but at the last moment, before the crowd of partygoers swallowed him up, he'd turned. They'd made eye contact. He'd smiled. And her stomach had flipped.

'Engaging in conversation with our rival creative director is a conflict of interest, wouldn't you say?'

Juliet had turned around. 'What? You mean that was . . .'

'Sykes,' finished Gabby, sneering contemptuously. 'Well who did you think he was? Prince Charming?'

Up until that moment Trudy had been uncharacteristically quiet. After her earlier burst of energy, she'd been lolling semi-conscious against a marble pillar, the soda siphon dangling by her side, her eyes half closed. But suddenly her head had jerked upright. Her eyes had focused. And looking straight at Gabby, her mouth had found its tongue.

'Why don't you just fucking shut the fuck up?'

At the memory, Juliet flinched and turned over in bed. At least after that the rest of the evening had been pretty uneventful. No more surprises. After Sykes had been thrown out, she'd spent the rest of the evening thinking about him. Reliving the evening; her surprise at discovering his identity – the driver of the silver sportscar, the man in the Gents, the mystery bidder, her rival for the MAXI account. What had Gabby called him? *The enemy*. She made him sound like some kind of Russian spy. This was a pitch for an ad campaign, not the Cold War. Trust her to behave like a drama queen as usual. Throwing him out of the ball. Making a huge scene.

And what about her own reaction? Two days ago she'd been furiously cursing and indignantly vowing all kinds of things she'd say in the unlikely event that she ever saw him again. She'd even gone so far as to call him the c word, which, even in these enlightened times, she never used. So 72 hours later, when she'd had every opportunity, what *had* she done? *She'd told him exactly what she thought of him*.

Except that wasn't exactly true, was it? thought Juliet, feeling hot and sticky and guiltily fidgeting underneath the duvet. She hadn't told him *exactly* what she'd thought of him at all. Instead she'd flirted. Quite outrageously, if she remembered rightly. She'd giggled, smiled coyly, thrown back her shoulders and stuck out her chest, she'd sucked in her stomach and teetered on her murderous heels as if they were the most comfortable footwear in the whole world.

And she'd lusted.

Big time.

Just thinking about him now made her groin ache. She thought about the way he'd looked when he was soaking wet, his dishevelled hair, dark and dripping across his face. His shirt clinging to his chest like some wannabe Colin Firth. Like one of the heroes out of Violet's books. A female wet dream.

Will rolled over in his sleep and unconsciously threw out his arm, lassoing her body towards his. Juliet caught herself. What was she doing? Fantasizing about another bloke when she was lying in bed with her boyfriend? Her loyal, trusting, *faithful* boyfriend. Even if he had behaved like a prick, promising he'd go to the ball and then letting her down at the last minute, Will was the man she was in love with, and had been in love with for two and a half years. Lying spooned together, his arm clamped around her right breast, his hard-on pressed up against her spine, Juliet listened to his breathing. Slow. Steady. *Unaware*.

Christ, what if Will knew? she thought, guilt prickling her body like a heat rash. And then changed her mind. Knew what? It wasn't as if she'd actually done anything. So she'd met someone and been attracted to him. Big wow. It wasn't as if she'd shagged him in the bushes. Even though she'd wanted to.

Oh, bloody hell. There she went again.

Jerking her head, Juliet began matronly thumping her feather pillow with her fist as if she was trying to beat up her scurrilous thoughts, before flopping back down. Thirst pawed at her like a hungry dog, but she was too lazy to get up and go into the kitchen. She just wanted to go back to sleep.

In her ear, Will began talking in his sleep, gobbledygook punctuated with lots of furtive kicking. Juliet groaned. This was Will's playing-for-England-in-the-World-Cup dream. The one where he scored God knows how many goals and she woke up with shins the colour of aubergines.

Dog-tired, she wriggled as close to the edge of the

mattress as she could without toppling over onto the seagrass matting, yanked the duvet over her head, stuck her fingers in her ears and closed her eyes.

And tried not to think about anything.

Or anybody.

Chapter Sixteen

It wasn't that easy.

Arriving at her desk on Monday morning Juliet noticed she already had a voicemail message. Punching in the four-digit password, she wedged the receiver under her chin and took the lid off the cappuccino she'd just bought from Mario. She was about to scoop up the melted chocolate froth with her forefinger when she heard

'Hi . . .'

It was him.

Like a live fish, the receiver escaped from under her chin and fell, rattling around on the desk. Juliet attempted to grab it, trying not to spill her coffee, her heart pounding as if she'd just legged it down the escalators for the Central Line. Managing to catch it, she rammed it tightly against her ear. He was still talking.

'*. . . obviously I'll pay for your drycleaning . . .*' there was a heavy pause. '*After Saturday I've got some drycleaning of my own . . .*' Juliet winced at the image of Trudy doing her Robert de Niro in *Taxi Driver* impression with the loaded soda siphon, but it was forgotten when she heard his next sentence: '*. . . and if you're not doing anything tonight I'd like to take you out for dinner to apologize.*'

Dinner? Juliet stared absent-mindedly at her rapidly cooling cappuccino, all thoughts of scooping up froth forgotten as she listened to him reeling off his number.

In the background she could hear Dean Martin. Crooning out of her iMac speakers he was providing a fitting soundtrack. She turned off the sound and tried to calm down, but it was difficult. Juliet wasn't used to handsome strangers ringing her up out of the blue and asking her to dinner on a Monday morning. Correction: She wasn't used to handsome strangers ringing her up. *Ever.*

Unfortunately she wasn't going to have any time to get used to it happening the once either, as Neesha, her assistant, reappeared from the kitchen with a Diet Coke and two rounds of toast. Both for herself.

'Hey, I've just been hearing about the ball from Annette.' Twenty-one and a first-class honours graduate from Cambridge, Neesha had just joined SGC's training programme. Which, if Juliet remembered from her own experience, meant that so far her knowledge of advertising consisted of photocopying, changing the printer cartridge and doing the Pret à Manger run at lunchtime. 'Was it really that great or is she exaggerating as usual?'

Juliet knew Neesha had been gutted she hadn't been able to make her first ad party. Something to do with a big family Indian wedding that had been going on for three days at Claridge's.

'Oh, erm . . .' With her mind still trying to absorb Sykes's voice on playback in her ears, she groped around for words. 'Yeah it was . . . erm . . .' across the room she saw Seth and Danny sloping down the corridor. They were still wearing their musketeer costumes from Saturday night. 'Awesome.'

'Shit, what a shame I missed it,' said Neesha, biting into a slice of thickly buttered granary bread. 'Any tasty men?' Despite her father's attempts to set her up with a nice respectable Hindu, Neesha was determined to choose her own husband. Even if this meant arranging to meet her would-be suitors at Nobu, ordering everything she could off the menu including a couple of bottles of Cristal, not touching any of it, and leaving them to pick up the bill. One and a half grand later they didn't want to marry her either.

'Oh, a few,' muttered Juliet, shuffling a few of the faxes as a hint for her to go away. She didn't.

'By the way, some guy called for you this morning, wouldn't leave his name, wanted to be put through to your voicemail.'

'Oh, yeah . . . I er . . . I just heard his message.'

'He rang first thing, I'd barely got in the door. Must have been pretty urgent.'

Juliet jumped on the words. 'Really?' she yelped, before realizing Neesha was staring at her quizzically, 'I mean, yeah, yeah it was an urgent matter about an ad campaign.'

Neesha waited expectantly.

Oh shit, thought Juliet, now she was going to have to start really fibbing. 'Erm . . . it was about our pitch for the MAXI account,' she bluffed vaguely. 'You know, the usual stuff about doing some market research, asking the public what they want from a car.'

Neesha tutted impatiently, 'Isn't that obvious? To get from A to B.'

'And you want a career in advertising?' quipped Juliet.

Grinning, Neesha sat down at the desk opposite and turned her attention to devouring the rest of her toast and reading her emails.

Leaving Juliet alone with the voicemail message and the rewind button.

By 6 p.m. she'd listened to the message an embarrassing eight times before she'd got a grip and deleted it. She hadn't called him back. Even if she had been tempted (and no she wasn't, she'd kept telling herself) she hadn't had the time.

Work had been crazy. And that wasn't crazy in the sense of one of those 'you have to be crazy to work here' stickers that were always found in *the* most deathly boring places such as dentists' waiting rooms and local libraries, put there by staff in an attempt to try and persuade the public that their workplace was a wacky, creative, *Go-Go-Go* kind of environment, and not the hideously dull, brain-aching monotony that it so obviously was. This had been the real thing.

The frenzied, exhausting, maddening type of crazy that meant Juliet hadn't had a minute to herself all day to flick through the free copy of *Metro* she'd found on the tube, grab lunch, ring Trudy. Barricaded to her desk by a wall of scary-looking in-trays, she'd been too busy working on the brief for the MAXI account. The deadline for the first meeting with the clients was on Friday, but Gabby's pep-talk last week had left her in no doubt about her future at SGC if they didn't win the account.

In short, she wouldn't have one.

Staring at the screen of her iMac, Juliet tried to concentrate on the report she'd been emailed earlier in the day entitled 'The growth of the sportscar industry in the UK'. Hardly the most enticing title for a 300-page document. It was like reading the telephone directory, only with the added joy of pie-charts, statistics and bullet points. She stared harder, watching the text disintegrating into lots of tiny dots. She stifled a yawn. It wasn't helping that she was being distracted by the commotion coming from Gabby's office.

She glanced up. Through the glass walls she could see her boss pacing up and down, gesticulating wildly and shouting into her headset.

'No, Monica, you cannot go to your salsa class, you're babysitting Finn and Gypsy.' She was having another argument with her Polish nanny. 'What do you mean, I'm their mother? What do you think I'm paying you to be?' There was the sound of a headset being thrown against the wall, a door slamming and Gabby swept past, her long leather trench coat flapping behind her.

'Domestic headaches,' she barked, before stopping mid-stride and doing a U-turn. 'If Monica has the audacity to call again I'll ask Annette to put her through to your extension . . .'

Great.

'Tell her I've got an appointment at six to unblock my chakras and I'll be home by seven. Could you also make sure she's aware that I expect to find those children fed, bathed and in bed.' She stared at Juliet. 'Aren't you writing all this down?'

Juliet hesitated. What was she? An account manager or Gabby's Girl Friday? Irritated, she grabbed a pad of Post-it notes. 'Anything else?'

Her sarcasm was wasted.

'Well, actually there was one other thing.' Abruptly dropping her tyrannical boss act, Gabby came over all-best-friend-like and perched on the end of Juliet's desk. Her face visibly softening, she pushed her sunglasses onto her forehead and gave her an Oprah-look of concern. 'I wondered if you'd had any more contact with our Mr Sykes?'

Juliet fiddled with the paperclips in her desk tidy. 'No, of course not.'

'Splendid.' Cocking her head on one side her director laughed lightly. 'Call me cynical, but I suspect he was hoping to discover what our MAXI pitch is going to be, by flattering one of our key players.' Placing her perfectly manicured forefinger across her lips she leaned closer. 'But I'm sure nobody breathed a word, did they?'

Presumably I'm the nobody, bristled Juliet. 'There weren't any words to breathe,' she smiled thinly. 'Danny and Seth are still brainstorming.' She thought about their daily jaunts to Tower Records, Blockbusters and the pub for 'inspiration'.

Bestowing a syrupy smile upon Juliet, Gabby patted her hand as she would a dog. 'I'm sure you don't need me to tell you that it would be very unethical to have any kind of communication with the opposing team, as it were. But then who would want to go on that ghastly big wheel anyway?'

Suffocated by the cloying attempts at friendliness Juliet stood up and randomly grabbed something to fax. She felt queasy. Gabby might be vicious, but what if she was speaking the truth? Had Sykes only been talking to her to find out about their pitch? Had she been naïve to think he was genuinely interested in her? That he'd been chatting her up because he fancied her? Christ, how could she have been so foolish?

'I really must shoot.' Interrupting Juliet's spiralling descent into paranoia, Gabby stood up stiffly. That was enough office bonding for one day. She glanced at the screen of Juliet's iMac. 'Aah, the report. Make sure it's on my desk first thing, could you?'

It was a rhetorical question. Juliet tried not to think of how many pages there were left to get through. Whole chapters on speed restrictions, fuel emissions, hatchbacks versus coupés. She'd be there all night, *riveted*.

'Though I'll be amazed if I have any strength to read it,' added Gabby, briskly buttoning up her coat. 'It's this godawful jetlag. It's playing havoc with my sleeping patterns.'

Which must be a first for someone travelling from Switzerland, thought Juliet, leaning against her desk, watching her account director goose-stepping past the creative department and into reception.

96 . . . 97 . . . 98 . . . 99 . . . She waited until she'd counted to a hundred before switching off her computer. Sod Gabby, she had her own chakras to unblock. She pulled on her coat. Mondays were always a killer and she couldn't wait to go home. Tonight Will was at five-a-side practice and so she had the whole evening to please herself. To forget about the ball, Gabby, Sykes, work. She fancied chilling out, playing her old

Joan Armatrading CDs that Will hated, eating something delicious for dinner and soaking in a Radox bath until her skin went all white and wrinkly. Sheer bliss.

Throwing her bag over her shoulder she mouthed 'bye' to Neesha who was on the phone to a friend in Delhi. One valuable lesson Neesha had learned about working for an international advertising company was how much money she could save in international phone bills. Pausing from her outpouring of Gujarati she put her tiny hand over the mouthpiece. 'Where are you going?' she hissed. She was intrigued. Despite what Juliet might have thought, she hadn't bought the story about the phone call.

'Home.'

Neesha raised one eyebrow. A technique she'd learned from her mother to extract the truth from teenage sons.

'OK, I confess I'm lying, I'm going somewhere infinitely more exciting.' Picking up her bag, Juliet began walking away, fanning the flames of curiosity.

'I knew it,' pounced Neesha triumphantly. She'd known something was going on but she couldn't work out what. She was twenty-one, single and spent every weekend clubbing, yet she didn't have men with posh, sexy voices calling her at work first thing in the morning. Why would Juliet? She had a boyfriend. She bought David Gray CDs. *And she was thirty*. 'Go on, tell me. *Where?*'

'Ooh, it has fabulous food, fine wines . . .'

'The Ivy?'

'Tesco's,' yelled back Juliet, pushing through the swing doors and diving into reception, past Annette and Big Ears, who was now propped up on the counter like something from the back window of a Citroën Diane, and out through the revolving doors.

Outside it was glove-and-scarf cold and already dark. Not that London could ever be truly dark. Unlike the countryside with its silent, starry, sleepy black, this was city black. A blurring of noise, activity and light from pavement cafés, shops, restaurant windows and traffic that snaked along the narrow Soho streets. Looping a scarf Violet had knitted her around her neck, Juliet buried her mouth in the soft pink mohair, feeling her hot breath against her skin. Quickening her pace, she walked across Soho Square, and headed in the direction of Oxford Street.

Chapter Seventeen

Tesco was obviously *the* place to be on a Monday night. Heaving with shoppers, the aisles were jammed with men and women, accidentally bumping their wire baskets into each other, making eye contact over the fruit and veg, engaging in smalltalk as they waited in the queue at the cash register. Despite the unflattering strip lighting, this place was a better pick-up joint than All Bar One.

Seeing how busy it was, Juliet was tempted to walk back out as soon as she'd walked in. Having been waylayed by the lure of Claire's Accessories, rifling through racks of hairgrips, toe rings, tattoo transfers and glittery bangles, it was now past seven o'clock and her earlier enthusiasm to cook something fabulous was waning. She hesitated, then decided to brave it. She didn't want to end up back at the flat, trying to concoct something edible out of the shameful contents of the kitchen cupboards.

Grabbing a basket, she headed optimistically towards the organic section. At least tonight she only had to cook for herself. After five-a-side practice, Will usually went to the pub for a few drinks and something to eat. He wouldn't be home until late. Juliet felt relieved. After Saturday things were still strained between them. She'd wanted to talk about what had happened, he'd wanted to brush it under the carpet. Now they were in the middle of an uneasy ceasefire; nothing had been discussed. Neither had apologized. Resentment was breeding.

Despite her good intentions, the organic section was a big disappointment. Juliet felt only pity for the bruised and battered vegetables, and the sadly unappealing packets of frozen soya mince. Why did things that were good for you always have to be so unappealing? Doing a U-turn, she began wandering vaguely up and down the aisles, waiting for inspiration to grip her. A pizza? Too unhealthy. Jacket potato and salad? Too healthy. Steak? Pasta? Curry?

Juliet surveyed the rows of fridge cabinets, the aisles of tins, the Indian, Chinese and Thai sections. Sometimes there was just too much choice in life. She toyed with the idea of being adventurous in the kitchen with a recipe book and a wok, but then decided against it. She wasn't a domestic goddess. She'd stick to what she knew. Her favourite, dinner-party saviour. Mushroom and asparagus risotto.

Filled with instant enthusiasm, Juliet began piling the ingredients into her basket. Arborio rice, vegetable stock, a packet of dried sliced porcini mushrooms. She chose her vegetables carefully, four big, meaty portobello mushrooms, a bunch of fine-stemmed asparagus, a handful of golden-skinned shallots the size of conkers and a pot of purple basil. The most important ingredient she saved until last. *Parmesan*. Real, deliciously pungent Parmesan, not the tasteless white powder sold in tubs for people to sprinkle over their spaghetti Bolognese.

At the cheese counter she found exactly what she was looking for, a huge amber wedge of crumbly, moist cheese with a hard waxen edge. She bought a large hunk, resisting the urge to break off a piece to nibble, and made her way to the cash register, her basket jolting against her legs as she squeezed and weaved her way through the crowds.

Five minutes later, waiting at the end of the checkout queue she began having second thoughts. Did she really want to be bothered cooking? It was a lot of fuss just for herself. There'd be no-one to taste spoonfuls from the pan, to share the bottle of wine, to nip out to the late-night corner shop for Häagen-Dazs afterwards. Juliet stared doubtfully at the ingredients in her wire basket. Maybe she should put it all back and get something for the microwave. It would be a lot easier.

Easier still would have been eating out.

Sykes's voicemail message played back in her mind: . . . *and if you're not doing anything tonight I'd like to take you out for dinner to apologize* . . . Even though she'd promised herself not to think about it, to forget all about him, it was impossible. Standing in the middle of Tesco's, being pushed and shoved by impatient shoppers, Juliet's resolve began to weaken. Maybe Gabby had got it wrong. Maybe he did fancy her. OK so she wasn't Penelope Cruz but she was attractive, in a freckled, size 10-12, honey-highlighted kind of a way.

Juliet glanced at herself in the fridge mirrors. A pale-faced, dry-skinned, tangled-haired woman who needed her highlights doing stared back. London in February wasn't exactly conducive to looking good.

Looking away, she allowed her mind to slip back to Sykes. She wondered where he'd have taken her. Maybe an achingly hip restaurant in town that served Asian-fusion food at blow-a-fusion prices, or a bustling trattoria with battle-scarred tables and baskets of freshly baked focaccia. Juliet's mind was off on a roll, imagining what she would have worn, said, eaten. She knew she shouldn't, but it was difficult not to. It was so appealing. Intriguing. Desirable. A trolley stubbed her mock-croc boots. She grimaced at the reality.

Maybe she'd been a tad rash deleting his number. She wasn't going to be doing anything tonight, apart from singing along with Joan, sitting on the sofa stuffing herself with risotto and then floating in the tub like a beached whale. Perhaps she should have accepted his offer. It didn't have to mean anything. They could have just had dinner as friends.

Except they weren't friends, were they? Professionally speaking, Gabby was right, they were rivals. Personally speaking, they hardly knew each other. *We could get to know each other*, thought Juliet, feigning naïvety. She dismissed the thought as quickly as it had appeared. Who was she kidding? She didn't want to be just good friends.

Toying over whether or not to admit defeat and grab a takeout on the way home, Juliet was interrupted by the shrill ringing of her mobile. PRIVATE NUMBER flashed up on the display. Who was it? It wasn't a friend, she'd logged all their names into her phone. A thought stirred. Maybe it was Sykes? Maybe Neesha had given him her mobile number when he'd called this morning. She realized she was hoping. *Desperately*.

'Hello?'

'I think I'm pregnant.'

It was Trudy. Juliet's disappointment surprised her. She hid it guiltily.

'Don't tell me, you've put on a pound.' Under normal circumstances such a reaction would have been odd, even callous, but Trudy wasn't normal when it came to her health. She was a severe hypochondriac. This month alone there'd been a suspected brain tumour, deep vein thrombosis and a malignant mole on her stomach that, after a visit to her GP, had turned out to be an ingrowing hair.

'Jules, I'm serious.'

'Just like you were when you came back from India and thought you had rabies?' The basket was getting heavy. Juliet put it on the floor.

'OK, OK, so you can't get it from eating fish, how the hell was I to know? It didn't say that in my *Rough Guide*,' she rebuked sulkily. 'Anyway, this time it's for real.'

'Why?'

'I've been throwing up for two days.'

'You don't think it might have something to do with getting pissed out of your head on Saturday night, smoking too many joints and polishing off that tray of mini pizzas?' The man standing next to Juliet in the queue, wearing a tight black T-shirt and a sunbed tan, turned his gelled head to listen.

'This wasn't a hangover. I've had hangovers. This was different. I'm definitely pregnant. I just know it.'

There was no point arguing with Trudy. When she was convinced of a certain diagnosis there was no reasoning with her. Turning her back to her neighbour who was intent on eavesdropping, Juliet lowered her voice. 'How?'

'How do you think? The immaculate conception?' she snapped. 'I had sex, isn't that normally how people get pregnant?'

'Didn't you use a condom?' Juliet glared at the man, who was now making no attempt to hide his nosiness. She glanced in his basket. It contained two cauliflowers and half a dozen packets of cheese sauce mix. That said it all. A follower of the Ricky Martin school of fashion and a cauliflower cheese junkie.

There was a guilty pause at the other end of the line. 'I know, I know, I'm a bad girl,' Trudy confessed tetchily. 'Don't lecture me.'

'I'm not,' Juliet sighed. 'Look, I'm sure you're not pregnant.'

Drugs, condoms, pregnancy. It was better than *EastEnders*. Cauliflower cheese man couldn't believe his pierced ears.

'Why not? Do you think I've got rotten eggs?' demanded Trudy defensively.

Juliet was exasperated. 'I'm sure your eggs are fine, but I thought you didn't want to be pregnant. *You don't, do you?*' She was suddenly worried. Lust did weird things to the female psyche.

'Of course I don't.' Trudy was now wailing down the phone. 'But I am, I just know it. Fergus is Irish, they have like thirty children in a family. Just think of the Corrs.'

'Or the Nolans.'

'I'd rather not.'

In the background Juliet could hear music and someone shouting Trudy's name. 'Where are you?'

'At the BBC on a shoot. My cellphone's down so I've borrowed the celeb's.'

'Who's the celeb?' Despite her better judgement Juliet was intrigued.

'Some broad with a northern accent and a butt bigger than J Lo's,' she snarled dismissively.

Juliet grinned. Whenever Trudy got annoyed she got bitchy.

'Her agent insisted she was a size six, so now I've got four racks of clothes that won't get past her friggin' knees . . . oh can you hang on a minute . . .'

Putting her hand over the phone, Trudy could be heard telling her assistant to stick the dress on with gaffer tape 'nobody will know, everything's airbrushed anyway' before hissing, 'Sorry Jules, gotta go, but I'm about to leave, I'll be home in a half-hour. *To stress*.'

Juliet looked at her basket. Hypochondriac or not, spending the evening with Trudy was better than staying in by herself cooking risotto for one. 'Do you want me to come over?'

Trudy gasped with delight. 'Oh Jules, you angel, would you?'

'Sure.' She was about to hang up when Trudy interrupted.

'Oh, there's one other thing, you wouldn't mind doing me a favour would you?'

Juliet was suspicious. Why did she get the feeling she wasn't going to have a choice? 'What is it?'

'Could you bring a pregnancy test?'

'*A pregnancy test?*'

'Actually, could you make that two . . .'

'But . . .'

'Catch you later.' Trudy was gone before Juliet could get a word in edgeways.

Asking cauliflower cheese man if he'd keep his eye on her basket for a minute – 'Hey, no problemo,' he winked knowingly, making her stomach turn. 'I think you'll find the pregnancy tests are on aisle six' – Juliet dashed back down the aisles. Grabbing a couple of Clearblues, placed next to the condoms as a cursory warning, she made her way back to the checkout. She passed the wine section and grabbed a bottle of something white and alcoholic. Then had second thoughts. What if Trudy *was* actually pregnant? She seized a bottle of Shloer and, just so they had every option covered, a bottle of Gordon's gin. Just in case.

Seventy quid lighter and four carrier bags heavier, she emerged through Tesco's sliding doors into the frantic bustle of Oxford Street in rush hour. Laden down with shopping, she was tightening her grip on the handles and steeling herself to join the streams of tourists, commuters and pickpockets, when she heard the sound of a horn. She ignored it. It sounded again. This time she looked up.

'We've got to stop meeting like this.'

Directly opposite, parked on a double yellow, was a silver Aston Martin. The engine was still running. Sykes was leaning out of the window, his chin resting on his arm.

Completely unprepared to see him, Juliet felt a jolt of nervous excitement before her vanity kicked in. She was not looking her best.

'What are you doing here?' Wow, she really had all the great lines.

'Your assistant told me, I thought I might have missed you . . .' He half smiled and then added by way of explanation, 'You never called me back.'

'So you thought you'd stalk me?' she fired back, and then immediately regretted it. She hadn't meant to sound quite so venomous. Her coldness was a smokescreen: she was thrilled to see him again.

'Are you sure you don't want a lift? Those look pretty heavy.'

'They're fine, thanks.' Straightening up she ignored the plastic handles cutting into her hands and began walking in the direction of Bond Street tube, the bottles clanking against her shins, her mind racing. She kept her eyes on the ground, staring at the chewing-gum stained pavement, different people's ankles, listening to the sound of her heels on the concrete. Her mind whirled like the crisp packets in the gutter.

She expected Sykes to take the hint and drive away, but he didn't. Instead he crawled alongside the kerb. She could hear the faint purring of the engine. Sense him next to her. Feel him watching her. It was unbearable.

After steadfastly trying her hardest to ignore him for a few moments she stopped walking and turned to look at him. 'Look, will you just leave me alone. I don't want you ringing, I don't want you following me around, OK?'

She didn't mean it. Not one word. She could quite happily have him following her around every day. But she couldn't. She had a boyfriend. She had to put a stop to this before she did something she'd regret.

'Hey, I'm sorry. You're right. I'm acting like an idiot, it was a stupid thing to do.' He put the car into gear.

Fuck, he's really going to drive off. Juliet panicked. He's going to do what I asked him to do. He's going to disappear and I'm never going to see him again. Her alarm heightened. She grappled with her conscience. It was a struggle. She couldn't let him go. *She just couldn't.* Whatever the consequences.

'*Wait.*'

He braked.

She took a deep breath. Her last faithful breath. 'I don't suppose you'd be heading in the direction of Hampstead, would you?'

Their eyes met. It had begun. *They had begun.*

He smiled. 'Funny you should say that.'

Chapter Eighteen

The whistle blew to signal the end of the match.

There was a God.

Halfway down the pitch, Will gratefully gave up his futile attempt to gain control of the football. Slowing down to a weary jog, his heart hammering against his ribcage, he put his hands on his shaky knees and bent over to try and catch his breath. Sweat ran in rivulets down his reddened face and dripped onto the scuffed wooden floor. He was exhausted. Worn out. Completely done in.

Three-nil down at half-time, he'd spent the last half an hour frenziedly charging up and down the indoor sports hall at Rochester recreation centre. Puffing away like Ivor the Engine, with his lungs feeling as if they were going to burst and his heart as if it was going to give out at any minute, he'd desperately tried to score a goal. But he hadn't come close. The sole of his Nike trainer hadn't so much as scraped the black and white leather surface of the football, let alone kicked it. The opposing team had just sped away with it and left him trailing behind like somebody's grandad.

He took a deep breath of stuffy central-heated air. Jesus, he was really going to have to start going to the gym again. Shovelling cement all day in Mrs Parker-Hamilton's back garden in Barnes didn't count as exercise. He needed to lose a few pounds, get really fit. Losing seven-nil wasn't just embarrassing. It was mortifying.

He felt a slap on the back. It was Rolf, his friend, business partner and fellow five-a-sider. 'Hey, great ball control there, Will,' he joked, his eyes creasing up with amusement behind the tortoiseshell frames of his glasses as he tried to stifle a laugh. 'Word of advice. You're supposed to make contact with the ball. Not use telepathy.'

Straightening up, Will gave him the finger. 'I didn't see you scoring any goals.'

'Preserving my energies for the pub, mate.' He grinned good-humouredly and pulled out a chunky KitKat from his shorts pocket. 'Here, have a break,' he held it towards him.

Will pulled a face. 'Christ, how can you eat chocolate at a time like this?'

'At a time like what? So we lost. It's only a game. And anyway, it's for my blood sugar,' he protested, his smile fading. 'I'm hypoglycaemic.' He bit off a thick, milky chunk. 'Sure you don't want some?'

'No thanks, I'm watching my figure.'

'Why what's it doing?' quipped Rolf, his voice muffled.

'Ha ha, very funny,' retorted Will, jabbing the rotund stomach that protruded from Rolf's rugby shirt. At fifteen stone and five foot nine he was, as his wife Amber affectionately called him, 'a big lad'.

'Hey, gerrof . . .' Grumbling, Rolf swiftly finished off his KitKat in two mouthfuls, screwing up the wrapper and hastily getting rid of the evidence in the swingbin. 'Get your own beer belly.'

Pushing open the door to the changing rooms, Will found the air heavy with condensation and laughter, jeers and praise. Discussing tonight's practice, the other members of the teams were eagerly pulling off shorts and T-shirts, flashing hairy bodies, bruised limbs, spotty arses, dicks of all shapes and sizes. Keith, referee and stockbroker, Phil and Andy, midfields and bankers, Jeremy and Phil, the two defence players and owners of a thriving organic pizza business, Felix, goalie and entrepreneur. All the same age as him. All more successful than him. All richer than him. All better players than him.

Watching them charge boisterously into the showers, Will tried not to let it get to him. He felt like a kid who'd lost at a playground game. He glanced at Rolf who was hunched over on one of the wooden slatted benches, peeling off his socks as if he wasn't sure what he was going to find underneath. At least Rolf was as useless as he was. Though that wasn't much solace, he thought as he watched him popping a huge blister that protruded from his hairy big toe. The guy was as blind as a bat, had two left feet and only went to five-a-side practice so he had a bona-fide excuse to give to Amber for going to the pub afterwards. He wasn't interested in scoring goals, just downing pints.

'So how's the missus?'

'Fine,' nodded Will.

'So how did her big bash go on Saturday?'

'Fine . . .' He tugged off his trainers without bothering to unlace them. Who was he trying to kid? He'd been asleep by the time Juliet had got back, and the next morning he'd avoided mentioning the ball. He'd felt bad enough as it was without having to hear about what an awful time she'd had, how she'd been by herself all evening with no-one to speak to. He looked at Rolf, who'd now moved his attentions to the fluff in his bellybutton.

'Actually I don't know, I haven't asked her,' he confessed.

'Why not?'

'Oh, y'know, I'm still in the bad books for not going with her,' he half laughed, yanking his football shirt over his head and getting his hair caught in the buttons. Untangling himself, he emerged, naked, from underneath his shirt, his pale body looking even whiter under the strip lighting. 'Anyway, I wasn't exactly having a fabulous time myself, was I? Being stuck with you in a garden until gone midnight.'

'Hey, don't blame me, it was your fault for building the sodding pond,' fired back Rolf, pulling off his tartan boxer shorts. Two sizes too small, they left a perforated imprint around his belly.

'It was a Japanese lagoon,' retorted Will.

'It was nearly a bloody reservoir. It was about to flood the street when I called you. What was I supposed to do? Stick my finger in the dyke?'

'Only if she's blond,' yelled Felix, causing the other players to laugh gustily. He'd just got out of the shower and was brazenly strutting around stark-bollock naked, showing off his gym-honed muscular physique.

Rolf joined in the laughter half-heartedly so as not to lose face. Will rolled his eyes. He got on with the rest of the lads but sometimes they really were a bunch of tossers.

'You over-reacted,' accused Will. He was like a dog with a bone. He wasn't going to let this drop.

'Maybe I did,' shrugged Rolf. He was the first to admit he had a tendency to be a bit of a drama queen. 'But I deal with plants. I know how to treat greenfly and make box trellises. I don't deal with water features. If I see water spraying out all over the fucking place I panic. The guy's paying us seventeen grand to build him a Japanese garden. He didn't ask for Niagara fucking Falls.'

'The guy's a dick.' After arriving late in Kensington the other day, Will was still smarting from having to grovel for the rest of the meeting.

'We're in arrears with the bank, Will. He's a rich dick.' Rolf raised his eyebrows and looked pointedly at him. They smiled at each other. It gave way to laughter. It was a truce.

Calming down, Will felt embarrassed about his foul mood. He was taking it out on Rolf and that was wrong.

It wasn't his fault he was a crap footballer and, according to Juliet, a crap boyfriend.

Grabbing their towels they went into the communal showers. They were practically deserted. Most of the team members had already showered and were getting dressed, ready to head off to the pub. These were prompt, busy, efficient, Palm-Pilot-using, briefcase-carrying, suit-wearing men. They had deals to clinch, windows to fill, schedules to adhere to. This was valuable free time. To be spent discussing house prices and the Chelsea game over a bottle of red wine. They weren't going to waste it gossiping in some mildewy council-run sports centre showers.

Unlike Will and Rolf.

'So who did Jules go with, then?' Taking off his glasses, Rolf turned on the shower and groped around on the tiles for the soap dispenser.

'No-one.' Will jumped back from the jet of water. It was freezing cold. He frantically adjusted the water temperature.

Rolf whistled through his teeth. 'You want to be careful.'

'Of what?'

'Letting Jules go to a party all alone and vulnerable, looking sexy . . .' his voice trailed off purposely.

Will laughed. 'Stop trying to wind me up, it was a work thing.'

'Precisely. And you know what happens at office parties. Flirting behind filing cabinets, groping in the stationery cupboard . . .'

'And you'd know from experience, would you? You've never worked in an office, you're a bloody gardener.'

'A horticulturist,' corrected Rolf huffily.

'Same thing,' replied Will, closing his eyes and relishing the invigorating feel of the hot water pummelling his aching muscles. Well, actually it was pummelling his spare tyre. But not for long. Soon it would be a stonking great big six-pack. 'Anyway it wasn't in an office it was up at Sommerville House.'

'Oh, so it was a posh do.' Rolf began shampooing his head, scrubbing hard with his fingers as if he had a thick head of hair and not the receding bits of dandelion-clock fluff that covered the pink crown of his head. 'I bet it was free drinks.'

'Is that all you think about? Booze?'

'And large breasts.' Rolf laughed.

Shaking his head, Will stepped out of the shower and reached for his towel. 'How does Amber put up with you?'

'I ask myself the same question. It's either got to be the dazzling wit, my high-powered job, or my luxurious floating palace.'

'It's a mouldy old barge.'

'The term's houseboat,' smiled Rolf, drying his huge hairy belly. It made Will's love handles pale into insignificance. 'But then it could be my fabulous physique.'

'Yeah, right.'

'It took a lot of hard work to get this body. I wasn't born looking like this, you know.' He held up his meaty arm that boasted a mam-and-dad tattoo. Rolf was the only man Will had ever seen with cellulite. 'Just feel that bicep.'

Will grinned.

'Of course I'm only keeping the weight for Amber's sake.'

'How do you make that out?'

'It's a known fact that pregnant women can feel self-conscious about their body image in front of their partner. But Amber and I will be able to compare bumps. I'm doing it for her benefit.'

'*What?* You mean *she's pregnant*?' Will was shocked and delighted. It was no secret that Rolf and his wife wanted to have kids. Ever since he'd been best man at their pagan wedding in Cornwall five years ago, he'd been expecting to hear the news that he was going to be a godparent. 'Shit, that's great. Why didn't you tell me?'

'Because she's not . . . yet,' added Rolf optimistically. 'But give it a few months. The doc seems to think he's worked out what the problem is.'

'There's a problem?' It was the first Will had heard of it. But then that wasn't surprising. He and Rolf were like brothers, but they hardly bared their souls. They didn't talk about how much they loved their girlfriends, discuss recent arguments, confess their emotions and fears. They talked about how Manchester United was doing in the league, argued over how long it was going to take to finish a garden they were working on, took the piss out of each other over a few pints.

'It's my sperm.' Rolf said it very matter-of-factly, without a hint of embarrassment. Will was impressed. 'Don't worry, I'm not a jaffa. The poor sods are there, and they're swimming. But not very fast. More the doggy paddle than the front crawl. I need to put them in training. Cut out the booze, the fags, the bacon sarnies.'

'So you're not coming to the pub tonight?' Now he was *really* impressed.

'I didn't say that. The doggy paddle's thirsty work.' Rolf lit up a cigarette and caught Will's expression. 'I'm giving up tomorrow.'

'Are you two coming or what?' There was a shout from Keith, the referee. All suited up, he stuck his head around the locker room door.

'You go ahead, we'll meet you there. Which pub is it? The usual?'

'Nah, we thought we'd try somewhere different tonight. It's the big match and Felix says the Faithful Hound in Hampstead's got Sky.'

'OK, see you there.'

The door swung shut. Pulling on his Levi's, Will

shoved his kit in his gym bag. 'How is Amber? I haven't seen her for ages.'

Grabbing his bottle green denim jacket with the corduroy collar that he'd bought from Benetton about ten years ago, Rolf grinned. 'Wonderful as always. She's at Thai-Bo tonight. Says she's learning how to kickbox me into shape.'

Will laughed. Rolf and Amber had to be one of the happiest couples they knew. Even if she couldn't get pregnant. He was envious of their easy relationship.

'If I'd thought, I should have arranged for her to meet us afterwards. We could have gone for a bite at that Greek restaurant.' Rolf salivated at the thought of all that feta cheese, pitta bread and deep-fried calamari. Despite his chocolate fix he was still starving. But then he was always starving. This was a man who once ate nearly a whole turkey and all the trimmings on Christmas Day, and then an hour later went looking for a fish and chip shop that was still open because he was feeling 'peckish'. 'What's Jules up to tonight?'

Will felt a pang of guilt. He hadn't asked her. In fact he hadn't called her all day. For a brief moment he considered ringing her on her mobile and then he changed his mind. He'd wait until he got home and then he'd try to make it up to her. Of course he didn't say any of this to Rolf. Instead he pulled open the door and smiling confidently, winked laddishly.

'Staying in. Pining for me.'

Chapter Nineteen

He was gorgeous. Truly gorgeous. Undoubtedly more gorgeous than she'd thought he was the first time she'd seen him, if that was humanly possible. Juliet sneaked another look at Sykes. Hard to believe, but it was true.

Having accepted his offer of a lift, Juliet was sitting in the passenger seat trying to keep her eyes directly ahead as they drove through the rush-hour traffic. She was finding it impossible. Unlike the Tardis, the sportscar was alarmingly small inside and being so close to Sykes was unnervingly intimate. He was right next to her. Inches away. Just a bit of leather upholstery, her Tesco's shopping and a gearstick between them.

She couldn't resist the temptation to keep glancing at him out of the corner of her eye, trying to garner as much information as possible. What kind of shirt was he wearing? What about his shoes? His make of watch? How he held the steering wheel? Which radio station was he listening to? She checked him out, taking great care to make sure he didn't notice.

Of course he noticed.

'Your friend's a pretty good shot with a siphon.' Looking sideways at Juliet, he smiled. She was mortified. Being caught blatantly eyeing him up, she wanted to climb inside the carrier bags that were squashed around her ankles like potting compost. Instead she had to make do with looking out of her window so he couldn't see her redden. She wanted to feel cool and flirty. Instead she felt awkward and frumpy.

'You're lucky it was only a soda siphon.'

He laughed. 'Tell me about it. My ribs are still bruised.'

'Not to mention your ego,' she smirked, turning to face him. She couldn't resist.

Slowing down in the traffic, he lit a cigarette from the lighter in the dash. 'You've got completely the wrong impression of me, you know.' Shaking his head in amusement, he wound down his window to let the smoke escape.

'Have I?' she asked. What did he think she thought about him? She wasn't sure herself. She was still trying to work that out.

'A dickhead driving a penis extension.' Repeating the words that she'd said at the ball he stared ahead at the traffic, waiting for the lights to change.

Juliet cringed. Had she really said that?

'Believe it or not, I tried to find you the other night. I drove around Oxford Street looking for you but you'd gone.'

He looked for me? Juliet's heart jumped, but she stared ahead, not saying anything in case she gave away how pleased she felt.

'I did, honestly,' he protested, taking her silence as disbelief. 'I felt terrible.' The lights changed and they began moving again.

'Not as terrible as I did, believe me.' She thought about Valentine's night. It was hard to believe it was only a few days ago. She felt so differently.

Misunderstanding, Sykes agreed. 'I know, I saw you. You were soaking wet, you must have been freezing.'

'I was. *Very.*' She nodded in mock-seriousness. She couldn't resist winding him up a little. After all, he deserved it. She'd been the one forced to squelch home on the tube, while he drove off in his warm, dry car. She was getting her own back . . .

'Please, let me pay for the drycleaning,' he offered, suddenly sounding absurdly formal. Taking his eyes off the road, he glanced across at her and smiled ruefully. 'If only to make me feel better about the whole thing.'

Juliet was impressed. He seemed genuinely concerned. 'Don't worry, I think it's ruined.' She fingered the sleeve of her sheepskin coat. Before it had seemed so important and now she couldn't care less. So what if it was brand new? So what if it had cost her a small fortune? So what if she still had to pay the Visa bill? Forget Frankie and the power of love. This was the power of lust. Her hormones were going bananas.

She saw Sykes looking at her. The tanned skin of his forehead was furrowed, his dark eyes brooding. He looked so ridiculously handsome she nervously broke out laughing. 'Don't worry, it's OK, I won't hold it against you.' She watched his face relax, the creases ironing out around the corners of his eyes. But she wasn't going to let him off that easily. 'Even if I did want to kill you the other night.'

'And now?'

Now they were on a dual carriageway, they'd begun to pick up speed, racing past rows of shops, restaurants, supermarkets, their neon lights reflecting in the spray thrown up by the traffic on the windscreen. The sound of the engine roaring, some kind of jazz on the radio, the tyres against the tarmac. Everyday life seemed a million miles away. It was speeding away from her. She looked at Sykes. Flicking his cigarette out of the window, he was concentrating on overtaking a lorry.

And now I want to kiss you, she thought, but didn't say it. She didn't even let herself think it. She grinned. 'And now we're quits.'

'I'm gagging for a pint. Can't this bleeding thing go any faster?'

Wedged into the torn plastic front seat of Will's Land

Rover, Rolf was disgruntledly watching the London traffic speeding past them and munching his way through a packet of salted peanuts he'd bought from the machine in the sports hall foyer. 'I'm dying of thirst.'

'Will you shut up whingeing.' With the accelerator pedal completely flat to the floor, Will was sitting hunched over the steering wheel, as if trying to make the Land Rover more aerodynamic so that it would go faster. It was useless. It rattled along, its engine whining painfully, barely nudging thirty-five miles an hour. He was trying not to let it get to him but it was impossible. For years he'd zipped around London in his convertible sportscar, being the first off at the lights, racing along at 100 m.p.h. on motorways, and now he was reduced to hogging the slow lane, along with the double-decker buses and learner drivers.

'I can see it in tomorrow's *Evening Standard*. Horticulturist dies from dehydration. Driver of Land Rover accused of manslaughter.'

Will glared at Rolf. 'Well, you're not exactly helping, are you? If you weren't such a fat bastard we'd be doing at least sixty.'

Used to the insults, Rolf ignored him. Stuffing in another handful of peanuts, he began fiddling with the volume button on the stereo. Nothing happened. 'Doesn't this thing work?'

'If you're not careful you'll be walking to the pub,' snapped Will. He gave up trying to overtake and pulled into the left hand lane. The humiliation. He couldn't even overtake a cyclist. 'Anyway, I don't know what you're moaning about. You drive a bloody scooter.'

'It's a Piaggio,' huffed Rolf defensively. Like Will, he'd had to sell his car to raise money for the business. He'd consoled himself with the thought that he'd be able to buy a Ducati motorbike instead and fulfil his dream of being an Easy Rider. It was air guitar for a thirty-one-year-old. To dress up in leathers. To feel the thrust of the engine between his legs. The wind in his hair while he still had any left. Unfortunately, never having passed his bike test, reality had dawned and he was now the proud owner of a 50cc scooter. Not to mention learner plates, a luminous cagoule and reflector armbands. 'At least it's a lot faster than this pile of crap. I'd have been on my second round by now.'

'Shut up and give us a fag.'

Obediently, Rolf dug out a packet of Benson & Hedges and passed him one.

'This business better start making us some money soon. You're right. I can't drive around in this thing much longer,' admitted Will, groping around on the dash for a packet of matches. Finding some jammed down an air vent, he lit up. Just then his attention was caught. 'Now that's more like it,' he declared, dragging on his cigarette and enthusiastically jabbing his finger against the windscreen. 'Just look at that.' He let out a whistle. '*Bee-oo-te-ful*.'

'Who's beautiful? Where is she? I can't see her.' In an uncharacteristic show of energy, Rolf quickly jerked upright and squashed his face against the window, cupping his hands around his eyes, scanning the pavement.

'Keep your dick in your pants, I'm talking about a car. Look.' Will pointed ahead of them in the queue of traffic waiting at the lights. 'A 1972, soft-top DB6 Aston Martin. *Magnificent*.'

'Nah, too flash,' said Rolf dismissively, not bothering to hide his disappointment. Discarding the salted peanuts he helped himself to a cigarette.

'What do you know? That's not flash, that's a classic. A real James Bond car.' He glanced across at Rolf, who had his eyes closed, blowing smoke rings. 'Just look at the body. Have you ever seen curves like that?'

'I'm married to Amber, you wouldn't believe what's hidden under her aromatherapist's uniform.' Without opening his eyes Rolf chuckled proudly. He was reliving a bedroom moment. He did that a lot.

Will rolled his eyes. 'You don't understand about cars, mate. Believe me, that is a beauty.' He gazed wistfully as the lights changed to green and the car accelerated away up Hampstead Lane.

'Mmm,' muttered Rolf, unconvinced. 'At least it'd get us to the pub quicker, but then what wouldn't?'

'We'll be there in a minute.' Slowly following, they began chugging up the hill.

'I hope so. This window's stuck and I'm freezing to death in here.'

Will wasn't listening. He was watching the tail-lights disappearing into the distance. Imagining being behind the wheel. The roar of the engine. Feeling the speed and power at his fingertips. Racing along. Juliet by his side. Suddenly he felt sad as he remembered how they used to be when they'd first started seeing each other. Her snuggled up next to him, him laughing. He wondered where it had gone wrong. His thoughts were broken by Rolf.

'Don't the heaters work either?'

'No, mate.' He shook his head, feeling rather deflated. It was the story of his life.

'Nothing seems to work any more.'

'I haven't even introduced myself. I'm Sykes.'

'I know.'

He seemed amused. 'What else do you know?'

'That you're over here from Italy.' Feeling more relaxed, Juliet leaned back in her seat as they whizzed up Hampstead Hill. She released her grip on the carrier bags: she'd been holding onto them like a lifebelt for the entire journey, but feeling as she did right now, she didn't want to be saved, thanks very much.

'News travels fast. What else do you know?'

'That you're one of Montague & Murdoch's best creatives and they've sent you to work on the MAXI pitch.' She gripped the edge of the seat as they sped around a corner. 'And you drive too fast.'

He looked amused, but didn't slow down. 'I don't know about being one of their best creatives, but yeah, I've been living out in Verona for the last twelve months, doing some stuff for our sister company, eating too much pasta, getting a suntan.' He glanced at her and smiled. 'And now I'm back in London to work on the brief. Although I'm not sure for how long. If we win the contract it could be up to a year, but then again it might only be a few weeks . . .' he stared ahead at the traffic so he couldn't see her reaction '. . . if you've got anything to do with it.'

Juliet felt a pang. She didn't want him to go back to Italy. Now she knew what Gabby meant by a conflict of interests. 'My boss thinks you gatecrashed the ball to find out what our campaign strategy's going to be.'

There was a pause. Juliet felt her heart rev in time to the engine. His pause seemed to go on for ever. It was a huge, Grand Canyon of a pause. *Oh shit, Gabby was right.* He wasn't denying it. She felt suddenly stupid. He wasn't interested in her at all. It was all a ploy. He was interested in what she could tell him.

'It did cross my mind . . .'

She could feel a but coming. *She hoped she could feel a but coming.*

'. . . but no.'

Her insecurities screeched to a halt.

'I was with some friends having dinner nearby, you know what it's like. We'd had a few drinks and of course I knew about the party. I thought it would be a laugh to grab some cheap plastic masks from the newsagent's, brazen it out and see if we could get in. It wasn't supposed to be a big deal.' He turned his attention away from the road to look at her. 'Well, that was the idea.' His words dripped with significance.

Unnerved by how heavy the conversation had become, Juliet tried to brush over his remark with chitchat. 'Oh yeah, I saw you with your friends, the guy and the two blondes.' As soon as she'd said it she wished she hadn't. She didn't want to admit to having stared at him all night. But it was too late.

'So you *were* watching me.'

She blushed. 'How To Be Cool' by Juliet Morris. It would never be a bestseller.

Sykes smiled. But it wasn't a smug smile. He looked pleased. Even *chuffed*. 'That makes two of us, because I was definitely watching you.'

His words made it impossible for Juliet to ignore it any longer. Sykes was laying the conversation wide open for her to say something, to admit how she felt. Except now, faced with the opportunity, something was stopping her, preventing her from revealing the effect he was having on her. That he'd been having on her ever since she first saw him on Valentine's night.

With her mind turning itself inside out like a contortionist, she struggled to appear normal. But how could she? Normal wasn't racing through London in a fifty-grand sportscar, flirting with a man who was so sexy he was indecent, breathing in the pungent smell of leather and aftershave. Normal was sitting on the green velvet sofa from Habitat, next to Will who was trying not to nod off, eating Maltesers and squabbling over who had control over the TV remote.

Thinking about Will made Juliet flinch with guilt. What was she doing flirting with Sykes? She glanced at her alibi of carrier bags. She wasn't flirting, she was getting a lift, it was all perfectly innocent.

Except of course it wasn't.

Who was she kidding? She couldn't hide behind her risotto. She'd got into Sykes's car because he was dangerous, exciting, because when she looked at him, talked to him, *was near him*, he sparked something inside her. She was like a cat on a hot tin roof, and it felt amazing. He made her feel alive, scared, unsure. *He made her feel sexy*. Something that Will didn't, *hadn't* for a long, long time.

Had he ever? Juliet couldn't remember, it seemed so long ago. She'd been twenty-seven, now she was thirty. She'd grown up, changed from a girl with mousy-brown hair and a part-time waitressing job to pay the rent, into a woman with highlights, gym membership and a career.

And all she could think about was now. Right now. This very moment. Sitting next to Sykes. Wanting something to happen. She wasn't stupid, she knew where this was going to lead to, where this drive was going to take her, and it wasn't Hampstead.

It was infidelity.

'Do you want me to go any further?'

Juliet looked up.

'Along this road.' Sykes motioned to the street ahead. 'Whereabouts does your friend live?'

'Oh . . .' she flustered, feeling like an idiot. 'Just here.'

He pulled up outside a skinny Georgian house covered with ivy and left the engine running. For a moment nobody spoke.

'Well, thanks for the ride.' She forced a breezy smile, breaking the loaded silence. Phew, that had been a close call. She began gathering her bags together, fumbling for the door handle, all hopes of making a grand exit fast disintegrating.

'Do you want to go for a drink?' He motioned across the road. 'Looks like there's a pub over there. The Faithful Hound.' He smiled. 'Or maybe a coffee? So you don't think I'm trying to get you drunk and have my wicked way,' he joked.

But something told Juliet he wasn't joking. 'It's not a good idea,' she heard herself saying on autopilot.

He smiled apologetically. 'I thought it was one of my better ones.'

She fought with herself. She couldn't do this. She

was Juliet Morris, a nice, loyal, *faithful* girlfriend. She had to be honest. She had to tell him about Will.

'Look, there's something you should know . . .' On the verge of confession she hugged her shopping to her chest, forgetting about the rip in one of the plastic bags. Without warning it extended into a gaping hole, scattering the contents onto the floormat, around her ankles, across his seat. *Oh shit.* Horrified, she watched the Portobello mushrooms roll under the brake pedal, the bottle of Pinot Grigio clatter onto the gearstick, the packet of arborio rice break open and send a rainfall of white pearls showering around the car as if they were at a Mediterranean wedding.

But all that paled into insignificance as, in all the commotion, she saw the bright Clearblue pregnancy predictors launch themselves like missiles and shoot across the car towards Sykes. An ex-rugby player, he caught them with ease.

Silence.

He looked at the packets quizzically, reading the blurb down the side. 'Oh, I see,' he nodded, understanding flooding his face.

'No, you've got it wrong.' Juliet could hear herself gabbling hysterically. This isn't what was supposed to happen. This isn't what she wanted. Grabbing the predictors from his grasp, she stuffed them in her pockets, as if hiding them would make them go away. 'I'm not pregnant.'

'Hey, look, it's not any of my business, you don't have to explain.'

She could feel him slipping away from her.

'They're not mine. It's my friend. Well, actually, she's not pregnant either, at least I don't think so. She's a hypochondriac . . .' Her gaze fell on the bottle of Gordon's gin. 'It's an old wives' tale, just in case.' Stuffing the bottle in another bag, she tried to hide the Shloer. It was too late, he'd already seen it. 'Non-alcoholic, for my neighbour. She's a pensioner.' Juliet thought about Violet with her snowballs. Even at eightysomething she wouldn't be seen dead drinking Shloer.

Watching her flustering, Sykes broke into a grin. It spread across his face, crinkling up the corners of his big brown eyes, his mouth wide with warm amusement. 'Are you sure you don't want that drink? You look like you need it.'

Juliet ceased panicking. He was smiling at her. Smiling back at him she suddenly saw the funny side, how ridiculous it must have looked, how farcical after all that flirting, all that sexual energy. She started laughing. All the emotions that had built up over the last few days were released in bellyaching, watery-eyed laughter. The tension evaporated and without thinking she leaned towards him, giggling as she picked the grains of rice from the dark curls of his hair. It felt so natural. She hardly noticed that her hand was brushing against his face, their heads were almost touching.

Until he began kissing her.

'Happy now?' Pulling up in front of the Faithful Hound, Will turned off the engine.

'Lager, I need lager,' gasped Rolf, opening the door and falling out onto the pavement. It was even colder than inside the Land Rover, and rubbing his hands together, he set off towards the beckoning glow of the pub. He'd got to the door before he noticed Will wasn't following him.

'Will?' He turned round to see his figure silhouetted against a street lamp. Standing stock still on the pavement he was staring at something in the distance. 'Come on.'

Will didn't answer. He didn't even move.

'Will? What's up?'

What was up was he'd seen the Aston Martin again. It was parked across the street and still had the engine running. As he admired it his curiosity was aroused.

Wasn't that where Trudy lived? Maybe it was her and some fella? Maybe it was the bookie he'd been hearing all about from Jules? Intrigued, Will strained to see, scrunching his eyes into thin slits. He could just about make out the silhouette of a couple. It looked as if they were necking on the front seat.

He peered closer, concentrating on trying to see their faces. If she'd just move a little to the left . . . turn this way . . . a bit more . . . nearly . . . nearly . . . Nah, it definitely wasn't Trudy, the girl's hair was different, longer, more like Juliet's in fact.

Will smiled to himself. Whoever they were, they looked as if they were enjoying themselves.

'If you don't hurry up my balls are going to be frozen solid.'

Becoming aware of Rolf's pitiful whines, Will put him out of his misery by turning around.

'My sperm aren't going to be swimming anywhere,' pouted Rolf grouchily.

Shaking his head, Will began walking up the path. Reaching Rolf, he clapped his arm around his pudgy shoulder. 'Give it a few weeks and they'll be doing the Olympics,' he smiled as, forgetting all about the Aston Martin and its passengers, he entered the beery warmth of the Faithful Hound.

Chapter Twenty

'What have you been up to?'

Juliet froze on the stairs. 'Who? *Me?*'

Like a bouncer, Trudy was standing guard at the entrance to her flat, wearing her red and black kimono, gold embroidered Moroccan slippers that curled at the toes and her hair tied up with a pair of knickers that had seen a few wash cycles. She looked extremely pissed off.

'Erm . . . nothing. Why?' *Shit.* Had Trudy been looking out her sash window? Had she seen her with Sykes?

'So what took you so long?' Arms folded, *King and I* style, she glared at Juliet accusingly. 'You're damn lucky my waters haven't friggin' broken already.'

A whoosh of relief. She hadn't been caught. Nobody knew, not even her best friend. Mumbling apologies, Juliet staggered into the bombsite that was Trudy's flat, and dropped her bags on the overflowing coffee table. At least she assumed it was the coffee table. She couldn't be certain what was lurking under the camouflage of magazines, leftover cuts of fraying fabric, rancid aluminium takeout trays and coffee cups with a type of mould growing out of them that looked uncannily like oyster mushrooms.

'You've been ages.'

'I've been hours, not nine months.'

'Every second is an eternity when you're pregnant.'

'For Godsakes, will you stop being so melodramatic?'

As soon as she'd snapped, Juliet wished she hadn't. Usually thick-skinned, Trudy deflated like a punctured lilo. 'I'm sorry . . . it's been one of those days, ignore me.' Pulling out the pregnancy tests from her pocket, she held one out towards her in surrender. 'You don't know whether you are or not yet, anyway.'

'I will in sixty seconds,' she harrumphed, grabbing the predictor out of her hand and flouncing over the assault course of crumpled clothing and discarded shoes, into the bathroom.

Watching Trudy sitting on the loo ripping open the packaging, Juliet leaned against the doorframe. Giddy and off-kilter, she felt as if she'd just come off the big dipper.

Fuck, what have you done? What the fuck have you just done? she screamed silently to herself, her head reeling. Adrenalin was pumping and, trying to calm down, she brushed away the bead of perspiration trickling down her forehead. Even though it was cold in Trudy's draughty flat, guilt was bringing her out in a cold sweat.

She still couldn't quite believe it. What the hell had got into her? *Kissing another man – a man who wasn't Will* – and she wasn't talking a peck on the lips. She was talking snogging, necking, groping, *panting*. Oh fuck. A flashback hit, then another, and another. Lunging at each other on the front seats of his car like a couple of horny teenagers, they'd launched into a full-bodied clinch with tongues and everything. It had seemed to go on for ever, but it must have only been a few seconds before she'd pulled away, blurting, 'I can't do this. I've got a boyfriend, I live with him.'

She hadn't known how she'd expected him to react, but she'd expected some kind of reaction. Instead he didn't do or say anything.

'You don't seem surprised.'

Leaning back in his seat, running his teeth over his

bottom lip, Sykes had stared into the middle distance. 'Because I'm not. I'd be surprised if you were single.'

'*Why?*'

He turned to face her. 'Are you fishing for compliments?'

'No, I was . . .' she flustered hotly.

He interrupted. 'Well you should be. You know you're absolutely stunning, don't you?'

She'd reddened. What was she supposed to say to that? She wasn't used to such straight-faced compliments, especially not from someone as gorgeous as Sykes. There had to be a catch. She waited for the punchline.

There wasn't one.

'So why are you here?'

'I needed a lift.' It was a lie.

'Can I see you again?'

'I've told you, I live with someone.' Hastily jerking her fingers away, she fumbled for the handle on the door. It sprang open. She was so jumpy she nearly fell out onto the kerb.

'That's not a good enough reason.'

'Why not?'

He stared at her. The look he gave her was a good enough reason. 'What about Friday? You're not going to let me down, are you?'

She looked at him, puzzled.

'The London Eye. You're my date.'

Drunken memories of the auction flooded back.

'It's for charity.'

'Now that's not fair . . .' she protested, but felt secretly thrilled. If she needed an excuse to see him again, she'd just got one.

'It won't be that bad, you might even enjoy yourself.'

That's what I'm worried about, she thought, gathering her shopping together.

'I can't.'

'Didn't your mother ever tell you there's no such word as can't,' he teased.

She remained steadfast. It was a struggle. 'I've already told you, I suffer from vertigo.'

'I know the perfect cure.' He wasn't taking no for an answer.

'Does it involve snorting salt water up my nose, or drinking from the other side of the glass?' She tried to make a joke of it. Her voice wavered.

'That's for hiccups,' he grinned. 'If you meet me next week I'll show you.'

But she wasn't to be persuaded. With the ingredients she'd managed to salvage shoved into two straining bags, she climbed out of the car. She closed the door firmly behind her.

He gave up trying to convince her. Digging in his wallet he pulled out a card and held it out to her. 'Call me. If you change your mind.'

Fingering the edges of his business card she was tempted to keep it, to put it in her wallet so that she could keep pulling it out and sneaking a look at it. It took a lot to hand it back. 'I won't.'

Without waiting she began walking away. She didn't want to give herself the chance to change her mind. Illuminated by the pale street lamps, she began hurrying the few doors down to Trudy's studio, her stiletto heels playing percussion against the pavement. Behind her, she was aware of his car making a three-point turn, the rhythmical revving of the engine providing the bass line.

'Juliet.'

She turned.

Pausing before he drove away, Sykes was looking at her out of his open window. Amusement played on his lips. 'I think you're supposed to gargle the salt water.'

'Have you seen these instructions? They're like a friggin' novel,' huffed Trudy, tossing the concertinaed booklet on the multicoloured bathroom rag rug in disgust. 'Don't I just pee on the stick?'

Juliet sighed. Whatever happened to sixty seconds? This seemed to be taking an eternity. She looked at Trudy. Sitting on the loo with her legs crossed, she was waving the predictor around as if she was conducting *Charge of the Pregnancy*. It crossed her mind to tell her about Sykes, then she thought again. Now might not be the best time to confess her guilty secret. Trudy had a lot more on her mind than her best friend's dangerous liaisons.

'Let me have a look.' Picking up the instruction leaflet, Juliet scanned the small print. There were lots of anatomical line drawings to illustrate three easy steps: (1) Wee; (2) Wait; and (3) Watch. It couldn't have been more straightforward. 'If there's a blue line in the square window you're pregnant, if there isn't one you're not.'

'That's it?'

Juliet shrugged. 'That's it. Apparently being pregnant kills the brain cells, so I guess they have to make it easy.' She grinned as Trudy scowled.

Rolling up the sleeves of her kimono, she stared at the predictor, bracing herself. 'Well, I guess this is it.' Trudy was doing her damnedest to be brave. To pull herself together. Except she couldn't. Her stomach was threatening to revolt by expelling its entire contents all over her rag rug. And she was sweating. Profusely.

'Do you want a drum roll?' Juliet couldn't keep the amusement out of her voice.

'Jeez, don't I get a little respect? This moment could change my life. This could be goodbye Vienna.'

'Or goodbye life,' corrected Juliet, unable to resist winding Trudy up. She wasn't the maternal type. She got broody over Manolo Blahniks, not babies.

Trudy glared at Juliet. She'd been worrying herself sick about this moment all day. Seeing big, fat pregnant women in Gap T-shirts and elasticated sweatpants wherever she turned, tripping over three-wheeler baby buggies hogging the pavements, hearing the strangulated cries of newborns that looked like shrivelled-up baby birds. She'd glimpsed the nightmarish breeding, broody, breast-feeding, crack-nippled baby world, and it was horrifying. Forget Dante, this was her version of hell. Yet all Juliet could do was fool around. 'You're not taking this at all seriously, are you?'

'I am, I am.' Perching her bum on the chipped enamel edge of the claw-footed Victorian bath, Juliet protested. 'It's just that only last month you thought you were going through early menopause.'

'I had hot flushes,' protested Trudy sulkily.

'*You had the flu*.'

Trudy acquiesced begrudgingly with her silence.

'So how do you explain Polly being late?' Folding her arms, she stared accusingly.

Juliet couldn't help smiling. For someone who was happy to talk about all bodily functions in gory detail, Trudy could never bring herself to say the word 'period'.

'By how many days?'

Trudy fidgeted uncomfortably. 'A few,' she muttered, unusually tight-lipped. She began fiddling with the dozen different types of shampoo, nail polishes, hair depilatories and disposable razors that littered the macramé-and-wooden-beaded hanging shelf. All with their lids off, covered in gunk and dust, they vied for space with two dead, crispy brown spider plants.

'How many's a few?'

She stopped fiddling. 'One.'

She saw Juliet's expression.

'It'll be two by tomorrow.' She made a stab at justifying herself.

Juliet groaned. 'That's not how it works. By tomorrow you'll probably be saying howdy-doody to Polly.'

'Gawd, would I be pleased to see Polly. I'd throw her a welcome home party.' Tugging off the pair of knickers that was acting as a makeshift Alice band, Trudy ran her fingers through her knotted mane. 'Not that I hate children. Babies are adorable . . .'

Juliet's eyebrows rose disbelievingly.

'. . . just as long as they're somebody else's.' There was a pause and, taking a deep breath, Trudy stared at the predictor in her hand. It was like a scene from *The Deer Hunter*. She was about to play Russian roulette with a loaded pregnancy test. The bathroom extractor fan whirring above her like helicopter blades, the halogens in the ceiling shining down on her like spotlights. Her nerves were fraying and she played for time. 'Can you imagine me? I'm not what you call Earth Mother material, am I? I can't even boil an egg, and babies don't eat takeout, do they?' she asked desperately, a terrible thought manifesting. 'I'd have to learn how to cook, wouldn't I? Or at least learn how to make that funny-looking mush.'

'No, that's what comes out the *other* end.'

Trudy went white. She looked paralysed with fear.

'Look, even if you are pregnant, and I'm one hundred per cent you're *not*,' added Juliet hurriedly as her friend's expression morphed into Munch's *Scream*, 'you don't have to go through with it.' As soon as she'd said it, she wished she hadn't. Being a hypochondriac, Trudy was also shit scared of operations. The morbid statistic of people dying under anaesthetic was one of her dinner party favourites.

'OK, let's get this show on the road.' Taking a deep breath, Trudy screwed up her eyes in concentration and stuck the predictor between her legs. Under her breath she began quoting her own style of First World War poetry. 'If I should be pregnant, think only this of me: That there's some corner of my closet; That is for ever a size eight.'

'Shall I put a CD on?' Juliet was trying to lighten the atmosphere.

Trudy waved her away. Rocking on the toilet,

hugging herself, she had an alarming resemblance to Arthur Fowler when he stole the Christmas club money.

Unearthing an Elvis CD, Juliet stuck it on the stereo. 'Suspicious Minds' began blasting out of the speakers. Juliet cringed as the King himself began warbling about being caught in a trap. They probably weren't the best lyrics for the situation.

But Trudy wasn't listening anyway. Her hand shaking, she was holding out the predictor at arm's length. They both stared at it.

Chapter Twenty-one

Five seconds ticked agonizingly past. Ten. Thirty. A whole minute. Nothing was happening. Juliet crouching on the multicoloured rag rug, Trudy still on the loo, they huddled together, their heads close.

'How long have we been?'

Juliet glanced at her watch. 'One minute and ten seconds . . .' Looking up at Trudy, she broke into a smile. 'Looks like it was a false alarm.'

'Give it another few minutes.' Trudy's hand shot out and she dragged Juliet down by the hem of her jacket as she tried to stand up. 'Just to be certain.'

They waited, watching the unexploded time bomb.

'Maybe you need a drink,' suggested Juliet. Prising herself from Trudy's grasp, she moved towards the tiny kitchenette.

'I'm all out of JD!' hollered Trudy. Since Fergus had gone awol she'd drunk the place dry. Including the minibar bottles she nicked from shoots for emergencies.

'Don't worry, I came armed,' yelled back Juliet, rustling through the contents of her carrier bags. 'You've a choice of either gin, wine or . . .' fishing out the Shloer, she stuck her head around the bathroom door and held up the bottle sheepishly. 'This.'

'Dear God, it's started already,' wailed Trudy, with her head in her hands. 'Not being able to drink, having to make do with just the tonic. I'll be an outcast from society.' She looked as if she was about to cry. 'It's enough to turn a girl celibate.'

Juliet was taken aback by this outpouring of emotion. Standing at the doorway, gin in one hand, the offending Shloer in the other, she regretted joking around. Nothing ever really got to Trudy. Things annoyed her, amused and angered her, sending her spinning into neurotic monologues, vehement arguments or hilarious laughter. But nothing ever really affected her. Nothing got under her skin. Worried her. *Made her cry*. Trudy boasted a stiff upper lip the British would be proud of and, in the rare cases when something did upset her, she'd never admit it to anyone. Always making a joke of things, she deflected her true feelings with humour.

But tonight was different. She hadn't budged from the toilet seat for the best part of twenty minutes and she'd turned ashen. Perhaps, as her friend, she should stop fooling around and be more supportive. OK so Trudy had cried wolf more times than she could remember, but maybe she was right this time. Maybe this time there really was a wolf in baby's clothing. *Maybe she really could be pregnant*.

'I need a beer.'

'We don't have any beer. But there's Shloer,' she waved it hopefully.

Trudy threw her a murderous look. 'Give me a gin, on the rocks.'

Juliet was doubtful. 'Is that wise?' She wanted to say 'in your condition' but she stopped herself. She was getting as bad as Trudy.

Trudy was in no mood for criticism. 'Make it a large one.'

Arguing wasn't a good idea and Juliet dived back into the kitchenette. Picking carefully through the mouldy packets of bagels and astonishingly large range of pickles, she discovered a couple of cocktail glasses lurking behind a six-pack of Quavers, and grabbed them. She looked in the fridge for some ice. An igloo of titanic proportions was rising out of the freezer section. Hacking off a few shavings with a bottle opener, she poured in a glug of gin and threw in an olive. She tried not to think about why it was called mother's ruin. She passed one to Trudy. 'I think it's safe to come off the loo now.'

'You could be right.' Grinning triumphantly, Trudy hoisted herself up from her throne – slowly, as her leg had gone to sleep – and gulped back a mouthful of gin.

Then spat it out all over her kimono.

Spluttering, she held up the predictor, her eyes unblinkingly wide, her face a ghoulish white. There could be no mistake. In the little square window a line had appeared. A big, bold and very blue line.

And Trudy had just crossed it.

'How are you feeling?'

Ten minutes later they were sitting on Trudy's squidgy sari-covered sofa, eating wedges of Parmesan, pickled gherkins and cheese Quavers. The food cravings had started early.

'Pregnant,' deadpanned Trudy, biting into a gherkin.

After the sudden shock of discovering that her neuroses had been proved right, Trudy had gone into one. Knowing her friend well enough not to intervene when she was having a tantrum, Juliet had hovered around near the fridge, sheltering behind a bottle of Pinot Grigio. Polishing off a couple of glasses she'd watched Trudy kick her beloved shoe collection around the flat, wailing and swearing without pausing for breath until, purged, she'd suddenly pulled herself together, plonked herself on the edge of the sofa and started eating. She hadn't stopped since.

'I should tell Fergus.'

'And decide what you're going to do?' asked Juliet gently.

'Are you crazy? I know what I'm going to do, I'm going to get rid of it,' she spat. There was no hint of sentimentality. Juliet wasn't surprised by Trudy's decision, but she was being particularly harsh, even for her. Juliet also noticed she was punching the cushion.

'Are you going to ring him?'

'I already have. For the last two days. The bastard hasn't returned any of my calls.' Munching a handful of Quavers Trudy tried to look unconcerned, but the rash on her chest gave her away. It always appeared in tiny beetroot bumps when she was upset.

'Oh Trude, I'm sorry, I had no idea.' Juliet felt terrible. She'd been so caught up with everything that had been happening in her own life, she hadn't even thought to ask how it was going with Fergus. She'd assumed Trudy was having lots of sex, lots of fun and enjoying herself. Instead she was getting pregnant and being dumped.

'Don't be, I'm fine. Honestly.' Trudy was lying. She wanted her mom. She wanted to bury her head in her mom's big Jewish bosom and cry her eyes out. She tugged open her fourth bag of Quavers.

She wasn't fooling Juliet. 'I'm sure you'll feel a lot better after a few days, once you've had time to think about it.'

'What's there to think about?' said Trudy, eyeing her suspiciously.

Juliet knew she was going to have to choose her words very carefully here. Putting down her glass of wine, she reached for Trudy's hand. 'Well, the abortion and everything. I mean, don't you think you're being a bit hasty? You might feel differently tomorrow. It's all a bit of a shock, it probably hasn't even begun to sink in yet.'

'Don't you get it? That's the whole point. I don't want it to sink in,' snapped Trudy, pulling her hand away roughly. 'Don't you understand? I want to get this . . . this . . .' staring down at her stomach she couldn't bring herself to say the word, '. . . this mistake outta me.' Her voice breaking, she jumped up from the sofa and took a few deep breaths before she began speaking quietly. 'I don't want to be a single mom, Jules, I just don't. That was never the gameplan.'

'But who says you'll have to be? Maybe you and Fergus will get it together . . .' Juliet was trying to inject a note of optimism.

She was shot down in flames. 'What? And play happy families?' snorted Trudy cynically. 'Are you crazy? Fergus is twenty-six years old. He's a baby himself. We aren't meant to be together, it was just a bit of fun.' Suddenly aware of the irony of her words, Trudy shook her head wearily and looked at her reflection in the gilt mirror. She felt as if she'd aged about a hundred years. 'I know what you're thinking. That I'm a selfish heartless bitch, and maybe I am.' Shrugging, she swallowed hard and continued before Juliet could protest. 'But I like my life the way it is . . . *the way it was*. I've got my own flat, I know it's way too small and as messy as hell but it's mine, and then there's my clothes business which is beginning to really take off. I even like not having a steady guy – which I know you probably find it hard to understand – ' Juliet felt a stab of guilt. ' – but I'm not dumb either. I'm thirty-seven and I know it could be my last chance to have a child. But that doesn't make it a good enough reason to have one. You have to really *want* to be a mom and I don't. Not yet anyway. Babies come later.' Wiping away a gunk of mascara from the corner of her eye, she put on a brave face, adding, 'Along with the rich husband, nanny and a personal trainer to get rid of all that pregnancy flab.' She laughed, trying to make a joke of it. 'I don't want to be alone, no guys for miles, sitting in by myself counting my stretchmarks.' Grabbing a lipstick she applied two perfect arches of scarlet.

Juliet went along with her and smiled, but she had the impression that Trudy was trying to convince herself as much as her.

'C'mon, let's go out, I need something decent to eat.' Bundling herself up in her canary yellow velvet coat,

Trudy stood by the door jangling a huge bunch of keys. All dolled up in her lipstick and heels, she was like a vase that had been smashed and quickly glued back together. From a distance she appeared like she always did, but looking closer Juliet could see the cracks.

'What about risotto?' Remembering her shopping, Juliet prised herself off the sofa.

'Rice?' Trudy looked horrified. 'Gimme a break. I'm pregnant, not desperate.'

Trudy seemed to make a remarkable recovery. Like a boxer getting back up on his feet, she bounced back into the cynical, foul-mouthed Yank that Juliet knew and loved, and happily began bitching away about the 'fat-fannied-celeb' on today's shoot as she locked her flat, climbed down the umpteen flights of stairs to the front door, and clippety-clopped down her path. Unlatching the rusty gate that was hanging onto its hinges for dear life, she ushered Juliet into the street and moved swiftly on to the pros and cons of Chopstix versus Domino's. It was a difficult decision. Right now she could murder the crispy duck with a sweet chilli dipping sauce, but then again if they ordered two Mega Feasts they got a free portion of garlic bread and a two-litre bottle of Diet Coke, which, considering it also came with a choice of extra toppings, was probably a much better deal, wouldn't you say?

Juliet didn't say anything. Walking alongside Trudy, yessing and noing at all the right times, she noticed something fluttering in the gutter, just ahead of her. A small white card. Zoning out of Trudy's monologue which had moved on to the option of KFC, she watched as the white card flipped over and balanced on the grilles of the drain, threatening to fall in.

'Hang on a minute.' Her curiosity aroused, she crouched on the pavement, her fingers groping for the card like a robotic arm diving for coins in one of those glass booths in a seaside amusement arcade. She thought she'd lost it. Until she felt her fingers touch the edges and, grasping it, pulled it towards her. Angling it towards the street lamp, she squinted to make out the lettering. Covered in dirt and wrinkled from the puddle of rainwater, it was still possible to make out the type: *Roberto Alexander Thatcher Sykes. Art director. Montague & Murdoch, Piazza Camaldi, Verona*.

Juliet's memory reared its deceitful head. This was Sykes's business card. He must have dropped it when she handed it back to him, or perhaps it had blown out of his car window when he'd driven away. Either way, the card had found its way back to her. Like its owner, it was persistent. She stared at it.

Having realized that Juliet was no longer listening to her, Trudy stopped yakking about curly fries and looked at Juliet. 'What's that?'

'Oh, nothing,' muttered Juliet, stuffing it in her pocket hurriedly. She'd throw it away later. Standing up, she brushed the dirt from her knees and linked arms with Trudy.

'What was that you were saying about extra toppings?'

Chapter Twenty-two

Flipping Sykes's business card over and over between her fingers, Juliet sat at her desk, deep in thought. It was Friday and nearly four days had passed since she'd kissed Sykes. *Kissed Sykes.* Her stomach flipped as she remembered. She stopped herself. That kiss had been a one-off, an indiscretion, a mistake. It was everything she knew was wrong. This kind of thing happened to other people, it didn't happen to her. And it wouldn't happen again. When she'd climbed out of his car and said goodbye she'd meant it. She wasn't going to call him, she was never going to see him again, and she wasn't going to change her mind.

But that was then and this was now.

Now temptation was knocking seven bells out of her conscience. Two voices arguing loudly inside her head. *Ring him! I can't. Why not? Because I'm not going to be unfaithful! Go on, you know you want to. No I don't want to, I'm not that type, I love Will . . . But? But?* temptation was yelling, banging its fists inside her head, *But what?* Juliet looked at the card, struggling with her conscience. *But I can't stop thinking about Sykes.*

Groaning, she dropped the card onto her keyboard and rubbed her eyes hard with frustration. She couldn't get him out of her head. She felt like an addict who'd had her first taste and wanted more. Even with the flurry of activity engulfing her office, Trudy's unplanned pregnancy, Will unexpectedly apologizing about going awol before the ball, she hadn't been able to think of anything but Sykes. Her mind was like a needle on a scratched record, it kept going back to the same groove, kept getting stuck. *Sykes, Sykes, Sykes*. Juliet allowed herself to take a deep breath, but it was no use. Time had a knack of chipping away at resolutions, especially hers, and his silence was obsessing her. What was he doing? Where was he? Who was he with?

Opening her eyes, she gazed through the large sash window opposite her desk, out across Soho Square. Nudging four o'clock, dusk was falling. Streaks of clouds hung across the skeleton trees and roofs of buildings like big fat bruises. Dark blue and purple, they were slowly turning darker as the light disappeared, as if someone was turning down a dimmer switch. Absent-mindedly she began watching the tiny matchstick figures in the streets below. It was tonight he'd invited her to the London Eye, yet he hadn't called, emailed, or shown up outside any more supermarkets.

Part of her was relieved. Even for charity a thousand pounds was a hell of a lot to pay for a ride on a glorified big dipper, and Danny and Seth had ribbed her mercilessly about 'that devil getting his money's worth'. But a part of her was gutted. And it was a very big part of her.

Juliet continued staring out of the window. Like a Lowry painting come to life, people were scrambling across roads, along pavements, jumping in taxis, driving cars. Maybe one of them was Sykes? Maybe that was him, crossing the park, walking to her office. She peered harder. Or maybe it was some fat ugly bloke who looked absolutely nothing like him, and she was going round the bloody twist. She glanced accusingly back at the card. She knew she should have left the thing to drown in the gutter.

* * *

'*Well?*'

Startled, she looked up to see Gabby bearing down upon her. Dressed head to toe in Prada black, she was feverishly rubbing Bach's Rescue Remedy on her wrists. 'Are you ready? It's time for the meeting.' Receiving no reply, Gabby scowled. A worm-like vein was beginning to bulge disturbingly down the middle of her forehead. Jabbing her hands on her cleverly – and very expensively – disguised hips, she gasped impatiently. 'Does the MAXI account ring any bells?'

'Oh . . . yeah.' Christ, she'd been miles away. For the last few days Danny, Seth and Magnus had been holed up in the Creative Department surviving on takeout pizza, full-strength Malboros and fear, trying to come up with a groundbreaking ad campaign. Today was crucial: they were to meet with their possible clients for the first time, to pitch their ideas. If the clients liked them they were through to the next round, if they didn't – she glanced at Gabby who was circling her desk, arms flapping, like a huge black crow – it was back to looking for a job in Monday's *Guardian*.

Juliet banged her ankles on the edge of her desk as she hastily stood up. 'I'll be right there.' Decisively scrunching up Sykes's card, she tossed it in the bin. She had more important things to think about. Like her career.

Forty-five minutes later and it was looking as if she might not have one for much longer. It had all begun so promisingly. Lots of shaking of hands and bowing of heads as the group of immaculately dressed Japanese clients from BMZ filed into the boardroom. Being an ad agency, the traditional floor-to-ceiling bookcases, button-back chairs, venetian blinds and large polished mahogany table had been dumped in favour of red plastic padded walls, matching pouffes and a round table made of clear Perspex that mushroomed up from the stainless steel floor. It was SGC's take on the traditional 'you must be crazy to work here sticker' and had been designed to look like a mental asylum cell. An achingly trendy one.

The Japanese clients had seemed suitably impressed by the décor. Oohing and ahhing, they'd sat cross-legged on the pouffes and begun cheerily helping themselves to the complimentary Evian and M&S sushi, politely enthusing about the food and making compliments about the miserable British weather. Even Mr Yokoko, the head of BMZ, who was unable to speak English and had brought along his interpreter, had made lots of favourable grunts as he'd tucked into another cucumber roll and pickled ginger.

But then Danny and Seth had taken centre stage.

Fuelled by lack of sleep, a six-pack of Red Bull and fresh intake of class A drugs in the Gents beforehand, they'd launched into their pitch. Moments later Juliet had been gripped with the same feelings she'd had when watching Tara Palmer-Tomkinson on Frank Skinner. Mortification fuelled by astonished disbelief.

For the first few minutes she'd clung onto the hope that it was just nerves. Sniffing loudly, their dilated pupils making their eyes look like saucers, they'd fumbled around with slides and storyboards, chattering nonsensically and working their way through three packs of Orbit sugar-free gum. Half an hour later and all hope had been extinguished. Watching Danny jigging up and down on his AirMax trainers, his fingers jabbing the air like Ali G, the words 'digging' and 'grave' sprang to mind. The pitch was slowly turning into a suicide mission – and Danny was taking SGC down with him.

Glancing around the table, Juliet cringed. Perched bolt upright, the Japanese clients had stopped smiling long ago and were unflinchingly stony-faced. Mr Yokoko looked more animated, but that was only because he'd lost interest at the first mention of Eminem and was now leafing through his Harrods gift catalogue picking out monogrammed cheese truckles and golfing umbrellas for his family back in Osaka.

Listening to Danny winding down like a clockwork toy, Juliet knew she had no option. With Gabby already having jumped ship, it was up to her as the account manager to try and salvage something from the wreckage. Such as her job.

'So Mr Yokoko, as you can see we've come up with a . . . er . . .' Rising up out of her seat she glanced across at Danny. Having finished his presentation, he was standing triumphantly by the projector, unaware that the clients had somehow failed to get to grips with his 'street' campaign: 'take a rapper, a gangland shoot-out, and the MAXI as the getaway car, throw in some computer graphics, some vintage Beastie Boys tracks or even Eminem rapping a voice-over, and just look what you've got!'

A complete disaster, thought Juliet, wondering how this pitch could have been the same one they'd run by her a few days earlier. Back then, enthusiastic, sober and *awake*, Danny and Seth had used their charisma and talent to present an idea that was fresh and invigorating. Now, moronic, trollied and verging on the unconscious, they had left her to stand alone in front of the clients, struggling for words and with no option but to use the ad man's descriptive airbag, '. . . a groundbreaking concept'.

There was no response. Except the kind of eerie silence that only ever happens in the few seconds before large institutions are demolished.

And then Gabby gave a polite handclap.

'Well, thank you very much for coming . . .' Unable to conceal the gloating in her voice, she stood up and was primly shutting her files when she was interrupted by a loud, '*Whoooh, wasn't that something?*'

It was Magnus. Leaping up from his pouffe, he declared, 'As you can see, here at SGC we're all extremely proud of our efforts. Obviously we're still a long way from the summit but base camp has been established and the final assault beckons.' Grabbing his microscooter, he zipped over to Danny, clapping him on the back while at the same time forcibly shoving him out of the way. 'I'm sure you'll agree those ideas were truly inspiring, but – and it's a very big but, gentlemen – as always, we've saved our best idea until last.' Dramatically ripping the storyboard off the stand he flung it over his head, bellowing, 'And what you're going to hear next, gentlemen, will blow you out of the water.'

The rescue mission had been launched. Magnus's thunderous voice caused Mr Yokoko to break off from choosing tartan bathtowels and look up, narrowly missing being decapitated by a storyboard skimming over his head. For a moment he didn't react, then he jolted upright and started clapping excitedly. This was the Magnus effect.

Now they had a true pro at the helm, Juliet watched bemused as Magnus launched into an energetic description of an entirely new concept.

'We're thinking Italy, we're thinking passion, we're thinking tiny cobbled streets . . .'

'Like *Coronation Street*,' butted in Gabby, furious that Magnus was attempting to steal the show. She got it completely wrong.

The Japanese contingency looked blank.

'Like *The Italian Job*,' corrected Seth, the copywriter, throwing her a filthy look. This was one of their earlier ideas that had been rejected for not being off-the-wall enough. Now they embraced it with vigour, clinging on to it like a liferaft.

'Ahhhhh.' There was a collective sigh of recognition from the BMZ team.

'Don't forget to blow the bloody doors off,' grinned a delighted Mr Yokoko.

'*Absolutely*,' enthused Magnus, slamming the desk, his Buddha beads rattling. 'Got it in one.' Jumping backwards he formed a circle with his hands and gave an impression of looking down a camera lens. 'We're thinking close-up of car – ' he narrowed his eyes in concentration – 'zigzagging through a market – ' he began zigzagging around the conference table on his microscooter – 'an upturned stall spills tomatoes across the street – ' he made a sudden screeching noise. The clients jumped, while Gabby rolled her eyes skyward. She really couldn't be doing with all this bullshit creative malarkey.

'The car swerves down a flight of steps . . .' Magnus paused for impact. 'Oh yes, Mr Yokoko, your car's *got balls*.'

There was a moment's hush as the interpreter translated. But instead of being offended, Mr Yokoko broke into a huge beaming grin and began nodding vigorously, repeating 'car's got balls' in agreement, causing the rest of his team to take his lead until the whole boardroom was chanting the words like a mantra.

Like a rock star revelling in his audience, Magnus waited until there was calm before he continued. 'The car passes restaurants, diners, waiters – ' he broke off to wipe away a strand of hair that had escaped from his fez. 'We're thinking pizza, pasta, Parmesan, garlic, carbonara, tomatoes, tiramisu . . .' Magnus's love affair with food was no secret, hence the paunch that was pressing up against his salwar kameez. 'Hey, we can even throw in a few nuns, maybe a shot of the Vatican. Get the religious angle, show the punters this car is *God given*.'

Juliet couldn't help but smile at his marketing tactics. Until she caught sight of Gabby's face. She was practising her Medusa look. It didn't need any rehearsing.

'You see Ferrari doesn't have the monopoly on Italian style.' Panting after his exhaustive pitch, Magnus wedged himself on the edge of the boardroom table.

Shaking his head, he put his facethisclose to Mr Yokoko's. 'And so we can use it. We can give the MAXI passion, sex, hot blood, Latin lovers – hell, we could even try and get Penelope Cruz,' he roared, leaning back on his elbows and dousing his face with Evian.

'Isn't she Spanish?' sneered Gabby. Fortunately she was drowned out by the sudden enthusiasm.

'Robert de Niro!' came a cry.

Magnus nodded frantically and slapped his thighs: 'Yes!'

'Al Pacino.'

'Yes.'

'Sophia Loren.'

'*Yes!*'

Juliet tried to look serious. It wasn't easy when Magnus was beginning to sound like Meg Ryan faking orgasm.

'Michael Caine,' gasped Mr Yokoko, getting into the swing of it but obviously not getting it at all. 'Don't forget to blow the bloody doors off.'

'Erm, well, the celebrities aren't finalized,' coughed Magnus, moving swiftly on. 'But it's a truly incisive strategy, one that gives us a chance to do some really famous work, and *for you* to launch a groundbreaking product.'

The meeting was over. Mr Yokoko gathered up his Harrods catalogue and began bowing and shaking hands enthusiastically. As did the rest of his group, who surrounded Magnus and gave him a hero's reception. Everybody looked pleased. Even the account planners, who were avidly discussing how SGC were going to do more research, market surveys and meet again in a few days.

Everyone except Gabby, who after the *Coronation Street* faux pas had been forced scowling and furious into a back seat. Juliet glanced over at her, just in time to catch her surreptitiously swigging her Bach's Rescue Remedy behind the lid of her briefcase.

'Erm, Juliet?'

As everyone began filing out of the boardroom, Magnus called her back. Hopping from one Birkenstock to the other, he was fiddling with his pinky ring and looking uncannily like Prince Charles. He cleared his throat nervously. 'So, er, how's your friend, the American?'

Juliet thought about Trudy. After discovering she was pregnant, she'd bounced back with alarming buoyancy and had spent the last few days planning her abortion with the same determination and enthusiasm that other people reserved for planning a holiday in the Caribbean. 'Oh, bearing up.' God knows why, but every time she spoke to Magnus, her vocabulary suddenly went all jolly hockey sticks.

'Splendid, splendid.' He nodded, his Adam's apple bobbing up and down rapidly.

They looked at each other. Neither said anything.

'Well, if that's it I better get back to my desk,' she began.

'Erm, I was actually wondering . . .'

'Yes?' Juliet waited expectantly.

Reddening, he pulled out a large paisley hankie from the sleeve of his salwar kameez, and began vigorously blowing his nose. Listening to him honking like a goose, Juliet assumed he'd lost his nerve, so she was surprised when he suddenly announced, 'I'm having a few friends over for a fondue and yoga evening next week. I thought Trudy might want to join us. Having told me all about how she couldn't live without Ashtanga.' Briskly wiping his fleshy nostrils, he smiled as he reminisced. 'A girl after my own heart.'

Trudy. And yoga? Juliet baulked. This was a woman who howled with cynical mirth at the sight of Life Centre devotees (she called them cult members), strutting around with their rolled-up yoga mats and freshly squeezed juices with a Madonna air of superiority, spouting on and on about how a few headstands and a bit of deep breathing had transformed their life. As far as Trudy was concerned, the only time she touched her toes was when she was painting them with scarlet nail polish.

But not wanting to shatter Magnus's illusions, she promised to pass on his invitation and the telephone number that he scribbled down on the back of a 'Rebirthing made easy' flyer and checked four times to be absolutely sure. Then she made her way back across the office. Which is when she noticed that a crowd had gathered by the window.

Neesha, Annette, Stuart from computer services, Danny and Seth, even a motorbike courier in full-face helmet and leathers, his walkie-talkie emitting loud crackly noises, were all bent over her desk as if they were in a rugby scrum. As Juliet walked up to them they all sprang back.

'Blimey, Will must love you,' whistled Neesha, in between mouthfuls of Marmite on toast.

'Or you've had a huge row,' butted in Annette jealously. Big Ears looked suddenly feeble. In the battle of the gifts, hers had just been obliterated by a ginormous package that had arrived by taxi, addressed to Juliet Morris.

Wrapped in shimmery blue tissue paper and elaborately tied with scarlet ribbon – and not the cheap, thin, shiny imitation stuff sold in packs of three at WHSmith that curled when you dragged a pair of scissors along it, but yards of luxuriously thick, gold-edged velvet – was a huge box. It engulfed almost the entire length of the frosted glass work surface.

Juliet gawped. So did everybody else.

'Well, go on then, open it. We're all waiting,' chivvied Neesha, licking the Marmite off her fingers in anticipation.

'There isn't a card,' butted in Annette, before Juliet had a chance to look for one. She'd already searched herself. Thoroughly.

'Yeah, c'mon, put us out of our suspense,' drawled Danny. Now that he'd bounced back from having nearly cost SGC their biggest client, his swagger had returned with full force. Sipping a cappuccino, he was leaning against the filing cabinet, trying to appear uninterested. But even he was curious. This was a lot better than the uninspired Interflora bouquets that usually arrived in all their cellophane mundanity.

With an audience clustered around her, watching her reaction, Juliet felt acutely embarrassed. She didn't like being the centre of attention. She stared at the present in disbelief. It had to be a joke. Will had never sent her anything before. It wasn't her birthday, or their anniversary. She looked at the package doubtfully. But then again he had apologized the other day, without any tricks, or fooling around. Maybe he was turning over a new leaf.

Realizing there was no way she was going to be able to skulk off to open her present in private, she began tugging at the ribbon. Everyone moved closer. Standing on tiptoe Annette leaned so close that her Wonderbra-and-stiletto-combo nearly caused her to topple over. Even Gabby, seeking solace from the dreadful meeting by nipping out to have a few botox injections, paused to see what was going on.

Trying to appear blasé, Juliet tore at the paper as if she was used to this kind of thing, not an excited novice who wanted to peel off the wrapping and keep it for ever as a memento. Underneath was a large, flat, white cardboard box. Seth whistled between his teeth as Neesha let out a squeak. Even Gabby made a strangulated growl, before immediately clapping her hand over her mouth in annoyance.

Juliet stared open-mouthed. Across the lid were five large embossed letters.

'Blimey, how much does your fella earn?' tutted Annette. She was totally peeved. She made her mind up to shove Big Ears through the shredder when she got back to reception. And Stevie as well if he didn't get himself down to somewhere like Tiffanys sharpish.

'Not enough,' muttered Juliet, who'd got over her initial reluctance and was feverishly pulling off the lid and fighting through the layers of purple tissue paper to see what was inside. Her hand touched something soft, like suede, or was that fur? Grabbing whatever was in the box, she pulled it out. A chocolate brown shearling coat unfurled like a cloak. She gave up trying to hide her astonishment. This was the most beautiful coat she'd ever seen. It had to be the most expensive coat she'd ever seen. And it was, undoubtedly, a coat that Will had never seen.

Which could only mean one thing.

Sykes.

There wasn't a note but she didn't need one to know it was from him. To replace the coat he'd ruined. She was impressed.

'Put it on then,' cried Neesha and Annette like a Shakespearian chorus.

She knew she shouldn't. Her independent streak told her she couldn't possibly accept it, it was too much, it must have cost a fortune, she had to send it back. But the shopper within her fought back. *Not before she'd tried it on*. This was the kind of item she'd normally gaze at in its security-tagged glory, unable to brave the frosty shop assistant who knew damn well she could never afford its outrageous price tag and only wanted to put it on so she could swan around the changing room pretending. But now she didn't have to pretend.

When she draped it over her shoulders and pulled the collars against her face, it swirled around her ankles, soft and luxurious like an ermine robe. Not that she'd ever tried on an ermine robe of course, but that's how she imagined it would feel. Wrapping it around her, Juliet dug her hands deep into the fur-lined pockets. And felt something. What was that? Intrigued, she pulled out a tangle of elastic and material.

There was a *phwoar* from Seth and Danny.

'Ooh, kinky!' shrieked Neesha, impressed.

What the . . . ? Dangling from her hand was a blindfold.

Staring at it, Juliet suddenly started laughing. 'No it's not.' She looked at her watch. There was still time. Ducking under her desk she rescued the card that lay screwed up in the bin, and grabbed her mobile. 'It's a cure for vertigo.'

Chapter Twenty-three

'Uggh, these digestives have gone all soft.'

At the other side of town, in a small cobbled mews in the heart of Kensington, Will and Rolf were taking a tea break. Huddled from the afternoon drizzle under a leaky tarpaulin, sipping from flasks of lukewarm Tetley's and eating chocolate biscuits, they were surveying how far they'd got with their Japanese roof garden. On very official-looking checked graph paper Will had designed an area of tranquillity, filled with a decorative lily pond, footbridge and the sound of wind chimes. It was a whole, hopeful, architect's dream away from the drone of a churning cement mixer, and the desolate landscape of sacks of gravel, broken paving stones and ripped-up turf that lay before them.

Not that Will was actually noticing the building site at his green-wellingtoned feet. In fact he wasn't thinking about gardens, Japanese or otherwise, he was thinking about Juliet. His apology about the ball hadn't gone down as well as he'd expected. Instead of giving him a hug, laughing about how daft they'd both been and happily curling up with him so that they were like two cats on the sofa with a bottle of wine, she'd given a stiff little smile, said, 'Don't worry, it's fine,' in the kind of staccato voice that meant it was anything but, and made some excuse about needing an early night.

And then I'd got it completely wrong as usual, thought Will, wondering how on earth he could have thought she was giving him the come-on. Shaking his head he stared out at the late afternoon drizzle. Even now, days later, he was still smarting at the memory of following her into the bedroom in his boxers, ready for action. Only to find her firmly tucked up in bed, lights off, pyjamas on, and body language that told him they weren't coming off thank you very much. Jesus, he was such an idiot. Talk about misreading the signs. How on earth had he managed to see a green light, when it had been a red light, a stop sign and a 'no entry' sign all rolled into one?

Will sipped a plastic cup of stewed, syrupy tea. Having finished off his flask of the trendy, organic, politically correct and outrageously overpriced coffee that Juliet always insisted on buying, he'd moved reluctantly on to Rolf's choice of refreshment – tooth enamel stripper – and began mulling over the last couple of weeks. He was miffed. And confused. What was going on? How come his 'sorry Jules, I was a right prat' speech had failed to make a difference? He took another gulp of tea. It was all because of stupid Valentine's Day. She'd been cool to him ever since. Pondering, Will drained the dregs from his cup. Actually, digging his head out of the sand for a minute, if he was honest with himself, really honest with himself, she'd been rather cool for ages. Well, not cool, just distant.

'Do you think the bloke that lives here has got any biscuits?'

'Um . . . what?'

'Biscuits,' repeated Rolf loudly. 'You know, custard creams, rich tea, jaffa cakes. These have definitely gone off.'

Snatching the packet of McVitie's away from Rolf, who was intent on digging down to the bottom to find a crunchy one, Will rounded on him. 'Does Jules seem all right to you?'

Disgruntled at being robbed of his chocolate fix, Rolf

glared sulkily. 'Yeah, 'course.' He began pouring himself out another cup of tea. 'Juliet's always been a bit of all right,' he guffawed, cheering up at his feeble joke. 'Now can I have those biccies back? Otherwise I'm going to have to go inside and have a root around the kitchen cupboards. I've hardly eaten anything today and I'm starving.'

Will ignored his pleas. 'No, I mean normal. You know, *happy*?'

Rolf was perplexed. What had brought all this on? He furrowed his forehead, his balding scalp wrinkling up like a rubber swimming cap, and gave it some thought.

'You don't have to think about it for too long,' huffed Will, after a few minutes' silence.

Leaning back on his upturned bucket Rolf dug out his cigarettes. After telling Amber he'd kicked the habit, he'd gone from twenty to thirty a day and taken to hiding them in his Piaggio crash helmet. 'Are you saying being normal is being happy? Because in that case, most people probably aren't normal.'

'I'm not asking you to get all philosophical on me,' interrupted Will irritably.

'I'm just saying . . .'

'Well, don't.'

Rolf lit up sulkily. 'If you're looking for just a straight yes or no answer, instead of an intelligent discussion – ' he complained, about to launch into one of his monologues. Until he caught Will's expression and thought better of it – 'then yeah, I s'pose she always seems to be pretty happy to me, though I haven't seen much of her lately.' Taking a long drag, he filled his lungs to the brim. Boy, that was good. Fags together with those nicotine patches Amber had bought him gave a serious high. Why hadn't he tried it before? All that misspent youth wasted on Es and acid trips. He breathed out. Reluctantly.

'Anyway, why all the questions? What's up?'

Will shrugged. 'Nothing.' His voice came out a tad

too high to be convincing. He cleared his throat self-consciously. Talking about his relationship made him uneasy, but something was niggling at him. Actually it was more than niggling, it was beginning to bug. Could it be that this was about more than just Valentine's Day? More than just that stupid ball? Could there be something up? *Really* up? Looking at Rolf who was sitting up, pretending to beg like the scavenging dog that he was, he shoved the McVitie's back in his paws, sighing.

'I know what all this is about.' Nudging Will roughly in the ribs, Rolf dislocated his jaw like a snake so he could fit in a whole biscuit.

'You do?'

'Yeah.' Rolf chewed jubilantly. 'It's what everything's always about. *Sex*.' Puffing happily on his cigarette, he winked laddishly behind his tortoiseshell frames. 'Been complaining about your centre forward action, has she?'

Why did I ever open my big mouth? Will grimaced, listening to his friend baying like a donkey. That was another thing about Rolf, he had no shame at laughing at his own jokes. Especially if they weren't funny and no-one else was going to.

'Leave it out.' He knew Rolf was only messing about, trying to wind him up. The problem was it was working. Without realizing he'd touched a nerve. He and Jules hadn't exactly been ripping off each other's clothes recently, had they?

Suddenly noticing that Will was looking deadly serious, Rolf's laughter trailed away guiltily. 'Sorry, mate. I was just having a bit of a laugh.'

'Yeah, I know . . .'

'So, c'mon, what's up? Has Jules finally realized she's too good for you?' Believe it or not, this was Rolf's way of trying to cheer him up. He hadn't seen Will looking this fed up for a long time.

'Something like that.' Grabbing a chocolate digestive

before they all vanished, Will broke it in two and numbly shoved half into his mouth. 'She's still not forgiven me for not going to that stupid fancy dress ball . . . or Valentine's Day, come to think of it.'

'Why don't you send her some flowers?'

'Isn't that a bit naff?'

Rolf shrugged. 'Women love naff. Red roses, diamonds, Posh & Beck's wedding . . .' He paused to swig back his tea. 'I mean, do *you* know a woman who doesn't know all the words to "Angels"? *Even worse*, they still request it on the radio. I mean, for Christsakes, it came out about *ten fucking years ago*.'

Will didn't look convinced. 'Not Juliet. She'd think all that was a load of sentimental rubbish. She's always going on about how important it is to be independent, to have a career, to be taken seriously. She was really pleased when she got her pay rise, because she said that at last she could afford to start paying half the mortgage. She said she wanted us to be equal partners.'

'You're telling me she doesn't cry at the end of *Officer and a Gentleman*?'

'Bawls her head off. Every time,' nodded Will, realizing Rolf might just have a point.

Rolf laughed triumphantly. 'What did I tell you?' Dunking a biscuit in his tea, he began licking off the melted chocolate.

Will was beginning to feel doubtful. Pulling out his tobacco, he began rolling up. 'Maybe you're right. Perhaps I should suggest a weekend away. We could drive down to Brighton or maybe even go up to Yorkshire. Actually, that might not be a bad idea. I haven't seen my parents for ages.'

Rolf looked as if he was about to choke on his biscuit. '*Christ*, Will, you've got no idea, have you? Being stuck in that rustbucket of yours, freezing to death and for what? To stay at some poxy B&B with plastic eiderdowns and a cold shower? Or to have to put up with your old man for two days? That's not a weekend away, it's a bloody punishment.' He laughed heartily to himself. 'A way to a woman's heart is to spoil her. Your fantasy might be a pint, a chicken masala and a copy of *FHM* with Cat Deeley on the front cover . . .' Rolf paused. 'Actually, make that the one with the cute little Scottish bird, whatshername?'

'Gail Porter,' prompted Will. 'Least it was before she got married to that musician bloke . . .' His voice tailed off as he sheepishly remembered looking at her wedding photos in a copy of Juliet's *OK!* And, even worse, *reading* the accompanying sycophantic text. Luckily, Rolf didn't quiz him on how he knew this information. He was too shocked by it.

'She's married?' he gasped, looking distraught. As if this now put her out of his bounds. 'Jeez, that's sacrilege, that is.'

There was a moment of silence as they exchanged lustful looks. Even Will, devoted boyfriend that he was, had fallen under the pint-sized presenter's spell. What man could resist her charms? Especially after they'd been so magnificently – *and amply* – projected onto the Houses of Parliament.

'Anyway, as I was saying . . .' Dragging heavily on his cigarette, Rolf moved off the subject before they embarrassed themselves by salivating: 'a woman's fantasy is being whisked away on a world of four-poster beds, white towelling bathrobes and all those fiddly little bottles of shampoo.' Tugging down his jumper which had ridden up to reveal his belly, he continued. 'It's basic caveman stuff. Look at Richard Gere. The guy wears a poncy white uniform, struts into a factory, kidnaps some poor girl *without even asking her*, when she's right in the middle of doing something. And women go crazy for it.' Rolf laughed in disbelief. 'If you ask me, you've got to take control, show 'em who's boss. Take me and Amber. She knows who's in charge in our relationship.'

'And who might that be?'

A female voice interrupted their conversation and they looked up to see the very woman herself, Rolf's wife Amber, leaning against the french windows. 'The front door was ajar, so I didn't bother ringing the bell,' she explained. 'And now I'm glad I didn't.' With her tiny frame dwarfed in a shaggy cream Afghan, she folded her arms, her green eyes flashing accusingly.

Caught red-handed, fag in one hand and an empty digestives packet in the other, Rolf paled. How long had she been standing there? He'd been so enjoying himself, tucking into tea and biscuits, he'd forgotten they'd arranged for Amber to come over after work. They had an appointment at some wacko naturopath she'd met at her yoga class, to try and increase his sperm count. Not that he didn't feel enough of a wanker already.

'Is that a cigarette? *And are those biscuits?*' Her voice rose.

Rolf coughed nervously. 'A momentary lapse. *Princess.*'

'You're supposed to be on a detox.'

'I am, I am,' jabbered Rolf. 'Bananas, grapes, apples . . . that's all I've eaten all day. Practically.'

'Er, what was that you were saying about showing 'em who's boss?' Will grinned. He couldn't help himself. Any minute now Rolf was going to start genuflecting.

Throwing him a filthy look, Rolf hurriedly zipped up his lime green cagoule and, crouching down with a great deal of difficulty, began studiously wrapping his flared cords around his ankles and fastening on bicycle clips.

'Er, I was thinking, after we've been to this old hippie – ' He saw her expression – 'I mean spiritual mediator, do you fancy grabbing something to eat? I've heard there's a wicked Indian on the corner . . .'

Shaking her head in exasperation, her hennaed curls bouncing against her pink cheeks, Amber pushed Rolf through the french windows. Laughing, she looked back at Will, who was watching, amused.

'Lingerie.'

'What?' He looked puzzled.

She smiled. 'I overheard.'

'Oh,' Will cringed. The embarrassment.

'And I think you should buy Juliet some underwear.'

Will blushed. Seriously, he could feel himself colouring up like a lava lamp. He pulled a face.

'Christ, I'm not buying Jules knickers, she'll think I'm a dirty old man.'

'No she won't,' Amber laughed good-naturedly. 'She'll think you love her.'

Will didn't say anything. This was all getting way too touchy-feely for his liking. Couldn't they talk about something else. Religion? Politics? Anything?

'Er, sweetheart, are you ready?' It was Rolf, popping his head back around the doorframe.

Amber threw him a murderous look. '*In a minute*.'

He shrank back hastily, as she turned to Will. 'If you want me to come shopping with you, just call. You know me, any excuse to shop.' Smiling mischievously she disappeared inside.

Waving goodbye, Will called out to Rolf, who was lurking in the corner like a naughty schoolboy. 'See you later, mate.'

Rolf nodded gruffly. Will couldn't help smiling. 'Hey, are you all right?' He feigned concern.

Checking that his wife couldn't hear, Rolf visibly relaxed. 'Yeh, sorted, mate, sorted,' he grinned, his cocky swagger returning now that he was out of ear-shot. Grabbing his crash helmet he stole a drag of Will's roll-up and inhaled sharply. Beckoning towards Amber's retreating figure he winked confidently. 'What did I tell you? Putty.'

Chapter Twenty-four

'Don't look down.'

'I don't intend to.'

With her hands across her face, Juliet peered between her fingers at Sykes who was leaning against the curved glass wall, grinning at her. Over his shoulder, London's skyline stretched out before her. Glittering in the darkness like an eiderdown of multicoloured fairylights, it was breathtakingly beautiful. *And equally terrifying.*

'Whoah.' Feeling her body sway with a sudden bout of dizziness, she put out her arm to steady herself.

'Don't worry, I've got you.'

Feeling Sykes's arm around her waist, his breath against her cheek, Juliet smiled uneasily. That's what she was afraid of.

Juliet had met Sykes less than an hour ago. After receiving his present her mind had been made up. Now she had the excuse that she so desperately needed. Now she *had* to call him, *had* to see him, if only to tell him she couldn't possibly accept it, to give it back. Unsurprisingly he'd adamantly refused to take no for an answer. 'If you want to argue, you'll have to meet me at the London Eye.' This time she hadn't been able to resist.

Without giving any explanation, she'd left work and rushed all the way on the tube to the Embankment. The choice of venue amused Juliet. The London Eye. On a

Friday night. *Out of choice*. She'd always regarded it with haughty disdain, a pointless tourist attraction like the ill-fated Millennium Dome. No Londoner would be seen dead on it. But there she was, sitting on the Circle Line all wrapped up in the sheepskin coat like a big, furry, guilty secret, nearly bursting with nervous excitement. God help her, she'd thought to herself, watching the stations go whizzing by. Lust had turned her into an American tourist.

Racing up the escalators she'd paused for a moment on the other side of the Thames, gawping up at the huge Ferris wheel for the first time. It rose into the sky, lit up like some fabulous fairground attraction. Perfect for a first date, she'd thought as she'd glimpsed Sykes, leaning against the railings, waiting for her.

Seeing him again, her stomach had done a loop-the-loop. *Wow*. He was waiting for *her*? He looked too good to be true, like something out of a Calvin Klein ad. Giggling nervously they'd gone through ridiculously polite introductions as if they were meeting for the first time: pecking him on the cheek and asking how he was – 'Fine, fine' – avoiding eye contact as he told her how great she looked.

'Oh God, I look a mess,' she'd laughed dismissively. 'A mess' actually being a look created after a frantic half-hour in the ladies' loos, applying lashings of mascara and lipstick and contorting herself underneath the automatic hand-dryer mounted on the wall, trying to blow-dry her hair straight. 'I came straight from the office.' Buzzing from his compliment, she'd struggled to hide her delight. She'd forgotten how fabulous it felt to get some attention. To be told she looked attractive. Will barely noticed she was alive these days, let alone how she looked.

A steward had greeted them. If greeted can be used to describe a bad-tempered woman with a mullet hairdo and the kind of triangular, Girl Guide uniform that would put anyone over the age of ten in a bad temper, snarling a curt 'follow me' and setting off briskly.

Exchanging amused glances and stifling laughter, Juliet and Sykes had followed behind like naughty schoolchildren. Bypassing the queue zigzagging wearily around the maze of metal barriers, they'd jumped straight to the front; passing the people who'd been waiting for hours in the light drizzle, who'd stared at them with a mixture of envy and puzzlement.

Trying to pretend she hadn't really noticed the Japanese tourist taking their photo or the gang of teenage girls who, chewing gum and nudging each other, had shyly asked Sykes if he was 'that actor, Rufus Sewell', Juliet had walked with him to the boarding dock. But she'd been nervous. By now her excitement had begun trickling away like sand through an egg timer, leaving her wondering if she wasn't making one very big mistake. What was she doing agreeing to meet Sykes? And at London's top tourist attraction? It was hardly discreet. What if someone saw her? *Them?*

Standing on the platform, waiting to get into their private capsule, she'd tried to push her fears to the back of her mind. Unfortunately, at that precise moment a pensioner in a pink pac-a-mac had come to a different conclusion about why they were getting VIP treatment and yelled out, 'Good luck, I hope you'll both be very happy.'

Oh God. Juliet had blushed the colour of the woman's pac-a-mac. That's all she needed. Some old dear thinking they were getting married on the London Eye. Unable to look Sykes in the eye, she'd put her head down and stared at her boots. Things couldn't be further from the truth.

'You are about to embark on the journey of a lifetime.' As they stood on the platform waiting to board and the glass pod inched slowly towards them, the uniformed steward had begun her rehearsed speech with about as much sincerity as an *OK!* magazine interview. 'The Millennium Wheel is a feat of British engineering and took years to complete . . .' her voice droned on, but Juliet had suddenly zoned out.

And zoned in on the glass pod that she was stepping inside. On the hundreds of tiny white fairy lights strung from the windows, the huge picnic hamper and two dozen red roses. Crikey, was this for real? Was this for her? Had she just stepped out of her life and into someone else's by mistake? One belonging to a character played by Meg Ryan?

Overwhelmed, Juliet had stared at the hamper, the lights, the flowers. Until that moment, she'd always thought roses were hackneyed. Years of seeing horrible, cheap buds packed tightly in cellophane being sold in plastic buckets at the side of the A40 had given them a bad press. But these were the real McCoy. Wonderfully long-stemmed with dewy petals that looked as if they'd been fashioned out of velvet, they were tied together loosely with raffia string. Clamping her jaw shut, she'd turned to Sykes. Now it had been his turn to shrug dismissively, 'Sorry it looks a bit Santa's grotto, but they wouldn't allow candles. Said it was a fire hazard.'

Any doubts evaporated. Juliet had felt as if she'd just died and gone to heaven. And guess what? *Heaven looked just like Santa's grotto.* Surprise changed to delight. There was a fine line between tacky and romantic and Sykes had got it just right. What could so easily have been an excruciatingly embarrassing Hallmark-card-with-teddies-on-the-front gesture was suddenly the most romantic thing anyone had ever done for her.

'. . . and the breathtaking views of London stretch over twenty-five miles . . .' The steward's voice had continued wafting into their bubble. '. . . so enjoy the ride, because in thirty minutes you'll come back down to earth.'

With the doors sliding closed behind them, Sykes had reached for her hand. Interlacing his long tanned fingers through her woollen knitted ones, he'd grinned wryly. 'Wanna bet?'

Now, five minutes later, they were gliding high above the River Thames. Even being frightened to death of heights, Juliet had to admit it was pretty amazing. Literally watching the world go by, she could see in all directions. Straight over there, to the left a bit, the historical dome of St Paul's was poking out from in between modern office buildings. That way was the towering glass edifice of Canary Wharf. Straight in front of her she could see a close-up of the clock face of Big Ben. And below, thousands of people going about their lives, leaving offices, catching cabs, drinking cocktails in bars.

Yet here she was. Alone with Sykes in a giant bubble, suspended high in the sky. Pulling away from him, Juliet leaned against the glass wall of the pod and took a glug of champagne to calm her nerves. It wasn't just the vertigo that was making her dizzy.

'Feeling better?'

'A little.'

'You know there's always the blindfold.' He tried not to smile, but his eyes shone, teasingly.

'What do you think this is? *Nine and a Half Weeks?*' It came blurting out.

He laughed. Thank God. But she couldn't help wishing she had some sort of a script so she'd know what to say next, how to act.

It was all so weird. The last time she'd been with Sykes they couldn't keep their hands off each other but now it was almost as if it had never happened. It was as if they were on a first date. And she felt woefully out of practice. What did people say on first dates? What did people do with their hands? How did people stop their stomach from making really revoltingly loud gurgling noises? Juliet cursed her digestive system. Did it have to choose this precise moment to start squirting gastric juices all over the baked potato and cottage cheese she'd had for lunch? Well did it? Really?

She glanced over at Sykes. He'd taken off his jacket to reveal a snugly fitting black shirt with the kind of cuffs that needed cufflinks, undone the collar, rolled up the sleeves and was leaning against the glass, staring out at the views. His body language was so laid back, so relaxed. So unlike my own, thought Juliet, suddenly aware that not only was she fiddling anxiously with the strands of hair at the nape of her neck, but her legs had mysteriously wrapped around themselves like two curly fries. What was he thinking? What was going on in his head? Uncrossing her legs she drained the rest of her champagne. She could ask herself the same thing.

'So, what do you think?' He swivelled round to face her, catching her off guard.

'Er . . . pretty amazing views.' She smiled, forcing herself to look away. Her gaze fell on the Fortnum and Mason hamper. The man certainly knew how to picnic. There wasn't a soggy egg sarnie or packet of Walkers cheese and onion in sight. Just a beautifully arranged display of strawberries, grapes, mangoes, about ten different types of cheese (and not one of them looked like Cheddar), oysters, gravadlax, bottles of champagne and, if she wasn't mistaken, she could spy a jar of caviare under the linen napkins.

In normal circumstances – and there wasn't anything remotely normal about tonight – Juliet would have been shrieking excitedly and diving into the hamper with gusto, armed with a cheese knife and a bottle opener. But tonight she wasn't hungry. Unusually for her, she'd lost her appetite.

'It's a shame you didn't think of everything,' she teased.

He raised his eyebrows, questioningly.

'We haven't got a picnic blanket.' See, he wasn't perfect after all.

'Oh well that's easy.'

Now it was her turn to raise her eyebrows questioningly.

'Take off your coat.'

'Scuse me?'

'Your coat, take it off.'

'Isn't the man supposed to take off his coat?' she protested, vaguely remembering something she'd done in history about Walter Raleigh taking off his coat for Elizabeth I, or maybe it was Sir Francis Drake? Or was he the one with the potatoes? She realized her mind was playing tricks. Throwing up useless bits of information to fend off having to think about what was actually happening.

'I thought you didn't want it?' he mocked.

Why do I have to be such a bloody feminist sometimes? thought Juliet, remembering how insistent she'd been about not being able to accept such an expensive present, how it was very kind of him, how she wouldn't feel right, how her mud-stained coat was perfectly fine. Blah, blah, blah. Why couldn't she have just said thanks like any other normal female in her right mind would have done?

Except she wasn't in her right mind.

'OK, OK, you win.' She shrugged, pulling off the coat reluctantly. Feeling naked in just a flimsy dress and boots, she passed it to Sykes. It was like handing over a child. Call her shallow, but she'd got seriously attached to her Gucci sheepskin, thanks very much.

Immediately he laid it down on the floor.

'You can't do that,' she yelped.

'Why not?'

Not wanting to sound like Victoria Beckham, Juliet

stopped herself from gasping, 'But it's Gucci.' She didn't want Sykes to think he could impress her with designer labels. She wasn't like Trudy who, whenever she read those questionnaires about 'what three things would you save if your house was on fire?' always fired back, 'My Gucci, Chanel and Manolo Blahniks . . . in that order.' Even so, a three grand coat spread out on the floor tested even her high street resolve.

'I think it makes a pretty good picnic blanket, what do you think?'

'I think you're mad,' she smiled, shaking her head as he sat down on the floor and looked up at her with those big, brown Botticelli eyes of his. *And I think if I'm not careful, I'm going to fall for you. Very, very hard.*

Chapter Twenty-five

Listening to the slam of the front door and the whining buzz of Rolf's Piaggio whizzing over the cobbles, Will stubbed out his roll-up and began packing up. It was time for him to go home too. Grabbing his rucksack and mangy old fleece he stepped inside the kitchen. Christ, the bloke who owns this pad has some money, he thought as he clattered across the Italian marble floor tiles, oblivious to the trail of dirt he was leaving behind him.

Leaning over the *faux*-granite sink, he began washing the dirt off his hands. Like everything in this house, no expense had been spared. Forget IKEA units, a four-slice-Dualite toaster and the great British mug-tree, this was a state-of-the-art stainless steel affair. Complete with concealed lighting that shone beams of light onto the cooker and integrated microwave as if they were museum pieces, it was filled with every mod con imaginable.

But no food, thought Will, drying his hands on his T-shirt and having a quick snoop inside the huge fridge that took up nearly a whole wall. Completely empty apart from a couple of bottles of champagne and one of those expensive-looking jars full of mixed olives and bits of orange peel, it was a whole world away from his own fridge, crammed with half-eaten cans of baked beans, Budweiser six-packs, Philadelphia Light and Jules's Optrex eye masks.

I bet the owner of that fridge never has problems

with his girlfriend, thought Will, closing the door miserably and walking into the hallway. I bet they're eating out together every night, drinking champagne, going to fashionable gallery openings and buying expensive art – he stared at a six-foot-high sculpture made of old bits of coat hanger and screwed-up crisp packets – even if it was a load of pretentious old bollocks.

He cut across the living room. This had all the trappings of trendsville – polished wooden floorboards, leather armchairs, a couple of reclining Buddhas, candles that showed no signs of ever having been lit, a *Costes* CD on top of the Bang & Olufsen hi-fi. Spying a shelf neatly lined with *Time Out* guides, a *Hip Hotel* coffee table book, and other volumes, he picked up Nelson Mandela's autobiography and leafed through it. As someone who'd started it about twenty times but never got further than Chapter 1, he was grudgingly impressed to see that, judging by the folded corner of page 514, someone was actually reading it all the way through. Not only that, but they were even making notes in tiny neat handwriting in the margin.

Putting it back, he descended the spiral staircase that led to the front door, mulling over what Rolf and Amber had said. Maybe he should take Jules to a five-star hotel for the weekend. He had to admit, it was very appealing. He could do with a bit of five-star treatment himself. The only problem was money. Right now he didn't have any, well not enough. Alternatively, there was always flowers and champagne . . . He thought about it. No, he couldn't. It was too corny, what would be next? Cuddly toys and helium balloons? Which only left Amber's suggestion: underwear. But he couldn't buy her that. It would be like getting socks for Christmas.

Dismissing the idea, Will flicked off the lights. No, they were both wrong. The Beatles got it right. *All You Need Is Love.*

He loved Juliet.

And he didn't need to buy her a pair of poxy knickers to prove it.

Champagne, oysters, caviare.

Juliet eyed the contents of the hamper spread around her on her makeshift blanket. Mmmm, she thought, as she savoured a mouthful of champagne. She could get used to this.

The first champagne bottle already lay empty, and she'd drunk most of it. Now they were on a second bottle. As always, conversation began flowing in direct ratio to the amount of alcohol and, having given in to temptation and sat down next to Sykes, it hadn't been long before she was feeling much more relaxed.

How could I have ever been nervous? she thought to herself, all warm and fuzzy-edged as Sykes told her about his Italian mother and English father. How he was born in Italy but brought up in London until, at seven years old, he'd been packed off to boarding school in Kent where the teachers had called everyone by their surnames. He'd been known by his ever since. 'Well, Roberto Alexander Thatcher Sykes is a bit of a mouthful, isn't it?' he laughed ruefully.

'At least it's different,' grinned Juliet, 'a one-off.' Just like you, she thought, sipping her champagne as he continued filling in the blanks. Revealing that he was thirty-three, single and an ex-rugby player, 'hence the lump on the bridge of my nose', and loved nothing more than driving his car, eating chocolate, 'I know where you women are coming from', and smoking. 'I keep trying to kick the habit but not a lot comes close to a glass of wine and a cigarette,' he smiled, looking at Juliet in such a way that she couldn't help wishing she was one of the things that did.

Seeming to read her thoughts, Sykes's face suddenly became serious and he added quietly, 'I'm glad you came tonight. Since I first saw you on Oxford Street I haven't been able to get you out of my head.'

What? Juliet dived on a strawberry for distraction. She hadn't expected her wish to be granted. He smiled, dare she hope, shyly? 'Sorry, am I embarrassing you? Is that a stupid thing to say?' He looked down at his hand, turning the smooth silver ring around his finger.

Stupid? Juliet felt as if she was having an out of body experience. Here she was, with a man who not only happened to be absolutely gorgeous, romantic, funny, sexy but who also happened to be telling her, totally off his own back and without anyone putting a gun to his head, that he couldn't stop thinking about her. 'No,' she answered, shaking her head. She felt the same way.

'You really mean that?'

Juliet's heart did a funny kind of hiccup. 'Yeah,' she murmured. Unable to look at him, she stared down at her hands. She wasn't used to being in this kind of situation. Feeling completely out of her depth she'd been trying to play it cool but she couldn't hold out much longer. Sykes was sweeping her off her feet. Quite literally. 'Yeah,' she nodded, louder this time. Looking up, she stared at him decisively. 'I really mean it.' *There. She'd said it.*

'So tell me. If you've got a boyfriend, why were you by yourself that night?'

Being abruptly reminded of Will, Juliet hesitated. She'd been asking herself that question ever since. 'I don't know.' She wasn't being entirely truthful. Deep down she suspected that she did know, but didn't want to admit it. To face up to the possibility that he wasn't in love with her any more. 'And I don't want to know,' she added, feeling uncomfortable. She didn't want to be reminded of Will, of reality, of her conscience. She didn't want to break the spell. 'Can we change the subject?'

'Fine by me.' Reaching out, Sykes casually brushed the strands of hair that had fallen over her face. It was only the slightest touch but Juliet felt the sexual tension tighten a notch. Until that moment they'd barely gone near one another, but now he was leaning towards her, his fingers were stroking her neck, making soft, swirly patterns just underneath her earlobe. He looked at her intently, his lips slightly parted. She stared back, almost forgetting to breathe.

'What are you doing next weekend?'

'*Next weekend?*' Juliet's voice came out much louder – and much higher – than she'd expected. She felt a crushing disappointment. Next weekend was a whole week away. She wasn't going to see him until then. *He didn't want to see her until then.* Insecurities began duplicating like bacteria under a microscope, and she sat up stiffly, putting a marked distance between them. 'Erm, I'm not sure, I'll have to check my diary.' She was lying. She already knew there was nothing in there but lots of blank pages and some Tesco's coupons. For some peculiar reason, her mother had been sending them to her ever since she'd hit thirty.

Sykes didn't seem to take offence. 'Well, if you're not doing anything, I was wondering if you'd like to have dinner. I know this great little Italian. Alfredo, the head chef, does the best risotto. You've got to taste it to believe it.'

'It can't be any better than mine,' she fired back. She couldn't help herself. Rejection was mutating into arrogance.

'Oh yeah.' He was smiling. 'I'll tell him you said that.'

'I'll tell him myself.'

'So you speak Italian?' He seemed amused.

Which made her even more annoyed. 'No.'

'Well, then you're going to have trouble because Alfredo doesn't speak English.'

'Why not?'

'Because he lives in Verona.'

'And he works in London? That's a bit inconvenient, isn't it?' she quipped, thinking she was being rather witty.

'Who said the restaurant was in London?'

Silence.

And then a clatter as the penny dropped. 'You mean . . .'

Cocking his head, Sykes gave her a long, lazy, crooked smile.

'You bastard.' She punched him on his shoulder.

'I couldn't resist,' he laughed. 'You're really cute when you're annoyed.'

This time she tried punching him with both fists, but he caught her by the wrists. Juliet didn't try to struggle. Three years of triceps pulls at the gym and she was still pathetically weak. Which is really rather lucky, she thought, quite enjoying being at his mercy as he bent towards her and kissed her lightly on the mouth.

'I'm going back to Italy for a few days. I need to sort some things out. And I want you to come with me.' He kissed her again. This time harder.

Juliet's mind was racing as she felt his lips moving against hers. 'Italy? Where would we stay?' she gasped, coming up for air. Christ, she could really say some dumb things at times.

But Sykes didn't seem to notice. 'My apartment's being rented, so I'm afraid it would have to be a hotel.'

Juliet tried not to laugh. He was apologizing for having to stay in a *hotel*?

'Well? Will you come?'

He threw the question down like a gauntlet. He was challenging her to a full-blown affair. Was she going to accept?

Juliet felt the breath catch in the back of her throat. Sweat prickling on the palms of her hands. *So this was it.* She couldn't put it off any longer. Decision time. Trying to steady herself, she took a glug of wine as her mind whirled on a roulette wheel. Red or black. Yes or no. Saying no would be to play it safe. It would mean she could leave now with no real damage done. It was just a kiss, a sheepskin coat, a ride on a stupid tourist attraction for charity. Drunken flirting that got out of hand. Easily dismissible. Forgotten about. In a few weeks she could convince herself it never happened. Will would never have to know. Nobody would ever know. And her life could go back to how it was. *But if she said yes?*

The possibility plunged her into a whirling pit of emotions. A part of her was yearning to shout yes, to rush headlong into the unknown, to play dangerous. To have an affair. She loved Will, but God, she loved the way Sykes made her feel. Just looking at him now made her belly flutter like the kites on Hampstead Heath. Tugging at their strings, like Sykes tugged at hers. She didn't know what to do, what to think, what she wanted, and yet, for all her confusion, she was sure of one thing. She didn't want her life to go back to how it was. Not ever.

'Only if I can have a separate room.' It was an attempt at a compromise. Unable to make a decision, she was playing for time. Except she wasn't really. Because what Juliet didn't realize was that she'd already made her decision. She'd made it the first time she'd accepted that lift outside Tesco's.

'You can have a whole separate floor if you want,' he smiled, letting go of her hands and wrapping his arms around her. Pulling her towards him.

Juliet felt a rush of adrenalin. She'd forgotten how fantastic it was to just kiss someone. To be kissed. Why did couples stop kissing like this after the first few months? Stop snogging on the sofa? French kissing on dance floors? Why did sex shove kissing into the back seat? It was such a waste, she thought, feeling Sykes's five o'clock shadow rubbing against her face, his tongue inside her mouth, his nose bumping against hers. When it was pretty damn fabulous, all by itself.

Juliet couldn't remember how long they stayed like that. Curled up together on her sheepskin. She could have stayed like that for ever if she hadn't heard a noise and looked up. To see with horror that they were back on the ground and in full view of a gaggle of schoolchildren who were giggling and pointing at them from the next capsule.

'Oh my God.' Ducking, she tried to hide from about twenty pairs of curious thirteen-year-old eyes.

'I don't know . . .' considered Sykes. 'I think a full moon's kind of romantic.'

'Huh?' She peered out from behind his broad shoulder just in time to see a gangly teenage boy pull down his trousers and proudly squash two round, white and very spotty adolescent bumcheeks up against the glass. It was a view that wasn't in any London Eye brochure.

Juliet shrieked, before clamping her hand over her mouth and looking at Sykes. He looked at her. For a split second there was quiet, before their faces contorted into huge grins and with loud snorts they burst out laughing together.

Chapter Twenty-six

Juliet was on a high. Since making her decision to go to Verona, almost a week had passed in an intoxicating blur. Juliet loved the word intoxicating. It described something she'd assumed her life had grown out of, until Sykes had come along, pushing all the right buttons and stirring up emotions she'd been hankering after for months. Giddy excitement, nervous anticipation, exuberant exhilaration. And a gnawing frustration.

Sykes had gone away on business to Manchester for three days, and when he returned they'd both been so busy working flat out on their respective pitches for the MAXI account it had been difficult to see each other. Embarking on an affair was dangerous enough, but with a member of a rival ad agency the stakes were even higher. Apart from a few snatched minutes in a busy Starbucks, a furtive half an hour in a hotel bar, a snogging session in his car that had been teenage in its intensity, Juliet had had to satisfy her desire with his endless text messages, flirty emails and phone calls on her mobile telling her he couldn't wait until the weekend.

And Will? Juliet didn't know what to think. So she didn't. After her evening at the London Eye she'd pushed him to the back of her mind and tried not to think about him. It had been alarmingly easy. These days they barely saw each other, barely spoke to each other. In fact, in the last week the only conversations she'd had with Will were to decide what takeout they were going to order, and to tell him where the clean towels were. As crazy as it sounded, somehow, by not having to lie to him, she'd almost convinced herself she was doing nothing wrong.

It was as if she and Will were intimate strangers. Living in the same flat, sleeping in the same bed, sitting on the same sofa, sticking to the same routine. And bathed in an impenetrable Readybrek glow, Juliet felt she was leading two entirely separate lives. As if she was a double agent. With Will she was Jules the stuck-in-a-rut long-term girlfriend, whose hobbies include washing up, watching videos, and spooning under the duvet. But with Sykes she was Juliet the swept-off-her-feet lover, who enjoys drinking champagne, sexually charged conversations, and being kissed.

Just about everywhere.

Sometimes Juliet would be sitting at her desk, rushing to catch a bus, swimming lengths in the pool at her gym, queuing up at Pret à Manger, and she had to catch herself. She'd never expected this to happen, never wanted it to happen. But it *was* happening. Her. And Sykes. *Having an affair.* She couldn't believe it.

Neither could Trudy.

'You're having an affair? With the man at the ball? *With Cary Grant?*'

'His name's Sykes. And it's not an affair. We haven't slept together.'

Trudy slammed down the soy sauce. 'Yet.'

Juliet had arranged to meet Trudy at Wagamama's. In retrospect it probably wasn't the best place for a confessional, considering they were in a busy Japanese restaurant, sitting shoulder to shoulder at a long trestle table, alongside people slurping large bowls of miso soup and struggling with their vegetable dumplings as they battled to master the art of eating with chopsticks.

Out of the corner of her eye, Juliet could see a single white thirtysomething male sucking up ramen noodles as if he was a six-year-old eating Heinz spaghetti.

'Are you going to fuck him?' demanded Trudy. It was an accusation, not a question. 'Or should I say *make lurrve*,' she scoffed loudly, putting on a Barry White voice.

Juliet didn't say anything. She felt suddenly embarrassed. Actually, she had been calling it that in her head all week, but hearing Trudy say it now, out loud, it sounded ridiculously corny. Like the dialogue from one of Violet's books.

'Oh my gawd, you are calling it that, aren't you?' Trudy caught Juliet's expression.

'No,' she lied, her cheeks reddening. She fiddled with the neck of her jumper. It was beginning to irritate. A bit like Trudy. 'Anyway, it's not about sex.'

Trudy raised her eyebrows. As did the woman to her left with a small toddler, a little girl with blond pigtails who immediately started up a singsongy chant of 'sexsexsexsexsex' as she made shapes with her noodles.

'Then what is it about?'

Juliet hesitated. She was reluctant to go into it. She'd already been ridiculed.

'Go on, I'm interested,' encouraged Trudy. She sat back on her chair and attempted to drink her foul-tasting fresh juice. God, she hated these healthy-eating places. No Diet Coke. No MSG. No E numbers. No wonder everything tasted so sodding awful, she thought, looking around the packed restaurant, where everyone else seemed to have the opposite opinion.

Looking at Trudy, who was waiting expectantly, Juliet's desire to talk about Sykes got the better of her. All week she'd been walking around with this great big secret inside of her, and it was a relief to be able to tell someone finally. Even if she wasn't getting the response she wanted. She sighed. 'Where do I start? He's romantic, he's gorgeous, he makes me feel amazing.'

Rolling her eyes, Trudy made a gagging noise and stuck her fingers down her throat. 'Oh purrrleasse, spare me the violins.'

Juliet scowled and dug out a crispy wonton. 'If you're going to be such a bitch, then forget it, we'll talk about something else.'

Trudy was taken aback. In seven years she'd never known Juliet to snap at her. Her immediate reaction was to back down, but she changed her mind. Her best friend was playing a dangerous game, and it was up to her to try and stop her from getting hurt. 'Hey, I'm sorry. I just think you're making a big mistake.'

Juliet was defiant. 'Well I don't.'

Trudy's patience finally broke. 'For Christsakes Jules, the guy's a player. A smooth operator. *You don't even know him*.'

'Neither do you,' snapped back Juliet.

Seeing there was no point arguing, Trudy gave up, shaking her head. 'Jeez, this guy's really got to you, hasn't he?'

'He hasn't *got* to me,' rebuked Juliet. 'I happen to like him.' It was the understatement of the year.

'So what are you going to do?' Trudy was trying to be very adult and mature about all of this, but it was difficult. She was still reeling from discovering that Juliet was having an affair. Juliet. *Of all people*. Loyal, faithful, shockable Juliet. She was staggered. Monogamy was her middle name.

Staring into her bowl of chilli chicken ramen, Juliet took a deep breath. 'I'm going to Verona with him. This weekend.'

Trudy nearly choked on a vegetable dumpling. 'You *cannot* be serious.'

Juliet's silence confirmed that she was serious. Very serious.

'Jules, what the hell are you doing?'

'Having some fun, enjoying myself. *What you're always telling me to do.*' She threw it back at her.

'I didn't tell you to go out and fuck some other guy.'

'I haven't,' she hissed loudly.

'*Yet,*' repeated Trudy.

They glared at each other across their paper table-mats. The woman with the toddler fidgeted and attempted to shuffle further along the bench, away from the foul-mouthed American and her unfaithful friend. Unfortunately her two-year-old daughter was having fun building houses out of a pile of sticky rice and started crying. Juliet's jaw clenched tightly shut. She wished she'd never said anything. Trudy's reaction wasn't what she'd expected. Wasn't she supposed to be a confidante? Wasn't she supposed to support her? Be excited for her? *Agree* with her? She'd turned into enemy number one.

Trudy spoke first. 'What about Will?'

'What about Will?' she fired back, defensively.

'Well he is your boyfriend. You do live with the guy.'

'Since when have you been so bothered about Will?' Juliet pushed her food away from her. Her appetite had disappeared. 'You're the one who's always telling me he's a shithead.'

Trudy sighed, wishing that for once she'd kept that big fat Yankee mouth of hers zipped up. 'OK so maybe he can be a shithead *sometimes,*' she admitted, somewhat reluctantly. Bitching about a friend's boyfriend was OK when they'd had a row, but being faced with the possibility that her friend might actually follow her advice and leave the boyfriend was alarming. She didn't want to be responsible for breaking up a relationship. And despite everything she said about Will, she genuinely liked the guy. 'But he's an adorable shithead.' She leaned closer across the table. 'He's a shithead *who loves you.*'

Juliet put her head in her hands. She didn't want to hear this. Not now.

But Trudy wasn't going to let her off lightly. 'You're playing a dangerous game.'

Juliet looked up defiantly. 'I know and it's fantastic.'

Trudy gasped. 'So what do you think's gonna happen? And I'm not talking about this weekend,' she added quickly. 'I'm talking about long-term. In the future.'

Juliet shrugged. For the first time in her life she'd been refusing to think that far ahead. She'd done that for thirty years and she was bored with it. She looked up at Trudy. 'You're the one who always says live for the moment.'

'Yeah, and look where that got me,' she smiled sadly. 'Thirty-seven, single and pregnant.' She shook her head. 'Believe me, you don't wanna go there. You had it right all along. *You and Will.*' She paused and lowered her voice. 'Don't throw away what you guys have got together on some crazy fling. It's not worth it.'

Juliet chewed her bottom lip. 'It's not just a fling.'

Trudy shook her head. 'So what is it? Happy ever after?'

Juliet was ignoring her.

'Because happy ever after doesn't exist, Juliet. Not in the real world.'

'Maybe not in your real world,' she hit back, and then immediately wished she hadn't. 'Oh shit, I'm sorry . . . I didn't mean it, I was just . . .'

'Hey, it's OK,' breezed Trudy, shrugging off any hurt feelings. 'You're right. What have I got to look forward to?' She smiled ruefully.

Juliet squeezed her hand, feeling suddenly guilty. Trudy was always so bloody tough and resolute, it was easy to forget she was under immense pressure. Fergus hadn't been in touch and it had been left up to her to sort out the mess she was in, to arrange doctor's appointments and clinic appointments, while having to hold down two jobs and get on with the rest of her life. Her impassive and rather nonchalant attitude to what was happening never ceased to amaze Juliet. She couldn't even begin to imagine how she'd cope in the same situation. Most likely she'd be a nervous wreck, crying on Trudy's shoulder.

Yet here they were talking about Sykes, her weekend in Italy, how amazing he made her feel. Juliet realized she was being incredibly selfish and appallingly tactless. She tried to smile supportively at Trudy.

Feeling wafts of sympathy coming from Juliet, Trudy tried to deflect them with sarcasm. 'Maybe I should get my Psion to check. Oh no, hang on, I think I can remember. Now let's see . . . next week there's my abortion – oh, and this weekend it's a fondue and yoga evening. *How fabulous*.'

Juliet couldn't help smiling. 'You called Magnus?'

'He called me. God knows how he got hold of my number.' Spotting the waiter, she motioned for the bill, before turning back to Juliet who was looking sheepish. Trudy narrowed her eyes accusingly. 'You *didn't*.'

'Well, he kept asking. He looked so sincere . . .'

'So do con men when they're robbing old ladies of their life savings,' retorted Trudy. She was not feeling big on the male species at the moment.

'What did he say?'

'I had twenty messages of mumbling and coughing a lot. In the end I thought the guy was going to choke to death so I picked up.'

'So?'

'So Saturday is me, cheese and a leotard.' Trudy rolled her eyes. 'And before you say it, don't. I can hardly believe it myself. God knows what's happening to me. I'll be hugging trees next.'

Paying the bill, they stood up and climbed the stairs towards the exit. After the artificial light of the restaurant, it was disorientating to step outside onto the street, with all its noise, brightness and bustle.

'I better get back to the office,' said Juliet, resisting the temptation to give her best friend a hug goodbye. After years of standing stiffly, hands rigidly by her side, head recoiled, Trudy had finally confessed to Juliet at Christmas that she hated these shows of affection, and could she please just wave in future? 'I'll call you after the weekend.' Trying to hide her obvious excitement at the thought of it, Juliet headed off down one of the back streets, towards Soho.

'Don't do anything I wouldn't do,' Trudy called after her. But it was forced cheerfulness. Watching her friend trotting through the busy crowd of shoppers, her hair swinging in a shiny curtain, her hips wiggling in what looked suspiciously like a new pair of trousers, she sighed. It was like watching a lamb going to the slaughter.

'You're going to Italy?' Bare chested, Will stood at the bathroom door, a toothbrush jammed between his white frothy lips. He didn't like the sound of this. Not one little bit. 'When?'

Juliet hesitated. Her lunch with Trudy earlier had cast doubts on her decision. Perhaps she was right, perhaps she should break the whole thing off now, perhaps . . .

'Tomorrow,' she heard herself saying out loud.

'*Tomorrow?*' Reaching over to the sink, he spat out a mouthful of Colgate froth. It missed and hit the soap dish. He didn't notice.

Or rather he's pretending not to notice, thought Juliet, watching him bend his head underneath the cold tap and swill out his mouth.

'That's a bit sudden, isn't it?' Grabbing a towel, Will began vigorously drying his chin.

'I know, but it's work. For the pitch. Magnus's orders.' One lie after another. They were tripping off her tongue with alarming ease.

Will looked put out. 'I can't believe it. We could have gone away this weekend.'

'We never go away for the weekend.'

'Yes we do.' Screwing up the towel, Will rammed it down the back of the radiator. It hung there precariously for a few seconds, before sliding to the floor. It lay in a soggy heap.

'Like when?' Bending down, Juliet picked it up irritably.

Will dug around in his brain. 'Er . . . what about that time we went to the Cotswolds?'

'That was Christmas 1999.'

Trust Jules to nitpick. 'Well, yeah, all right . . . but we had a good time, didn't we?'

'Yeah,' nodded Juliet. 'We had a good time.' Staring at the towel in her hands, she picked at the loops of fabric, remembering the landlady thumping on the floor when they'd been having sex, the days spent stuffing their faces with cream teas, playing mini golf in the pouring rain. And laughing. That's what she remembered most of all. Lots and lots of laughing.

Looking up at Will, who was tugging on an old crumpled T-shirt with WASTED emblazoned across the chest, she smiled sadly. 'But that was over a year ago.'

It was eight o'clock and they were getting ready to go to the cinema. Finishing work early for once, Will had suggested they go to that Will Smith film he'd been wanting to see for ages. To his surprise Juliet had agreed. She'd even agreed to go for an Indian afterwards. Chuffed, he'd jumped in the bath and had a quick shave, leaving Juliet pacing guiltily up and down the living room, rehearsing how she would break the news that she was going to Italy. Wishing she'd told him earlier. Wondering why she hadn't.

'Well I don't know about you, but I'm ready.' Put out by Juliet's unenthusiastic – and very sarcastic – reaction to his suggestion of a weekend away, Will huffily sprayed two squirts of deodorant under each armpit, scooped up his *Exchange & Mart* that was wet and wrinkly and swollen to twice its size from being dropped in the bath, and stalked past her into the living room. 'The bathroom's all yours.'

Pulling a CD from the jumbled mass of silver discs and empty cases on the shelf, he stuck it into the stereo and pressed PLAY. Grabbing the remote, he flopped onto the sofa and glanced at the time on the video recorder. 'By the way, we've got to leave in fifteen minutes,' he yelled out grumpily. Usually he couldn't care less about timekeeping, but Juliet's news had left him feeling rather peeved and, if he was honest, more than just a little bit jealous. He was eager to get going. Pressing the volume button until it was as loud as it would go and the bass was making all Juliet's photo frames, vibrate, he opened his *Exchange & Mart* at the section marked 'Sportscars'.

Let her go to Italy. He didn't care. Not one little bit.

Fifteen minutes? To shower, wash her hair and tackle the kind of clean-up operation only ever seen on the news after an oil tanker had capsized? Sticking her hand behind the shower curtain, Juliet turned on the hot water and surveyed the bathroom.

It was a Will-zone.

Thick with steam that no extractor fan had a hope in hell of extracting, wet sploshy footprints that led out across the floorboards like something left by a yeti. Bathwater that had drained away leaving, not only a dirty great big ring around the white enamel, but her prized bottles of Space NK products. With their tops off and swollen with bathwater, they were lying at the bottom like the aftermath of a shipwreck.

Freshly shorn bristles decorated her toothbrush and toothpaste, while a fine carpet coated the sink. Nail clippers lay where he'd dropped them, complete with a scattering of toenail cuttings for her to impale her bare feet on like splinters. The toilet roll holder was empty – yet again – but Will, being thoughtful, had precariously balanced a fresh roll on top of the previous cardboard innertube, obviously intending for Juliet to try and remove the one below without knocking it off, as if she was playing Jenga. He'd even thought to discard his clothes on the floor like jumble, making little piles of screwed up socks and muddy jeans, creating his own work of art not unlike something from the Tate Modern.

Once upon a time, Juliet would have told Will in no uncertain terms to clear it up, but now she was resigned to it. Scooping everything up, she shoved the whole lot in the overflowing laundry basket. Once upon a time Will used to make her feel like a sex goddess. She turned off the hot tap, and began running in the cold. Now she felt like his bloody cleaner. And, whatever Nigella might say, there was no such thing as a domestic goddess, she thought, unravelling Will's Calvin Kleins that had somehow managed to wrap themselves around the bottom of the radiator.

Exactly fifteen minutes later she emerged freshly showered and pink cheeked. Tying up her hair that was still damp and tousled, she'd put on her favourite pair of faded jeans and a simple white T-shirt. A smear of raspberry lip gloss completed the look.

Walking into the living room she saw Will sitting on the sofa. Barefoot, he had his feet up on the coffee table and was wearing an old checked shirt he'd had for years. Chunks of sandy hair that he kept saying needed cutting were falling over his furrowed brow. He kept playing with it, twisting it around his forefinger as he stared at the photographs of sportscars. He always did that when he was concentrating.

Juliet stared at him. Oblivious to her presence he was singing away to one of his favourite old Jam CDs, nodding his head in time, one hand beating out as if he was drumming. Watching him, her heart twisted itself inside out. He looked so vulnerable, so much like the man she'd fallen in love with. So much like the man who'd fallen in love with her. Kind, sweet Will. He was her best friend, her boyfriend, her partner in crime. They'd been through so much together, loved so much together. What had happened?

At that moment his CD started jumping, kangarooing over all the scratches. Tutting, Will turned it off. The room fell silent. As it did, he looked up and noticed Juliet standing there.

For a moment Will didn't say anything.

Neither did Juliet.

For a moment she thought he was going to tell her how nice she looked, ask her what perfume she was wearing. *Tell her how much he loved her*. And in that moment she would have changed her mind, she would never have gone to Verona, and in years to come would have been happily snuggled up in bed with Will when she'd have suddenly remembered a guy called Sykes who she once nearly threw it all away for.

But instead Will scowled and asked grumpily,

'What took you so long?'

And in the blink of an eye, the moment was gone.

Chapter Twenty-seven

'*Ciao bella*.'

Stepping out of the dimly lit bustle of Verona airport, Juliet was greeted by a stretch of spotlessly clean lavender-blue sky, bright, ice-white winter afternoon sunshine, and a group of cab drivers leaning against the bonnets of their cars, smoking cigarettes and waiting for fares. At the sight of a lone attractive female wheeling a suitcase, waves of hair spilling from underneath a fake fur hat as she paused to tilt her head to the sun, they broke from their banter and eyed her appreciatively through their black Mafia shades.

'*Ahhhh, bionda dove vai?*'

So this was Italy. Juliet smiled to herself as she bathed her face in warm rays, listening to the chorus of catcalls. She didn't understand a word of Italian, but she knew exactly what the cab drivers were saying. The funny thing was, instead of feeling annoyed and telling them to sod off, which would have been her usual response in London, she was flattered. The torrent of Italian was irresistible, it sounded so sexy, so romantic, so passionate. 'Cheer up luv it might never happen,' from a group of beer-bellied workmen at Shepherd's Bush roundabout on a grey, rainy Monday morning, didn't have the same effect somehow.

'I can't let you out of my sight for a minute, can I?'

Squinting, she shaded her eyes from the glaring sunshine and saw Sykes. Having finished at the foreign exchange, he was striding through the sliding doors folding a thick stack of lire into his shiny crocodile skin wallet. *God, just look at him, how can anyone look so gorgeous?*

Juliet sighed, longingly. All week she'd been planning what to wear and on the advice of Trudy, who'd called her on the mobile when she was on the way to the airport to apologize for being less than supportive the day before, she'd gone for the Julie-Christie-in-*Dr-Zhivago* look and bought a furry hat from Accessorize in Duty Free. But instead of feeling chic, she wasn't sure she didn't in fact look like an oversized sheep. She felt too contrived. Unlike Sykes, who was walking towards her wearing his Persol sunglasses and a black woollen Armani coat which was flapping open to reveal the silk lining. With a Mulberry leather holdall slung casually over his shoulder, he oozed effortless style.

They'd met earlier that afternoon, after she'd left work early with some excuse about a dentist's appointment, and caught a cab straight to Heathrow, Terminal 3. Seeing him now, she was reminded of the expectation she'd felt, her stomach full of butterflies as they'd held hands like a couple of honeymooners, checked in to their business class seats, and been asked to put their baggage on the weighing scales. Followed by a mixture of awe and embarrassment when she'd seen that Sykes had somehow managed to magically vacuum-pack his weekend wardrobe into something not much bigger than her filofax. She'd been so indecisive about what to bring, she'd ended up packing everything in one of Trudy's cast-offs. A transatlantic suitcase the size of a large American fridge, it had squeaky wheels. *And it was tartan.*

At Verona she'd watched it thudding down the baggage carousel, squashing Head bags and Samsonite wheelies in its wake and realized the real reason why all the presenters on the holiday programme went on about travelling light. And it had nothing to do with ease or convenience. It was because it was sexy. Infinitely more sexy. No wiggling through the airport lounge for her, wheeling a chic little black trolley. Oh no. When Sykes had disappeared off to change some money, she was left grappling with a very un-chic piece of luggage. Dragging it behind her through Customs, she'd felt as if she was moving house – and it was dressed in a kilt.

Catching up with her, Sykes slipped his hand around her waist. 'You need to be careful of Italian men.'

'Oh really?' Gladly leaving behind that particular humiliating memory, she grinned. 'Does that include you?' she joked, but she was deadly serious. The intensity of her feelings for Sykes put her on an incredible high, but she knew they also brought with them a dangerous vulnerability.

He smiled in response. But it was the kind of annoying, secretive smile that gave nothing away. Juliet tried to read what he was thinking in his eyes, but it was impossible. The sunglasses he was wearing were the type with really dark lenses favoured by film stars, to avoid eye contact with their adoring public.

Instead, his answer was to grab hold of her.

'Mmm, you smell gorgeous,' he murmured, burying his face in the nape of her neck. As he did, Juliet caught their reflection in the tinted arrivals lounge of the airport. For a second her mind flitted back to Valentine's Day, Oxford Street, standing alone in the pouring rain and seeing herself in a shop mirror. Never could she have imagined in that moment, that only a few weeks later she'd be standing in the warm Italian sunshine with a new Gucci coat wrapped around her shoulders and Sykes's arm wrapped around her waist.

Sykes hailed one of the cabs. Climbing into the back seat Juliet listened to him giving directions in fluent Italian. As someone who could only remember the dregs of O level French, she was impressed. And very turned on. It was such a cliché, she knew she should be ashamed of herself, but it was irresistible. *He's irresistible*, she thought to herself, trying to banish all the Italian stallion jokes, legends about Latin lovers and Madonna's 'Italians Do It Better' T-shirt from her mind as they sat hips touching, thighs pressing, anticipation building.

They set off towards their hotel. Their driver obviously thought he was Ayrton Senna reincarnated. Accelerating down the autostrada at over a hundred, Juliet gripped the leather seat, watching the blur of countryside through the window as Sykes chatted on his mobile.

'Sorry darling, do you mind? I've just got to catch up with a few people, let them know I'm back in town,' he'd explained.

'No, course not . . .' she'd begun, before she was interrupted by him yelling, '*Aaayye, Marco, come stai*?' down his Nokia. If she'd felt a seed of disappointment she hadn't shown it. It would be silly, she'd thought to herself, gazing out of the window. Just because she'd switched off her mobile as soon as she'd reached Heathrow, that didn't mean he had to. After all, she couldn't expect him not to get in touch with his old friends.

Exiting sharply off the motorway, their cab ploughed through the nondescript low-rise buildings, tatty shops and sixties blocks of soulless flats that made up the outskirts. Staring at the mud-coloured blocks of concrete, Juliet's heart sank. Was this it? Her great expectations looked in danger of turning into one big anticlimax; then she caught a glimpse of a huge circular wall looming up in front of them. The famous Roman arena.

Excitement flooded back as the arena disappeared entrancingly from sight and they plunged through the city walls into the shadowy labyrinth of narrow cobbled streets, past ancient buildings with beautifully carved stonework, intricate window arches, wrought iron balustrades. And then as suddenly as they'd started, they stopped, lurching to an abrupt halt outside a very grand hotel that had been shoehorned into a skinny little side street.

Juliet stared wide-eyed out of the window. In one of his many emails to her that week, Sykes had described their hotel as 'cosy'. Looking at Colomba D'Oro, with its flags flying overhead, red carpet decorated with hotel insignia running up the front steps, highly polished brass proudly decorating the mahogany doors like a display of medals, *cosy* wasn't a word that sprang to mind. My God, thought Juliet, there was even a uniformed doorman who looked uncannily like Pavarotti.

Even so, she tried not to appear too impressed. After all, it wasn't as if she hadn't stayed in four-stars before, and a couple of five-stars on SGC expenses. Nevertheless, she had to admit to herself that she was impressed. Very impressed.

This was, as Trudy would have said, a result.

'OK, ciao, ciao.'

As the doorman held open the door of the cab, Sykes flicked his mobile shut, grinning. 'My friends are very intrigued to know more about the mysterious woman I'm with.' Stepping onto the red carpet, he tipped the cab driver. 'They can't wait to meet you.'

'*Meet me?*'

'Don't tell me you're feeling shy,' he laughed, pushing his sunglasses up onto his head.

'No, I just . . .' Juliet's voice trailed off. She'd assumed it was going to be just the two of them, together, all weekend. Now it looked as if she would have to share him.

'Just what?' Sykes was looking at her.

She hesitated. She could hardly play the role of a possessive girlfriend, could she? Shaking her head, she smiled. 'Nothing.'

Feeling the spikes of her boots puncturing the carpet like an advancing hole puncher, she followed Sykes inside. This was one of those boutiquey kinds of hotels that only people who subscribed to *Vogue Traveller* would know about. Discreetly decorated with vases of fresh white lilies, a caramel-coloured leather sofa tucked snugly into the corner, the day's newspapers arranged like a decorative fan, and a bowl of cocoa-dusted truffles on the reception desk, it was a world away from musty old British B&Bs and chintzy country manors.

The kinds of place Will used to take me, thought Juliet, unable to stop the memory popping into her head as she watched Sykes handing his Visa card over to the receptionist who was looking positively orgasmic at the sight of this handsome male smiling down at her.

Signing the hotel register, they handed over their passports and took an old-fashioned elevator, the kind with concertina-grilled doors that reminded Juliet of Agatha Christie novels, to the top floor. True to his word, Sykes had booked two rooms, albeit interconnecting.

'And before you ask, the door does lock,' he grinned, dismissing the heavily sweating porter whose complexion had turned the colour of Parma ham and who looked as if he was about to keel over from lugging Julliet's suitcase up five flights of stairs. It was too big for the lift. 'Just in case you think I can't be trusted.'

Juliet laughed nervously. A week of flirting, sexual innuendoes and fancying Sykes rotten had created a level of sexual tension that was fast becoming unbearable. Part of her wanted to just grab him there and then and rip his clothes off. To shag him and have done with it. The other part of her was revelling in all the teasing and lusting. In the waiting and anticipation.

As Sykes began taking off his coat and lit up a

cigarette she glanced around the two rooms. They looked more like suites, with pieces of antique furniture dotted around, a chaise-longue, claw-footed coffee table, tassled lamps, a writing bureau with neat piles of vanilla notepaper and envelopes. Juliet had never understood that. Why did hotels always have stationery? Who the hell ever went on holiday to sit in their hotel room writing letters? Who cared, she thought to herself, realizing she was asking herself stupid questions to avoid looking at two very significant pieces of furniture. *The Beds*.

Standing in the middle of the rooms, she could see them both at once. Each one was ginormous, heaving with plumped-up pillows, heavy brocade bedspreads, the promise of clean white sheets. Yet while hers looked safe and snug in its innocence, the one in Sykes's room looked like a den of iniquity and rampant sex. It eyed her challengingly.

Will you, or won't you?

She looked away hastily. Opening the French windows that led out onto a pretty balcony, she stepped out and took a few breaths of cold air. Part of her couldn't believe she was here. That she'd actually done it. She was in a foreign country, in a hotel room, with Sykes. Only a few hours ago she'd been in her own bedroom, kissing Will goodbye as he was leaving for work. Listening to him telling her how much he was looking forward to having the flat to himself, to enjoying a weekend of football, boys' nights in and vindaloos. Proving to her just how little he cared. Eradicating any last-minute doubts. Convincing her she'd made the right decision.

And now she was finally here. Teetering on the brink of an affair, of being unfaithful, of making love with a man that the phrase weak at the knees was made for. After all that anticipation, all that build-up, all that nervous energy. It was Christmas Eve for grown-ups, she thought, staring out at the skyline. Which begged the question: If they slept together, would it suddenly turn into Boxing Day?

'Calling Romeo?'

'*What?*' She turned around.

Sykes was leaning against the French windows. 'Juliet – on her balcony. "Wherefore art thou . . ." ' his voice tailed off as he waited for her to cotton on.

'Oh, yeah,' she smiled. 'I mean, no . . . I was just getting some fresh air. It's beautiful here.' She gestured to the panorama of rooftops. Endless row upon neatly stacked row of terracotta tiles, stretching away to the skyline like a field of rusting corn on the cob.

'The real thing's just around the corner.'

Juliet didn't know if it was her, but she seemed to be reading two meanings into everything he was saying. 'Sorry, you've completely lost me,' she explained, feeling incredibly nervous. Like a virginal thirteen-year-old, not a been-there-done-that-thirty-year-old.

'Balcone di Giulietta,' he explained in Italian. 'Verona's biggest tourist attraction. You know this is where Shakespeare set *Romeo and Juliet*, don't you?'

'Of course,' protested Juliet, trying to look offended. To be truthful, it was so long since she'd read the play at school it had completely slipped her mind. But now, being reminded she felt a thrill. The greatest love story of all time, being set right here. It appealed to every slushy-weepy-indulgent-un-PC-*Sleepless-in-Seattle* bone in her body. It must be fate. 'But I didn't know there was an actual balcony. I thought it was just a legend,' she confessed.

'Apparently it's based on a true story.' Joining her outside, Sykes began gently brushing his hand against the side of her neck, doing that tracing thing with his fingertips. Juliet shivered, even though she was wearing a furry hat and a sheepskin coat. 'In the thirteenth century Bandello, an Italian poet, wrote about two feuding families who lived here in the city, and the tragic love affair between their son and daughter . . .' he broke off, laughing quietly to himself, 'Christ, that's what living here for a year did to me. I've turned into a tour guide.'

'Mmmm,' murmured Juliet, feeling like a cat and wanting to close her eyes, lift up her chin and start purring. Before Sykes, she'd never have believed that the little bit underneath her earlobe was an erogenous zone. She forced herself to get a grip before she got carried away. She couldn't cave in and jump into bed the moment they arrived in their hotel room. *Could she?* 'So are you saying Shakespeare stole someone else's idea?' With a great deal of effort, she swung her thoughts back to the conversation.

'I wouldn't say stole it, just borrowed it, changed it a little, made it his own.' Sykes continued stroking her neck. 'It happens all the time,' he muttered quietly.

'Can we go and see it?'

Breaking away, Sykes stopped to look at his watch. It was nearly four in the afternoon. 'Yeah, why not.' He began walking back inside.

Juliet opened her eyes. She felt a stab of disappointment. She hadn't meant that minute. After the huge build-up over the last few days they were finally alone together. Wasn't he supposed to be throwing her onto the bed and making mad passionate love to her? *Or at least thinking about it?*

'But don't you want to unpack first?'

Unpack? Now? She watched Sykes unzip his holdall and take out his toiletry bag, a large thick paperback, a small handful of clothes. She looked at his clothes. All folded up neatly in plastic dryclean-only bags. He began removing their wrappers and hanging them up carefully. Shirts around padded hangers, trousers held by the hems and folded underneath. *Crikey*. She was used to checking in her room, dumping her suitcase, having a quick pee and dashing straight out again. She always left the boring job of unpacking until after she'd grabbed her fix of shopping, sightseeing, and drunk the first ice-cold gin and tonic of the holiday.

In fact Will never used to bother unpacking at all, thought Juliet. He always said he never could see the point of taking it all out to put it all back in again. She thought about how he used to drive her crazy by leaving his suitcase in the middle of the floor for her to trip over, and pulling things out to wear in creased, screwed-up dribs and drabs.

'There's some extra hangers here if you need them.' Sykes rolled the holdall up neatly and popped it onto a shelf. He held out a handful of wooden coat hangers. 'You'll probably need them,' he grinned.

'Oh, yeah . . . thanks.' Taking them from him, Juliet watched as he disappeared into the bathroom to 'freshen up'. Pulling off her hat and coat, she dropped them onto an armchair. She glanced at her suitcase, lying on its side in the middle of the room like a beached whale.

And suddenly felt a bizarre affinity with Will.

Chapter Twenty-eight

In the end they decided to leave the sightseeing until the next day. Shakespeare's Juliet may have had nothing better to do than stand on her balcony, but by the time this Juliet had finished the mammoth task of unpacking, it had already begun to grow dark. Instead, Sykes suggested going for a drink.

'I know a place that does a great martini,' he said as they left the hotel an hour later. He looked at her in a way that always made her stomach sit up and beg. 'They stir the alcohol together instead of shaking, so they don't bruise the vermouth.'

'Do they bruise gin and tonics?' she laughed as they walked down the front steps. Excited at the prospect of experiencing her first taste of an Italian city, and the evening that lay ahead, she'd just broken her own record for getting ready. And in *my* room, she mused, thinking about Sykes's tempting offer of his shower which was 'big enough for the both of us'. 'Maybe later,' she'd smiled, trying to play it cool and flirtatious and not let him see how nervous she was. Despite fantasizing about this moment all week, now it was here and she was right in the middle of it, she'd felt it was a bit too soon *and she was a bit too sober* to be contemplating taking all her clothes off in front of him.

'Look, if you don't want to go . . .' Sykes looked affronted.

'No . . . I mean yes . . . of course I want to,' she rushed in, suddenly realizing he thought she was making fun of him. She made a mental note to stop joking around. She always did it when she was nervous. It was a habit she'd picked up from Will, but not everyone shared their sarcastic sense of humour. She reached for Sykes's hand.

'Caffé Filippini's probably the best piano bar in Verona,' he continued defensively.

Now it was Juliet's turn to jump to the wrong conclusion. 'A piano bar?' she echoed, imagining an old guy playing Gershwin on a baby grand, potted palms, bellhops, lots of hush. She'd assumed they'd be going to a funky hangout with a vibrant Latin atmosphere. Immediately she wished she'd worn something different to her jeans and PORNSTAR T-shirt.

Amused by her worried expression, Sykes softened. 'Don't worry, it's not the Ritz,' he laughed, as they continued walking down the narrow side street. The sound of their feet on the cobbles intermingled with the buzz of scooters, their horns echoing down the alleyways. The aroma of fresh coffee wafted out from the tiny espresso bars squeezed in between lingerie shops, a wine merchant's, a skinny chemist's shop with a window full of designer sunglasses. 'In Italy that's what they always call bars. Don't ask me why, I've never seen a piano yet. And I should know. It was my local the whole time I lived here.'

'Whereabouts did you live?' Juliet was intrigued. In the last week she'd started to learn more about Sykes, to discover his habits, his views, *his history*. But she was still filling in the gaps about what kind of life he'd led before he'd driven his car right into hers.

'Not far from here.' Turning out of shadows, they entered a brightly lit main road. 'Across the other side of the arena.' Juliet looked to where he was pointing and saw a huge archway ahead. A childhood memory of Floella Benjamin's *Play School* voice singsonging, 'let's look through the arched window' sprang unexpectedly to mind. And doing just that, she saw a wide piazza stretching away towards the impressive Roman amphitheatre, its own tiers of rose-pink arches lit up against the navy sky.

'Wow, is that for real?' she gasped, feeling as if the whole of Verona had unexpectedly opened up before her like a double-page spread. A Canaletto painting come to life.

'I know, it's hard to believe. The whole thing looks like some kind of computer-generated graphic, doesn't it?' agreed Sykes. 'But then that's *Gladiator* for you,' he added drily.

They headed towards it, passing row upon row of restaurants and busy pavement cafés. Despite the still cold night air, people were sitting outside, bundled up in furs and hats, sipping espresso and chatting, the embers of their cigarettes dancing around like fireflies in the distance. 'We'll have to come back in the summer, when they have open-air opera concerts in the arena.' He looked at her, suddenly filled with enthusiasm. 'I went last year, on a really hot evening in July. Everyone was chilling out, drinking wine and listening to *La Traviata*. The atmosphere was just incredible.'

'Mmmm, yeah.' Juliet nodded, trying to remain totally calm when her mind had just taken a skydive from 30,000 feet. Sykes was talking about coming back to Verona with her in the summer. What did that mean? Was he implying *that he wanted this to be much more than just an affair*?

Juliet was taken aback. Until that moment, neither of them had spoken about the future. Who knew what lay ahead? Everything had been happening so quickly, so unexpectedly, it was impossible to make sense of it, and so she hadn't. Instead she'd allowed herself to be carried along on a wave, to 'live for the moment'. A phrase which, until she'd met Sykes, she'd thought meant buying something expensive from Joseph. And it had been an exhilarating release. All her life she'd planned and organized, analysed situations, avoided unnecessary risks, and made rational, logical, long-term decisions. It was adult. It was sensible. *And it was boring*.

Unlike now.

Holding hands they weaved their way among the crowds, pausing to peer in shop windows, to buy some cigarettes at a *tabachi*, to gaze up at the intricate frescos adorning the façade of nearly every building which, lit up by the street lamps, made a kind of public art gallery. Snuggling up contentedly against Sykes's shoulder, Juliet listened to his stories about what it was like working in Verona, spending weekends at Lake Garda when the city sweltered in the August temperatures, going skiing in the Alps at Christmas. How different he'd found working in an ad agency in Italy, how much he'd loved their passion, their style and their three-hour lunches, and how much he'd missed London, his friends, 'a really good Sunday roast', and his creative team in Soho, with their hard-nosed attitudes 'and their coke habits'.

Intrigued to know if he'd had any Italian girlfriends, she edged around asking him about his love life – Sykes knew about hers, but she knew barely anything about his.

'There were a couple of flings, but nothing serious,' he shrugged.

Flings? Juliet's ears pricked up. What did he mean by flings? Did he mean *affairs*? A small flicker of fear and, considering she was the one with a live-in boyfriend, a very large and ridiculous stab of jealousy planted themselves in her heart. She was about to try and get him to elaborate, when he announced, 'Well, this is it, Piazza Erbe.'

She'd been so intent on finding out about Sykes's romantic history, she'd barely noticed they'd entered a large picturesque square surrounded by the kind of magnificent historical buildings that would send an

American tourist into apoplexy and that boasted battlements, porticoes and statues of mythical gods that peered down from the balustrades like nosy neighbours. The centre of the piazza was filled with umbrella-covered market stalls that had long since closed up for the night, while around the edges dozens of lively restaurants and bars overflowed out onto the marble paving stones.

'*Aaayyee*, Sykes!'

A bellowing voice. Sitting outside one of the bars Juliet saw a man with a goatee waving. He was with another man and two raven-headed women.

'Who are they?'

'My friends. I said we'd meet them here for a drink.'

'Your friends?' Juliet's heart sank with a thud into her LK Bennett boots. She wanted to get to know Sykes better. But not like this, she thought, feeling unexpectedly nervous. In today's society, meeting his friends was as bad as meeting the parents. They'd either love her, or hate her.

'Hey, don't look so worried.' He grinned, squeezing her hand. 'They're going to love you.'

Juliet tried to look enthusiastic, but even at this distance she could see the women were worryingly stunning. All at once she felt incredibly – and uncharacteristically – insecure. She stopped herself. She was being ridiculous. If they were Sykes's friends, they'd be really cool. And an even more cheering thought – they were probably two couples.

By the kiss the skinny brunette placed on Sykes's cheek, Juliet knew this woman was no half of any couple. Her attentions were firmly aimed at Sykes, who was returning the kiss and smiling. 'Mmm, you smell gorgeous.'

Watching on the sidelines Juliet felt a prickle of doubt. He'd said the same thing to her earlier. 'Juliet, I want you to meet Gina, Marco, Lucca and Stephanie.'

So what, it didn't matter, she thought hastily. It was probably just a coincidence, she decided, plunging into a round of smiling and kissing. As expected, the two men made a huge fuss, the girls less so. In fact Gina, the woman who'd had her lips stuck to Sykes's stubble as if she was attached by superglue, looked her up and down as if she was buying a slave, and then proffered a limp hand. Juliet shook it uncomfortably. Thrown in at the deep end, she was frantically trying to work out what relationship everyone had to each other. Were Stephanie and Lucca an item? Had Gina been one of Sykes's 'nothing serious' flings? Was Stephanie giving her daggers or was she just being paranoid?

One thing she did know for certain was that both women were immaculately turned out with their perfectly arched eyebrows, sharply cut bobs and magenta manicured fingernails. They were probably the type who carried stainless steel eyebrow tweezers and emery boards in their Prada clutch bags in case of rogue hairs or nail breakages, she thought, sitting down and hiding her own sensibly short fingernails in the pockets of her sheepskin coat.

'So, you are the famous Juliet?' Stephanie smiled. Or was that a snarl? mused Juliet, watching Stephanie's blood red lips part to reveal surprisingly dodgy teeth.

'Well, I'm not *the* famous Juliet,' she tried joking. None of the Italians laughed. Sykes didn't seem to notice.

Accepting a cigarette from Gina, *who'd insisted on lighting two and passing him one*, Sykes had plonked himself down next to Marco and Lucca, who were clapping him so boisterously on the back anyone would have thought he'd been choking, and pouring out torrents of Italian. Juliet remained sitting uncomfortably next to Stephanie who tossed her curtain of hair over the side of her face, thus making it virtually impossible to attempt any kind of conversation. Not that I'd have much luck anyway as no-one's speaking

English, thought Juliet, realizing that her entire knowledge of the Italian language consisted of either pasta dishes os fashion designers. Trying to construct some sort of a sentence with *spaghetti arabiatta* and *Valentino* and no verbs would be tricky. Even with her best *Goodfellas* accent, it probably wasn't a good idea. First impressions and all that.

After sitting there for a few minutes, which seemed interminably long to Juliet, boredom and thirst got to her. Clearing her throat, and feeling very Jeeves and Wooster, she interrupted like some kind of terribly English butler.

'Erm, anyone for a drink?'

The men stopped talking. The two women blew cannons of cigarette smoke at her. Sykes broke into an apologetic smile. 'Oh, sorry darling, you know what it's like, catching up with old friends.' He leaned across the table and stroked the side of her face. Christ, the man was so bloody sexy, she thought, immediately forgiving him for talking to Lucca and Marco and ignoring her. Out of the corner of her eye, she saw Gina throw him a murderous look. Yep, Gina was definitely one of those flings.

'You stay and get to know everyone better. I can sort out the drinks.' Slipping his wallet out of his breast pocket, he made to stand up.

'No, no, you carry on . . . catching up.' Protesting hastily, Juliet stood up and gave a little smile around the table. The last thing she wanted was to be left alone with his friends. Although Marco and Lucca seemed quite amiable – they kept glancing across at her and beaming delightedly – Stephanie and Gina weren't exactly welcoming. 'Back in a minute,' she hey-hoed, weaving briskly through the tables towards the bar before any attempt at chivalry could stop her.

She stretched it to ten.

What was she doing? Why was she being so insecure

about Sykes? Feeling so jealous of Gina? Ordering a martini for Sykes, two Americanos for Lucca and Marco, *two ice-creams* for the ice queens themselves and two extra large gin and tonics – both for herself – Juliet hitched herself up on a barstool. She couldn't remember the last time she'd felt like this. Being with Will for so long had lulled her into a blissful state of security. Now she'd been thrown back into those shark-infested waters surrounding new relationships. Not knowing if she and Sykes were going to make it to dry land, having to keep one eye over her shoulder as she clung onto her man.

Now you're being ridiculous and very hypocritical young lady, she scolded, and then promptly cheered herself up by helping herself to the delicious picky things on the bar. You're the one with the boyfriend. It's probably Sykes who's feeling jealous and insecure. Dipping a crostini into a bowl of tapenade, she glanced outside. She could see him entertaining his friends with some anecdote or other, holding their attention like a magician at a children's party. Well that shot her theory down in flames, she thought to herself. Never had she seen a man looking so confident and self-assured.

Alone at the bar, Juliet turned her attentions back to a large bowl of fat purple olives. She wasn't alone for long. This was Italy, and she was an attractive female. Within minutes a little crowd had gathered around her and she soon discovered she was enjoying rather a laugh with the locals, and the handsome bar staff who practised their English in a Joe Dolce kind of accent, asking her about '*Lorndorn*' and pouring her a glass of prosecco 'on thee 'ouse'. By the time she'd carried the drinks back outside, she was feeling much better.

'Juliet's in advertising too,' said Sykes as she sat down, a little unsteadily. That first drink had really gone to her head. The second was providing back-up.

'Is that how you two met?' Until now Juliet had

presumed Lucca couldn't speak English. In fact he spoke it perfectly.

'Sort of,' replied Juliet, sipping her gin and tonic thirstily.

'Do you work for the same company?'

'No we're rivals.' Sykes grinned at her across the table.

She grinned back. So what if she didn't like his friends? It didn't matter one little jot, she thought, staring dreamily, and a little tipsily, into Sykes's eyes.

'Really? How interesting.' Gina perked up. Until now she had been sitting stiffly slicing tiny chips off her ice-cream with a teaspoon and chainsmoking Fortuna cigarettes. 'Does that make you enemies?'

The way she said 'enemies' confirmed to Juliet that she'd well and truly made one in Gina. She consoled herself with the fact that enemy number one was wearing a rather naff pair of leather trousers that belted high up around the middle, the kind only forty-something South Kensington blondes or rich European women with red lipstick and gold earrings would wear. Trudy always howled with bitchy merriment and called them Ivana Trump trousers.

'Not in the bedroom,' laughed Lucca, elbowing Sykes in the ribs in a nudge-nudge-wink-wink blokeish kind of a way.

Sucking up gin like a Hoover, Juliet realized she was going rapidly off Lucca and his ridiculous goatee, which perched on his chin like a small greying brillo pad.

'Oh, you are *so funny*,' screeched Stephanie, as everyone burst into near hysterics.

Except for Juliet. 'We're both trying to win the same campaign at the moment, aren't we, Sykes?' Now everyone was speaking in English, she felt she should at least try to make an effort at some kind of sensible conversation. If only to try and put a stop to Lucca's appalling schoolboy humour.

'And who's going to win?' Stephanie flicked her bob over to the other side and did that funny snarly thing again, with those funny jagged teeth of hers. She looked like a Hallowe'en pumpkin. If only Trudy was here, mused Juliet, remembering the many times she'd been witness to her pulling a poor orthodontically challenged soul to one side in a bar. Watching her launching into a lecture about how it was 'never too late to wear braces' which usually began with the opening gambit: 'Do you think Julia Roberts was born with a smile like that?'

'Yes Juliet, who do you think will win?' echoed Gina, grabbing back her attention.

She looked at the faces around the table. Everyone was staring at her expectantly. Fuelled with gin, she felt a surge of cockiness. 'I will.'

'Whooaahh!' There was a torrent of Italian, as the men did a little drum roll on the cobbles with the leather soles of their shoes. '*Aaaayyyyye*, Sykes, are you going to let a woman beat you?' Like a couple of backing singers, Gina and Stephanie joined in a chorus of laughter.

'I doubt it very much,' he smirked. 'You're going to need something a little bit special to win this campaign.'

'Are you saying SGC doesn't have something a little bit special?'

'The robotic talking dog in the Pedigree Chum ad was hardly groundbreaking,' laughed Sykes. His laughter rankled. Juliet was now feeling definitely drunk and lairy. 'It's set in Italy and it's a spoof of *The Italian Job . . .*' she boasted, before clamping her hand over her mouth. 'Oh shit, I shouldn't have said that.'

'Don't worry, you're among friends,' laughed Lucca.

Was that supposed to console her? She looked at Sykes. Dragging hard on his cigarette, he winked at her. She relaxed. What was she worrying about? By now the alcohol had well and truly kicked in and she winked back, not noticing the muscle in the side of Sykes's jaw twitching in agitation.

Quickly she sucked up the dregs of her drink. 'Shall I get another round in?' Used to British pub culture, she hadn't realized that no-one else was getting even slightly drunk. It was only when she'd stood up that it dawned on her that the others had barely touched the first round. Even the ice-creams were uneaten. Sitting upright like Gina's La Perla cleavage, the two vanilla scoops were refusing to melt in their owner's arctic presence.

'I thought perhaps we could go and eat.' Sykes stubbed out his cigarette and took a sip of martini.

'All of us?' Juliet tried to keep the disappointment from her voice.

'No, just you and I.' He spoke quickly in Italian to his friends. 'But if you want I'll change the reservation for later and we can stay with these guys longer. That's if you're not hungry, yet.'

Juliet didn't need persuading. 'Hungry? *I'm starving.*'

After saying their goodbyes, they walked to the restaurant. It wasn't far. Sykes held her as she wobbled uncertainly on her stilettos – cobbles might look very romantic, steeped in history and all that, but Juliet was beginning to find that they were murder to walk on. Her heels kept getting wedged between the cobbles and each time it chipped away at the leather. She decided that tomorrow she was going to forget about trying to look stylish, and ditch the high heels in favour of her trainers.

'What did you think of that lot?' They'd paused outside the restaurant to look at an elaborately carved fountain. 'Crazy, aren't they?'

Juliet nodded, watching the water gushing out of the serpent's mossy mouth. Well she couldn't say they were bloody awful, could she?

Luckily, she didn't have to say anything as Sykes

tilted her head and kissed her. He tasted of cigarettes and alcohol. It was very erotic. If he was this good at kissing, how good was he going to be in bed?

'They told me how great they thought you were.'

Feeling his hand slip underneath her coat, his warm fingers finding the gap of bare skin between T-shirt and jeans, she felt the tension inexplicably evaporating. What was the matter with her? Ever since they'd arrived in Verona she'd been so touchy. Feeling sensitive about the silliest things: Sykes calling his friends in the cab, about unpacking her suitcase while he watched CNN in his room, his relationship with Gina and Stephanie.

With his hands moving up her spine, underneath her bra strap, around to her breasts, she became aware of the sensations of her body. The way her back was arching, her breathing was quickening, her heart was thudding. No wonder she was feeling sensitive. Being with Sykes put her into a heightened state of awareness. It was as if every emotion was magnified a thousand times. Colours seemed more vivid, food tasted more delicious, that cup of coffee was the best one she'd ever tasted. And that was saying something, as she'd been in Garfunkels at Heathrow airport at the time, she thought, trying to keep her mind on anything that was vaguely mundane. Anything to stop her from thinking about his hands, which were circling her nipples, the erection she could feel pressing against her through his jeans.

'You OK?' Now she was leaning against the wall and he was kissing her neck, around to the nape, along her collarbone.

'Yeah, fine,' she murmured. She was lying. She wasn't fine. Fine was cool, calm and collected. An easy shrugging of the shoulders, a mediocre film, a bottle of Penfolds wine. It was OK, but nothing special. And she felt special. *Everything felt special*.

'Do you want to know something?' He looked up at her.

She nodded, dumbly.

He hesitated.

She waited.

'I'm afraid I might fall in love with you.'

Sykes's words came tumbling out, and for a split second Juliet didn't register what he was saying. She could see his mouth moving, hear words, but she didn't string them together in a sentence. *I'm. Afraid. I. Might. Fall. In. Love. With. You*.

She did now. Her stomach flipped.

'Shhh. You don't have to say anything,' he whispered. But he didn't give her any choice anyway, as he began kissing her again. Deeper this time. More urgently.

Juliet didn't mind. Not one little bit, she thought, letting herself be carried away. She was intoxicated – God, she loved that word – intoxicated by Sykes, by his body, hard and muscular underneath his cotton shirt, by the opalescent moonlight that cast a silver sheen over the fountain and made it seem almost ghostly. Or maybe it was just the gin, she mused with typical self-deprecating humour, as their lips finally broke apart.

Sykes remained wrapped around her.

'Do you want to forget the restaurant?' It was a loaded question.

Juliet hesitated. Food was definitely not on either of their minds. She found her voice. 'Do you want to come back to mine for a coffee?' she teased nervously, and then wished she hadn't. There she went again. Joking around.

But this time he laughed. 'Yeah, something like that.'

She looked at him. Seeing the lips that she'd just kissed, the face she kept seeing inside her head every time she closed her eyes, the broad shoulders she'd snuggled up against. He was so fucking sexy he made her physically ache inside. Oh God. Juliet knew where this was heading and she knew she had no control over it. Up until now it had been flirting, foreplay, fantasies, *frustration*. But not any longer.

She didn't care about the consequences, she couldn't resist. *She didn't want to resist any longer.* Her head was in soft focus, but her body was crystal clear.

She fancied him. She wanted him.

She craved him.

So what the bloody hell was she waiting for?

Chapter Twenty-nine

Will didn't remember Yorkshire ever being this cold. Or this dark. Or this windy. It had been all right driving up the M1, just a bit gusty when he'd turned off at Leeds, but by the time he'd driven past Skipton and spotted a sign for his parents' tiny village in the Dales, a force ten gale was blowing.

Rubbing the ice off his windscreen, he rattled down the winding country lanes, trying not to be buffeted into the drystone walls, or a farmer's field. His nerves were fraught. Rabbits scurried in front of him, hedgehogs appeared from nowhere as he plunged blindly into the cavernous darkness, guided only by the flickering light weakly projecting from his headlamps.

Suddenly something loomed ahead of him. *Fuck*. What the hell was that? Jamming on his brakes he swerved to avoid a huge white thing in his path. As he did he heard a familiar bleat. Fucking hell, it was a bloody sheep. Revving the Land Rover out of a muddy ditch, it crossed his mind that everyone always complained about what a nightmare it was to drive in London. Obviously they'd never been to the Yorkshire Dales. Cranking into first he lurched back onto the tarmac, avoiding the sheep that was still standing in the middle of the road, giving him the dead eye. In the city all you had to avoid were pedestrians and couriers. Up here it was like driving through a bloody wildlife park.

* * *

Going to stay with his parents for the weekend had been a last-minute decision. When he'd left for work that morning, Juliet had still been packing. Her flight wasn't until the afternoon and seeing her getting ready, wet hair wrapped up in a turban, clothes all over the bed, he'd been determined to show her how fine he was with the whole situation. 'Actually, this weekend should be quite a laugh. I can't remember the last time I had the flat to myself. Maybe I'll throw a wild party,' he'd joked, kissing her awkwardly goodbye. Everything seemed to be awkward between them these days.

Leaving work early, he'd arrived back at the flat ready for a weekend of slobbing and debauchery. An hour later, after flicking his ash in her favourite 'I hate yoga' cup, making a fried bacon sarnie – a rare treat in the two years since Jules had moved in with her Linda McCartney sausages and that bloody awful Quorn stuff – and eating it on the new sofa *without a plate*, Will had finally admitted it to himself.

He didn't want to be in the flat by himself all weekend.

Now he had the chance, he didn't actually want to spend his Saturday with Rolf watching football, he didn't want to get pissed on beer and mop up his hangover with fried food. To be honest, it didn't taste half as nice as he remembered, he'd thought, putting down his half-eaten greasy bacon sarnie with disgust and staring forlornly at the TV.

When he'd been hit with a sudden impulse. Sod it. If Juliet could go away for the weekend, so could he. He'd checked his watch. Five o'clock. If he left now, he'd probably make it in time for supper. Decisively turning off the telly he'd hurriedly packed a few things in a holdall – most of it being his dirty washing – and grabbed his keys. Yep, the more he thought about it, the more determined he became. He didn't need five-star hotels, fabulous food and Italian sunshine. Will had thrown his coat on huffily. Absolutely not. Slamming the front door he'd strode manfully towards the Land Rover. In fact, given the choice, he'd much rather have the spare bedroom, his mum's home cooking and the Yorkshire drizzle. Shivering in zero temperatures, he'd turned the key in the ignition. *Definitely*.

Marilyn Barraclough had been watching out of her kitchen window for the past hour. Taking a break from her vigil, she flicked on the kettle. She was so excited. It was exactly six months on Sunday since she'd last seen her son, round about the time he'd set up his new business. She'd lost a lot of sleep about him giving up his job, and a good one at that, but turning self-employed seemed to be the thing these days. What did they call it in London? Ah yes, freelance.

The kettle quickly boiled and clicked off and she poured water over the Nescafé granules, clicked in two Sweetex and a dab of soya milk. She'd made the switch from semi-skimmed after reading that soya helped to prevent osteoporosis, much to the disgust of her husband Jim, who kept moaning about it curdling. Making sure no-one was looking, she opened the cupboard, surreptitiously helped herself to a couple of chocolate fingers and, holding the hot mug between her clasped hands, settled back down to her position in front of the window.

Will had barely pulled into the gravel drive when he saw his mum, popping out of the porch like a jack-in-a-box, arms folded tightly across her Shetland wool chest. That was one of the weird things about Yorkshire women, mused Will, they always had their arms folded. Watching her, hovering on the front steps with George the ginger tomcat weaving around her ankles, a surge of love swelled up inside him. Had he really left it so long to see his old mum? He was never going to do that again.

'Just look at your hair. Don't they have scissors in

London?' It was the first thing she said as he climbed out of the Land Rover. Will smiled. It might have been six months but nothing had changed. Still going on about his hair. It would be his clothes next.

'And what about those jeans? Halfway down your backside,' she tutted exasperatedly. 'Have you not got a belt?'

'Hello, Mum.' Throwing his arms around her in a big bear hug he breathed in her scent. A familiar, comforting mix of Lenor, onion gravy and Chanel No.5. 'How are you?'

'As right as I can be, living with your father,' she laughed good-naturedly, pretending not to like the fuss and pushing him indoors, out of the blasts of icy northeasterly wind. 'He's in the front room, watching that car programme he likes,' she added, gesturing from the hallway where she was insisting Will take his boots off and hang up his thick leather coat.

As his mum disappeared into the kitchen, Will padded across the carpet in his socks, riddled with holes made from that one nail in his flat, and softly pushed open the stripped pine door. Stretching ahead was the living room, low-beamed and cosy, filled with too much furniture and too many photographs of Will and his sisters: christenings, birthdays, graduations. And then he saw his dad. Lying full stretch on the sofa, in front of the woodburning fire, he was staring intently at the TV, his chin squashed so low his half-moon glasses were almost balancing on the bushy grey moustache that lay across his top lip like a ferret.

Will paused. He'd told his mum not to tell his dad about his impromptu visit – the plan had been to surprise him – but suddenly Will realized he was the one who'd got the surprise. Seeing his dad, prostrate on the sofa, watching telly, he'd just been struck by a thought. *Like father, like son*. And the surprise wasn't exactly a pleasant one.

To put it bluntly, and his father usually did, Will and

his father didn't see eye to eye. His childhood had been a constant battle. Being a typical northern grit bloke, Jim Barraclough had always dreamed of a son to share his love of engines, cars and all things mechanical. Instead he'd produced a teenager who wanted to sit in his bedroom, reading, drawing and playing records – far too loudly. Will, meanwhile, had struggled to grow up with a dad who quoted the views of the *Daily Mail* verbatim, whose reaction when he'd told him he wanted to be an architect was, 'Are you soft? Drawing's for poofs', and who ate his tea every night at five o'clock before nodding off in front of the telly. It had taken the best part of thirty years for them to even start accepting each other.

Even so Will had always sworn he'd never turn into his dad, but looking at him now, he could see he was doing exactly that. Lying on the sofa after work, eating something Juliet had cooked, falling asleep in front of the news. Will shuddered. Now he could see what Juliet had to put up with. No wonder she was pissed off with him so much these days. He couldn't blame her. *The poor woman had been living with his dad.*

His thoughts were broken by a voice. 'William?' Jerking upright, his dad cricked his neck and turned to look over a cushion. 'Oh, hello son. I thought it was you from the draught. Do you never learn to shut doors?' but he was smiling as he said it.

'Hello, Dad.' Will stuck his fingers in his pockets and nodded in acknowledgement. Hugging was strictly not for men up north.

'Have you brought that lovely girlfriend of yours?' Pushing his glasses up his nose, Jim Barraclough peered around him, looking for Juliet. As a man with two daughters and a very attractive wife, he was a ladies' man in the real sense of the word.

'No, Juliet's had to go to Italy. A work thing,' added Will, in response to his father's raised eyebrows.

'My word, these career women . . .' gasped his mum,

walking into the living room holding a tray out in front of her as if she was trying to rein in a frisky horse. 'At her age I was a housewife with three young children.' She chivvied Will into the reclining armchair and plonked a tray on his knee. 'Roast beef and Yorkshire pudding, your favourite,' she beamed, handing him a knife and fork. It was all Will could do to stop her tucking a piece of kitchen roll underneath his chin.

Watching his wife fuss around another man, even if it was his son, Jim felt more than a little disgruntled. He was used to receiving all the attention in his own house. 'And what's wrong with being a housewife?' he interrupted, grumpily. Since his wife had hit the menopause she'd become a born-again feminist. He was sure it was something they put in those HRT patches, because a lot of his friends at the golf club were having the same trouble. His poor friend Brian was still getting over the shock of seeing his sixty-one-year-old wife in a nude calendar for the Women's Institute.

'Nothing, dear,' she soothed, winking at Will. 'Dirty nappies were much more fun than trips to Italy. It was Italy you said, wasn't it?'

Will nodded warily, trying to change the subject. 'Yeah, she would have loved to come up for the weekend,' he heard himself fibbing. He quickly justified it to himself: he was doing it to spare his parents' feelings. 'But you know how it is in advertising.'

His mum didn't have a clue. Her only experience of ads were the ones in between *Emmerdale* that allowed her to nip into the kitchen to make a cup of tea, but she nodded anyway. 'So how are you and Juliet?' She was never one for pussyfooting around.

Will speared a potato guiltily. 'Oh great, great.'

'When are you going to make an honest woman of her then, eh?' asked his dad, reaching for the *Daily Mail* and flicking to the TV listings.

Will scowled. Any excuse for a dig. Now he remembered why he'd put off visiting for six months. 'Jules and I are fine as we are,' he replied, attacking his roast beef with his fork. Admittedly things weren't so fine, but his father was the last person he was going to admit it to.

'Aha, you mean she's turned you down,' guffawed his dad, heartily enjoying himself.

'No, I mean I haven't asked her,' said Will, tight-lipped, feeling himself beginning to get annoyed.

His dad stopped laughing and stared right at him. 'Well, why not?'

Will was going to fire back a suitable answer until he realized that, actually, *he hadn't got one*. Why hadn't he ever asked Juliet to marry him? Because two out of three marriages fail? Because it was old-fashioned? Because it was what other people did? Because he didn't love her enough?

To be honest, there wasn't a reason: he'd just never really thought about it. They'd never talked about getting married; in fact, thinking about it now, the only time he'd ever heard Juliet mention weddings was when they'd driven past Chelsea and Westminster Register Office and she'd whooped with mirth at the puffball ensemble being worn by the bride.

'Jim, leave him alone, he's only just got here.'

Will turned to see his mum, coming to the rescue with a cup of tea for her husband. Laughing, she passed it to him. Together with the box of chocolate fingers. His favourite.

'Well, I was just wondering . . .' Jim's voice tailed off as his wife sat down next to him on the sofa and cuddled up to him. 'Three grown-up kids and still no grandchildren,' he tutted. 'I would have thought you'd have provided us with a few by now. Your mother's dying to start knitting, aren't you, Mam?'

'Don't call me that,' she scolded, swatting him good-naturedly, and shaking her head to his offer of a biscuit. 'I can't, I'm on a diet.'

'Why? You look smashing, Marilyn. Doesn't your mother look smashing?'

Will nodded, smiling and watching his parents laughing. Forty years and they were still going strong. Looking at his mum, her face lit up underneath her blusher, it dawned on him that, whatever he might think about his dad, he must be doing something right. Juliet didn't look at him like that and they'd only been together for two and a half years. He felt a twinge of sadness. Of regret. He'd been neglecting her. And not just her.

'Do you want to go for a pint afterwards?' Interrupting his parents' cosy laughter, Will spoke to his dad.

Taken aback by the suggestion, he looked up, surprised. William had always turned his nose up at the local village pub. 'Oh, I didn't think you'd want to bother, like.'

'Maybe have a game of darts or something?' They both knew this was more than just about the pub. This was Will holding out the olive branch.

Digging him softly in the ribs, Marilyn stared at her husband. Forty years of knowing someone so well translating into one look. Turning to Will he nodded, a smile faintly creeping over his moustached lips. 'Aye son, that would be grand.'

Chapter Thirty

Mmmmmm.

Floating in that blissful world between sleeping and waking, Juliet gently eased open one eyelid. Through her lashes she slowly began to focus on her surroundings. On the shafts of sunshine seeping into the darkness from underneath the wooden shutters, picking out the burnished gilt of the chaise-longue, a creamy ripple of cotton sheet, her bare feet peeping out from underneath.

Mmmmm, how funny, she mused, feeling deliciously warm and toasty, that she'd never noticed her right foot was so much bigger than the left. She gazed dreamily. Almost twice the size in fact. *And* much more tanned. And . . . eugghhhh . . . Beginning to feel more awake, her vision started to clear. What was that sprouting out of her toes? It looked almost like swirls of dark hair.

Swirls of dark hair

Juliet wiggled her toes. Only five glittery toenails wiggled back.

Her eyes snapped wide open. Her body went rigid. Keeping her head stock still on its feather pillow, she moved her eyes, like a portrait in a haunted house, and peered sideways. *At the very tanned, very hairy, very naked and* . . . she hesitated for a second before surreptitiously pinching the edge of the sheet between finger and thumb, lifting it a couple of inches and, feeling like a peeping Tom, sneaking a look underneath. It was pretty dark under there but sitting proudly on a clutch of pubic hair was a circumcised, purple-veined, shiny-headed penis. Standing to attention it was giving her a full, morning glory salute . . . *very well-endowed body of Sykes lying next to her.*

Jesus. Fucking. Ada.

Hastily letting go of the sheet like a burglar getting rid of the stolen goods, Juliet's stomach began doing a weird flipping thing, like a fish out of water. Her mind started rewinding frantically as if it was a video playing backwards. Last night. Kissing by the fountain. In the hotel lift. In Sykes's room. In her room. In the bath. *They'd had a bath together?* Oh yeah, that was after cracking open that bottle of champagne from the minibar, and before they'd finally fallen onto her bed, naked and slippery with soapsuds. Before he'd proved that there really was a great deal of truth in that T-shirt Madonna used to wear. *Before they'd made love.*

At the memory of last night, she paused for the guilt to wash over her, to drown her in a tidal wave of regret and shame. Unexpectedly, it didn't. Despite her request for separate rooms, from the very moment she'd accepted his offer of a weekend in Verona, Juliet had known she was going to sleep with Sykes. But thinking about it and doing it were two very different things.

She didn't feel bad. She didn't feel odd or wrong or guilty that she was lying in bed with a man who wasn't her boyfriend. On the contrary, thought Juliet, feeling those warm sensations flooding back into her body again. She'd never felt better about herself.

With this admission, her stomach ceased flip-flopping around. Her limbs relaxed and, wiggling onto her side, she snuggled her face deep into the pillow and gazed at Sykes. Fast asleep, he was lying perfectly still. His long lashes tightly closed, his lips firmly together, his hands across his chest, he wasn't making a sound. He wasn't snoring, making weird farmyard noises, kickboxing or whirring his legs incessantly underneath the sheets as if he was out in front of the Tour de

France. He wasn't lying face down in the pillow, mouth hanging open, spit oozing out to form a little wet patch.

He wasn't Will.

No, he's just perfect, thought Juliet, looking at Sykes the way people look at a work of art, or a fabulous painting, or a beautiful woman. He could be a model, or even an angel, she thought, enraptured. *Or he could be dead*, popped up a thought, as she realized that she'd never known a man to be *so* still, *so* silent, when he was asleep. In fact, now she came to think of it she couldn't even hear him breathing.

She stared intently at his chest, and after a nanosecond of panic, was relieved to see it was rising and falling. And then was embarrassed that she could ever have thought such a ridiculous thing. Of course he was still alive, for Godsakes. What did she think was going to happen? Some kind of divine retribution? That God's punishment for her having an affair was going to be discovering her lover dead in bed the next morning?

Juliet gave a long, satisfying yawn and stretched out like a cat. It was far too early to be suffering from Catholic guilt. Especially when she wasn't even a Catholic, she thought, feeling very unreligious and letting her eyes run unashamedly up and down Sykes's body. It had to be the best body she'd ever seen. With his flat ridged stomach, big tanned chunky pecs, broad shoulders and the smattering of dark hair that covered his chest, Sykes had her perfect kind of physique. It was a physique that belonged to a man who knew how to operate all those complicated weight machines in the gym. *This is a man who must live in the gym*, she thought, comparing it to her own body, which looked pale and sort of squidgy.

Lying naked next to the kind of body she'd last seen advertising a stomach cruncher in the *Mail on Sunday*, Juliet knew she should, by rights, be feeling horribly insecure. She was used to Will and his hairy back, skinny legs and love handles that made the bit of cellulite around the tops of her thighs pale into insignificance. But Sykes's sex appeal was catching. He made her feel as if she was the sexiest, horniest, most gorgeous woman in the whole wide world. He was doing for her what no amount of new clothes, make-up and eyecream could do. He made her feel as if she was unique. Important. *Gorgeous*. It was addictive. And very romantic, she thought, gazing up at Sykes.

At that moment his eyes blinked open. Deep chestnut irises gazed back at her. A slow smile curled across his face, revealing two rows of perfect white teeth. It was the kind of confident smile that could only belong to a man who knew he had a fabulous body (now that Sykes was awake, there was no pulling the sheet up around his ears for him, or suddenly sucking in his stomach like a vacuum-cleaner bag) and who knew, from satisfied customers, that he was absolutely fabulous in the sack. This wasn't a man who was going to wake up the morning after with a hangover and a sheepish apology about coming too quickly, thought Juliet as, without saying a word, he twined his arm around her naked waist.

Warm bare skin, against warm bare skin. *Mmmmmmm*. As she felt his hands moving lower, his head nuzzling, his tongue licking, Juliet closed her eyes and sighed happily to herself. *Mmmmmmmm*. She felt as if she was in a parallel universe. As if she'd sidestepped her normal life, and like Mr Benn putting on a fancy dress costume, entered a different world. Though it was doubtful Mr Benn ever got to visit *this* kind of world, she thought to herself, groaning as Sykes's dark curly head moved down past her belly button. *Very doubtful indeeedddmmmmm*.

It was nearly three in the afternoon when they finally made it out of bed. Juliet could have stayed there all day, enjoying a wonderfully continuous loop of making love, ordering room service, making love, ordering room service. But eventually, sunshine, whirring Vespas and the smell of fresh coffee from the street below proved too tempting. Juliet was a cheesy tourist at heart, and Sykes's stories of sweeping Renaissance gardens, amazing churches and the famous balcony were too irresistible. Even more irresistible – if that was at all possible – than remaining cuddled up in her private little world of 300 count white Egyptian cotton sheets, croissant crumbs and, without putting too fine a point on it, one very big hard-on.

'God, it's so beautiful here, it's almost unreal.' Juliet was strolling hand in hand with Sykes across the Ponte Piatra, a thirteenth-century bridge that straddled the river. Rays of sunshine were bouncing off the water, reflecting glittery, twinkly patterns on the windows of the buildings. With her mittened fingers squeezed warm inside his leather ones, she felt a warm happiness welling up inside her. Last night Sykes had told her he could fall in love with her, and right at this moment she couldn't help thinking that maybe, just maybe, she could fall in love with him. She couldn't remember the last time she'd felt so happy. In fact she felt so ridiculously happy, it did seem unreal. Any minute now and cartoon birds would be tweetering around her head.

They were heading back into the city after spending the last few hours being regular tourists, sightseeing, taking photographs, sipping cappuccinos. Juliet had been getting so carried away, she'd even found herself contentedly choosing postcards, before it had suddenly dawned on her. Who the hell did she think she was going to send one to? Her mum and dad? Trudy? *Will?* She conjured up the image of him getting drunk with Rolf, watching football, eating Indian takeout for breakfast, lunch and dinner. Stuffing the cards hastily back into the carousel, she'd ignored the frowning shopkeeper. What was she going to write: *Wish you were here?*

When hunger had struck, they'd chosen one of the many pavement cafés, eaten great big slices of pizza and joined in the spectator sport of people watching. Here in Italy it seemed to be a national obsession. Juliet didn't blame them. Everyone looked fabulous. The men were immaculately dressed, the women incredibly glamorous. And with figures to die for, thought Juliet. Looking at their tiny waists and perfect complexions, she'd been struck by the irony that while all her female friends in London were obsessed with diets avoiding wheat, dairy products and caffeine, here in Italy all the women were on a diet of pasta, gelati and espresso.

And looking amazing for it.

The observation prompted Juliet immediately to give in to her cravings, and stopping off at one of the many gelati stalls, she indulged in chocolate ice-cream scooped high in a sugar-coated waffle cornet. Licking the mouthwateringly thick, dark swirls, she followed Sykes into a busy pedestrianized street lined with designer shops. At the far end a large crowd was swarming, blocking the wide paved street.

'What's going on?' She looked at Sykes, but he was gazing at a shirt in a shop window. At least she thought he was, until she saw him fiddle with his collars and realized he was checking out his reflection. He did that a lot. Still, at least it made a change from being with someone who hadn't paid any attention to their reflection for the past six months. Or hers, she thought. And then she felt annoyed that she was thinking about Will again.

'Have you seen all those people?' She prodded Sykes's elbow to get his attention.

'People?' He turned to look where she was pointing. 'Oh yeah, that's the entrance to Juliet's house and her balcony,' he said matter-of-factly. 'And that's the queue to see it.'

'Can we join it?' she suggested eagerly, and then caught his expression. 'You don't want to.' Her voice fell flat.

'It's not that I don't want to . . .'

Juliet could feel a 'but' coming on.

'But it's just that I'd promised a few colleagues I'd pop in this afternoon, clear some of the things I left lying around there on my desk. I left for London in a bit of a rush.'

'Sure,' she nodded coolly. Considering he'd been the one enthusing about it ever since they'd arrived, it was slightly niggling that he didn't want to go and look at it with her. 'You've probably seen it a dozen times anyway.'

'Something like that.'

His evasiveness annoyed her. 'Look, why don't I meet you back at the hotel in a couple of hours. Gives me time to do some shopping as well.' As she was suggesting it, Juliet realized that it actually wasn't a bad idea. Normally she'd have already been inside most of the shops, joyfully hammering her credit card. But she'd been so caught up with Sykes, she'd barely thought about shopping. It was a first. The thought hit home. *Crikey, it must be lurve*.

Sykes seemed surprised by her reaction. 'You don't mind?'

'Not if you'll lend me your camera,' she answered, smiling ruefully. 'Well I can't leave without taking a picture of that, can I?' She held out her hand expectantly, only for it to dawn on her that he was looking rather hesitant.

'Actually, it's quite tricky to use.' Reluctantly he pulled the dinky silver case out of his pocket. Juliet glanced at it. It was one of those new expensive state-of-the-art digital jobbies with a zoom lens and a million different features on it that only a professional photographer would ever need. But it still had the basics. A hole to look through and a button to push.

'I'm not trying to be David Bailey. I only want to take a snapshot of the balcony,' she laughed, surprised to see that Sykes was still looking hesitant. And not saying anything. In her embarrassment, she continued joking. 'Don't worry, I won't drop it.' She was beginning to wish she hadn't mentioned it. She'd never thought about it before, but Sykes was quite anal when it came to his belongings. Her mind threw up a memory of him unpacking. Very anal in fact.

'Yeah, 'course, you're right.' Changing his mind, he broke into an apologetic smile and calmly handed her the camera. Before pulling up the collars of her coat, he leaned towards her. For a moment Juliet thought he was going to kiss her, but instead he stuck out his tongue and licked the side of her face. 'You've chocolate ice-cream on your cheek,' he laughed, before turning away and striding off towards the arena.

Touching the side of her cheek Juliet smiled and looked through the viewfinder of the camera. She watched his retreating figure, the angular shape of his shoulders in his black woollen overcoat, the swaying of his hips. Following him with her eyes across the square, through the crowds, she waited for him to look back before he disappeared from view so she could take a photograph.

He didn't look back.

Chapter Thirty-one

Left alone, Juliet's first impulse was to join the queue of sightseers. But, as is the nature of first impulses, it was swiftly succeeded by different, stronger, and seemingly more appealing ones. In this case called Gucci and Prada. Followed by Miss Sixty, Diesel, and a gorgeous shoe-shop that she couldn't pronounce the name of. A language barrier that didn't stop her buying a pair of calf-length boots. Not to mention the soft, buttery leather clutch bag that was as impractical as it was irresistible. Hell, she was in such a shopping mood she even waltzed into Benetton and had a good rummage through the neatly folded candy-coloured jumpers. She was nearly even lulled into buying one.

Until she stopped for long enough in between the pistachio-ribbed turtleneck and the lemon angora shortsleeve, to draw breath from the magic of Italy and get a grip. This was still Benetton, and if she wasn't careful she was going to go back to London looking like one of those suburban early-thirties mums who had flabby upper arms, streaked hair that involved a rubber cap and a hair salon called Upper Cuts, and jauntily drove around town *in a Ka*. Juliet hastily yanked on her clothes. She was having an affair, not a lobotomy.

Outside she realized it was getting late. The light was dimming and she was half tempted to head straight back to the hotel. After all, it would be dark in a few minutes, and she wanted to spend a long time getting ready. Having skipped dinner the night before, Sykes had made reservations at his favourite restaurant for that evening. Even so, she hesitated.

The balcony beckoned. Being called Juliet she'd grown up with Shakespeare's legacy. She'd only been seven years old when her mum had allowed her to stay up late to watch Olivia Hussey playing Juliet in the Zeffirelli movie version and, even now, she could still clearly remember being curled up on the sofa in her Twinkle pyjamas, desperately wishing she could hurry up and grow up so she could fall in love with her own Romeo. Just as clearly as she could remember the teasing she received from her classmates when they were studying the play for O level – having to endure all the acne-ridden boys yelling 'wherefore art thou' at her down the corridors was no fun for a fifteen-year-old. And then Leonardo di Caprio and Clare Danes had to come along ten years later and the jokes had started up all over again. Juliet checked her watch. It was late, but not too late. She'd lived with the legendary love story for too long. She couldn't leave Verona without paying homage to her namesake, could she?

The answer was no, and armed with her shopping bags – the cardboard type with rope handles that swung confidently by her side when she walked – she headed happily towards the crowds. Although it was late afternoon, they were showing no signs of abating and she was quickly swallowed up by a line of people filtering slowly through the gates, into a deep, round brick arch, every inch covered in scrawled inscriptions, carved hearts, scrabbled poetry, declarations of love, from incurable romantics from all around the world.

Which includes me, thought Juliet, smiling ruefully as she shuffled forwards out of the darkness into a small walled courtyard that was being filled with a tangerine glow. And there, straight ahead, up a little, on the right was the balcony. *So that was it?* Juliet stared. It was much smaller than she'd imagined. Less dramatic. Like the time she'd seen Madonna at HMV on Oxford Street and had been struck by how nondescript she'd seemed, how the hype and fame were so much bigger than this tiny little woman with a pale face and bleached hair that needed the roots doing.

Even so, the balcony still exuded a special kind of magic. The sun was sinking low into a blushing sky, sending shafts of light through the intricately carved rooftops. The faded reds and pale yellows of the buildings were intensifying into burnt siennas and roasted ochres, as if rust was seeping through the plaster and coating the balcony in a rosy glow. Cricking her neck to stare up at the carved stonework, Juliet was buoyed up by a feeling of hope and vindication. It was a romantic silent reminder of a bygone age, high above the bustling hub of modern day life.

She smiled. Perhaps Trudy was right, perhaps in today's society romance was outdated, but that just made it all the more precious if you could find it. And if believing that made her an old-fashioned romantic, then so what. There were plenty of other old-fashioned romantics like her. Bloody hundreds of them, she thought, glancing around and watching couples taking pictures of themselves on the balcony, giggling at how corny it was, yet still kissing into the lens. One for the scrapbooks.

But not her scrapbook, she thought, glancing down at the camera in her hand, aware that she didn't want a photograph after all. *She'd been here before.* The date might be different – then it had been 14 February and now it was March; the venue was different – Soho and now Verona; and even the man had changed – first Will, and now Sykes – but she was still in exactly the same place. Alone in a sea of couples.

The chiming of a church clock interrupted her thoughts. Christ, was that the time? She had to get back. Leaving the courtyard, she set off towards the hotel, walking quickly across the cobbles, her billboard bags swinging by her side. Just not as high this time.

'Do you think they have an English translation?'

After staring blankly at the menu for a few minutes, Juliet peered around its leather-bound spine at Sykes. 'I don't want to look like a Brit abroad, but it would be nice to know what I'm eating,' she whispered, feeling suddenly like Eliza Doolittle with Henry Higgins.

'Don't worry, I'll order for you,' he smiled, leaning back in his chair. 'I'd recommend the risotto I was telling you about in London. Alfredo makes the best risotto in town.' Flicking his ash in the small silver ashtray, Sykes watched the waiter swoop on it like a magpie and take it away. It was replaced by an identical clean one. 'In the world, probably.'

Tucked away in the corner of an elegant restaurant, Juliet and Sykes were finally enjoying their first 'official' dinner date. It was very formal, *frighteningly* formal, with pinstriped walls heaving with heavy gilt-framed pictures, soft classical music playing, disturbingly bright lighting from the huge chandeliers and a slightly older clientele. It was Sykes's favourite restaurant.

It was a bit of an old-fashioned restaurant really, thought Juliet, who'd recovered from her earlier feelings of loneliness by dissolving them in a long warm bubblebath and the glass of champagne Sykes had given her. But hey? So what? She'd been looking forward to this moment for a long time. It didn't matter that the restaurant might not exactly be one she'd choose, it was obviously very exclusive, she'd thought as one white-coated waiter held out her chair for her, while a second almost identical white-coated waiter flourished a menu under her nose. She'd looked at it as if she knew what she was looking at. She hadn't. It was all in Italian, of course. But then this wasn't the kind of place that needed a tourist translation.

'Actually, I feel like the pasta,' she murmured,

running her eye hopefully across the handwritten pages. As luck would have it, a familiar-looking phrase jumped up from the page. 'Tagliatelli ai funghi.' She announced it triumphantly, knowing exactly what that meant. And her accent wasn't that bad either.

Sykes looked amused. 'In Italy, pasta's a *primo piatto*,' he smiled, and then seeeing her puzzled expression, explained in English, 'An entrée.'

'That's OK,' she shrugged happily. 'I'm sure there'll be enough. I'm not that hungry.' Grinning, she turned her attention to the wine that had been poured for her by the waiter hovering at her elbow. Sykes had chosen it, but she didn't particularly like red. It stained her teeth purple and always made her mouth feel as if she'd been eating rhubarb, but it was better than nothing. In fact the wine doesn't taste that bad, she thought, taking a large gulp and feeling it weave a warm path to her empty stomach.

'But you can't go to an Italian restaurant and just order pasta.' Sykes traced his fingertips lightly across her bare arm. Juliet was wearing a strappy black dress dotted with tiny sequins that she'd bought ages ago but had never been anywhere smart enough to wear before. It was one of those super-glam, super-impractical dresses that hugged and squeezed in all the right places, making her feel like a vamp. A bloody freezing vamp, she thought, wondering why it was so cold in the restaurant.

'To really enjoy an Italian meal you need to try all the different courses, all the different flavours,' continued Sykes. 'You don't have to eat huge quantities, just taste a little of each.'

'You mean I should do as the Italians do,' smiled Juliet, thinking how persuasive he could be. Glancing around the restaurant, her eye fell on a large white fish that was being expertly filleted for the table of diners opposite. 'Maybe I'll have the fish.'

'Hmm, the fish is good,' he nodded, 'but I really do

think you should have the risotto. Trust me on this one.'

Juliet could see she wasn't going to win. 'OK, OK,' she grinned, giving in laughingly. 'I'll have the risotto. But this better be good.'

Snubbing out his cigarette, Sykes gave her one of those smiles that always made her feel there was a hell of a lot more hiding behind it. 'Oh, it will be,' he murmured, chinking his glass against hers.

The food arrived hidden under large silver domes which were then removed with a flourish by the pompous-looking waiter. Creamy swirls of *tagliatelli ai funghi*, golden rings of *calamari fritti*, wafer-thin slices of *carpaccio* and the famous *risotto ai frutti de mare*. Happy and glowing, Juliet savoured every mouthful. Sykes was right, it was truly delicious, but then as far as she was concerned she could have eaten baked beans on toast and it would have tasted delicious that evening.

Courses came and went along with their topics of conversation, another bottle of wine miraculously appeared, was uncorked and poured into their glasses. Listening to Sykes telling her a funny story, she suddenly realized time had played its trick of speeding up, and they had reached the dessert stage. Happy and glowing she stared as the waiter wheeled out an archaic dessert trolley.

'Gelato, panforte, or zabaglione,' suggested Sykes. 'What do you fancy?'

'You,' she giggled loudly, unable to resist. A couple of diners turned around, but Juliet didn't notice as she was focusing on draining her glass. The wine waiter stepped forward to fill it up again, but Sykes put his hand over the rim.

'I think you've had enough,' he was laughing.

'Hey, don't be a spoilsport,' she protested, giggling louder and trying to pull the glass away. But his fingers closed around the edges and held fast, as his smile faded. 'No, seriously.' She suddenly saw that he really *was* serious. She swallowed, her laughter trickling away. She'd only had three glasses, and she'd eaten a three-course meal. OK, so perhaps she was a bit giddy, but she wasn't *drunk*. Not anything like she used to get with Will when they went out for dinner.

As evidence, pictures of her thirtieth birthday last year flashed up in her mind. The Japanese restaurant complete with a Japanese Elvis impersonator that Will had booked for her as a surprise. Rolf, Amber and Trudy springing out from underneath the table like three big, excited kids. Everyone getting completely wasted on sake. Having hysterics when Will had drunkenly grabbed the microphone and made a complete fool of himself by performing a hip-wiggling karaoke duet with the King himself. Gazing up at him shaking his hips and curling his lip, and thinking what a daft idiot he was. And how this daft idiot was the guy she wanted to spend the rest of her life with.

She lit up one of Sykes's cigarettes and dragged on it heavily.

'Since when did you start smoking?' His face was tight.

'Just now,' she retorted, inhaling as if it was her last breath. She felt a headrush. She'd gone away for the weekend with a man she'd known for a few weeks, to Italy, expecting passion and romance. Not to have her glass covered up and told what she could eat, thanks very much. And the risotto wasn't a patch on hers anyway, she thought, puffing away silently as Sykes stiffly asked for the bill.

'And a large bottle of Pellegrino,' he added, speaking in English for her benefit. And his own. 'No doubt you'll be needing it for your hangover tomorrow.'

Juliet stared at him. Was he lecturing her? Bristling, she stubbed out her cigarette and stood up, ready to leave.

Forget tomorrow. This hangover had started already.

Chapter Thirty-two

Violet switched off the Hoover with the sole of her tartan slipper. The drone fell silent, allowing strains of Jimmy Young on the radio to filter through from the kitchen windowsill. Golden Oldie hour – her favourite. Stiffly bending down, wincing at the arthritis twanging in her knees like someone plucking the strings of a banjo, she tugged out the plug. So much better than that old carpet-sweeper, she marvelled, never failing to be impressed at how just by pressing that bit there, the extension lead coiled quickly back inside, all neat and tidy.

Violet was giving her flat a thorough spring clean. She was expecting visitors. Puffing away on a cigarette and humming merrily along to Dean Martin crooning 'Everybody loves Somebody', she gave her nest of tables an extra-generous squirt of Pledge.

Well, just one visitor actually.

Her doorbell chimed loudly. She paused from her vigorous polishing. Like a squirrel on the lookout, she jerked upright, a yellow duster dangling from her bony fingers. She cocked both ears. *Ding-a-ling-a-ling-a-ling-a-ling*. There it went again. Padding softly across the front room, straightening her favourite painting, *The Crying Boy*, which hung in pride of place over the coal-effect gas fire, she peered tentatively through the nets hanging like white doilies from the bay window, straining through her thick prescription lenses. *He was early*.

Violet nearly had a heart attack. She wasn't ready. She hadn't started making the corned beef sandwiches yet, or popped out to the corner shop for some of those Mr Kipling's French Fancies. She hadn't even put the kettle on. Quickly untying her pinny, she took her Avon lipstick from her handbag. At least there were some advantages to losing her eyesight, she grimaced, shakily applying a thick frosting. She could almost fool herself into believing she looked twenty-one again.

Ding-a-ling-a-ling-a-ling-a-ling.

'Coming.' Her voice wavered, as she hastily clipped on a pair of diamanté earrings. They'd been a present from Albert when they'd first got married. But he wouldn't have minded, she reassured herself, trying to flatten her white wispy candyfloss hair into some kind of shape. Albert always wanted her to look her best, whatever the occasion.

Satisfied, she pattered onto the hallway lino. She could see the outline of a figure through the wobbly glass panes of her front door. Stubbing out her cigarette in the geraniums, she smoothed down her dress, slid back the safety chain and turned the latch.

'Why, don't you look a picture.' A tall West Indian man was standing on her doorstep. Looking dapper in a herringbone suit, a navy silk cravat and matching handkerchief in his top pocket, he gave her a smile that would have outshone Blackpool illuminations. Taking off his Panama hat to reveal two snowy white tufts of hair on either side of his bald head, he held out a small plant, its tiny teardrop blue petals, bright and shiny against the plastic terracotta pot. 'It's an African violet,' he explained. His deep, velvety voice still bore a faint American accent.

Violet tittered shyly and went all pink-cheeked. 'Oh, Errol, you shouldn't have,' she protested, not meaning a word of it and proffering her powdery cheek for him to kiss. She felt quite giddy. In fact ever since first meeting Errol at the local pensioners' club a couple of weeks ago, when he'd asked her to join him in a game of gin rummy and spiced up their polystyrene-cupped coffees with whisky from his small, silver hip flask, she'd been all of a tizz.

For a moment they beamed at each other, until Violet remembered herself. 'Oh, look at me, forgetting my manners. Please, do come in,' she flapped, standing to one side to let Errol cross the threshold. As he did, she glanced into the street to see if anyone was looking. No, it was empty. Oh hang on, what was that? She could hear music. It sounded like an ice-cream van. *In March?*

Crooking her neck to see over her hedge, Violet squinted hard. That was funny, it was coming from that white car outside William's flat. Actually, wasn't that William in the driver's seat?

'My, you've got a lovely home here, Violet.' Errol's voice snapped her back.

'Oh . . . er . . . thank you,' she smiled, dragging her attention away from the goings on across the street to see her gentleman visitor standing politely in her hallway, stooping low so as not to bang his head on her tasselled lampshade.

'Please, go through. Can I tempt you with a cup of tea?'

'I don't suppose you'd have anything a little stronger? It sure is cold out there.'

Closing the front door, Violet looked up at him shyly. 'A *snowball*?'

Errol broke into a wide grin. 'Why, that would be lovely.'

The shame of it. The humiliation. The stomach-churning mortification. Will was dying with embarrassment. Ducking his head low over the steering wheel of his mother's VW Polo, he eyed the parking space behind him in his rearview mirror.

But he had no option.

Swallowing hard, he put the gearstick into reverse. Immediately a hideous electronic jingle struck up with alarming jauntiness.

Daaa-da-da. *Daaada*. Daa-da-da. *Daaadadada*.

Slamming his heel down on the accelerator pedal, he raced backwards as any street cred he might have had committed suicide. What the hell was his mother thinking of? Driving around in a car that sounded like an ice-cream van every time it was put into reverse. Instead of saying 'Look out, car reversing' it yelled, 'Look out, here comes a complete twat.'

Daa-da-da. Daaada. Daaa-da-da. Daadadada.

On and on and on it went, without any let-up. It was relentless. It was torture. It was . . .

Oh. My. God. Will groaned the groan of the undead.

Just as he was thinking things couldn't get any worse, he'd now suddenly realized something even more terrible. Being piped out of his arse on loud-speaker wasn't just any old lift music. *It was the Lambada*.

Will had just driven back from Yorkshire. His Land Rover had conked out on his parents' driveway, but luckily his mum had kindly loaned him her car for a few weeks. Well, he'd thought it was lucky, but now he wasn't so sure. Not after enduring five hours on the motorway listening to a radio that would only tune into Pennine FM, or his mother's range of cassettes – a grand total of two – *Phantom of the Opera* or *Chas and Dave's Bumper Medley*. Bumper medley actually being a codeword for never-ending, nightmarish two and half hours of 'Rabbit, Rabbit, Rabbit' mixed into the riproaring, spoon-playing 'My Old Man's a Dustman'. Yep, he'd been that desperate.

Thankfully turning off the engine, and reminding himself never to try and parallel-park *ever again*, he clambered out of the car, stretching out his legs. Coming back here after being in Yorkshire, he felt different. Revitalized. Clearer. Despite his initial misgivings, he'd really enjoyed his weekend, meeting up with his two sisters who were now both living in Leeds, catching up with a few old mates, spending time with his parents. For the first time in years, he'd got on great with his dad. They'd felt more like mates than father and son, in fact he'd discovered his old man was actually quite a laugh.

But one thing had been missing. *Juliet*. He'd tried to call her a few times but her mobile just went on to voicemail and he hadn't a clue what hotel she was staying in. Even worse, Will realized guiltily, he'd never thought to ask. Climbing the front steps he dug out the key and pushed open the heavy front door. Walking on the moors, with nothing for company but the bright, brittle blue sky, broodingly empty landscape and the family's silver-backed lurcher, he'd really had a chance to get his head together. It was the first time in months he'd had the chance to really think, and being in Yorkshire had brought a few things home to him.

Stepping into the hallway of his flat he flicked on the light. The bare bulb shone back at him, reminding him for the thousandth time to get a new shade. He'd never really put their relationship under the spotlight before and now he had he was surprised by the intensity of his feelings. I love Jules, thought Will suddenly, bending down to pick up the mail. I love her to bits. Truly, madly, deeply – to borrow the title of that dreadful piece of rubbish with Alan Rickman that she likes so much. I love her more than anything else in the world. Because, when it all comes down to it, Jules *is* my world.

Blimey.

Bowled over by his emotional revelation, he walked into the empty living room and surveyed the mess he'd left behind. How could he have made such a mess in just a few hours? But instead of ignoring it he began a clean-up operation, picking up old coffee mugs, three (*three?*) dirty socks, Friday's screwed-up newspaper; wriggling free a piece of stale toast that had wedged itself between the floorboards.

Pausing for a rest, he found himself looking at the shelf above the fireplace, at the jumble of photo frames all vying for space. Skimming his eyes across them, one caught his attention. It was a picture of him and Juliet on St Charles Bridge in Prague, grinning like a couple of lovesick teenagers, their arms wrapped around each other like silly string. It had been their first weekend away together and he'd asked some old guy with an accordion to take their photo. It wasn't the most flattering of either of them – the top of their heads had been cut off and it was a bit out of focus – but it was the first photo of them together. When was that taken? A year ago? Two? Christ, it must be longer than that. He looked at the dust on their faces. We look so different, younger, together, *loved up*.

No sooner had the thought registered than Will was hit by the sobering truth. He was losing Juliet. Their relationship was disintegrating. It was trickling away through his fingers, like fine topsoil. He had to do something, and he needed to do something fast before it disappeared for ever. He was thirty-three years old and his life was a mess. He was a mess. He was in debt, overweight, a slob, he was driving his mum's car, for Christsakes. He'd let himself go, *he'd let everything go*.

Looking down at all the crap he was holding in his hands, he marched into the kitchen and threw it defiantly in the bin. Things needed to change around here. And it was about time he started doing something about it.

Sipping her in-flight Bloody Mary, Juliet gazed out of the aircraft window. At the dazzling sunshine, feathery white blanket of clouds, uninterrupted hyacinth sky stretching out as far as the eye could see . . .

'Excuse me, madam, I think you might have dropped this.' A voice interrupted her daydreams and she glanced up to see an air hostess. Beaming broadly, she was dangling something small and furry between her finger and thumb. It looked like a small dead animal.

Juliet almost wished it had been. Anything but that bloody awful Dr Zhivago hat. 'Oh, thanks.' Returning the beam, she took the item from her and reluctantly stuffed it down the side of her seat. She looked at it with the expression of a woman who stares at herself in the mirror, trying to work out what possessed her to buy that pair of hipster flares/sequined boobtube/denim mini with the cheerleader kickpleats. She decided to pass the blame to Trudy. It was all her idea anyway, she decided, struck by the thought that her best friend's fashion tip might well have been an attempt at sabotaging her weekend.

But what about her weekend? thought Juliet. Although Trudy had insisted on keeping up appearances, with her abortion looming next week, she would no doubt be a nervous wreck. And some best friend I am, Juliet thought, feeling a stab of guilt. Where have I been when she's needed me? What could I have possibly thought was more important than being there for her?

The answer lay right next to her. Out of the corner of her eye she looked at Sykes. Reclining all the way back in his club class leather chair, he was plugged into his headphones, watching an old episode of *Men Behaving Badly* on his personal video screen and eating his in-flight meal. He'd been like that ever since they'd boarded. Actually, tell a lie, he'd taken off his earphones once to ask her if he could 'have those nibbles if you're going to leave them'. It was a whole different world away from their outbound flight when he'd been ordering champagne, lavishing her with attention and compliments, enthusing about Verona. Two hours and ten minutes of kissing, giggling, whispering, *lusting*.

Juliet looked away and stirred the brown swirls of Worcester sauce into her tumbler of lurid scarlet pulp. They'd checked out of the hotel after breakfast and taken a cab straight to the airport. 'I can be a terrible insomniac, I didn't want to disturb you,' she'd replied when Sykes had asked why she'd waited until he was asleep before going next door to spend the night in her own room. Tilting her chin, he'd gently kissed her, murmuring, 'Sweetheart, it's more disturbing to wake up and find you're not there.' Feeling his lips against her, she'd felt suddenly awkward. He was being so nice, why on earth hadn't she told him the truth?

Probably because I'm not sure what it is any more, she pondered, distracted by watching the air hostesses animatedly trading boyfriend troubles by the club class loos. Last night, lying awake by herself in that great big antique bed, in that great big unfamiliar room, she'd felt tired, yet unable to sleep. Her mind had begun running away with itself, hopping from one thought to another, scrutinizing, replaying, dissecting, analysing, obsessing. It had been an amazing weekend, a whirlwind couple of weeks, but now the dust was beginning to settle and shapes were beginning to appear, tiny doubtful shapes. Sykes's friends, the restaurant, *sex*.

Juliet fidgeted in her seat. As great as it was, even that had seemed different last night. More a case of excellent textbook sex, faultlessly and professionally performed, like a gymnastic display worthy of six tens. It wasn't the amateurish, messy, up-a-bit-down-a-bit lovemaking she and Will shared. With fanny farts (hers) and real farts (his), jiggly bits and saggy bits, yelling and huffing, laughing and orgasming. *Or not*, she mused, a smile spreading over her face as she remembered how when they'd first slept together, he'd saved both their embarrassment by joking around and announcing that his nickname was 'the fastest shooter in the west'.

Er, hello? Juliet brought herself up short. What was

she doing? She was 33,000 feet in the air, returning from a weekend with her lover – in fact her lover was sitting right next to her on the bloody aeroplane – and here she was, fondly thinking about her boyfriend. Taking a trip down memory lane. Reminiscing. Any moment now and she'd be calling the air hostesses over and proudly showing them the passport photos of Will she kept tucked into her wallet.

Trying to take her mind off things she pulled out her in-flight magazine and began flicking through it. Tacky duty-free souvenirs, advice on how to avoid deep vein thrombosis, an article on the history of Verona . . . Her interest aroused, she stared at the black and white photographs showing the arena at the turn of the century, café-filled piazzas, Juliet's house. It looked just as it had yesterday except . . . Juliet looked closer. Hang on a minute, where was the famous balcony? Thinking there must be some mistake, she read the caption underneath: *Juliet's balcony of the legend never actually existed. It wasn't until some years after this photograph was taken that it was finally built as a tourist attraction*.

And realized she was the one who'd made a mistake.

Staring at the words, Juliet felt an intense childish disappointment. Like the time she'd discovered Santa Claus didn't really exist, but was just an old bloke in a red nylon suit. She swallowed a bitter mouthful of Bloody Mary. She felt a bit foolish. There she'd been, believing the balcony was this great romantic symbol, and it wasn't real at all. It was just a con. A great big fake, put there for all those millions of tourists who flocked to Verona every year, wanting a focus for their romantic fantasies. They probably didn't care if it was the real thing or not. They wanted it to be. And by suspending their disbelief they could believe in the illusion. For a few moments at least.

A thought struck and she snuck a look at Sykes. Was it the same with Sykes? Was he the real thing, or had she been fooling herself? Had the whole weekend just been an illusion? A romantic fantasy that was just that – a fantasy? A suspension of disbelief? Of *reality*?

Her thoughts were broken by feeling something in her lap. Looking down she saw Sykes's hand had moved from his armrest and was sliding over her knee, up her thigh; his fingers were curling around hers, interlacing between them. Holding his hand, Juliet dismissed her doubts. She was being oversensitive and reading too much into things. It was the disappointment that the weekend was over, the uncertainty of what lay ahead, and a godawful hangover that was conjuring up all these doubts and insecurities. Making her feel so confused.

Sipping her drink, she gazed back out at the clouds, watching them turning thicker and greyer as they began descending. Even so, she couldn't ignore the niggling feeling in the pit of her stomach. There was no getting away from it. If Friday *had* been Christmas Eve, then today *definitely* felt like Boxing Day.

Trudy was gazing at a different kind of view. Avocado-coloured porcelain, a limescale-covered U-bend, the bits she'd missed with the brush. All signed by the creator himself – Armitage Shanks.

'Eueeurgghhhh.'

With her head stuck down the toilet bowl, she retched violently. There went her breakfast Pop Tarts, her lunchtime smoked salmon bagel, her three cups of black coffee. Funny how they weren't so appealing second time around. Wiping her chin with the sleeve of her kimono, she flushed and stood up. Shakily. Holding onto the radiator for support, she grabbed the smudgy, fingerprint-covered bathroom mirror and angled it towards her. Unfortunately it was the magnifying side. Staring back at her were a pair of huge swollen bloodshot eyes, pores so enlarged her face could have been mistaken for a colander, and a complexion the same colour as the bathroom suite.

She felt the bile rise in her throat.

And they called this blooming?

Trudy had just endured the weekend from hell. Held hostage in her flat by haywire hormones, food cravings and killer breasts that had taken on a life of their own, she'd blobbed on Magnus's offer of yoga and lain under the duvet feeling like an undiscovered corpse, watching old movies and working her way through her home delivery menu. Which she then promptly threw back up again. God only knows why they called it morning sickness, she was projectile vomiting 24 hours a day. It gave a whole new meaning to the Slimfast diet.

She'd consoled herself with the thought that the nightmare would soon be over. From the moment she'd discovered she was pregnant, every waking moment had been taken up with getting herself un-pregnant. A not-so-merry-go-round of doctors, examinations, waiting rooms, forms, doctors. In fact she'd seen more doctors in the last fortnight than she'd seen in her entire life. And for a hypochondriac, that was saying something.

First stop had been her GP. A pensionable man who'd eyed her disapprovingly from beneath his enormous bushy eyebrows which were in dire need of topiary. Had his wife never tried to attack him with the garden shears? she'd mused, waiting for him to put her out of her misery and offer her a quick-fix abortion. Except he hadn't. What he had done was sniffily inform her that there was a six-week waiting list on the NHS. After witnessing his sanctimonious smile, Trudy had been tempted to attack him with those goddamn shears herself, but instead she'd taken matters into her hands another way.

Leaving the surgery she'd gone back to her flat, armed herself with a black cawfee, her phone and the Yellow Pages, and begun asking the question every American citizen would ask in time of crisis.

'Do you take American Express?'

After three phone calls she'd ended up choosing a private clinic in Harley Street. All major credit cards were welcome, and they even offered to throw in a free D&C at no extra cost. The woman on reception made it all sound relatively simple – she even had a choice of abortion, medical or surgical. She'd chosen the latter. It was quick, final, and much more detached. Just like having her tonsils out, or an ingrowing toenail removed, she'd thought at her initial consultation where she'd been relieved to discover it was all white and sterile. Brisk, efficient and businesslike. And not at all emotional, she'd thought, lying on the white plastic examination bed as the doctor performed an ultrasound and informed her that as she was only four weeks pregnant she had to wait a fortnight before her abortion. More than ever, Trudy was determined to remain unemotional about the whole thing. Emotions just got in the way and made things messy. Her life was messy enough.

But now it's all sorted out and all that's left to do is sign on the dotted line, she thought, stepping over the mess on the kitchen floor and grabbing a bottle of flat Diet Coke. Taking a gulp, she savoured the sweetness, imagining what her father would say if he saw her drinking 'cavity juice'. But then what would he say if he knew she was pregnant? She hadn't told her parents. She hadn't told anyone apart from Juliet. Not even Fergus, even though she was seriously considering it after discovering she was going to have to shell out £400. Four hundred pounds? It was a pair of Jimmy Choos. Two pairs in the sales.

Just as she was feeling herself getting all wound up at the unjustness of it all, Trudy was distracted by her reflection in the full-length mirror. No make-up, slept-in hair, kimono with bits of puke on the sleeve. Mmmm, very attractive. For a moment she stared at herself, before, unable to resist, she turned sideways, pulling the embroidered satin tight against her stomach. Trudy stared at it. For a moment she tried to imagine what it would be like to be heavily pregnant. To wear elasticated waistbands, and walk like a duck. To shop in Mothercare instead of Harvey Nics. To choose names and prams. To have no pelvic floor muscles. To have a baby. *Her baby.*

She let go of her kimono and it fell open to reveal her bare freckled tummy. She gazed down at it. Hesitating. Before rubbing it protectively, she held her hands gently against the warm, soft skin. The enormity hit her like a ten-ton truck. *Life was, quite literally, in her hands.*

For a split second she almost grasped a different ending to this story. A happy ending. Suddenly catching herself, she jerked her hands away, briskly tying her kimono around her in a double knot. Jeez, what the hell was she thinking? All these hormones flying around were making her into a sentimental old sow. She already had an ending and it was booked and paid for. Sniffing defiantly, she was about to take another swig of Coke when she felt a familiar wave of nausea beginning to wash over her.

Ohmygawd. Not again.

Scrambling frantically into the bathroom, she threw herself on the mercy of Armitage Shanks. And as far as she was concerned it would be a very happy ending.

Chapter Thirty-three

According to the automated voice, the express train from Heathrow to Paddington only took fifteen minutes. Juliet felt as if it was one of the longest journeys of her life. Huddled up in the chewing-gummed corner of the central-heated carriage, sipping a cardboard cup of bitter takeout coffee that bore no resemblance to the real stuff she'd been drinking for the last two days, she attempted to read someone's discarded Sunday papers. It was only when she realized she'd been reading the same sentence over and over again, and had no idea what it was talking about, that she gave up. It was useless. Her mind was all over the place.

The weekend was over. Gone. Finished. And now . . . *Thud*. That was the sound of Juliet coming down to earth. Doing a Dorothy from *The Wizard of Oz*, waking up from an exciting Technicolor world, only to find herself back in the drab reality. It was the opposite feeling of coming out from a darkened cinema into bright sunshine. She was coming down from the biggest high she'd ever been on and, when thinking about some of the drugs she'd played around with at university, there'd been some pretty big highs. But they were nothing compared to the one she'd been on all weekend. In fact for the last couple of weeks. An unbelievable trip that had ended the moment the wheels touched down on the tarmac at Heathrow.

She and Sykes had said their goodbyes in the arrivals

hall. They'd agreed in Verona it would be less risky, and a lot easier, if they made their separate ways home from the airport. But when he'd actually kissed her outside the garishly lit WHSmith, promised to call, and then promptly boarded the pink hippopotamus bus to take him to the long-stay carpark, it had felt anything but easy. It had felt cold and detached. Like two colleagues saying goodbye after a business trip. Which was ironic, she'd thought to herself as she'd headed down the escalators towards the train platform, as that's exactly what she'd told Will her weekend was going to be. Only then, of course, she'd thought she was lying.

Reminded of Will, the guilty monster that had been lying low inside Juliet all weekend suddenly raised its deceitful head. Closing her eyes, she took a deep breath. She'd been trying not to face up to it, but she coudn't ignore it any longer. Whatever had happened between her and Sykes didn't change the fact that she still loved Will, and she didn't want to hurt him. She caught herself. She couldn't believe she was actually thinking such things. It was such a cliché. Over the years she'd heard those same lines in a thousand soap operas, read them in countless magazine 'true-life stories', consoled endless girlfriends over endless bottles of wine who'd been told the same things by their now 'ex' boyfriends. And she'd never, ever believed them. *Now she was the one thinking them.*

But a hell of a lot had happened in the last few weeks, and things weren't black and white any more. They were messy, confused shades of grey. Parts of her still loved parts of Will. Or was it just the memory of him that she still loved? She didn't know. But one thing she *did* know was that whatever her feelings were for Will, they had nothing to do with her feelings for Sykes. They were completely separate. Even if they seemed so completely intertwined.

Opening her eyes, she glanced at her watch,

following the second hand around the face as it ticked away, agonizingly slowly. Five minutes to go. Now four minutes and fifty-five seconds . . . fifty-four . . . fifty-three . . . fifty-two. She felt as if she was on some kind of countdown. Sitting on that train, her life with Will in London edging closer and closer, suburb by suburb, her weekend with Sykes in Italy creeping further and further away. Until step by step she was going to find herself walking back into the flat she and Will shared, back into the life they both shared, and she was going to have to tell lies, *and she was going to have to pretend it never happened*.

At the thought, Juliet's stomach felt as if it had just stepped into an elevator and plummeted a hundred floors. Oh Christ, she'd never meant for this to happen. What was she supposed to say? How was she supposed to act? This wasn't in the rules, was it? How to behave with your partner after spending a weekend with your lover. She winced. *Lover*. Whereas before that word had seemed illicit and exciting, now it just sounded like something from a bad Channel 5 movie. As if she should be wearing Lycra and red lipstick, not a woolly jumper, trainers and hair scraped back in a ponytail. She'd even taken her make-up off in the loos a few minutes earlier, getting rid of any evidence, so that Will wouldn't suspect anything. His name triggered her heart to start hammering loudly in her chest with anticipation. Except this time it didn't feel arousing or exhilarating.

It felt terrifying. Trudy's words of warning were coming back to haunt her. She wasn't cut out for this. She'd never cheated in her life, not even on her homework. She was a nice, normal, kind, responsible person who didn't drop litter, who cried at *Animal Hospital*, who actually *rang* those phone lines and donated money for *Children in Need* instead of just sitting on the sofa, slagging off Gabby Roslin. She wasn't the cheating type. But then, who was? Footballers? Film stars? Those bloody suburban housewives driving around in their Kas? Leaning her forehead on the cool pane of glass, Juliet stared out of the window. But it was so dark outside all she could see was her reflection. And the answer, which she suddenly realized was staring her right in the face.

'That'll be fifteen quid, love.'

Paying the driver, Juliet lugged the suitcase onto the pavement and closed the door. She hesitated for a moment, watching the black cab driving off down the street, before turning away and walking up the front steps. Well, here goes. Putting her key in the lock she gave a little shiver – and it wasn't the cold.

The first inkling she got that something was up was when she turned on the light in the hallway. For nearly six months it had needed a lampshade, ever since Will had taken down the old one saying he didn't like it, and never replaced it. Neither had Juliet, who'd quashed her initial impulse to go out and buy a new one. She was fed up with always being the one who did everything around the flat. This time it was up to Will. And so she'd left it. Until the bare 100-watt bulb wasn't just a bulb any more, it had taken on a much deeper significance. It had become a symbol of Will's couldn't-be-arsedness, an illness that had spread through their entire relationship.

So what was that? A cure? she thought, staring up at something suspended from the ceiling. A dome of green – nay, *peacock green* – material, that was ruched and, dare she say it, *tasselled*? It looked bizarrely familiar. It also looked suspiciously like a lampshade. Even if it was a hideous one. Juliet circled beneath it, her neck cricked in examination. Nevertheless, aesthetics aside, it was still a lampshade. *Blimey*.

Abandoning her suitcase by the radiator, she tugged off her boots and coat and pushed open the living room door with trepidation. Which is when she got her second surprise. Expecting a vista of aluminium take-out trays, dirty plates, stagnant coffee cups and empty beer bottles – the general boys' night in landscape – she was completely unprepared for a vision of tidiness. Diagonal cushions balancing plumply on their corners, a polished coffee table, CDs in their cases, a vase of white lilies. *There was even a distinct smell of air freshener.*

Juliet felt as if she'd walked into the wrong flat. It was immaculate. Spotless. *Suspicious.* Where was the pilau rice trodden underfoot? The public house stench of overflowing ashtrays? The carpet of Sunday papers that Will always left all over the floor as if he was about to start decorating? Talking of which – where the hell was Will?

As if on cue, she heard the sound of a key. The front door slamming. Footsteps. And then before she knew it Will was walking into the room. Standing in front of her. *In a tracksuit.* 'Hi.' Catching his breath, he brushed away a bead of sweat trickling down his forehead, and smiled his familiar schoolboy smile.

Juliet stared. It was the third surprise. A triple whammy. 'Hi,' she replied, her voice unexpectedly coming out in a much higher pitch than usual.

A gap yawned open where conversation should have been. With the hellos over they looked at each other, both seeming absurdly nervous.

'So how was your weekend?' They both spoke at the same time, and then laughed. It released some of the pressure and they smiled, almost shyly, at each other.

'It was interesting . . .' Juliet felt herself nodding. Feverishly. She stopped at once. 'How about you?'

Taking up where she'd left off, Will began nodding. 'Yeah, the same. Interesting.' Visions of Yorkshire flashed by in his mind.

They remained standing, facing each other across opposite ends of the coffee table. It reminded Juliet of when they'd first met at the housewarming party. Hovering over the cheese'n'biscuits, making polite, but loaded, conversation.

She broke the pause. 'So what's with the tracksuit?'

'Oh this,' he shrugged, doing that thing of pretending he hadn't noticed he was decked out in a blue and white striped Adidas ensemble. As if he usually walked around looking like one of the Gallagher brothers. 'I've been to the gym.'

'*The gym?*' echoed Juliet. 'On a Sunday evening?' The surprises were coming thick and fast.

'Yeah, why not?'

'But I thought you weren't a member any more. I thought you said it was a waste of money.' She realized she was gabbling.

'I changed my mind,' he replied simply, grabbing his ankle and doing a calf stretch as if to prove his point.

Juliet watched him, not knowing quite what to make of it all. Will was acting really strangely. She couldn't put her finger on it, but she'd gone away on Friday and come back two days later and he was different. Yet, in a funny way, *familiar*.

Looking at him, she suddenly realized why. She'd just seen a spark of the old Will. The Will who used to go for a run in Hyde Park every morning before work. The Will who used to be a good half a stone lighter, who used to wear white linen shirts and not the first screwed-up T-shirt he could find that wasn't covered in dried-on toothpaste and masala dhal, the Will she'd spent weekends with enthusiastically doing up the flat, sanding floors in hideous boiler suits (which was obviously why they'd got the name) and goggles, escaping the sawdust by going out to bars and restaurants.

The Will she'd fallen in love with. And who'd fallen in love with her.

Catching herself, she glanced around the living room. Except even the old Will hadn't been tidy.

'I'm just going to jump in the shower . . .' Interrupting her thoughts, Will finished stretching and began walking out of the living room. 'I really worked up a sweat on that five-mile run . . .' With his back to her, a small smile allowed itself to briefly surface. Relief, satisfaction, *hope*. Quickly hiding it, he paused in the doorway and turned to face her. 'Oh by the way, I thought maybe afterwards we could go out for something to eat.'

Now this was just too much. First the lampshade, then the tidiness, then the gym . . . Juliet looked into Will's pale blue eyes, half-hidden by his shaggy blond eyebrows. Something was definitely up.

A wave of paranoia gripped hold of her. Did he suspect? She dismissed it as quickly as it had appeared. Of course he didn't. If he did he'd hardly be tidying up the flat, would he? Then, like a line of dominoes, a second thought struck. Had he been up to something? No of course not, that was her, not him. Then a third thought. *Perhaps he was just trying to be nice*. Juliet felt winded by her conscience. Of all the three, that one made her feel by far the worst.

'Would you mind if we stayed in?' As she said it, she couldn't believe she was saying it.

'But the table's booked . . .' Will's voice trailed off. This wasn't the reaction he'd been expecting. He thought Juliet would jump at the chance to be taken out for dinner. That he'd be able to wine and dine her and put everything right back to how it used to be.

'It's just that I'm feeling pretty tired. I was going to run a bath.' She could almost smell Sykes oozing out of her pores. Feeling suddenly dirty she was gripped by a desire to wash him away, along with the guilt and the remorse. Except of course she couldn't. She looked at Will. The last thing she felt like was going out for a candlelit dinner. She caught herself. How times had changed. 'You don't mind, do you?'

'No of course not.' He hid disappointment. 'I might

just be able to rustle you up some cheese on toast. *If you're lucky*,' he added, grinning.

Will's cheese on toast was a bit of a speciality. He used to make it for her when they'd first met, it was the perfect hangover cure. Thick white sliced bread, toasted on just one side, Wensleydale cheese – grated not sliced – grilled until it was bubbling and just turning brown, and then – this was the best bit – a garnish of HP sauce before being popped under the grill for a few seconds to seal in the flavour. Mmmmm. Her mouth watered at the thought. Sod risotto, it was just what she fancied. 'Can I have three slices?' Despite everything, she felt herself relaxing.

'Three slices?' he whistled between his teeth. 'I don't know about that. I said if you're lucky, not if you're a greedy pig.'

Breaking into a smile, she threw one of the plumped-up cushions at him.

He caught it, laughing, before slowly his smile faded. Hugging the cushion to his chest, he looked at her. 'I've missed you.'

For once he wasn't joking around. He meant it. Juliet knew that the moment she glanced up and caught his expression. And he knew that she knew.

They stared at each other and it was as if the fog had finally lifted. As if for the first time in months, they could finally see each other again.

Juliet took a deep breath as the realization hit. 'I've missed you too.'

Chapter Thirty-four

Once Trudy had made her mind up about something there was no way anyone was going to change it. She was going to tell Fergus she was pregnant. Why? Because as the father, she wanted him to know so that he could offer her support, strength, love in this difficult time?

Gimme a break, she thought, locking the door to her flat. This was Fergus she was talking about, the guy who'd legged it after his full Irish breakfast and had never been heard of again. The only thing he could offer her was £200, which was half the cost of the abortion. If that sounded heartless she didn't care. Why should Fergus have his fun and not have to pay the consequences? Trudy was angry. And the more she stewed about it, the more resentful and revengeful she became. As far as she was concerned, if Fergus could stick his dick in her fanny, he could friggin' well stick his hand in his wallet.

Which is why she'd made her mind up to confront him, and nothing, and nobody, was going to stop her. Not even Juliet. Although it didn't stop her trying.

'Are you sure it's a good idea?' It was Monday afternoon and Juliet was at work, hiding out in the Ladies, smoking a cigarette. She'd started again. Sitting on the plastic lid of the loo, she fiddled with her mobile to get a better reception. 'You haven't spoken to Fergus for weeks.'

Trudy wasn't taking no for an answer. 'I'll pick you up outside your office at six.'

Juliet looked at her watch. It was 5.30 now. 'Where are we going?'

'Gambling.'

'*Gambling?*'

'Well don't say it like that,' snapped Trudy, touchily. 'You've been doing it all weekend.' And before Juliet had a chance to argue, she flicked shut her mobile and tossed it into her gold snakeskin pumpbag. Cantering down her front steps, she spotted a cab and dived into the road to flag it down. There was a screech of tyres as the driver slammed on his brakes and slid to a standstill inches from the toes of her bubblegum pink stiletto boots. Without apologizing for nearly having caused a major pile-up, not to mention having nearly sent the cabbie head first through the windscreen, Trudy yanked open the door and, gathering the swathes of her lilac fake fur coat around her, clambered inside.

'Where to, darlin'?' The driver eyed her up in his mirror, his earlier desire to launch into an angry monologue forgotten at the first flash of fishnet thigh.

'Wimbledon dog track, please.' Pulling out her compact mirror Trudy flicked it open and looked at herself. Dissatisfied, she groped around in her pocket for her red lipstick. She already had some on, but she firmly applied another thick coat. Now she knew why they called it warpaint.

'And step on it.'

Cross-legged on the loo, Juliet stared at her mobile. She'd been in the office since eight that morning, sitting in solitary confinement behind her desk, wading through piles of paperwork she'd recklessly abandoned on Friday afternoon. The final deadline for the MAXI account was only days away, and by the end of the week they'd find out if they'd won it or not. Everyone was holding their breath. Promotions were hanging in the balance, reputations were at risk and people's careers were on the line. Even Gabby was uncharacteristically subdued. The tension in the air was overwhelming.

Ironically, Juliet found it a relief. She wanted to be overwhelmed, to have her mind filled with advertising contracts, to be kept busy, not to have time to return emails, or text messages, or phone calls. *To have no time to think.* About Sykes, or Verona, or last night. Eating cheese on toast, laughing at Frank Skinner, lying in bed with Will, not pretending to be asleep when he'd started kissing her, undressing her, making love to her . . .

She stopped herself right there. Trudy was right, she had been gambling. Playing poker with her life. For so long Will had felt like an eighteen. Solid, dependable, but not a twenty-one. And then she'd met Sykes. What was he? Juliet took a drag of her cigarette and thought about the last couple of weeks. About how she'd been faced with a choice. To stick or twist. Gamble or play safe. The stakes had never been higher. She could win, or she could bust and lose everything. A flashback of Will last night flared up again, lying curled around her like a big, warm post-coital blanket. And what had she done? *She'd twisted.*

Juliet stared at the embers of her cigarette and suddenly felt sick. She didn't want it any more. Standing up, she flicked up the lid and dropped it into the toilet bowl.

Over an hour later the black cab turned a corner by the sprawling mock-Tudor pub on the bridge, and Wimbledon stadium loomed up ahead. From the outside it resembled a huge warehouse. A hulking grey building constructed of concrete and corrugated iron, it was covered in graffiti and peeling bill posters.

Despite its ominous appearance, Trudy and Juliet were relieved. But then anything would have been a relief after spending forty-five minutes stranded on the back seat watching their money drain away as the meter clocked up, fielding banter from Dave the chirpy cabbie. After unsuccessfully trying to chat them both up, he'd spent the entire journey regaling them with stories of his recent 18–30 holiday to Tenerife and his fortnight spent riding the inflatable banana and dancing the drunken night away in clubs filled with foam and 'top-notch birds in bikinis'.

'Can you wait?' Trudy shouted at Dave as they pulled up at the entrance. Now they were here, she wanted to get this over and done with as quickly as possible. She was like an SAS hit squad – in and out with no mess, and hopefully no casualties.

'Are you sure you can afford me, darlin'?' Puffing out his chest in his shiny, striped football shirt, Dave brushed back his gelled hair with his sovereign-ringed fingers and winked at her in his rearview mirror. 'I'm not cheap.'

'No kidding?' Diving out of the taxi before he could argue, Trudy smiled scathingly. 'It must be your after-shave then, honey.'

Sticking his head out of the window, Dave watched her stalking across the carpark with her friend. He cackled to himself. He always liked the ones who played hard to get.

'Are you sure you want to go through with this?' Eyeing up the hardcore punters jostling through the turnstiles, Juliet's doubts magnified. 'We don't have to go in there, you know.'

'But I want to go in there.' Trudy was resolute. 'I want to get this over and done with.'

'But don't you think it's a bit . . . er . . . *public*?' Juliet had visions of a Jerry Springer-type showdown.

'Jeez, Jules, what do you think I'm gonna do in there? Cause a scene?' Flicking open her mirror, Trudy checked her reflection for the umpteenth time. 'I can be subtle. *When I want to.*'

At the ticket booth they paid the ancient man with a craggy kind of face that looked remarkably like a Maris Piper potato – one that had been in the bottom of the cupboard for too long and had begun sprouting hairy tufts in nooks and crannies – and pushed through the clanking turnstiles into what was grandly called the 'Players' Lounge'.

A brightly lit bar area opened up, highlighting the swirling fog of cigarette smoke and shabby, battle-scarred walls painted a colour that appeared to have been inspired by Colman's mustard. Furthermore, in another interior design first, the carpet was burgundy and flowery. Covered in tab ends, beer stains and torn-up betting slips, it clashed nicely with the lurid yellow décor. Not that any of the punters seemed to mind. Clustered around the wall of TV screens displaying the odds, a mostly male crowd were jovially drinking beer from plastic pint glasses and smoking.

'Well it doesn't look like he's here, we must have missed him,' said Juliet, trying to sound despondent and not over the moon at the thought of leaving. The place was horrible. Testosterone was dripping off the walls and they were being stared at in a way that was uncannily similar to that classic scene in *American Werewolf*. The one where the poor old American walks into the aptly named pub, The Slaughtered Lamb, on the Yorkshire moors and is menacingly warned that he isn't welcome in these parts. Juliet scanned the room. This was no film but the sentiment was the same. She linked Trudy's arm. 'Come on, let's go home.'

'But we've only just arrived,' wailed Trudy, not going anywhere. Her thick skin acting like body armour, she moved further into the bar, a woman on a mission, scanning the room.

'Hmm, you could be right.' Her resolve wavered.

Juliet felt a chink of hope.

'Hang on a minute.' The penny dropped. '*You've never met Fergus*.' She glared at Juliet accusingly.

Juliet smiled sheepishly. 'So I haven't,' she admitted. 'What does he look like?'

'Like all bastards. Tall, dark, handsome,' quipped Trudy, breaking into a rueful smile. 'You can't miss him.'

Feeling the soles of her boots sticking to the carpet, Juliet loyally accompanied Trudy, who was advancing across the lounge, marching past the flashing slot machines and the white Formica fast food counter, towards the grandstand. Her Crystal Tips hairdo darting from side to side, her eyes on radar, Trudy was on the lookout. So Fergus couldn't be bothered to return her calls? Didn't want to see her any more? Well tough. He was going to have to face her now. He couldn't get rid of her that easily.

Entering the grandstand, Juliet was relieved to find this had a completely different atmosphere. More a 'come and enjoy an evening's entertainment' rather than 'come and get your head kicked in'. Floor-to-ceiling windows gave an unrestricted view onto the racetrack, enabling people to watch the racing in the warmth, while a restaurant, spread over tiers of white-tableclothed tables, was busy with diners tucking into three-course meals as they gambled.

Following Trudy down the stairs, Juliet saw that it was arranged in some kind of a class system. The best seats at the front were reserved for the greyhound owners, ruddy-faced men with sideboards the size of lamb chops and wives with Gloria Hunniford hairstyles and faces caked in Ultra Glow. Behind them, halfway up, sat the corporate clients. Rowdy cityboys who thought it was still the eighties and prayed to the god of Gordon Gekko. Ostentatiously smoking cigars and drinking champagne they were showing off to those on the outskirts. They needn't have bothered. Drinking lager and eating ketchup-soaked hotdogs, these tattooed blokes and their gold-jewelleried girlfriends were having a great time, taking the piss out of the suits and watching them making complete dicks of themselves by unwittingly gambling away their huge bonuses.

'Julie, is that you, luv?'

Trying to keep up with Trudy who, despite her four-inch heels, was cantering down the stairs, Juliet faltered. Glancing behind to her left she saw a row of curly blue rinses. A platinum blond head bobbed forward.

'It's me, you daft beggar.' It was Violet, beaming cheerily and waving a cigarette. Juliet watched the long finger of ash disintegrating and sprinkling the heads of the people sitting in the tier below like dandruff.

She smiled. 'What are you doing here?'

'Having a flutter, what does it look like?' she explained, slurping a snowball. Violet looked as if she'd been on the snowballs all evening. All dolled up in her fur coat and cameo brooch, her crayoned eyebrows had smudged and her bright fuchsia lipstick was bleeding into her salmon pink face powder. 'I come every week with t'pensioners' club.' Tipsily she turned to the blue rinses sitting on both sides of her like backing singers. 'This is Betty, Edna and May . . . and this is Errol.'

A distinguished-looking man in a blazer took his pipe out of his mouth. 'Vi's a natural. She's already up thirty notes,' he boasted proudly.

'Well, I do like to study form,' she giggled, patting Errol's arm. He gazed at her adoringly as she wedged her glasses firmly up the bridge of her nose and turned her attention back to Juliet. 'Are you with William?'

Guilt stabbed. 'Er . . . no . . .'

'Oh, that's a shame. I wanted to ask if my lampshade fitted,' she smiled happily, not realizing she'd just landed Will right in it. 'When he came over on Sunday and asked if he could buy it off me, you could have knocked me down with a feather. Fancy, a young man wanting something of mine.' She chuckled at her *double entendre*, before leaning forward and whispering, 'To be honest, I was glad to get shot of it. I never liked it.'

Juliet smiled, but her mind was clicking things into place like a Rubik's cube. So that explained the sudden appearance of the tasselled monstrosity in the hallway. Will hadn't gone out and bought it, it was a pensioner's cast-off. No wonder it looked so bloody familiar. She looked at Violet, who'd begun nattering to Errol as if Juliet wasn't there. 'She's one of those career women, you know, all modern like, and she's living over the brush with a wonderful young man, though if you ask me . . .'

She interrupted. 'Sorry Violet, I'm with a friend. I can't stay and chat.' Stalling her disappointment, she added, 'But I'll drop in tomorrow from work. I can read you t'rest of *Bittersweet Dreams*.'

Violet's reaction was unexpected. 'Oh, that load of nonsense,' she pooh-poohed haughtily. 'Errol's taken it back to t'library for me.'

If Juliet wasn't mistaken, by the look they exchanged, Violet was getting her fix of romance elsewhere.

Leaving Violet and Errol flirting unashamedly, Juliet hastily said her goodbyes and dashed down the stairs and out through the side doors to the racetrack. Outside there was a crowd of people bundled up in winter coats and scarves, milling around on the concrete steps where half a dozen bookies had set up their stalls.

The race was beginning in five minutes and the greyhounds were being paraded past, their skinny bodies illuminated by the floodlights. A buzz of excitement ran through the crowd as money started changing hands, thick and fast, causing a favourite to emerge and the odds to alter. Scanning the crowd for Trudy, Juliet noticed a young girl nervously placing a five-pound bet, a bulldog of a man handing over a large wad of notes, a drunk reeling around with a can of Special

Brew in his gnarled hand gabbling incoherently – a gambler who'd gambled away his life.

And then she spotted Fergus. At least Juliet assumed it was Fergus. Working in partnership with one of the tweed-suited bookies, he was crouched behind a betting board meticulously logging the money that was being taken. Despite wearing a skanky old benny hat pulled low over his ears and a blue donkey jacket with plastic elbow patches, there was something dangerously attractive about him. He reminded her of the boys who used to work on the dodgem cars when she was a teenager. The swaggering, sexy, charming, irresistible travelling fairboys who, with their rockabilly haircuts, homemade tattoos and Doc Marten boots, broke the hearts of hormonal, fifteen-year-old virgins up and down the country.

At the same time, across the other side of the crowd, a hormonal thirty-seven-year-old was having her heart-strings severely tugged. Trudy had seen Fergus as well, and she was taken aback by the effect he was having on her. Watching him standing up and stretching his long, denim-clad legs, her bravado wavered. She caught it before it crumbled. Steadfastly pulling up her furry collars, she hid her clenched fists deep inside her pockets and began striding towards him, rehearsing what she was going to say.

But then events took an unexpected turn.

A pretty redhead sprang into the frame. With her frizzy perm, gelled back into a high ponytail, swinging jauntily and gold hoops all the way up her ears, she seemed to appear from nowhere in a tiny denim jacket, a black Lycra miniskirt and bare legs that had mottled in the sub-zero temperatures, like curdled milk. Skipping up to Fergus, she giggled as he bent down to kiss her on her plump, upturned lips.

Trudy froze. Watching them nuzzling together, she crumpled. Underneath her foundation, the colour drained from her face, her mouth shrank, her shoulders slumped. Wearing not a scrap of make-up, the redhead exuded the confidence and had the poreless skin of youth. This was not someone who spent thirty quid on anti-feathering lip treatments. Who woke up in the morning and had to wait a good half an hour for her face to 'settle'. Who'd resorted to using Preparation H to try and shrink her eyebags. This was the reason he hadn't called. This was the competition. And she looked about seventeen.

Suddenly Trudy felt really old. An ancient, wizened-up late thirtysomething in designer clothes. She felt as if she was in one of those time-release films that begin with a flower in full bloom, only to show it quickly wither and decay. Her neuroticism took a stranglehold. Juliet had been right all along. This was a bad idea. What was she doing here?

Without warning, reality struck with full force. She was fooling herself. She hadn't come all this way to ask Fergus for money towards an abortion, she'd come because deep down she wanted Fergus to give her a big, hairy bear hug and tell her everything was going to be OK. This was the biggest thing that had ever happened to her. *She was pregnant.* Shouldn't the father-to-be be cracking open the champagne? Shouldn't her mother be crying with delight over the phone at becoming a grandmother? Shouldn't she be getting lots of attention, fuss and hand-knitted bootees from relatives she'd never heard of?

Shouldn't she be in love?

Trudy's sentimentality caught her off guard. For years she'd poured scorn on all that slush, dismissing the picture perfect ideal of happy families as a load of bullshit. Yet here she was wanting it so much that it hurt.

'Trude, you're shaking, are you OK?' Having spotted her in the crowd, Juliet finally caught up with her after pushing through the swarms of people.

'Sure, honey, you know me, I'm always fine,' she said briskly. Juliet's concern brought her to her senses. She was going soft. The hormones were playing havoc. Being pregnant really did kill the brain cells. 'You were right. Let's get outta here.'

She was about to turn back, when she looked up. The redhead had disappeared but Fergus had clocked her. He looked shocked. And defensive.

Knowing she couldn't turn back now, she left Juliet and walked over to him. 'I need to speak to you.'

He continued staring at her for a moment, before he found his voice. It was gruff. 'I'm busy,' he replied dismissively.

'Well, I'm pregnant,' she snapped back, unable to stop herself. It came out a lot louder than she intended. A few people standing nearby stopped chattering and turned to see what all the commotion was about.

'It's not mine,' he fired back at point blank range.

His words hit their target and Trudy struggled not to flinch. Digging her fingernails hard into her palms, she looked into his dark eyes, searching for some sign of the easy, kind, lustful rogue she'd got to know these last few weeks. OK, so they were hardly love's young dream, but they'd spent time together, slept together, had a laugh together. Surely that counted for something?

But nobody was laughing now.

She tried to be reasonable. 'Can we go some place and talk?' People were beginning to stare. Not just those around her, but the crowd inside. She could almost feel the thousands of pairs of eyes behind the windows, watching them from the comfort of their ringside seats.

'What's there to talk about?' spat Fergus. 'If you're in the club, it's your problem.'

Wham. In a split second Trudy's opinion of Fergus changed for ever. What had she been thinking? She didn't want him, she despised him. What on earth had she ever seen in him? He was a loafish, sexist, immature loser. And he wore acrylic jumpers that had gone all bobbly. Trudy was mentally chastising herself when the redhead reappeared clutching two polystyrene cups of coffee.

'Ere, what's going on? Are you all right babe?' Passing Fergus a coffee (three sugars, plenty of milk) she clung possessively to his arm and threw Trudy a dirty look. 'What do you want with my fiancé?'

'*Fiancé?*' It was news to her.

The redhead waggled her left hand. The cubic zirconia glinted menacingly. 'We're getting married, aren't we babe?'

'*You're getting married?*' Trudy couldn't stop herself. Shock was turning her into an echo. Where was her wit? Her putdowns? Her acid tongue?

'Sure are.' Smiling proudly as if she'd just won the jackpot, the redhead patted her stomach. Only then did Trudy notice the bump underneath her denim jacket. It was at least four months bigger than her own. 'We're having a register office do after the baby's born.'

Nobody said anything. The redhead looked at Trudy. Trudy looked at Fergus. Fergus looked away.

It was Trudy who finally spoke.

'Sorry, I made a mistake.' Her voice was low, almost a whisper, but there was no mistaking the steely resolve. 'I thought you were someone else.'

A cheer rose up from the crowd.

As the winning greyhound crossed the finishing line, the crowd began surging towards the bookies. Squeezed and jostled, Trudy found herself elbowed out of the way by a middle-aged man impatient to claim his winnings. Pushed apart by the human barrier, she turned to Juliet and, linking arms, they boldly walked out of the racetrack, through the turnstiles, and away from Fergus who stood with the redhead wrapped tightly around him, watching her leave.

* * *

Dave the cabbie was still waiting for them in the carpark. His head buried deep in 'Readers' Wives', he looked up jumpily as she reached for the door handle. 'Back any winners?' he gasped, sticking his mag under the sun visor and crossing his legs to try and hide his huge erection.

Trudy slumped into the back seat. She'd been holding it together, resolutely clinging to that brave face of hers all night, all weekend, all fortnight – since the moment that blue line emerged in that tiny window – and she couldn't do it any longer. A tear betrayed her by spilling onto her cheek, but instead of briskly wiping it away, she let it trickle a path through her blusher and plop sadly onto her fur collars.

Shaking her head, she glanced at Juliet and smiled resignedly. 'No. Only losers.'

Chapter Thirty-five

Juliet dropped Trudy off outside her flat in Hampstead. She'd offered to stay the night on her sofa to keep her company, but Trudy wouldn't hear of it. Sniffing, she wiped away a splodge of mascara that had stuck to her cheek in an engaging Pierrot effect. 'You go home to Will. I want to be alone,' she declared in a very Garbo-esque tone of voice, before adding, 'Not that any woman can be alone if she has a Dolly Parton CD.' She looked at Juliet, a puckish smile breaking through the tears. 'I can feel a "Jolene" evening coming on.'

Juliet understood. Over the years she'd experienced a couple of Trudy's Jolene evenings. Unlike most other females who chose friends, Chardonnay and Malboro Lights, whenever Trudy was upset she dealt with it by locking herself away and listening to 'Jolene' on continuous play for several hours at a time. It was a form of therapy for her. For her long-suffering neighbours, it was more a form of torture.

'What about Friday? Do you want me to come to the clinic with you?'

Trudy tutted exasperatedly. 'Will you stop fussing? I'll be absolutely fine. A quick hoover and I'll be as good as new.' She waved her hands, as if shooing away a cat. 'Now, will you please go home? Go on, *get outta here*.'

Juliet could see no hope of trying to persuade her but, comforted by the knowledge that at least she was leaving her friend in the capable hands of Dolly, she waved goodbye and leaned forward to tell the cabbie her address.

Except she didn't.

She had no intention of going home.

As soon as Trudy was out of sight, she asked the driver to give her a few minutes and fished out her mobile. Sykes had called her earlier, but as she was with Trudy, she hadn't answered. It wouldn't have been a good idea. Best friend or not, discovering Fergus had been unfaithful, wasn't going to make her the most sympathetic person to Juliet's situation. She dialled his number. She wasn't going home, because she had to see him. She *needed* to see him. Picking at the bits of skin around her fingernails she listened anxiously to the ringing tone. A few seconds later and it would divert to voicemail. 'Come on, pick up, pick up,' she hissed desperately.

'Have you been avoiding me?' he greeted her teasingly.

'Of course not,' she protested, trying to keep her voice steady.

'Where are you?'

She threw the question back. 'I was going to ask you the same thing.'

'In a bar around the corner from my house, getting something to eat. I've just finished a workout at the gym and I'm ravenous.'

'Can I see you?'

He paused to drag on a cigarette. 'You don't need to ask.'

Juliet could hear him smiling down the phone.

She relayed the address of the bar to Dave, the cabbie. It was in Kensington, only a few miles away, but as always when she was in a desperate hurry, every traffic light changed to red, every zebra crossing conjured up a pedestrian, every roundabout attracted a queue. She could feel the urgency rising in her throat, and she forced herself to sit back and relax. Folding her arms she stared determinedly out of the window, and tried not to notice the sweaty handprints left behind on her sheepskin coat.

Eventually, the cab turned off the main road and into a small side street. The exhaust echoed loudly against the narrow walls and the swirls of fumes formed white patterns in darkness. The pub was on the corner. Handing over a £20 note, Juliet climbed out into the prickling cold and, hesitating for a moment, peered up at the Churchill Arms. The bevelled glass windows emitted a warm glow onto the pavement. It was a pub she'd walked past a thousand times, on her way home from shopping in Kensington, but had never been tempted to go inside. She smiled at the irony. How times change.

Listening to her heart thudding loudly in her ears, she walked towards the main entrance. And then hesitated. Unscrewing her small pot of raspberry lip-gloss, she ran a smear over her lips with her finger, shook out her hair and fiddled with the collars of her shirt. Pushing back the heavy door, she entered the smoky warmth of the pub.

It was one of those gastro pubs, bare floorboards, chalkboards featuring tonight's menu, deep scarlet walls, leather sofas, ambient lighting. Being a Monday night it was fairly quiet, a few regulars at the bar watching sport on the mute overhead TV, a couple in front of the open fire eating food. Music was wafting from the speakers. She recognized the music. It was the same *Buddha Bar* CD Will had bought her for her birthday last year. At the time she'd loved it, but now its novelty had worn off. She heard it everywhere. Like lift music, it was always playing in every bar, shop and Starbucks she walked into.

'Hey, what took you so long?'

She saw Sykes around the far side of the bar, tucked away in the corner. It was the kind of place nobody could see, unless they were looking. The kind of place you'd sit if you were having an affair.

Juliet looked at Sykes. His hair was still wet from the gym, and he was wearing a blue linen shirt that was half unbuttoned, and a pair of jeans. She noticed they were Versace. 'I hope you don't mind, I've already ordered my food,' he smiled, standing up and brushing away a drip of water drizzling over his forehead from his dark damp curls. Juliet felt herself staring. He looked as gorgeous as always. 'I was going to wait, but . . .' he shrugged apologetically.

'But I was sitting in traffic,' she replied, walking towards him and trying not to stare. She couldn't help it. Her eyes travelled upwards from his denim crotch, black leather belt with a silver buckle, the waistband of his Calvin Kleins peeping over the top. Her gaze rested on the bare triangle of chest where his shirt gaped open.

'If you want to order something now it should be ready the same time as mine. We can eat back at my house, it's only around the corner.'

She smiled, feeling unexpectedly nervous. 'Don't worry, I'm not hungry. I didn't come here to eat.'

'So what did you come here for?' he murmured, curling his hand around her midriff. Pressing her against his warm, damp body he leaned forward to kiss her.

She pulled away abruptly.

Taken aback he stared at her, his forehead furrowed. 'What's wrong?'

'This.' Her heart was pounding. She attempted to clarify. '*Us*.' She stepped back to put more space between them, waiting for the inevitable row.

Except it never materialized. Instead Sykes merely sighed. It was the battle-weary sigh of a man who'd been here before. 'Talk in sentences, Juliet.'

She bristled at his condescending sarcasm. Jamming her hands in her pockets, she began twisting the nylon lining into knots. 'I want this to be over. I can't see you any more.'

'Is that why you came to see me?' Appearing almost amused, he slid his wallet out of his jacket breast pocket. 'I'll get us both a drink.' Leaving her standing, he walked across to the bar.

Juliet watched him in disbelief. That was his reaction? For the last 24 hours she'd been in a state of anxious turmoil. Unable to sleep, unable to work, her mind had been running around in circles, like a dog trying to catch its tail. Round and round it had whirled. Will, Sykes, London, Verona. Clashing emotions, deep-seated resentments, doubts, hopes, desire, guilt, sex, *love*. Until exhausted she'd finally surrendered to her decision.

She and Sykes were over. She'd known that the moment the wheels of the 737 had touched down at Heathrow. In fact, if she was truly honest, she'd known long before that, she just hadn't admitted it to herself. She hadn't wanted to break the spell.

But *she* hadn't.

It had broken all by itself the moment she'd walked back into her flat and seen Will. Standing there in that ridiculous tracksuit, in that ridiculously tidy living room, with that ridiculous lampshade making tasselled faces at them from the hallway, she'd realized he'd changed. Or was it her that had changed? And she'd realized she couldn't lose him. Whatever problems they had to fix, she couldn't give him up. She couldn't give up on them.

Which is why she'd needed to see Sykes. And all the way over in the cab she'd been rehearsing what she'd say, what he'd say, how she'd explain, building up to this great big showdown. But there hadn't been one. The beginning might have been one big adrenalin rush, but the ending was a bit of an anticlimax. No argument, histrionics, tears, raised voices. Just a nonchalant shrug of the shoulders.

It was an unexpected blow to Juliet's ego. These past few weeks had hurled her through a big dipper of emotions and, rightly or wrongly, what had happened between them had had a huge effect on her life. Hadn't it to his? Hadn't she meant anything? Didn't he care? She stopped herself. Christ, what the hell was she thinking? *She was dumping her lover.* What did she want him to do? Try and stop her? Break down in tears and beg her not to go? Turn incandescent with rage and challenge Will to a duel?

The thought turned her blood cold. Of course she didn't. She didn't love Sykes. It wasn't her feelings that were hurt. Just her vanity.

'Are you going to join me?' Breaking off from her thoughts Juliet looked up to see Sykes reappear with two glasses and an unopened bottle of champagne. He smiled sheepishly. 'Old habits . . .'

She didn't smile back. 'What are we celebrating?' she asked sulkily, thinking how ironic it was that she was the one who felt miffed.

Peeling off the gold tinfoil, he deftly eased off the cork with the expertise of a man used to opening champagne bottles. Not like Will, who could never resist making a big drama out of it. Shaking up the bottle as if he was a Grand Prix winner and screwing up his face as he held it out at arm's length. Yelling 'Stand back' as the cork popped off with a mini-explosion, torpedoing across the kitchen as champagne sprayed out like a burst water main.

Filling two flutes without spilling a drop, Sykes held one out to her. He clinked the rim of his glass against hers. 'Verona.'

Juliet sat down. She had that surreal feeling of being catapulted back through time. *Verona*, God, that seemed like so long ago. Another world. Mutely, she sipped the amber bubbles. They tasted bittersweet.

'Verona was special. We had something there.'

Despite having a whole weekend of memories to

choose from, her mind flicked back to the courtyard of Juliet's house, standing alone among all those tourists, gazing up at the balcony. She looked up from staring at the bubbles fizzing to the surface. 'But it wasn't real.'

'Does it have to be?' he murmured, leaning across the table. Extending a hand, he gently stroked the side of her face.

Juliet understood. Sykes wasn't looking for a relationship. He didn't want the reality of it. In his own way, he was as big a romantic as she was. He wanted the giddy sexual rush, the excitement, the thrill, and he was offering her the chance to have it too. She didn't have to make a choice, she could continue as before. Going out with Will and seeing Sykes.

Except it wouldn't be like it was before.

Sykes would be her bit on the side. It would be about lunchtime shags and dirty weekends, furtive phone calls and seedy drives in the country. All the old, worn clichés sprang to mind, and Juliet recoiled from them. That was never what she'd wanted. It hadn't been about sex. She'd meant what she'd said to Trudy. As naïve as it might sound with the knowledge of hindsight, for Juliet, Sykes had been about that elusive high that grabs you at the beginning of a love affair and sends you spinning. About that giddy feeling in the pit of your stomach that makes you catch your breath, about exhilaration, romance, feeling special. *About the desire for something out of the ordinary*.

But now it could never be any of those things.

Sykes's fingertips moved to that little patch underneath her earlobe. Just like he used to. Except this time it didn't tingle. Reaching up, she lightly brushed his hand away. 'Yeah, it has to be real. To me anyway.'

He smiled ruefully and leaning back against the wooden bench, lit up a cigarette.

She hesitated. There was just one more thing. A hunch she wanted to satisfy. 'Tell me. Is Gina an ex?'

Blowing smoke down his nostrils, he allowed a sheepish smile. 'Was it that obvious?'

'Just a little bit.' She shook her head, remembering that night with his friends. Now it seemed so trivial, she couldn't believe she'd felt so insecure.

'That's where I went on Sunday afternoon, when I left you. I went to meet her.'

It all fell into place. So that's why he'd wanted her to go sightseeing by herself. Juliet listened without saying anything. How quickly they'd moved from lovers to acquaintances.

'We didn't sleep together if that's what you're thinking.'

'I'm not.' She was surprised that he thought he had to explain. Surprised by how little she cared. 'So are you going to get back together?' It was a surreal conversation.

'Maybe.' He dragged hard on his cigarette and for a moment she noticed how knackered he looked. The lids of his eyes were almost bruised with fatigue. 'If I move back to Italy, who knows?'

'Excuse me? Are you the Thai green chicken curry and boiled rice?' It was one of the bar staff. Juliet watched as he walked across the bar and put the takeout on the table in front of Sykes, noticed the carrier bag on the seat next to him with a couple of bottles of Evian, toilet roll, an *Evening Standard* and a copy of *FHM*. Her gaze returned to Sykes. His perfect profile, the dark curl of hair falling onto his forehead as he leaned forward to flick his ash in the ashtray, his eyes flicking over the TV screen above the bar as the sports results came on. And all of a sudden it was as if everything dropped away.

Behind the impressive sportscar, beautiful Armani suits, designer house, the flattery and gorgeous looks, Sykes wasn't anything special. He was just another thirtysomething bloke, going home to spend a night in with a takeout and the telly.

* * *

It was time to leave.

'I want you to take this back.' Standing up, she took off her coat and laid it over the back of a chair.

Looking away from the TV, Sykes turned to her. It was almost as if he'd forgotten she was there. 'I don't think Gucci will let me,' he smiled.

'Well you can always use it as a picnic blanket,' she smiled back. Putting down her champagne flute, she began resolutely walking across the bar, to the exit.

'Juliet . . .'

She glanced back.

'I hope you find your Romeo.' He was looking at her in that no-hard-feelings kind of a way. She didn't answer. Instead she continued walking across the bar. She stood back to let some people inside, before stepping out into the cobbled mews. She took an invigorating lungful of frozen air. And standing alone in the silent darkness, whispered to herself: 'I already have.'

Chapter Thirty-six

It was Friday morning and Will was standing in the bathroom doorway, peering through a gauze of steam at the silhouette behind the leopardskin shower curtain. Long skinny legs, the smooth curve of stomach, a neat little waist that could have been made to measure for his arm, and then the nicest bit of all, *that lovely round bottom*. Mmmmm.

He gazed at it admiringly. That had to be the most perfect bottom. It wasn't too big – like those stonking huge pear-shaped backsides he often saw on the high street, mushrooming out of grey stretch leggings like a fleshy atom bomb with VPL – but then it wasn't too small either, like those skinny supermodel bums in magazines that were as flat as pancakes. Looking at this particular bottom Will felt like one of the three bears. No, this one was just right.

Unable to resist, he reached out and, pulling back the swathes of plastic curtain, grabbed it with both hands.

'*Agghhh . . . ?*' Caught in the middle of shampooing her hair, Juliet let out a shriek and twirled round in surprise. With soapy water streaming down her face, she untangled the strands of hair clinging like seaweed across her eyes and, her mouth wide open like a blow-up doll, blinked hard and fast. Seeing Will, she gasped indignantly. '*You bastard.*' But she was smiling.

He smiled back and leaned towards her, planting a kiss on her soapy shoulders. 'Mmm, you taste good.'

'It's citrus and guava,' she retorted deprecatingly,

holding up the bottle of shampoo as evidence in her soapy hands.

'Mmm, yeah, *very fruity*,' nodded Will, adopting his Sean Connery accent and pretending to lick his lips in rapture. 'I think I'd like seconds.' Grabbing hold of her slippery waist he gave her another kiss, this time on the lips. '*Now* I can understand why fruit first thing in the morning is so good for you,' he muttered, raising one eyebrow.

Juliet had to smile. Will was always getting his James Bonds mixed up. One minute he was Sean, the next he was Roger. She slapped him goodnaturedly. 'Gerroff, you're going to get soaked.' She laughed as the spray from the shower-head rained down over his woolly arm. 'And you're going to be late. I thought you had a deadline to finish that Japanese roof garden today.'

'It's practically finished,' he protested. 'Apart from a few bedding plants and a little bit of clearing up, and Rolf's going to take care of that. It'll give the lazy sod something to do.' Loath to withdraw his arm, Will couldn't resist running his hand downwards to the little dip in the base of her back and across the outside of her thighs. 'Which means I get to take the day off.'

'You're taking the day off?' Juliet couldn't believe her soap-filled ears. 'But you never take the day off.'

He shrugged mysteriously. 'I felt like a change.'

Turning to let the water rinse through her hair, she stared at him. 'Are you feeling all right?'

'Never better.'

Juliet narrowed her eyes, trying to work out what was going on in his head. Over the past week Will had turned over a new leaf. Going to the gym, discovering the laundry bin, *discovering her again*. Perhaps this was just another one of those leaves. Squeezing a dollop of shower gel into the palm of her hand she began lathering up her shoulders. 'Well, you might not have to go to work, but I do. We presented our reworked campaign for the MAXI account yesterday and we're waiting to discover if we've won it or not.' She began lathering her boobs. 'Now shoo.'

'Spoilsport,' whined Will, being shooed away reluctantly from his real-life wet dream as she yanked back the shower curtain. 'Don't forget, I'm taking you out for dinner tonight,' he added, listening to the splashing behind the plastic leopardskin and feeling somewhat left out.

Juliet's voice was loud above the spray of water drumming against the enamel bathtub. 'Are you *sure* you're feeling all right?'

He grinned to himself. No, he didn't feel all right. And it felt fantastic. Deep in thought he stared at the silhouette. 'I'm in love with you, Jules.'

Above the noise of the shower, his words caused Juliet's heart to miss a beat. With the water streaming down her face, she stopped what she was doing. Will had never said that to her before. Up until the past few months he'd always told her he loved her, but this was different. This meant something else.

Like a seal, she popped out her dark wet head, wiping a trickle of water away from her face. With steam swirling in between them it reminded Juliet of a scene from an old black and white film she'd once watched with Trudy, where the couple saw each other again at a railway station. In fact she was beginning to think how romantic it was, when Will leaned across to kiss her, whispering, 'Are you sure you don't want me to do your back for you? You haven't seen my loofah action.'

A huge grin broke across her face. Trust Will. Kissing him, she stood up. 'You can show me later,' she winked, before disappearing back behind the tempting vinyl veil of the shower curtain.

'Heeeyyyyyy, good morning London. It's just turned 8.30 a.m. and this is Billy and the breakfast crew, bringing you that Friday feeling.'

Trudy awoke with a start.

Flinging her arms out from the toasty confines of her eiderdown, she vaulted naked out of bed, yanked back her purple velvet curtains and tugged open her creaky sash window. It had finally arrived. Gripping the sill, she thrust out her head and chest like a ship's figurehead and, closing her eyes, inhaled great big lungfuls of Hampstead Heath air. Forget the 4th of July. Today was Independence Day.

'*Phewpheeww.*'

A chorus of wolfwhistles. Snapping open her eyes, she looked down to see a troupe of builders hanging like trapeze artists from the scaffolding on the white stucco house opposite. Clutching thermos flasks of tea and breakfast butties, they were staring across at her in delighted bewilderment. In what had to be a first, they were truly lost for words. 'Show us your tits' seemed a tad defunct. Eventually one found his voice – *and balls* – to holler: 'Nice pair!'

About to respond with her customary four-letter greeting, Trudy paused to glance down at the cream-coloured mammaries that rose from beneath her collarbone like UFOs. Actually, they had a point, she thought begrudgingly. Gazing at them now, she realized with a burgeoning sense of cheeriness that they were the boob job she'd always wanted. Looking up at the goggle-eyed workmen, she adopted a page three pose. Arching her back, shaking her slept-in hair and flashing a Trojan smile, she yelled, 'I know . . . And guess what? *They're all mine.*'

Will dug his hand deep in his pocket, and let his legs stride out. It was just after 9.30 but instead of being where he usually was at 9.30 a.m. on Friday morning – stuck in a traffic jam or knee-deep in mud and cement – he was walking through Holland Park with a big silly grin on his face. The sun was shining, birds were singing, bushy-tailed squirrels were scampering across the path, there were even tiny green buds appearing on the branches of trees. Listening to the satisfying sounds of his feet rhythmically crunching on the gravel, he took a deep, jubilant breath. Yep, spring was definitely in the air. And that wasn't all, he mused, unable to resist humming along to Louis Armstrong's 'What a Wonderful World' that was providing the soundtrack in his head.

He was happy. He was on cloud nine. *He was in love*.

Will couldn't remember the last time he'd felt this good. Since coming back from Yorkshire, something had fundamentally changed and it had nothing to do with circumstances – it was between him and Juliet. He'd changed towards her and she'd changed towards him. They'd both still been busy at work, stressed out about deadlines and working long hours, but now instead of getting home, trading a few sentences about what to eat for dinner, whose turn it was to do the washing up or the size of the phone bill, then flopping in front of the TV, they'd made time for each other.

They'd talked, listened, laughed, loved. And done a serious amount of shagging, added Will, saving his thoughts from getting just that little bit too slushy. Being a new sensitive man was perfectly OK, but that didn't mean forgetting about the – how could he describe it? – more basic physical pleasures in a relationship. Not that making love with Juliet could be described as basic. Far from it. It had to be the most special thing he could imagine.

Staring out across the expanse of grass, Will revelled in the feeling of space. Holland Park wasn't quite as spacious as the Yorkshire moors but, for London, it was the best place to get away from it all. A place away from the clutter and noise of everyday life, that gave him a chance to think about things, see things clearer. He'd been doing a lot of that recently, which is why he could now see the size of the rut they'd been in. That was the funny thing. At the time he hadn't even realized they were in a rut. Hadn't seen that they'd been heading in one direction only, and that was towards the edge. But thankfully he'd woken up just in time and saved their relationship from plummeting over it.

Striding out across the dewy grass, Will felt like a bit of a superhero. He felt taller and broader, more confident. More attractive even, he considered, noticing a couple of teenage girls staring at him. He sucked in his stomach. And winced. Ouch, that hurt. It was no good, he was going to have to let it all hang out. His muscles were still in agony from all those crunches his new personal trainer at the gym was insisting he do to shed the 'thirtysomething' pounds he'd put on. Actually it was more like a stone that had somehow managed to creep up on him while he wasn't paying attention. Along with a lot of other things, he thought, heading towards the exit onto the high street.

Will had lived through a life-changing week. A week that had really opened up his eyes and made him see the bigger picture. He'd finally made peace with his dad, and by doing it he felt as if he'd experienced some kind of revelation. Nobody liked their parents interfering, but they'd been right. Why hadn't he ever asked Juliet to marry him? Now he knew the answer. Because he'd been scared. He'd been scared of growing up, taking responsibility, of moving forwards. Scared of becoming like his parents.

But now, for the first time in his thirty-three years he was thinking seriously about his future, and he wasn't talking about turning self-employed, buying a car or going on holiday. He was talking about Juliet. *His future with Juliet.* And the funny thing was, he'd suddenly realized just how much a part of him *wanted* to be like his parents. Forty years later and they were still in love. It wasn't a bad act to aspire to.

Nearing the gates, Will looked across the park and saw a couple. The woman had hair a bit like Juliet's and she was with her boyfriend, or her husband, who looked about the same age as himself, if not – dare he say it – *younger*. They were both holding the hands of a little boy in a stripy jumper and red Mickey Mouse wellies. He couldn't have been more than about three years old and they were swinging him up and down, and he was laughing, a giggly, tinkly, unstoppable laugh that most people grow out of. But not the people holding the little boy's hands. They were laughing too. Smiling and chattering, and whooping as a tiny pair of Mickey Mouse feet flew into the air.

Watching them, Will knew unequivocally that's what he wanted. He wanted to spend his life with Juliet, to argue with her, laugh with her, cry with her, to hold the hands of their children and send them whooping and laughing into the air. To look at her from across the other side of a room, or a party, or in the fruit and veg aisle of a supermarket, and know that this warm, funny, sexy, gorgeous woman he couldn't take his eyes off, was the woman he was going to grow old with.

Noise from the busy main road interrupted his thoughts and he looked up to see gates and the traffic, shops, pedestrians, and the woman bundled up in an Afghan coat waiting outside the newsagent's on the corner. Chatting animatedly on her mobile, she glanced up with a sixth sense that someone was looking at her, saw Will, and started waving manically and jumping up and down in her moonboots.

Will smiled. Everything Amber did was manic, she was one of those hyper-vegan types who had more energy than any meat-eater he'd ever known. God knows where she got it from, but the way she was dashing across the street to meet him, she was obviously getting it from somewhere.

'Bang on time.' Her curls springing up and down

around her face, Amber strained on tiptoe to give Will a kiss.

'Did you think I'd be late?'

'I'm married to Rolf,' she grinned ruefully as explanation. 'So? Are you ready?' She eyed him challengingly. 'Amber McGinty, your own personal shopper, at your service.' Clicking her heels together she did a mock salute.

Will found himself wondering what he'd got himself into. When he'd taken her up on her earlier offer and called her, he hadn't envisaged 'Operation Amber'. He could see a whole exhausting day stretching ahead of him. Now he understood why Rolf always looked so knackered.

But Amber didn't notice his dubiousness. She was highly excited. This was her most favourite pastime. 'OK, now we need to check if we've got everything,' she bossed, linking arms and propelling him down the high street. 'Money?'

Will nodded mutely.

'Chequebook?'

He nodded again.

'Visa card?'

And again.

'*Willpower?*'

Smiling wryly, he found his voice. 'Now that's something I've got plenty of.'

Chapter Thirty-seven

'So when are you going to marry me?'

Entering the bustling warmth of Mario's Coffee Shop, Juliet broke into a smile as the big bearlike owner greeted her with his usual morning proposal.

'Today, eh?'

Waiting in line, she was about to reply but, on this particular morning, his wife Marie came to her rescue.

'Ayyyee, leave her alone,' she chastised, slapping her husband's furry knuckles with the roll of clingfilm she was using to cover her bowls of sandwich fillings. 'Can't you see?'

'See what?' protested Mario goodhumouredly, winking at Juliet across the counter.

'Mario. Alfredo. Brambilla. Is there something wrong with your eyes?' Gasping at the ignorance of her husband, Marie threw her chubby hands in Juliet's direction. *'She's in love.'*

Standing in the middle of the coffee shop, squeezed up next to half a dozen people, quite a few of whom happened to work in her office, Juliet blushed the colour of her mohair scarf. Was it that obvious?

Her mind threw up images of the last few days. God knows what had happened during Will's boys' weekend while she'd been in Verona – he hadn't spoken about it once and she hadn't asked him; as far as she was concerned that weekend was definitely best left in the past – but he'd been different. But then she'd been different as well. That night, when she'd gone to see

Sykes and told him it was over, she'd felt a huge weight lifted from her shoulders. What had started out as an exciting affair had suddenly felt like an albatross around her neck. Now, looking back, she felt only an overwhelming sense of relief that she'd made the right decision before it was too late. She'd had one hell of a lucky escape. She could have so easily ended up losing Will, and for what? A romantic fantasy? A six-pack in a suit? Flattery and a Gucci coat?

Recurring feelings of guilt and foolishness flushed over her. They did that a lot. Trudy's take on it was that they'd fade with time. 'You had a fling. You got away with it. Now forget about it.' It wasn't so easy. Part of her desperately longed to tell Will the truth and ask for his forgiveness. But she knew she couldn't. Telling him would be selfish. Confessing might absolve her guilt and make *her* feel better, but it would only hurt Will. In a perverse kind of a way, by not saying anything, she felt she was protecting him as much as she was protecting herself.

'Well, 'eez one lucky fella.'

Juliet looked up to see Mario holding out her cappuccino and toasted cheese bagel. She smiled, feeling faintly ridiculous. Mario was like an Italian version of Cilla, only without the teeth. Any minute now and he'd be talking about buying a hat.

She paid with a fiver. Giving back her change, Mario gave her hand a squeeze. It was unexpectedly gentle, considering his hands were calloused and the size of shovels. He smiled, his black Pavarotti eyebrows almost eclipsing the flirtatious twinkle in his eye. 'If ever you change your mind . . .'

Laughing, she stepped out onto the pavement and began heading towards her office. Somewhere, in the middle of the night, the season seemed to have changed. It felt much warmer and untangling her scarf, she unfastened the top buttons on her sheepskin collar. Having given back Sykes's extravagant present, she'd reluctantly dug out her old coat from the back of her wardrobe. Only to be pleasantly surprised. It wasn't as bad as she'd thought. The stains had faded and after a good once-over with a suede brush it looked pretty good. To be honest, she'd forgotten how nice her coat actually was. OK, so it wasn't Gucci, but so what? It might not have the glamour factor but it was definitely much more her. Will had obviously thought so too as, for the first time in a long time, he'd noticed what she was wearing. 'You look great. Is that new?' he'd asked, bundling her up in a sheepskin hug and kissing her. Feeling her mouth trace the familiar contours of his, she'd murmured happily, 'Sort of'.

Sipping her coffee Juliet was about to take the short-cut across the square when her eye caught a flash of silver down a back street. She glanced across automatically. It was the sun reflecting off the paintwork of a car. But, wait a moment. *Was that . . . ?* For a fraction of a second Juliet could have sworn it was Sykes's Aston Martin. Quickly shielding her eyes she tried to get a closer look but it was too late. Before she'd had a chance, the car had quickly swung into a parking space directly in front of an unloading goods van, and was completely hidden from view.

Part of Juliet told her to keep on walking. The chances of it being Sykes's car were highly unlikely, he worked on the other side of town. Why would he be near her office, at 10 a.m. on a Friday morning? And anyway, so what if it *was* him? They were over, he was history. A skeleton in her cupboard. A guilty secret. A mistake. She *didn't want* to see him again. But despite her reasoning, Juliet was intrigued. To tell the truth, although she liked to think it was a Poirot-twitching-of-the-moustache intrigue, in actual fact it was more of a blatant craning-her-neck-and-squinting-hard nosiness.

She hovered, half hidden by the wrought iron railings and bushes, sipping her scalding hot cappuccino. The steam from the cup made her nose run. Sniffing, she stared down the street, her eyes fixed resolutely on the back of the white minivan, willing it to move. It didn't. She watched the two tattooed blokes unloading crates and boxes, stacking them in piles on the pavement. This had to be the biggest delivery of ingredients to a pizza restaurant. *Ever.*

The seconds ticked away. Then a couple of minutes. Until, trying to drain the last frothy dregs of her coffee, it dawned on Juliet how ridiculous she was being. What the hell was she doing? She couldn't stand here all day, spying on her ex-lover who in fact probably wasn't her ex-lover at all. More likely some fat middle-aged banker in a Porsche. She tutted at herself. She had a job to go to, *and she was going to be late*.

Turning away she was hurrying towards her office when the echo of a car door slamming caused her to stop dead and twirl around. Only to laugh at just how ludicrous she was being. Just as expected, she thought, as a figure appeared from behind the lorry. It wasn't Sykes. It wasn't even a man. It was a woman.

It was Gabby.

The sight of her account director took Juliet completely by surprise. Gabby? Then she relaxed. Well, that solved that little mystery. Of course it wasn't Sykes. There was more than one silver sportscar in London and anyway, her account director would hardly be accepting lifts from him, would she? Shaking her head, Juliet turned away before Gabby had a chance to catch her lurking, and set off towards her office.

Trudy gave herself the once-over. Far too much lipstick, way too heavy handed with the mascara, *completely* over the top with the ponyskin cowboy boots. Perfect. Giving herself a little curtsy in the mirror, she dug out her coat from underneath a mountain of wet towels, reached for the sunglasses that were balancing precariously on the chock-a-block sink drainer, and flicked open the latch. After her Jolene evening she was feeling so much more like her old self. Dolly Parton certainly knew how to make a girl feel like a wonderful old tart again.

She was about to close the door behind her when the old-fashioned black telephone next to her bed gave a little shiver and began ringing. *Fuck it.* She ignored it. Today she was going to be far too busy to be sorting out shoots, juggling her diary with freelance work, discussing designs with clients – which is why she'd left her mobile recharging next to the toaster. It was vitally important that she arrived at the clinic in plenty of time; the last thing she needed was to miss her appointment by answering the phone. Firmly pulling the door shut, Trudy double-locked it, and began clomping down the stairs, two at a time.

Which is why she didn't hear the answering machine click on, her recorded message, or the voice on the other end of the line speaking urgently into the phone. 'Trudy, are you there? It's me, Fergus . . . I need to speak to you . . . Trudy? . . . *Please, if you're there. Please pick up the phone . . .*'

Walking into SGC, Juliet immediately sensed something was up. There was a change in atmosphere. A drop in temperature that was nothing to do with Annette and her command of the central heating control. It was Friday. It was the morning after they'd made their last pitch for their final, revamped ad campaign to BMZ and Mr Yokoko. After the last few weeks of hard work, late nights, tight deadlines – all the stress and tension – she'd assumed people would be either relaxed and chilling out, or in a buzzy state of anticipation. But instead, the mood of the office felt subdued and sort of *cool*.

Looking through the Perspex walls, she could see Danny and Seth already at their desks. She called over to them. 'Any news on the pitch?' She couldn't resist asking, even though she knew if it was good news the rest of the office wouldn't be soberly drinking instant coffee at their desks and flicking through the morning papers.

'Which news do you want, the good or the bad?' deadpanned Danny sitting cross-legged on his desk, eating the stale remains of the Marks & Spencer's chocolate caterpillar cake. It had been sitting in the fridge since Neesha's birthday in January. Any longer and it would have crawled out itself.

Watching him shoving in mouthfuls with his fingers, Juliet resisted her pessimistic side. 'Good.'

'Barratt, Boodle & Hopkins have been given the elbow, so now we're head to head with Montague & Murdoch.' He paused to pick off the Smarties. 'It's us or them.'

'That's great,' enthused Juliet. 'And the bad?'

'Rumour has it they've got a very – and I'm talking *very* – similar campaign idea to us.'

Juliet felt a small knot of fear in her stomach.

'What? You mean they've stolen it?' interrupted Neesha in mid-mouthful of granary toast.

'How could they have stolen it? It's not the bleedin' crown jewels, is it?' fired back Annettte, emerging from the ladies' loos.

Danny rolled his eyes. It was too early to enter into a conversation with Annette. And he was way too sober for Neesha. 'I don't know, it's probably a load of bollocks,' he shrugged, discarding the empty plate and wiping his fingers on his T-shirt. 'You know what it's like, industry gossip.'

As Juliet stood silently, listening to Annette, Neesha and Danny squabbling and trying to quash the seed of panic she could feel slowly growing inside her, Gabby swept into the office like the Grim Reaper. Perhaps she was just being paranoid, but Juliet felt sure she was looking directly at her when she demanded, 'Is Magnus in yet? I need to speak to him. It's urgent.'

Oh no.

The knot in Juliet's stomach doubled in size and wrapped itself up in her intestines.

Oh shit.

Paranoia gripped as a series of outtakes from the past few weeks began falling over themselves like dominoes. Gabby's warning about Sykes as a rival, his determined pursuit of her, Tesco's, the coat, the London Eye, Verona.

Oh fuck.

VERONA.

Juliet felt sick as she remembered. Having too many drinks and letting it slip about the pitch, his disappearance the next day 'to go to his office', even though afterwards he'd given her some excuse about visiting Gina, the way he'd taken it so well when she'd finished it. And what about just now? Had that been his car? If so, what the hell was her account director doing getting out of it? Gabby didn't like Sykes. She called him 'the enemy'. Juliet's mind spun so fast she felt dizzy. But what if he'd become *her* enemy? What if Sykes had arranged to meet her secretly to tell her something. A scorned lover getting his own back. *Betraying her to her account director.*

Juliet screeched her thoughts to a halt. *Now stop it. Just Stop It.* This was crazy. She was getting carried away. This was real life in a Soho advertising agency, not some blockbuster espionage flick starring Jeff Bridges. This was Soho Square, not *Arlington Road.* There would be an entirely innocent explanation. She watched as Gabby marched into Magnus's office without knocking and firmly shut the door behind her.

She hoped.

Casting her eye across the shiny brass plaque on the wall of the Harley Street clinic, Trudy paused to rub a perfectly manicured finger over the lettering. Anyone passing by would have presumed she was a woman pausing for reflection. Hesitating over her life-changing decision. Riddled with doubts and angst and guilt.

They would have been wrong.

Trudy was merely removing a smudge of polish, left behind by the cleaner. Complete and utter pig she might be when it came to her own flat, as soon as she stepped out the door she was fastidious about everything looking perfect. It was the stylist coming out in her.

Satisfied, she pressed the intercom. There was a pause before she heard a voice. 'Hello?'

'Hi, I'm Trudy Bernstein, I've got a 10.30 appointment.'

The door was buzzed ajar, and pushing it open she walked down the corridor and into the reception area. It reminded her of the kind found in mid-range chains of hotels. Lots of neutrals, cane furniture that had seen better days, a set of prints of nothing in particular. A woman behind a beige desk looked up and gave her a Claire Rayner smile. 'Hi, my name's Belinda and first I'd like to take a few details.'

'Details' turned out to be the usual name and address, plus a disclaimer that ran into four paragraphs. It was like filling out an application for a store card, thought Trudy, scribbling in the box marked X and handing over her Amex.

'Well, that's all the paperwork done.' Belinda – who was still smiling and had been doing so throughout the entire form-filling procedure – gave her a copy from the clipboard. 'Now are you having a local or a general anaesthetic?'

Trudy looked at her new-found friend with suspicion. Her chumminess might appear genuine, but it was as false as her fingernails. Part of the job, like typing and answering the phone. Standing behind her pine-effect desk, Belinda reminded Trudy of those super-chatty women who wore lipliner, sleeveless turtleneck jumpers with gold necklaces *on top*, and worked in nail salons. In fact the way she put the question, she could have been asking her if she was having a manicure or a pedicure.

'Local,' replied Trudy. Just the word anaesthetic gave her the willies. Not perhaps the best word to use under the circumstances, she mused, begrudgingly giving Belinda a weak smile. It felt churlish not to.

'Splendid.' Belinda looked delighted. 'It's so much easier to recover from. A couple of hours and you'll be back to normal.'

'Great.' Trudy nodded, wondering if it was just her, or if the situation really was that surreal.

'Now, if you'd just go to the room downstairs. A nurse will be waiting for you.'

'The Room Downstairs.' It was like the title of some awful book about children being locked in the cellar and tortured, thought Trudy, descending the neutral stair carpet to be greeted by a jolly-looking West Indian nurse. Yet another member of the happy brigade.

'Now, I just want to check your blood.' Smiling, the nurse firmly took hold of her hand. 'Don't worry, it's just a little prick, you won't feel a thing.'

Wincing, Trudy resisted the joke.

'Mmm, I like your bracelet.' Still smiling, she gestured to the Buddha beads Trudy was wearing around her wrist.

Trudy smiled weakly. They were *so* last season, but she'd dug them out that morning in a moment of superstition. Committed as she was to her decision to have an abortion, it still didn't prevent the terrifying statistics for operation theatre fatalities from constantly popping into her head. She needed some serious good karma to ensure she didn't end up another one.

'In my country, pink stands for love.' The nurse released her hand.

'Well they didn't do me much good then, did they?'

replied Trudy, and then immediately regretted it. Self-pity was the last thing she needed right now. A Scotch on the rocks *maybe*.

Another girl appeared from upstairs. Obviously the next appointment, thought Trudy, feeling as if she was on a conveyor belt. Paradoxically, this comforted her. That was exactly how she wanted it to feel. Emotionless. Mechanical. An everyday occurrence. She was just one of many hundreds, thousands, probably millions of women who had come through those doors. She wasn't the first and she certainly wouldn't be the last.

Leaving the nurse to take care of her next patient, she moved into the waiting area which was already fairly full of women of all ages, colours, sizes, races. Plonking herself on the rather tired brown corduroy sofa, she opened the copy of *Vogue* she'd bought at the station on the way, and turned immediately to the fashion pages. The latest models in the latest designer clothes, a bikini shoot in Bali, photographs of the latest catwalk shows. Trudy found herself flicking over them without really looking. Normally she'd have been consumed by these pages, but today she couldn't concentrate.

It irked her.

She'd been so determined to take this all in her stride, to be the picture of cool, calm and collected, she was annoyed at her emotions betraying her. Instead of checking out the season's must-have handbags her attention strayed to the women who, every few minutes, appeared from the door at the far end of the corridor.

Watching them, Trudy had a sudden reality check. She wasn't playing at being grown-up any more, putting on lipstick and heels, *this was for real*. Fate was staring her in the face and it didn't look like so much fun any more. Closing the smooth glossy cover, for the first time she faced up to what was going to happen to her without the mental airbrushing.

These were the women who'd had their abortions. Who'd gone through it. Women who portrayed the whole range of emotions from the physical pain of those holding their stomachs, to the emotional. From the smart fortysomething businesswoman sobbing, to the dreadlocked teenager whose face was flooded with relief. It was a universal experience and yet it was an experience that was intensely individual.

And what's mine going to be? she asked herself, watching the teenager take out her mobile phone and begin text messaging. Who was she sending it to? Her boyfriend, or a friend, or her mum? Trudy didn't know, and she realized all of a sudden that she didn't know a lot of things. For so long she'd lived with the determined belief that she was going to sail through this with nothing more than a stomach ache and an entry on her Amex statement. But now?

Now an unthinkable thought was tugging, trying to unearth a part of her that, for all of Trudy's life, she'd buried deep under tons of gritty realism, cutting sarcasm, stubbornness and sheer single-mindedness. The part of her that had gently cradled her naked belly, that had wanted Fergus to wrap himself around her in a big bear hug and tell her he loved her, that had allowed a tear to fall in the back of the cab. It was this secret, hidden self that had put on a crazy old Dolly Parton record. And, when she was certain no-one could see her, had collapsed on the bed, and sobbed her bloody heart out.

'Ms Trudy Bernstein?'

Her thoughts punctured, she jerked upright. The nurse was smiling at her, calling her over. It was her turn.

'If you'd just like to go through there and put on the robe.'

Trudy stood up, only to feel her legs tremble beneath her. For a second she feared they were going to give way, until her self-preservation kicked in. Walking across the waiting room, she reached out and curled her fingers around the smooth silver handle. It was cold to the touch. She hesitated. Then opened the door.

Chapter Thirty-eight

Sitting on a chrome barstool at an unashamedly posey cocktail bar in a West End hotel, Will turned to Rolf and Amber next to him. 'So what are you drinking, red or white?'

'Oh, thanks mate,' beamed Rolf. Having just silently freaked out at the prices on the drinks list, he was delighted not to be the one having to buy the round. Five pounds for a beer? Eleven for a vodka and orange? Think how much beer he could buy for that down the offy. But now he was suddenly a lot more interested in the wine list. 'Hmmm, I could murder a glass of the South African Shiraz.'

'But he'll have mineral water,' piped up Amber, smiling sweetly and pecking Rolf on the cheek. 'What did the doctor-woctor say?'

Will felt his toes curl. Listening to the way Amber and Rolf spoke to each other in those funny googoo voices adults always used for babies was hideously cringeworthy.

'No alcohol, remember?'

Rolf smiled as if he was in pain. 'How could I forget,' he muttered under his breath. He looked as if someone had just grabbed him by the balls. But then Amber, quite literally, had.

It was 6.30, and after an exhausting day spent shopping, Will had gone to the bar to meet Juliet. Although she didn't know it yet, he'd made a reservation in the hotel's restaurant for that evening as a surprise. It would be the first time they'd been out for dinner since before Valentine's Day, and after the mess he'd made of *that*, he'd decided to pull out all the stops and go for the 'wow' factor.

And this was definitely wow. Jaws dropped, not just at the exorbitant prices, but at the pristine white décor, abstract sculptures, much-written-about stainless steel bar, and the celebrities who'd been spotted propping it up drinking lychee martinis. To be honest, it wasn't Will's kind of place. It was trying that little bit too hard. Even the loos hadn't been spared. Constructed of smoked glass and the kind of uplighting that would make even the likes of Natalie Imbruglia reach for her concealer, they were so minimalist in their fixtures and fittings they'd done away with anything as silly as door handles. So if you actually wanted to use the toilet, you had to spend a good five minutes doing a kind of Marcel Marceau impression to try and locate the doors.

Amber and Rolf appeared to have no such misgivings. Perked up by the complimentary sushi on the bar, Rolf was regaling her with one of his anecdotes. Having finished pruning the last bonsai on the Japanese roof garden, he'd buzzed over from Kensington on his moped to pick up Amber. He wasn't supposed to be staying, in fact he'd only gone there so he could give Amber a lift to her – sorry, their – meditation class, but he'd managed to be persuaded to stay for a drink.

If the truth be told, it had been more a case of 'try stopping him'. Rolf wasn't looking forward to his meditation class. Paying some old hippie a tenner to tell him to sit still and not speak had cleared his mind of everything but two words: 'taken' and 'ride'.

'So what did you buy?' he asked, pausing momentarily from wolfing down cucumber rolls and motioning to the bags that formed a small mountain around their barstools.

'Er . . . actually most of those are mine, pumpkin,' confessed Amber, attempting to create a diversion by folding her arms tightly so as to push out her cleavage. Supposedly having accompanied Will in an advisory role, she'd ended up doing most of the shopping.

'Just to keep you company,' she'd explained, staggering to the cash desk weighed down with armfuls of Jigsaw jumpers.

The cleavage trick seemed to work. Instead of continuing his line of questioning, Rolf squeezed her thigh lustfully and announced, 'We should probably be making a move. Got a busy night ahead of us.'

'What? Meditation?' smirked Will.

'And the rest,' smirked back Rolf, ducking as Amber swatted him like a mosquito and began giggling in the high-pitched nervy way she always did when she was turned on.

Wasting no time, he began zipping up his anorak, grabbed his helmet and all Amber's bags, while she planted a White Musky kiss on Will's cheek. 'Juliet's going to love it,' she whispered encouragingly.

'I hope so,' Will murmured. Because there was no way he was doing this again, Will thought as he watched Amber turning and striding ahead, chivvying Rolf. As much as he loved her, she was bloody hard work.

'Oh, by the way, I almost forgot.' As Amber disappeared into the foyer, Rolf turned round.

'What?' Will knew what was coming next. He often used the same excuse to Juliet. Pretending to have forgotten something meant there was something he hadn't done and couldn't be arsed to do.

'About the Japanese job. The client didn't make it back in time to settle the bill . . .'

Will rolled his eyes. They were so deep in debt he daren't even *think* what Rolf was going to say next.

'. . . but he said that he'd leave us a cheque.'

Will visibly relaxed.

'He's going back to the house to pick up his passport on the way to the airport, I think he's flying to Europe or did he say New York . . .' Rolf paused. 'Well anyway, it just means one of us has to go over there tonight and pick it up. That way it can go in the bank tomorrow morning and be cashed by Thursday. Get some of our creditors off our backs.'

'One of us?'

'Well I have been there all day,' huffed Rolf. 'You were the one who took the day off. To go shopping with my wife. *And my money*.'

Will pulled a face. He'd planned a romantic evening with Juliet. The last thing he felt like doing was picking up bloody cheques.

Rolf tried to use his powers of persuasion. He didn't want to have to go back there either. 'Oh c'mon, it'll take five minutes. And it's practically on your way home . . .'

Surrendering, Will smiled and sipped his red wine. He really felt like a cigarette but this wasn't the kind of place for roll-ups. Cigars? Yes. Cocaine. Definitely. Baggy old Rizlas stuffed with Drum? Only if people thought it was a joint. 'Go on, go to your meditation class.' He waved him away. 'Amber will make you suffer if you miss it.'

'That's what I'm hoping,' he winked.

'*Rolfie*.' Amber could be heard howling in the foyer.

'You better go. It's the call of the wild.' Will grinned.

'Tell Juliet we're sorry we missed her.'

'I will.'

'*Rolfeeeeeee*.'

'Just coming, princess.'

Watching the retreating figure of Rolf, Will looked at his watch. Juliet was fifteen minutes late. Crossing his mind that she might be getting her own back, he dug out his mobile.

* * *

Hurrying across Soho, trying to avoid bumping into the early evening crowd, Juliet thought she could hear the faint ringing of her phone. Stopping to find it in her bag, she looked at the illuminated screen. It was Will.

'Jules? Where are you?'

'Two minutes away.' Which really meant five.

'Is something up?'

Could he tell? She hesitated, then denied it. 'No.'

'*Jules.*' For once, Will was being insightful.

She gave in. 'OK . . . but I don't want to tell you over the phone.' Dashing across the street, she dodged a minicab. 'I'll tell you when I see you . . . I'll be there in five minutes.'

'I thought you said two?'

'Order me a drink, a strong one.'

Ending the call, she dug her bare hands in her pockets, flinching as the material pressed against her fingers. They were sore, but then it was hardly surprising after she'd been sitting at her desk all day, doggedly chewing, picking and biting them in nervous agitation. She'd even had to resort to making a make-shift plaster out of Sellotape as her thumb had started bleeding all over her in-tray.

A head wind had whipped up. Putting her head down into her fur collar, Juliet broke into a trot. Compared to the suffocating tension of the office, it was a relief to be finally outside in the anonymous buzz and noise of Soho. After watching her account director going into Magnus's office that morning, she'd turned into a bundle of worry and neuroses. What was she saying in there? What were they talking about? *Who* were they talking about? Keeping vigil outside, she'd pretended to start work on a couple of new accounts they'd acquired, half-heartedly typing out a few faxes, sending a few emails, until, after an hour, his door had finally opened.

Gabby and Magnus had emerged. They'd both looked serious, but while he'd seemed genuinely sombre, she'd looked pantomimishly serious. All Anne-Robinson-*Weakest-Link* frowns and gloating stares, she'd taken off her signature shades, revelling in every single dramatic minute. Juliet had watched as they'd walked towards reception, Gabby casting a regal eye around the office before disappearing into the lift. According to Annette, the official gossip line, they'd spent the whole day in a meeting in the chairman's office.

By the time the little clock on her iMac showed 18.10, it had begun to dawn on Juliet that maybe she'd jumped to the wrong conclusion. If she was in big trouble, surely she would have been summoned by now and presented with her P45? Not left sitting at her desk playing Patience on her iMac. Looking around the office she saw that most people had drifted off home. Neesha had already left to meet some suitor or other, Danny and Seth had buggered off at 4.30. She was practically the only one left.

She'd felt herself begin to relax as her rational side began to surface. All that panicking for nothing. It had been entirely innocent. It was just those pangs of guilt making her paranoid.

'Juliet, have you got a few minutes?'

With a start she'd looked up to see Magnus looming next to her. She'd been so deep in thought she hadn't seen him reappear from the lift and walk over to her desk. Or heard him. Those Birkenstocks of his allowed him to creep around without making a noise.

'Erm . . .yeah, I mean, no . . .'

'Could I see you in my office?'

Oh bloody hell. Juliet had felt a wave of fear. Magnus wasn't being his usual smiley, flirty, awkward self. Instead he was trying to be terribly official and managerial, a role which he was painfully uncomfortable with, hence the reddening of his already ruddy cheeks and the way he nervously tapped his fingertips together as if he was Prince Charles opening a hospital.

Her throat seemed to constrict and she forced herself to swallow. She'd been right all along. Her worst fears had been founded. Sykes had stolen their campaign idea, in fact he hadn't stolen their idea he'd been given it, thought Juliet in angry disbelief at her stupidity. Not that she could ever prove it as he would have changed it a little, made it his own. Like he'd said in Verona, 'it happened all the time'. But if that wasn't bad enough he'd vindictively decided to throw doubt on *her* integrity. Which is why he'd spoken to Gabby. Who'd spoken to Magnus. Who'd spoken to the head honcho. This was the executioner's order, she was going to be fired. After all those years of hard work and slog, all those endless applications, she was going to end up losing the job she'd fought so hard for.

It took less than a couple of seconds for all these thoughts to charge screaming through her head, then Juliet gave Magnus what she hoped was a smile of confidence and innocence. 'Sure. I'll be right there.' Resisting the urge to start clearing her desk, she'd walked the plank into his office.

Will looked up from making patterns in the ashtray with the end of his roll-up to see Juliet at the entrance to the bar. Flushed and messy-haired from the wind, she was quickly checking her appearance in the full-length mirrors, tugging at her skirt, wiping away a smear of eyeliner when she thought no-one was looking. Watching her frowning at herself, Will thought how wonderful she looked. Perversely, he always thought she looked the loveliest when she thought she looked her worst.

Catching Will's reflection behind her in the mirror, Juliet turned and walked towards him. Smiling, Will held out the lychee martini he'd ordered for her. Well, if it was good enough for Madonna . . .

Juliet took it from him and, before saying a word, took a large gulp.

Wrapping one hand around her waist, Will pulled her towards him. 'So?' Bemused, he gazed at her.

Still stunned by what had happened, Juliet savoured the sting of alcohol at the back of the throat. Connecting with Will's gaze, she took a big breath. It was difficult to even say the words.

'I've been promoted.'

Will's reaction was immediate. 'Wow, that's fantastic.' He knew just how much this meant to her. Whooping, he threw his arms around her shoulders, engulfing her in a huge hug. 'Well done, Jules, that's amazing.' He proudly cupped her face in his hands and gave her a kiss. 'I had no idea you were up for promotion.'

She shook her head incredulously. 'Me neither.'

And Juliet meant it. She could barely believe it. She'd been in a state of shock ever since Magnus had called her into his office, asked her to sit down and then proceeded to tell her, in fits and stammers, that Gabby had resigned and would she be interested in becoming their new account director? In fact, she'd been so taken aback, it was only after Magnus had continued waffling for at least another twenty minutes about benefits and pay rises, that she'd thought to ask why Gabby had left.

'She's gone over to the other side,' he'd replied simply. 'Head of accounts at Montague & Murdoch.' If Juliet hadn't been completely in shock by this point, this news would have tipped her into full-blown speechlessness. Luckily Magnus, being Magnus, was on a roll and she hadn't had to say anything as he elaborated on what had to be the biggest piece of office gossip since he'd gone native in Goa.

'As you probably know, there's never been any love lost between myself and Gabriella. Her ambitions are like most people's – power, money and acclaim – whereas my own are to master yogic breathing, learn how to give a damn good shiatsu massage, and of course, to create some brilliantly groundbreaking ad campaigns.' At this reference to his achievements, he'd proudly puffed out his chest. 'It would appear that a rather obscene pay rise and the chance to work in Italy with one of their hot-shot creatives, Roberto Sykes, was too tempting an offer.'

Work in Italy with Sykes? At the mention of his name, it had all become clear to Juliet. So *that* was why Gabby was in the car with Sykes this morning. She felt an enormous sense of relief. It had had nothing to do with her. Or Sykes, for that matter. He hadn't 'stolen' their campaign idea, *it was Gabby*. Magnus had said it himself. '*She's gone over to the other side.*' Gabby had turned traitor and sold their ad campaign secrets for the price of a new job and a huge great fat pay rise. And to get her own back on Magnus, Juliet thought, remembering that first meeting with BMZ and how Gabby had given Magnus a look that could have killed.

'So the rumours *are* true.' Juliet had finally found her voice. 'In the office everyone's saying Montague & Murdoch pitched the same idea as ours for the MAXI account. It was Gabby who told them, wasn't it?' Juliet had wanted confirmation from Magnus, but instead he'd broken into what the office called 'his Mona Lisa smile'. It was usually the cue that he was going to start quoting some Chinese proverb or Dalai Lama teaching from one of the many hundreds of 'life-changing' books crammed on his shelves. This time was no different.

'Gossip and rumours are dangerous animals. Be careful. Their growls frighten others, but they have been known to bite the hands that feed them.'

Juliet really hadn't known what he was going on about. It was like one of those clues from that awful treasure hunt programme with Anneka Rice that she used to watch as a kid. But Magnus was taking it all totally seriously. To make it appear more profound, he'd nodded sagely. A little touch he'd copied from the teacher in the *Karate Kid* videos.

'So it's true?' Juliet had persisted.

Magnus hadn't answered, but by his refusal to deny it he'd confirmed that it was. 'Why don't we just wait and see until after the weekend?' he'd smiled, attempting evasiveness. 'BMZ have promised to give us their decision on Monday. And anyway, don't dwell on Gabriella, concentrate on patting yourself on the back.' He'd slipped effortlessly back into his Tony Blair mode. 'You've done remarkably well, and I'm delighted to be the bearer of such wonderful news.' With that, he'd reclined back on his large leather pouffe and begun practising that yogic breathing.

'You don't seem pleased.'

Will broke Juliet's thoughts, and she zoned back into the bar with a jolt.

'What? Oh, yeah . . . I am . . . I am . . .' she nodded as if to convince herself. She was more than pleased, she was ecstatic, but it was difficult to take it all in. It had all happened out of the blue. 'It's just going to take a bit of getting used to. Me, Juliet Morris, *account director*.' There, she'd finally said it. For the first time, Juliet felt a little glow of pride. Hearing herself say the words out loud to Will, she finally allowed herself to believe it. This was for real.

And at the realization, a smile broke across her face. She knew it was going to stay there for days.

Chapter Thirty-nine

After two more lychee martinis and a bottle of Dom Perignon, which Will had ordered without daring to look at the price list, they continued their celebrations in the restaurant.

'Crikey, this is all very posh,' laughed Juliet, clinking glasses with Will as they polished off the last dribbles of champagne. They'd just eaten what had to be the most fabulous meal of their entire lives. With all the hype surrounding the restaurant, Juliet couldn't see how it could live up to its reputation, but it had, and more.

The starters of quail eggs, pine nuts and avocado had been so beautifully arranged she'd been sad to mess it all up with her knife and fork – but she had, with more than a little help from Will who'd dived in with his soup spoon to mop up the leftovers. The main courses had been something else. Roasted swordfish, coriander mash and caramelized red onions had appeared on spotlessly white plates, and in those elegantly stacked layers much loved by cookery books. In their own kitchen, she and Will veered more towards the more low-rise splurge on a plate look.

As the waiter cleared their table, Juliet grinned at Will. 'When you said you were taking me out to dinner I was expecting Pizza Express.'

'They were fully booked,' he quipped, leaning across the table and wrapping his hands around hers. Woozy with all that alcohol, his initial inhibitions about being in a very posh restaurant, under the watchful eye of formal cream-coated waiters, had disappeared along with the bottle of Dom Perignon. Unconcerned with who might be looking – and nobody was – he was enjoying being overtly affectionate. 'I feel like you're miles away over there,' he grumbled.

Juliet smiled. Will was funny when he'd had a few drinks. 'So why don't you come and sit next to me?'

'I don't know. Why don't I?' He grinned, picking up his chair and plonking it next to hers, much to the consternation of the waiter, who frowned at the mess Will was making of his carefully organized seating plan. 'Mmmm, that's much better.'

Laughing, Juliet glanced at the space where his chair had been, and for the first time noticed a billboard-sized carrier bag. Earlier she'd been too stunned about her promotion to notice anything. 'Aha . . . so that's what you've been up to all day,' she grinned, raising her eyebrows as one of the ever watchful waiters bent to pick it up and deposited it mutely next to Will. 'Don't tell me, you've bought something to wear instead of that mangy old fleece.'

'What's wrong with my fleece?'

Putting down her champagne flute, Juliet sighed in exasperation. 'It's full of holes . . .' Pausing, she pressed her mouth against his ear and whispered loudly. 'And it smells.'

Will smiled ruefully. 'Well, sorry to disappoint you, but no, I didn't.'

She pulled a face.

Retrieving the bag, he put it on the table. 'I bought a present for you, instead.'

Taken aback, she looked at it, and then back at Will. Juliet was puzzled. 'It's not my birthday, you know,' she said, a smile spreading across her face. 'Actually, if it was you'd probably have forgotten it.'

Draining his glass, Will shrugged. 'Fair point. I admit, I don't have the best track record for birthday presents.' Putting his champagne flute on the table, he fiddled self-consciously with the glass stem. 'I just wanted to buy you something. You know, after everything that's happened . . .' His voice trailed off, as the old feelings of embarrassment took over. He was a Yorkshireman. Even though he felt like being a soppy romantic, it would take more than a few martinis and a bottle of fizz to hammer out years of indoctrination in how not to show your feelings. He deflected the spotlight from himself, by gesturing to the bag. 'Well go on then, open it.'

Juliet stared at the inviting pink carrier. Now it was on the table she could see the logo printed on the side. *Agent Provocateur*. She was impressed. For a man who thought all women's underwear came in three-packs from M&S, *she was very impressed*. Excited, she peeped inside. A fuchsia, tissue-papered bundle lurked between the paper bag walls.

'Oh my God,' she gasped. 'Are you sure I should open it in here?' Gazing at the delicate package, Juliet had the same expression as the women who huddled around the window of Tiffany's, staring at the diamond rings. Will had never bought her underwear before. It was terribly sexist, and terribly clichéd, but tearing away a thumbnail of tissue paper and catching a glimpse of black lace beneath, she felt a thrill shiver up her spine. *It was wonderfully romantic*

Juliet loved it. She loved that he thought she was sexy enough to wear sexy underwear. She loved the thought that he'd made the effort to find out which was the best lingerie shop in London – and by best she wasn't talking Rigby and Peller, she was talking the erotic, glamorous and completely impractical kind of lingerie that wasn't made for comfort, or fit, or to wear under those work trousers with control panels and no pantyline. It existed purely to make a woman feel fabulous.

She looked back at Will. More than anything, she

loved the thought that he'd walked into the shop and bought her underwear. After two and a half years together, Juliet knew how embarrassed Will could get about stuff like that, and the fact that he'd done it showed just how much he cared. Even so, that didn't stop the sneaky suspicion that Trudy must have something to do with this. 'You chose this yourself?'

Will looked sheepish. 'I had a little help,' he admitted, trying not to redden as he remembered being in Agent Provocateur with Amber, who'd abandoned him and dived off to look at lacy G-strings. How he'd been left lurking behind the padded plunges, fingering the gel inserts and feeling as if he'd been cheated all his life, when he'd been swooped upon by the assistant as if he was a dirty old man.

'Looking for something in particular?' she'd bellowed as he'd blushed the colour of the scarlet corset. Fortunately, Amber had overheard (it would have been impossible not to) and come to his rescue. 'He wants something sexy, but not tarty. Romantic, but not corny. Perhaps something in black, sheer, but with embroidery and a little Chantilly lace. In a 34B, underwired or multiway, with a little padding if you've got it. And for the knickers either a high leg or a thong.' Will had listened in amazement. Thank God he hadn't attempted this without back-up. He had *no idea* it was this complicated.

'Oh, Will, thank you.' Putting her arms around him, Juliet kissed him tipsily on the lips, thinking how much she loved getting drunk with Will in restaurants, how lovely he looked in a white shirt instead of an old T-shirt, and how much she loved her new underwear.

Will kissed her back. *Mmmmm.* He'd always pooh-poohed this whole present buying thing, but perhaps he should do it more often. He broke away before it turned into a full-bodied snog in the middle of the restaurant. 'I got you something else as well.'

'More presents?' She was enjoying this.

'Now don't get too excited . . .'

Juliet reached for her champagne. 'Don't tell me, it's a new lampshade,' she laughed, remembering how she'd confronted him about Violet's tasselled monstrosity last week. And how they'd decided that it was so awful, they should leave it. After all, it was kind of symbolic . . .

'Something like that.' Digging into the pocket of his coat (he'd had to fight the waiter to leave it hanging over the back of his chair), Will held out something that was green and gold and shiny, with lots of glittery bits.

It was a cracker.

Juliet stared at it, bemused. 'There's a punchline, right?'

He shrugged. 'Pull it and see.'

Sighing, she played along. Putting down her drink, she clutched the gaudy tinfoil end of the cracker and pulled. The other diners in the restaurant turned round at the rather louder than expected bang, as did the waiters, whose expressions caused Juliet and Will to hoot with the kind of laughter reserved for drunken nights only. Giddily, she unfurled the crêpe paper hat and placed it skewwhiffily on Will's head, before leaning forward to pick out the small plastic toy that had fallen out and rolled behind the condiments.

Except it wasn't a small plastic toy. *It was a small velvet box*.

Abruptly, Juliet stopped laughing.

Wow. For a moment she couldn't do anything but stare at it sitting upright in the palm of her hand. *Wowee*. This wasn't what she thought it was. *Was it?* Hearing her heart loud in her ears, she slowly turned the box over, gazing at the small silver hinges, the navy blue velvet. Wanting to absorb every tiny detail before slowly easing it open.

A delicate antique ring nestled inside. A square ruby set simply in a gold band. It wasn't flashy, or trendy, or ostentatious. It was just perfect. Until now, every piece of jewellery Juliet owned was silver, she didn't even like gold. But this changed her mind for ever. This had to be the most wonderful ring she'd ever seen.

'It's beautiful.' Glancing up, she caught Will staring at her, chewing his lip and looking very, *very* nervous. As he had been for the last few moments as he'd waited for her reaction. Juliet noticed the pulse in his neck beating a drum roll. Oh God, this *was* what she thought it was. Juliet tried to swallow. It felt as if every single atom in her body was on pause. Suspended in the air. A freeze frame photograph. *This. Here. Now.* Now she knew the real meaning of the Wow-factor.

'I know what you're thinking . . .' Will's words brought everything back up to full speed. 'I always said I didn't believe in marriage, and I know that I went on about all those statistics and stuff if it was ever mentioned . . .' He swallowed nervously. He knew he was babbling uncontrollably but he was powerless to stop. He needed to get it all out in one big stream of consciousness. Any attempt at punctuation and he'd lose his nerve. 'And I know we've never really talked about it before, which is probably my fault as I always changed the subject if you ever mentioned it, not that you ever did really. I mean you've never been one of those women for whom walking down the aisle in those big tents is a lifelong ambition . . .'

Juliet watched him as he half laughed, then thought better of trying to make a joke and continued.

'And so I don't even know if you want to . . . with me, that is . . . In fact, knowing me I've probably got this all wrong . . .'

'Can I get a word in edgeways?'

Will fell silent.

Holding the small velvet box in her hand, Juliet looked directly into his big shaggy dog eyes. 'Yes.'

He hesitated. 'What? You mean yes I've got this all wrong, or yes you want to get married?'

Juliet suddenly started laughing. Only Will could make such a balls-up of a simple proposal. 'Yes, I want to marry you.' She grinned ecstatically. 'Though you can ask me if you want to.'

'Oh . . . yeah.' Clumsily wiggling the ring out of the box, Will paused to try and pull himself together. All that champagne had helped his nerves, but it wasn't much good for his co-ordination. Looking at Juliet's hands, he realized he didn't have a clue which finger it went on.

Seeing his hesitation, she helped by proffering her left hand.

Will gave himself a second. He took a breath before gently easing the ring onto her finger. It wasn't a perfect fit, but it was pretty near as damn it. He cleared his throat, feeling suddenly grown up.

'Juliet Morris, will you marry me?'

'Yes I will, William Barraclough.'

It was as simple as that.

For the next few moments they just looked at each other. Euphoric. Giddy. Drunk. Loved up. Incredulous. Engaged. No, rewind that bit. Juliet hated the word engaged. It reminded her of toilet cubicles. *She was getting married*. No longer would Will be her partner, or long-term boyfriend, no longer would their relationship be an 'Is this it?'

This *was* it.

She was going to be Will's wife, he was going to be her husband, and it was the most fabulous thing that had ever happened in her whole life. It leapfrogged right over her promotion. Knowing she was going to spend the rest of her life with this man, in his purple crêpe paper party hat, and the flushed red cheeks from those lychee martinis, and the bits of avocado he'd managed to squash down his shirt like a potato print. *This* was in a completely different stratosphere.

Rubbing her thumb down the side of his face, she smiled teasingly. She had to ask.

'Are you sure this isn't one of your jokes?'

Leaning towards her, Will gently, and firmly, kissed the smile on her face.

'I've never been more serious.'

Chapter Forty

Hurtling through the back streets of Soho in a boneshaker of a black cab, Will and Juliet cuddled up together, kissing like a couple of teenagers.

'Maybe we shouldn't have had that second bottle of champagne,' giggled Juliet, being jolted apart from him as the cabbie flung them around a corner.

'I think that's what my credit card company thought,' smiled Will ruefully, trying to ignore the enormous hard-on he could feel pressing against the button-fly of his jeans. Proposing marriage was a stressful business, but the exhilaration afterwards when Juliet had said yes was definitely worth it. He felt over the moon. And as horny as hell. He couldn't wait to get back to the flat. He gazed at Juliet. She was all drunk and delicious. Silently he thanked the Lord that he'd changed his views about buying underwear. It was like two presents in one. Only he got to open his when he got home.

'Did you see the waiter's face when your card was refused?' Juliet's voice petered out in a squeak as she dissolved uncontrollably into drunken laughter.

It was infectious. 'Did you see *my* face?' he protested in mock seriousness until, unable to keep it up, he started laughing.

Will had a funny laugh. His eyes crinkled up and disappeared, and he opened his mouth so wide that you could see his large number of fillings. But hardly any noise came out. It was a silent movie laugh, the odd squeak now and again. 'I take my girlfriend out for a romantic dinner, ask her to marry me, and she ends up footing the bill.'

'And you left that awful party hat as a tip,' reminded Juliet, wiping away a tear of laughter that spilled onto her cheek.

Holding his head in his hands, Will half laughed, half groaned. Christ, he must be drunk. What a naff thing to do. *And he'd thought it was funny*. Looking up at Juliet, he saw her gazing at the ring on her finger. Angling it towards the street lamps, so the ruby glittered in the orange light. He felt a glow of contented happiness. Why hadn't he done this months ago?

She caught him watching her. 'It really is a beautiful ring,' she murmured dreamily. 'Where did you find it?'

'Oh, you know . . .' he shrugged. 'It came out of a cracker.'

Juliet's mouth split into a grin. 'You bloody idiot,' she gasped, swatting his chest, before collapsing against him. With his arms around her, she snuggled up against his woollen shoulder and let her gaze drift absent-mindedly out of the window. The cab had slowed down in traffic and outside was bustling with lights and noise. A faint drizzle had started to fall and she could make out shapes of people standing on the edge of the pavement trying to hail cabs, staring enviously in through their window as they drove past, just as she'd done on Valentine's night.

Snug and safe, with the heat of Will's body seeping through her coat, Juliet knew that after everything that had happened, all the doubts, fears, mistakes and insecurities, she'd got what she'd always wanted. Finally she was on the other side of the glass.

She wasn't looking in any more. She was looking out.

'Is it straight across at the roundabout?' Heading towards Shepherd's Bush, the driver slid back his window to ask for directions.

Will nodded. 'Yeah . . . straight on . . .' before out of

the fog of champagne and euphoria, a fuzzy memory loomed. 'Oh . . . hang on. Could you hang a left here?' 'Hang a left' was Will's feeble attempt at trying to be matey with the cabbie, a baldheaded Buster Bloodvessel type who'd been listening to the wrestling ever since Soho. The cab braked sharply, and veered left. 'I need to go somewhere on the way.'

Thrown against him on the back seat, Juliet frowned. 'But I thought we were going straight home?' She squinted at her watch. 'It's nearly midnight.'

'I've just got to pick up a cheque for the roof garden.'

'Can't you do it tomorrow?' She slipped her hand underneath his shirt as a little gentle persuasion.

It didn't take much to persuade Will. He was severely tempted, but he was severely broke as well. He smiled apologetically, and made a mental note to kill Rolf when he next saw him. 'You don't mind, do you?' he asked.

Juliet pretended to think about it for a few moments, before answering, 'Well, I guess I'll finally get to see what you've been up to for the last few weeks.' Breaking into a smile, she jabbed him in the ribs. 'Though I don't see why business should come first.'

Grabbing her, Will did his 007 wink. 'Don't worry, we'll come later.'

They swung off the busy main road and into a small narrow mews. The noise of the exhaust ricocheted loudly against the garages as the cab jolted over the cobbles like a badly sprung mattress, grinding to a juddering halt at the dead end. Using some of the mateyness he'd built up with the cabbie, Will asked him if he'd mind waiting for five minutes – a favour he was only too happy to agree to, considering the wrestling was in the last round – and, shoving open the door, stepped into the darkness.

Juliet followed. 'Won't the owner be in bed?' she giggled, warm and fuzzy with alcohol. She stumbled slightly on the cobbles and clung onto Will.

He grinned with amusement. 'No, he's away on business.' Pulling a bunch of keys out of his pocket, he dangled them in front of her. 'We've got the whole place to ourselves.'

Avoiding a couple of bags of cement that Rolf had been too lazy to shift and had left behind on the cobbles, Juliet stood on the step as Will jiggled around with keys, trying to remember which was which. Waiting, she stared distractedly at the front door. Navy glossed and with the number thirteen in polished brass numbers, it was the type of door SGC always used in commercials at Christmas, festooned with a picture-perfect holly wreath. She couldn't help noticing it also had one of those trendy fish door knockers she'd once seen in a magazine. The cold tugged her attention back and she stuffed her hands in her pockets. She was relieved when Will finally got to grips with the Banham locks.

Pushing open the door he stepped inside and turned on the light, illuminating the scarlet hallway.

'Crikey, nice pad,' commented Juliet, closing the door behind her and following Will up the spiral staircase to the open-plan living room.

'If you like living in *Elle Décor*,' he quipped, flicking on the state-of-the-art-lighting as he moved through the house.

Juliet surveyed the room. Large and spacious, it was incredibly stylish. There was a marble fireplace filled with tall white church candles, a glass shelf neatly arranged with books with spines all aligned, two large reclining Buddhas, a real animal skin rug that lay across the floorboards. There was even an aquarium that doubled as a wall. But Will was right, it was just too fashionable. There wasn't a dodgy pair of curtains, or a chipped mug, or a tasselled lampshade in sight, she thought. It was textbook cool. Style that was less about personal taste or imagination, and a lot more about spending an afternoon in the Conran shop with a Platinum Amex.

'So what's this garden like?' she called out to Will.

'Well, it is pretty cool, even though I say it myself,' he admitted, before adding, 'Though not as cool as a promotion . . .'

'. . . or a proposal,' she corrected.

'. . . or getting married to you,' he corrected.

They both turned and looked at each other, before pulling faces.

'Oh God,' howled Juliet. 'We're starting to sound like Rolf and Amber.' Eyeing Will wickedly, she affected a baby voice. 'Pumpkin.'

'Princess.' He smirked, grabbing her and giving her a big wet sloppy kiss.

He pulled away, unlocked the French windows and flung them open. At first it was just blackness, but then he flicked another light switch. Juliet looked out in wonder. She was expecting something, but not this. Illuminated by subtle spotlights hidden underneath the decking, a tranquil Japanese garden seemed to materialize out of nothingness, as if a magician had pulled away the black cloth. A cleverly designed bamboo fountain, a rockpool full of carp and water-lilies over which arched a delicately carved bridge, and a simple teak teahouse hung with silver windchimes and shrine lanterns.

Juliet was momentarily lost for words. For months she'd moaned about Will working late, about the time he spent at his job, about putting his business before their relationship. She'd never really been able to understand why he'd given up his architect's job, his beloved sportscar and forty-five grand a year, to work his arse off in a garden, in the rain, in a scruffy old fleece and a pair of wellies. But now she could see what he could see. She could understand his dream. She felt the same buzz. Looking out at the garden was like seeing a little bit of magic.

She whispered quietly, 'It's amazing.'

'And so is this.'

She turned to see Will holding up a cheque. Leaning forward, she strained to read the small numbers printed in the amount box. 'Twelve thousand pounds?' she gasped, her eyes open wide. She'd had no idea.

Grinning, Will kissed the cheque. 'Seventeen thousand smackeroonies,' he whooped, grabbing her around the waist and twirling her around. Laughing and shrieking, they held on to each other as if it was some kind of mad, drunken, euphoric waltz. Spinning round and around, Juliet's promotion, Will's proposal, her ring, his cheque. One big fabulous merry-go-round. Until, so dizzy they were almost falling over into that very expensive carp pool, they ground to a staggering halt, eyes bright, smiles wide, catching their breath.

'God I love being drunk,' gasped Will, running his hand through his hair and swaying dangerously. He was the happiest a man could be. Never in a million years had he thought everything would work out so bloody fantastically. 'Here, take it, have a closer look.' He waved the little white slip of paper.

Revelling in Will's happiness, Juliet took it from him. Holding it to the light, she traced the one, seven, three noughts and dash with her finger, and the funny squiggly signature that was a bit like one of those heart graphs. Christ, some people had terrible signatures, they were just big messy scribbles, completely indecipherable. Abstractedly, she glanced at the name underneath.

Roberto. Alexander. Thatcher. Sykes.

An ice cold hand gripped her heart.

This was Sykes's garden.

This was Sykes's house.

Oh. My. God.

Her mind flipped out into freefall as the horror of the situation hit instantaneously. Whirling frantically, racing against time to try to piece everything together like a hideous jigsaw puzzle. It was as if spotlights were shining on the clues she hadn't noticed. The Nelson Mandela paperback that had sat neatly on his bedside table in Verona, now glared out from the bookcase, his brand of cigarettes by the telephone, her coat hanging behind the door. *Her coat?* Oh fuck, why couldn't he have hung *that* up in his wardrobe?

Her heart thumping like a piston, she darted sideways, pushing the door flat against the wall before Will saw it. He probably wouldn't notice it, never mind recognize it, but she couldn't take the risk. Now more than ever she knew Will must never know. She could never risk losing Will. With the alcohol draining from her veins, Juliet suddenly felt horribly sober.

'Come on, let's go,' she suggested, trying to sound normal when all she wanted was to get the hell out of there.

'Hang on a minute. Don't you want to see the meditation platform?'

She bit her lip and forced a smile. 'The cab's waiting.'

'Oh yeah . . . . Buster Bloodvessel.' Grinning, Will started turning off the lights and bolting the French windows. 'You know I've often wondered what this Sykes bloke's like. I've only met him the once and to be honest, I thought he was a bit of a prat. Even so, he does intrigue me. You know all he's got in his fridge is champagne . . .' Walking through the kitchen, he pulled open the door to show her. 'Actually, do you think he'll miss a bottle?' Waving one at her, he started laughing.

Juliet swallowed hard. 'Will, come on . . .'

Reluctantly putting the Cristal back and shutting the door, he sighed. 'But what I'd like to know is, does this kind of guy pull women? I mean, would you want to go out with someone who's got black and white headshots of himself framed in the bathroom, and listens to jazz . . .'

Juliet wasn't listening, she was concentrating on

trying to get Will out of there as quickly as possible. *Nearly there. Just a few seconds and they would be outside*.

'. . . and no, before you say it, I wasn't being nosy, I just wanted to put some music on the other day when Rolf and I were working, and all I could find was that bloody shite modern jazz . . .'

They were at the top of the spiral staircase. Juliet could have cried with relief. Only a few steps. They were so close she could hear the wrestling on the radio from the cab outside.

'Ladies first.' Standing to one side, Will smiled, bowing jokingly.

She gritted her teeth. But there was no time to argue. Putting one foot on the steel staircase, she heard her boots clatter in time with the thudding of her heart.

'Oh look.'

Will's voice struck fear in her stomach and Juliet twirled around. Something had caught his attention. Next to the lamp was an orange and black packet, the word 'Supersnaps' emblazoned across the front. 'I wonder where the flash sod's been, probably Monte Carlo.'

No, it was Verona, she screamed inwardly, flicking through her own mental photo album. Of Sykes with his camera, carefully setting his timer to take pictures of them together on the bridge, in the bedroom, in the bath . . .

Of Will leaning forwards, innocently reaching for the packet. 'No, Will . . . *leave them*.'

Yelling, Juliet jumped off the step and flung out her arm to grab the photographs from him. Her hand flailing against his, the look of surprise on his face as she knocked them from his fingers and they fell from his grip, freeing themselves from the packet as it flew through the air. Watching with terrifying helplessness as everything seemed to slow down. As frame by frame, the photographs fell. Fluttering, twirling, flipping and swooping. Kodak confetti scattering across the floor.

Shaking his head and laughing, Will crouched down to pick them up.

And then stopped.

Dead.

Chapter Forty-one

Silence.

A moment stretched into a void.

Will felt his body caving in around him. His whole life imploding. His future being wiped out. It was as if all his senses seemed to leave him, except for pain. A sharp, searing, gut-wrenching pain.

Cowering like a frightened animal, he crouched on the floor. Reaching out a trembling hand, he picked up one of the thirty-six photographs lying like ashes across his shoes. Shoes that, he noticed, were all scuffed around the toes. They needed polishing. In fact he was pretty sure he remembered seeing some black Mr Minit shoe polish underneath the sink, next to the Fairy Liquid . . . Unable to make sense of what was happening, his mind tried to focus on the mundane. To hide from the awful reality. But the comfort was short-lived. Will's fingers curled around a photograph, the corners sharp against his fingertips.

It was a picture of Jules, eating pizza in some café, wearing some stupid furry hat and a daft happy smile. There was a Roman arena in the background, blue sky, sunshine, a date branded in the corner. The weekend she went to Verona on a business trip. And there was something – *someone* – else.

Will's eyes flickered slowly across to the other half of the picture. He didn't want to look. He couldn't bear to look, but he couldn't stop himself. He had to look. At the dark good-looking man he recognized as his client, at his hands wrapped around Jules's waist, at his face half hidden by her hair, at him kissing her. It was the classic holiday snap of two lovers, on a romantic holiday.

Happy. Together. *In love.*

Will's face crumpled.

Juliet watched it. Standing silently in shocked disbelief, she struggled to try and think of what to say, of what to do, but there was nothing. No simple explanations, easy one-liners, quick excuses. All the reasoning she'd used before, to Trudy, to herself, crumbling and falling apart as she saw the expression on Will's face. Before it had seemed so easy, so right, so fun and exciting. She'd felt bored, ignored, unloved. Christ, now it all sounded so fucking pathetic. So inadequate. So *naïve*. A tear escaped and trickled silently down her cheek. No words could ever, *could ever* justify that look on Will's face.

'*Will* . . .' Her voice broke as she reached forward and tentatively placed her trembling hand on his shoulder.

At her touch he sprang back, stumbling to his feet. His wounded eyes met hers. His jaw clenched. His voice was low and deliberate. And desperately painful. 'Don't. Touch. Me.'

Juliet shrank back. The venom in his voice sent her reeling. Physically and emotionally. He'd never spoken to her like that before. Catching her balance, she steadied herself against the bookcase and tried again. 'I want to explain . . .'

Will exploded, his shock and hurt mutating into anger. 'You might think I'm a fucking wanker, but I'm not stupid, Juliet. I don't need a fucking explanation.' Screwing up his face, he spat out the words. Drowning in betrayal, he was clinging to his anger. It was all he had. He stepped backwards, away from Juliet, from the photographs that lay around his feet like some sick kind of shrine to his relationship. 'I don't need times or dates or places. I don't need to know how many times you've shagged him, or how good a shag he is . . .' He was shouting now and his voice was breaking. His face was white and blotchy, his eyes bloodshot. *'I don't need to know anything . . .'* He broke off, and with the sleeve of his coat he wiped away the tears that were spilling uncontrollably down his face.

Juliet felt physically sick. She'd never seen Will cry, not even when his beloved grandmother had died. He was always so laid back, always joking around, being stupid, making her laugh. She wanted the old Will back, the Will in the restaurant, the Will who'd put his arms around her in the back of the cab. *But he'd gone.*

Despite his insistence, she tried to explain. 'Will, it's over . . . me and him . . . I finished it, I told him I didn't want to see him any more. It was just a fling.' As she said it, she realized the bitter irony. Before she'd been so adamant in wanting to make Trudy believe it wasn't; now she so desperately wanted Will to believe it was.

'I don't care.' He shook his head wearily. He suddenly felt like some pathetic caricature of a betrayed husband.

'But I do.' She was crying now and her eyes were blurred with salty tears. 'I want you to know.'

'Well I don't. Don't you understand?' It's not all about what you want, Juliet, don't you get it? *It's not always about you.*' With his whole world collapsing around him, Will struggled to keep himself together.

But Juliet couldn't give up. 'I know that, and I know I've fucked up – ' she wiped her cheek. ' – but it didn't mean anything . . . it wasn't real . . . it was just . . .'

'Just what?' Shouting scornfully, Will sprang towards her, thrusting his face up close to hers. ' What is it they say? A picture says a thousand words?' Screwing up the photograph in his fist, he flung it at her. 'Well, there's enough fucking words here. What fucking else is there to say?'

Turning, he began to walk away from her towards the staircase.

'That I love you, Will. That I'm *in* love with you.' Panic screamed. She was desperate for him to believe her.

He looked back. The way he stared at her, it was as if he hated her.

'I pity you, Juliet. You don't know what love is. You don't have any fucking idea,' he shouted, his voice echoing loudly around the bare brick walls. 'You think it's Valentine's Day, and weekends in Italy. You think it's drinking champagne in some expensive restaurant and being bought stupid bloody underwear.' His eyes were swollen with crying and he was struggling to keep it together, to stop himself from completely falling apart. 'But that's just the trimmings. The decoration. *They're just gestures.*' Breaking off, he took a couple of deep breaths, trying to calm himself down. When he spoke, his voice was quieter. 'Without trust, and respect, and kindness, they don't mean shit.' Roughly brushing away bits of his fringe from his eyes, he stared hard at her. 'I thought love was about caring about someone day in and day out, about being there when it's fucking amazing, and still wanting to be there when it feels like crap. *I thought it was about for ever.*'

The disappointment in his voice was crushing and Juliet buried her face in her hands, her body convulsing with stomach-wrenching sobs that caused her to jerk and gasp for breath. She'd never felt pain like this. On the surface it was just an argument, but it wasn't the kind of argument she'd seen in movies, or TV, or in plays. It wasn't scripted and airbrushed and witty. It was raw and ugly and crude. It was about spit and snot and tears, about shouting and crying and hating yourself. About fucking up and not being able to put it right with a close-up kiss and a memorable one-liner. *About not having a happy ending.*

Suddenly aware of the band of gold on her finger, cold against her forehead, she looked up. It had to be worth one last attempt.

'Will . . . *please* . . . I'm so sorry . . .'

'I don't want a fucking apology . . .' He swore vehemently. Will knew his swearing was pathetic, but he didn't care. He wanted to kick and shout and swear and fight. He had no other way of venting his frustration against what was happening to him, *to them*. He felt so futile, so bloody helpless. 'I don't want *a fucking gesture*.'

'It's not a gesture,' wailed Juliet, her voice breaking with sobs. All she wanted to do was to put her arms around him, to stamp out the hurt, to put things back to how they were only minutes ago, but she was powerless. She'd caused all that hurt. She looked at Will, standing rigidly, an unwanted tear rolling silently down his face. Right at this moment she hated herself more than he could ever hate her.

Roughly rubbing the tears from her cheek, she gulped back emotion. Her face was swollen, make-up streaked across her puffy eyes, her nose running like some kid in a pushchair. And she didn't care. For once in her life she didn't give a shit about what she looked like. All she cared about was Will.

For a few moments neither spoke. It was eerily quiet in the mews, just the sound of their breathing, their ribcages rising and falling, their stifled sobs. The air hanging thick with hurt and anger. Raising her eyes, Juliet gazed at Will. He was staring down at the floor, his brows knitted together. Two people. One hurt.

Juliet's voice was barely a whisper. 'I love you.'

Will didn't react. For what seemed like eternity he just stood, silently, brokenly, in the middle of the room. Then dragging his eyes upwards he stared back at her.

'I don't love you.'

He spoke quietly, but his voice was hard and bitter. And like a soprano shattering glass, Juliet heard something snap deep inside.

It was the sound of her heart breaking.

Chapter Forty-two

'You look like shit.'

'I feel like shit.'

It was way too early on Saturday morning and Juliet was standing at the doorway of Trudy's flat. On the carpet beside her was a tartan suitcase. Just over a week ago she'd packed it to go to Italy with Sykes. Just over an hour ago she'd packed it and left Will.

Or rather, he'd left her.

It was so awful it wasn't even ironic.

'Cawfee's on.' Smiling supportively, Trudy waved into her cold, draughty studio. She'd heard all about what had happened when Juliet had woken her less than an hour ago, crying hysterically down the phone and gabbling nonsensically. Eventually struggling to hold it together long enough to tell her about Will proposing, finding the photographs, *finding out about Sykes*. To be honest, although Trudy wasn't going to admit it, it hadn't come as much of a surprise. Love triangles were the stuff of Shakespearian tragedies. People always got hurt. It was as inevitable as rain on bank holidays, rows in IKEA, and the fat lady singing. Who, by the expression on Juliet's face, was belting out her aria right at this very second.

Lugging her suitcase into the flat, Juliet crumpled onto the sofa. Still wearing the same clothes from last night, she hadn't showered, brushed her teeth or bothered to do anything with her hair. It hung limply from her head in knotted tangles. Which was a perfect description of her appearance. Anaesthetized by shock, she sat staring into space, tears seeping like smoke from a smouldering wreckage. She was a mess. Her life was in one great big awful mess.

After leaving Sykes's house last night, she'd gone home with Will in the cab. Nobody had spoken, neither of them had slept. At ten past seven that morning Will had emerged from the sofa, pulled on a T-shirt and jeans and smoked a roll-up in silence. At twelve minutes past he'd calmly told her they were over, unearthed his car keys and walked out of the flat, their relationship and her life.

Quick. Simple. Gone.

Over two and a half years of getting to know each other, finding out about each other's quirks and habits, building up memories, sharing experiences. Nearly a thousand days of laughing at stupid jokes, getting drunk, making love, rowing and making up again. Of discovering how much you like each other, how much you love each other. Of becoming best friends, lovers, a couple, Will & Jules.

Obliterated.

Will & Jules didn't exist any more. Juliet still couldn't believe it. It just didn't seem real. Was it really only last night she was ecstatically happy? Just a few hours since she was drunkenly kissing Will in the restaurant and he was asking her to marry him? It seemed so long ago. It felt like another life.

'Please don't say it.' She glanced up at Trudy who was padding around the kitchen in her pyjamas and a fur coat, rinsing out cups, trying to locate tea-spoons.

'Say what?'

'That you told me so.'

'Hey, come on, you know me. That's not my style.' Clutching a couple of 'I love New York' mugs, a cafetière and a box of Pop Tarts, Trudy reappeared and balanced everything precariously on top of the cluttered coffee table. 'People in glass houses and all that.' Sitting cross-legged on the floor, she waved the box. 'Do you want one? The toaster's gone and died so I'm afraid you're gonna have to eat them raw . . .' Unwrapping one, she held it up, angling it in the light. She pulled a face. 'Hmmm, maybe they do look pretty gross, but you know what?' She smiled optimistically. 'They're actually not so bad. Just a little chewy.'

Juliet shook her head. The thought of eating anything made her feel nauseous. 'No thanks, I'm not hungry.'

'Oh yeah, the heartbreak diet,' nodded Trudy sagely. 'Been there, done that, bought the T-shirt.' She began plunging the cafetière determinedly.

Juliet was hurt by her flippancy. Trudy could never have been where she was right at that moment. Trudy had never been in love. She said so herself. How could she possibly have any idea what it felt like to lose the person you love?

Unaware that she was being anything less than a firm shoulder of comfort and support, Trudy passed Juliet a mug of thick, dark treacly coffee. 'Do you want some Scotch in that?'

Juliet nodded. She couldn't help the smile that cracked her lips. It felt weird. Cradling the cup she felt the heat seeping into the palms of her hands.

Leaning around the back of the sofa, Trudy produced a bottle of Jack Daniels and began unscrewing the lid. 'So come on, tell me about what happened.'

Juliet sighed wearily. 'I've told you everything.'

'Don't you want to analyse?' Trudy was surprised. She analysed everything. And she meant, *everything*.

'There's nothing *to* analyse.' Juliet shrugged resignedly. 'It's happened. End of story.' For a few moments she stared into her coffee, fighting back tears, before looking up and forcing a smile. 'Anyway, let's change the record.'

'What do you want to listen to?'

'You.' With the cuff of her coat, Juliet blotted her eyes. They felt bruised and sore. 'And yesterday. Unless you don't want to talk about it . . .' her voice tailed off. Knowing Trudy she'd probably just want to put the whole abortion behind her, blot it out, pretend it never happened. 'I did try and call you a couple of times, but you didn't answer. I left a message.'

'I know. I got it, thanks.' Pouring a generous measure into Juliet's mug, Trudy screwed the lid back on the bottle.

'You not having any?'

'Jules, it's 8 a.m.'

'Since when has time come between you and Jack Daniels?' Juliet smiled weakly, taking a sip and feeling the alcohol burning a hot bitter path into her stomach. Looking at her friend, her face fell serious. 'Tell me truthfully, are you OK?'

Trudy allowed a smile. 'Never better.' Reaching over she took Juliet by surprise by squeezing her hand. 'Can I ask you a favour?'

'Of course you can. Christ, you do enough for me. I can't tell you how grateful I am to you for letting me stay here for a few days until . . .' Unable to finish the sentence, she tailed off.

Trudy tried to make a joke of it. 'Hey, my pigsty is your pigsty.'

Juliet smiled, rallying herself. She forced some enthusiasm. 'So c'mon, what is it?'

There was a pause. Trudy suddenly seemed nervous. Finally she spoke. 'Will you be godmother?'

It took a nanosecond for Juliet to register. 'What? . . . You mean? . . . *You didn't?*'

'I couldn't go through with it,' replied Trudy shaking her head. 'Actually that's not true. *I didn't want to go through with it.* For the first time in my whole life, I know what it feels like to fall in love. To be in love, and it's with this little guy.' She smiled unashamedly, protectively rubbing her stomach.

Juliet was unexpectedly moved. Never could she have believed fast-talking ball-breaking, hard-as-nails Trudy could be so gentle, so vulnerable, so romantic, *so in love*. This was a woman who always professed not to have a maternal bone in her body. A woman who called children stain devils. *A woman who was going to be a mum*. Juliet smiled in amazement. 'Trude, I had no idea,' she gasped.

'Neither had I,' admitted Trudy candidly. 'But sitting in that waiting room yesterday I realized that life throws all kinds of stuff at us, but we have a choice about how we deal with it. Whether we turn it into a positive or a negative,' she smiled ruefully. 'I know it sounds like earnest hippie shit, but it's true. I thought of all the reasons in the world why not to have this baby, but ultimately it was my decision. Either I could decide it was a mistake and have an abortion, or decide it was a gift and keep it.' Taking a gulp of coffee, she reached out and bit off a corner of Pop Tart. 'I went for the free gift option.'

Looking at Trudy, Juliet suddenly saw how right she was. In just 24 hours both their lives had dramatically changed, for better and for worse. But maybe that was because she was looking at hers in the wrong way. Maybe she was just feeling sorry for herself. Her mind replayed footage from last night, of the photographs fluttering through the air, Will laughing and trying to catch them, his face when he couldn't. Juliet put a line through that idea. No, there was no way anything positive could come out of that.

Trudy's story was a different one altogether. Seeing her friend so happy, Juliet couldn't resist giving her a hug. For once she didn't pull away. 'Oh Trude, I'm so pleased for you, that's fantastic, really fantastic.' Juliet truly meant it. It felt weird to be able to be so happy and yet so terribly sad at the same time, but it didn't stop her from being delighted things were finally working out for her best friend. She drained the last of her coffee then hesitated for a moment. 'But what about Fergus?' How to throw a spanner in the works, but she had to ask.

Rolling her eyes, Trudy shook her head in exasperation. For a woman spurned by the father of her unborn child in favour of another woman with his unborn child, she looked remarkably cheery. 'You're never going to believe this, but he's been calling non-stop. That's why I didn't answer the phone. The loser's had a change of heart and wants me back.'

'And?'

'*Purlease*,' she said indignantly. 'What do you take me for? I'm pregnant, not a schmuck.'

Juliet smiled. The sentimentality hadn't lasted for long. 'So how are you going to get rid of him?'

Trudy began gnawing on another Pop Tart. 'I'll tell him I'm in love with him. He'll run a fucking mile.' Gleefully she broke out laughing, jiggling her head up and down, her frizzy hair dancing around her head like a sea-anemone. Wiping away a tear trickling down her freckled cheek, she looked serious. 'But there is one huge problem I'm going to have to face now I'm keeping this baby.'

A list ran through Juliet's head. Being a single mum, telling her parents, Veronica and Larry, not having enough money, her busy job, finding space in her tiny studio flat. 'What's that?' she asked gently.

'Maternity clothes,' groaned Trudy. 'Jeez, do they suck.'

That afternoon they went for a walk on Hampstead Heath. It was Trudy's idea. Although she wasn't exactly the outdoorsy type, she couldn't stand seeing Juliet huddled on the sofa looking so upset. And anyway, after all those Pop Tarts she needed to burn off a few calories. According to the pregnancy magazines she'd bought yesterday ('Pregnancy magazines?' she used to shriek scornfully, her eyes reverting to her beloved

British *Vogue*, French *Vogue* and American *Vogue* on the shelf above) in a few weeks she was going to start showing what they termed 'a bump'. Nowhere in those magazines had there been any mention of a fat gut, or a jelly belly, or a spare tyre. Which is what she was going to end up with if she didn't start marching around the heath, pronto.

'You see, I said you'd feel better if you got some fresh air.' Thinking that she was beginning to sound like her mother, Trudy was now linking arms and propelling her up a grassy hill.

'Sorry I'm being so pathetic, I know,' apologized Juliet, who'd spent the last half an hour trudging zombified around the lake, working her way through a pack of full-strength Malboros and staring fixedly at a mobile that hadn't rung. Seven hours had dragged by since she'd seen Will. It felt like seven years. In desperation she'd convinced herself that perhaps he hadn't found the note she'd left telling him she'd gone to Trudy's, that maybe he'd forgotten her mobile number, that perhaps he was at home hoping she'd ring. And so she had. Except he hadn't been at home. Just the answering machine and their message. The message she'd recorded.

Listening to her own voice had been like listening to that of a completely different person. A confident, breezy, happy person. Probably because she was, then. '*Hi this is Will and Jules, we're not in at the moment, but if you leave a message we'll get straight back to you.*' She'd left several, at home and on his mobile. Slowly repeating her numbers, saying she loved him, asking him to call her back.

He hadn't.

'You're not being pathetic. You're being perfectly normal, whatever that is.' Wearing ski goggles, kitten-heeled alligator boots, a fur coat, rabbit hat and any other bit of dead animal she could find, Trudy was getting some strange looks from the happy families swarming around with their 2.4 children, Gap sweat-shirts and obligatory yapping dog.

'Oh look, kites,' she suddenly enthused, trying to hide the drips of scorn in her voice. If there was one thing she'd never understood, it was people and kites.

Pausing to watch a scattering of T-shirted people with ruddy triceps, gambling around on the grass verge as if it was the height of summer, zipping and whirring scraps of coloured nylon around in the sky, Trudy tried to make encouraging noises. 'Ooh, look at that one . . . and that big one . . . and the funny one with dangly bits . . .' she exclaimed, nudging Juliet in the ribs and hoping that a good *double entendre* would bring a smile to her face. Even if it was one of derision.

But Juliet only looked even more gutted. 'Will and I used to have a joke about kite flying . . .' she muttered, reminded of the first night they'd slept together.

Seeing that the supportive, consoling, encouraging friend bit was doing no good whatsoever in making Juliet feel better, in fact it only seemed to be making her feel worse, Trudy decided to change tack. 'Breaking up with Will might not be such a bad thing, you know.'

Dragging painfully on a cigarette, Juliet looked across at her, startled.

'Once you're over the shock, you'll probably realize it's just a case of only wanting Will because you can't have him.' Trudy was playing Devil's advocate. 'I mean it was only last weekend you were with Sykes in Verona. *Having sex.*'

Juliet's face burned. She couldn't believe what she was hearing.

Seeing her furious expression, Trudy shrugged apologetically. 'I'm sorry if you don't want to hear it, Jules, but it's true.'

Finding her voice, Juliet rounded on her indignantly. 'Fucking hell, Trude, how can you say that? How can you even *think* that? How I felt about Sykes had nothing to do with Will.' She scowled angrily.

Trudy was delighted. Anger was good. Indignation was good. Anything but that godawful blanket of sadness. She pulled a face. 'Oh c'mon, it's got everything to do with Will. *With you and Will.* If you'd been happy, and I mean really happy with Will, if you'd thought he really loved you, if he hadn't stood you up on Valentine's Day, and let you down at the ball, and fallen asleep on the sofa every night, and taken you for granted, and all that other stuff you used to moan about, you wouldn't have even looked twice at some player like Sykes.' She paused to draw breath. Juliet wasn't saying anything. She was chewing her lips agitatedly and looking the other way, staring at the murky grey London skyline. 'Look, I'm not saying Will's to blame for all this, but neither are you. You're being *way* too hard on yourself.' Her voice softening, she put a furry arm around Juliet's shoulder, expecting her to shrug it off angrily. But she didn't. 'Your fling, or affair, or whatever you wanna call it with Sykes, isn't the reason you and Will have broken up. It was going wrong long before he appeared on the scene. He was just a symptom.'

'But if Will had never seen those photographs . . .' protested Juliet quietly.

'But if there'd never been any photographs in the first place . . .' reminded Trudy firmly.

For a few moments they both stood in strained silence. Bathed in weak March sunshine they stared out across the heath, watching wiggling dots of walkers in the distance, divorced fathers on their access day buying '99' ice-creams for their cherubic four-year-olds and trying to get to know them again, young couples strolling along the paths, a hand in each back pocket, new mums trying to do a three-point turn with their shiny three-wheeler prams. Tens, hundreds, thousands of people they didn't even know. Strangers with lives, friends, hopes and worries. Just like theirs.

'He'll come round, you know what men are like,'

cajoled Trudy, feeling a touch guilty after her outburst. True though it was, perhaps she was being a bit hard on Juliet. Admittedly, she'd never seen her look this terrible. Her face was battle-scarred with dried-on tears, foundation and streaks of mascara, but it wasn't just about what was on the outside. It was about what was going on on the inside.

'He won't.' Tossing her cigarette to the ground, Juliet squashed it flat with the sole of her boot and immediately took out another. It was her last one. Digging out the small box of matches, she began striking one after another. Her hand trembled as she tried unsuccessfully to keep one alight. 'You didn't see his face.'

Leaning towards her, Trudy cupped her hands protectively around a dying flame. It flickered hesitantly, before making up its mind to burn brightly. 'Just give him a few days.'

Chapter Forty-three

So Juliet gave Will a few days. It sounded so easy. A few days. It was vague, flippant, *inconsequential*. 'See you in a few days', 'I'm going away for a few days', 'I'll have this report ready in a few days.' It could be anything from 48 hours to nearly a week because it didn't matter. It mattered to Juliet.

It mattered so much she could barely function for watching the clock. Counting off the seconds, minutes, hours that stretched with agonizing slowness as the weekend finally surrendered itself up to Monday morning and she got up from the sofa and numbly went through the motions of showering, putting on clean clothes, drying her hair, applying make-up.

It crossed her mind to ring the office and say she was sick. She *was* sick. She couldn't eat, she couldn't sleep, she couldn't think. Engulfed in a kind of waking nightmare she was reminded of one of Danny's T-shirts. It bore the slogan, 'Remember to breathe'. Juliet needed reminding. Just as she needed, craved, *yearned* for the comforting familiarity that going to work would give her. Walking through Soho, buying her cappuccino and bagel from Mario, chatting to Annette in reception, sitting at her desk and listening to Dean Martin crooning as she turned on her iMac. Juliet wanted to step back into her old world, and for a few hours at least, fool herself into thinking life was as it had been before.

So she walked to Hampstead tube station, rode down

in a lift, sat on a train, rode up on an escalator, walked out of Oxford Circus station and walked into the office. Everyone greeted her as they always did. A couple of grunts from Danny and Seth, a granary grin from Neesha, a rundown of Saturday night from Annette. Then she sat down at her desk, turned on her computer, sipped her cappuccino and kept herself busy all day. Working through lunch, talking to clients, returning emails and building a mental barrier that blocked out any incoming thoughts of Will. Convincing herself that nothing had changed.

When everything had changed.

At 5 p.m. Magnus called a meeting in the boardroom to explain Gabby's empty office and formally announced Juliet's promotion to account director. Showered with congratulations she smiled accordingly, thanking Magnus for his speech, laughing at all the usual derisory jokes from the creatives, saying how pleased and delighted she was.

It was all a lie.

Inside she felt numb. No flicker of pride or satisfaction, just a great big emptiness. It was brutally ironic. She'd wanted this promotion so badly, yet now it was hers, she couldn't have cared less.

Which was exactly how she felt when Magnus launched into his 'last but not least' speech, a verbal drum roll that led up to his second newsflash. '. . . These past few weeks have been bloody hard work, and we've produced some cracking good work, but now we can finally begin to reap the fruits of our labours. Because what I'm here to announce today, as well as Juliet's promotion which is so thoroughly deserved – ' he threw her a smile – 'is to say Jolly Well Done. We have lift-off. *We've won the MAXI account*, and so—'

The whole office erupted. It had been holding its breath for weeks and before Magnus could finish speaking, his words were drowned out in loud cheers, exuberant bawling, the kind of whooping you'd expect at an American baseball match, courtesy of the librarian-looking woman from accounts that nobody had ever heard speak before.

'Oh fuck I don't believe it man, I don't believe it man,' ranted Seth and Danny, punching the air and grinning at each other inanely.

'Wow cool, does this mean a pay rise?' chirped Neesha, making a mental note to delete her CV and recent job application forms from her computer.

'Champers, champers,' chanted Annette who'd abandoned reception and was racing wobblingly on her stilettos towards the loos to cake on the make-up in preparation for the evening's celebrations.

Everyone spilled out of the boardroom, all the usual backstabbing, bitching, grumbling and sniping replaced with grinning, joking, laughing camaraderie. Hurrying back to their desks they collected bags, coats, laptops, mobiles and, with the promise of free champagne at the bar around the corner, vacated the office faster than any fire drill.

'Juliet, are you coming?' It was Neesha.

'You go ahead. I'll catch you up. I've just got a few things to sort out.'

'Are you sure?' Neesha looked relieved. For a moment there she thought she might have to stay behind and actually do some work.

'Yeah, 'course.'

Grinning, Neesha hurried back up the corridor. Juliet watched her tiny figure disappear into reception and listened to the chime of the lift doors opening and closing. She was lying. She wasn't going. She couldn't face it. Seeing everyone around so happy and excited would be like watching a movie with the sound turned down.

Finding herself alone she noticed her hands were gripping the edge of her desk. Hanging on in there. Laying them flat on the cool glass surface she stretched them out starfish wide. She wasn't wearing Will's ring. Unable to face the inevitable questions from the girls in the office she'd threaded it onto the silver necklace she always wore underneath her clothes.

She stared at the space it had left behind. Thinking about the space Will had left behind. Wondering where he was, who he was with, what he was doing, what he was thinking. It had been three days and nothing. No phone call. Text message. Email. Just one big aching emptiness. An involuntary sob rose from her throat, loud against the silence of the deserted office, and sinking into her chair Juliet curled herself into a ball, buried her face in her chest. And cried. She cried for a hell of a long time.

A few miles away on a quiet West London canal were moored a dozen barges of different sizes and colours, some new and glossy, others looking slightly more weathered. One in particular stood out. Painted an unusual shade of lilac, it had a white roof on which were hand-decorated watering cans and long black plant pots crammed with brightly coloured winter pansies. Along one side in curly white lettering was the name, *Lavender Mermaid*.

Inside three people were sitting around a wooden table, drinking herbal tea and talking. Actually one was talking, the other two were listening. And had been for the last three days. 'I don't know what to do.' Stubbing out his roll-up, Will drained this third cup of rosehip tea under the watchful eye of his hosts and Samaritans, Rolf and Amber.

'Why don't you call her?' Leaning across the table Amber gave his shoulder a supportive rub. Putting his cup down on the polished surface, Will stared into the bottom of it. 'I can't . . . it's not that easy.' Just as this wasn't. Sitting here with his best friend and his wife, talking about his innermost feelings. But it was easier than trying to deal with it by himself. He'd tried for those first few hours on Saturday morning. Aimlessly driving around in the car with the radio turned up so loud it was all static and crashing bass. He'd been trying to block out the noise in his head, but it had been impossible. It had been deafening. Defeating.

At the canal he'd woken up Rolf and Amber and they'd appeared from their bunker, bleary-eyed and yawning. Then Amber had remembered shopping for an engagement ring and immediately jumped to the wrong conclusion as to why they were being dragged out of bed first thing in the morning, especially when she was on her most fertile period. Before he'd had a chance to explain she'd begun shrieking excitedly and it was only when she'd finally tired of hugging him in her Winnie the Pooh pyjamas, and Rolf had ceased jovially welcoming him to the henpecked husbands club and thumping him on the back in blokeish camaraderie, that Will had heard the sound of someone sobbing. And realized it was himself.

Rolf stretched back in his chair and folded his chubby arms. 'Why not? Juliet's called you. You said yourself she'd left half a dozen messages.' He caught Amber's eye across the table. She was urging him on. 'You two need to talk.'

'Perhaps if you'd done more of that in the first place,' murmured Amber to herself. Despite hearing Will's version of events, she still had loyalty to her sisterhood. She might not agree with what Juliet had done, but that didn't mean she couldn't understand why. Amber glanced at Rolf, who was using the torn corner of an envelope to free something stuck in his molar. She'd be lying if she said she'd never been tempted. She stood up. 'Why don't I make us some more tea.'

'Have you got anything stronger?' Will needed a drink. And he wasn't talking rosehip tea. Amber smiled apologetically. 'We're off alcohol at the moment, doctor's orders,' she explained, and then caught Will's expression and changed her mind. Sod it, there were always exceptions to the rule and this poor guy was one of them. 'I've got an old bottle of tequila if you're interested.'

Rolf's face morphed into that of a goldfish. *An old bottle of tequila?* Since when had Amber drunk tequila? And with whom? Paranoid questions began racing through his mind but Will interrupted.

'Tequila's good.'

Smiling, Amber disappeared into the pantry at the far end of the barge. Both men watched her until, making sure she was out of earshot, Rolf leaned towards Will. 'If it's any consolation, if Amber had slept with another bloke I'd feel exactly like you do.' Rolf had been taken aback to hear of Juliet's affair. It had really shaken him up and for the last few days he'd been extra-specially attentive to Amber, showing an interest in her new book on reflexology, listening to her new rebirthing CD, enthusing about his detox diet – and not cheating once. He'd even given away his secret stash of fags to the homeless bloke that lived on the corner.

'I just can't stop thinking of them together.' Will's jaw clenched tightly as he remembered the photograph of Juliet. The image was seared on his mind like a third-degree burn. With time it might fade but it would always leave a scar.

Rolf sighed. 'Well you've got to.'

Will shook his head in frustration. 'Christ, I feel like such a fucking idiot.'

'That's just hurt pride, mate,' consoled Rolf. 'I know it must be hard, but you've got to stop thinking like that. It's not going to get you anywhere.' He paused for a moment, deep in thought. 'And to think I gave that bastard some bloody lovely bedding plants,' he muttered, his eyes flashing furiously. 'Maybe we should jump him one night. I've still got a set of keys. We could wait till he comes home, rough him up a bit.'

A faint smile broke on Will's lips as his old humour surfaced. 'What with? Your Piaggio helmet? My spirit level? A couple of bags of potting compost?' He shook his head. 'Don't get me wrong, I could kill the bastard. And don't think I haven't thought about going round there, having it out with him, but for what? It was Juliet who cheated on me, not him,' he added sadly. Heaving a deep, cavernous sigh he stretched out his hunched frame. 'And anyway, I've never had a fight in my life. I'm not going to start now.'

'Hear, hear,' agreed Amber reappearing with the tequila. Swatting Rolf, she rested the chunky bottle on the table and began unscrewing the lid. Rolf couldn't help noticing it was already half empty. 'Honestly, what are you thinking of?' she gasped, opening a cupboard and producing three shot glasses. Rolf felt his brows knit together tightly. Where the hell had those just come from? Amber poured an amber glug into each shot glass, deftly cut up a lime and put a tub of sea salt on the table. Rolf watched. Either his wife had been a bartender in another life, or one of her hobbies was tequila slamming. *When he wasn't there*. She began handing around the glasses. 'Though I've got to admit, a duel is kind of romantic . . .'

'Don't you start all that romantic crap,' growled Will with such ferocity he caused Amber to jump back, startled, her hennaed curls springing. Seeing her expression, he sighed brokenly. 'Oh shit, Amber, I'm sorry, I didn't mean to . . .'

'It's OK, don't worry . . .' she smiled reassuringly, patting his arm and giving him a shot glass and a piece of lime.

'Just remember it's about what you want,' Rolf reminded Will, sipping his tequila as if it was the finest malt whisky. He was going to savour every drop. Having been on carrot juice, water and tea for the last three days he wasn't going to knock it straight back. Like Amber was doing, he noticed. And with the kind of wrist action that didn't belong to a novice. He looked back at Will. 'What do *you* want?'

Swallowing the tequila in one gulp, Will ran his teeth over his bottom lip. It tasted bitter. He sighed, running his fingers through his messy blond hair, pressing his fingernails hard against his scalp. His head ached, his whole body ached. He was engulfed in a blanket of despair, hurt, and the suffocating exhaustion that came with night after night of no sleep. Grabbing the tequila bottle he poured himself another shot.

'I want to get completely fucking blotto.'

Chapter Forty-four

Hurrying down the pavement, Juliet paused nervously to check her reflection in the wing mirror of an old Datsun parked at the side of the road. It looked fine, exactly the same as when she'd checked it in the darkened windows of the tube on the journey from Trudy's, a motorcycle's side mirror around the corner, the gilt-framed mirrors in the parade of antique shops further down the street.

It was Sunday afternoon and she was on her way to meet Will. He'd called. Finally. *Thankfully*. It had taken eight whole tortuous days but at ten o'clock that morning her mobile had started ringing and she'd known it was him. She didn't even have to look at the illuminated screen, or hear his voice, she'd just known. The relief had been overwhelming. The conversation had been brief and perfunctory: he'd asked her if she was free to meet for a coffee at their old haunt. Juliet had taken that as a good sign. Will couldn't hate her so much if he wanted to meet at a place that was so full of memories, surely? Maybe he'd changed his mind? Maybe, just maybe, he wanted to give it another go, to get back together?

Juliet had just lived through the worst eight days of her whole life. The weekdays had been bad enough, but the weekends were even worse. Only that morning she'd woken from another fitful sleep of dreaming everything was how it used to be, only to find herself wrapped up in a sleeping bag on Trudy's sofa. *Alone*.

The loneliness was crushing. Sunday mornings had always been about her and Will. Waking up together, her making coffee while he went to buy the papers, getting back into bed and sitting propped up against pillows, sipping coffee and eating croissants. She'd always taken it for granted. It was just something they did. Will used to joke that they were like an old married couple as they cuddled up together, her grumbling at him for scattering crumbs, dripping coffee and papier-mâchéing the duvet with scrunched-up pages, him laughing sheepishly and trying to get round her by telling her how gorgeous she was first thing in the morning.

Last week on the heath Trudy had said a lot of things that Juliet didn't want to hear. But after having time to think about it, Juliet had had to admit her friend had spoken a lot of truth. Things between her and Will hadn't been perfect. Far from it. They hadn't inhabited a rose-tinted world. There'd been rows and sulks and resentments, and for a long time she'd felt taken for granted. But it was only now Will was gone that Juliet realized just how much *she'd* taken for granted. How much she'd got it wrong.

It wasn't just the big romantic gestures that made a relationship, it was all the little things. Will giving her a random smile for no reason, a shared look that didn't need any explanation, putting his feet on her ice-cold ones to warm them up in bed. It was about him saving her all the olives off his pizza because he knew they were her favourite, pretending he couldn't see the huge red spot that had erupted on her chin in the night, not saying anything but giving her an unconditional hug when she was premenstrual and being a complete bitch. Small things. Important things. The truly romantic things. Yet the only small thing she had left now was the voice in her head whispering *Too late, Too late, Too late*.

At eleven Trudy had left the flat saying she was

going to try a new yoga class Magnus had invited her to as it was great for pregnant women. Think Madonna. Think Liz Hurley. Think pelvic floor muscles. Juliet hadn't believed her. Pregnant or not, Trudy hated yoga. And since when had she and Magnus become birthing buddies? No doubt it was just an excuse to escape from the depressing person who had lain mutely on the sofa since she'd got home from work on Friday night, surviving on nicotine and caffeine, allowing the TV to wash over her like an anaesthetic. Juliet hadn't blamed her. She'd wished she could get away from the depressing person too. Leave herself behind on the sofa to smoke herself to death.

And then, out of the blue, Will had called and asked if she'd meet him. She'd said yes immediately. But then she would have said yes if he'd suggested the North Pole. It had got her off the sofa, that was for sure. And in the shower. And in a mad panic as she'd tried on every item of clothing she had, and some of Trudy's, before deciding on an old pair of Levi's, her trainers and a toffee-coloured cashmere jumper Will had bought as a present for her when they'd first met. She didn't want to look as if she was trying really hard, but she was. Really, really hard.

Juliet knew it was pathetic. In the past Will had seen her in no make-up and her scraggy old pyjamas, he'd seen her lying in bed with flu with a Rudolph nose and a hot water bottle, he'd even seen her butt naked, pissed and on all fours, throwing up in the loo. It hadn't stopped him loving her. But neither had it stopped her from spending ages on her make-up, doing her hair the way he liked it, wearing his favourite perfume. Or from hoping, as she'd undone her necklace and carefully slipped the delicate gold ring onto her finger.

Reaching the café, Juliet paused momentarily to try and get herself together. She felt ridiculously nervous.

Taking a few gulps of damp air she stared at the outside. It looked different. Tatty and scruffy. The cracked paint on the door, the smears on the window, the name that had obviously been painted by a sign-writer with a bad case of the DTs. She looked at the shaky lettering. It was funny how when she'd been with Will she'd never noticed that before.

Pushing open the door, she stepped inside. She was early. Unbelievably, so was Will. He'd been there for the last fifteen minutes, hogging a whole table, never taking his eyes off the entrance as customers came and went. Even so, he was unprepared to see Juliet. Watching her walking through the door Will felt a lump in his throat. For some reason he'd been expecting her to look different but she looked just as she always did. Beautiful. Not that he noticed what clothes she was wearing or if she was wearing make-up, or even if she'd washed her hair. She was Jules. That was enough.

Juliet saw Will waiting for her. The effect was instantaneous. Deep breaths, deep breaths, deep breaths, she told herself as she began making her way towards him. It was surreal. Seeing him in such familiar surroundings she could almost convince herself that it had all been just a bad dream. For those few moments that it took to walk across the crowded café she could fool herself into believing that when she reached the other side Will would smile and kiss her and they would drink coffee, read the papers, chat about nothing in particular.

But it hadn't been a bad dream, it was real, and instead Will stood up self-consciously. She smiled awkwardly. So did he.

It was a start.

Juliet sat down and looked at Will. He looked terrible. She felt a stab of guilt. 'It's good to see you, Will,' she greeted him quietly.

Averting his eyes he sort of nodded his head, but didn't answer.

She tried again. 'How are you?'

He looked up. 'I've been better,' he replied acerbically. Not very adult, but he couldn't help it. How did Juliet expect him to be? Happy? Fine? Having a good time?

Juliet began chewing off her lipstick. This was even harder than she'd expected. She watched as he began fiddling with a sugar packet. Tearing it into little tiny pieces so the brown granules spilled out onto the table.

He sighed. 'Look I called you because I wanted to tell you to your face.'

His words kicked her hard and flat in the stomach. She fought with her voice to keep it low and steady. 'Tell me what?' she asked, looking him bravely in the eye.

Will met her gaze. And held it. 'I want you to move all your stuff out of the flat . . .' his voice tailed off. After some serious soul-searching he'd finally made up his mind but saying it was so fucking hard. 'Look, there's no point dragging it out. We might as well make a clean break. It's over.'

It's over. Juliet repeated the words in her head. They were the same words she'd said to Sykes. She wondered how many people had heard those words. Millions probably. As her mind tried to run away and hide, a tear burst free, splashing onto her hands like a drop of rain. She looked at Will. 'Just like that?'

He reacted angrily. 'No it's not *just like that.*' Will was bitter. Juliet didn't have a clue what he'd been going through. He glared at her. 'Don't turn this around. I wasn't the one who was unfaithful.'

Juliet couldn't speak. She didn't want to speak. There was nothing to say.

Her silence goaded him. 'Just tell me one thing, Juliet. *Why him?*' He'd vowed to himself he wouldn't ask. He didn't want to know. He didn't want to fill in the details, to give his imagination anything else to feed upon. But now, looking at Juliet, he couldn't help himself.

Juliet just shook her head wearily. 'I don't want to talk about him.' She didn't want to tell Will about Sykes. There was no point. It would only hurt him. It would only hurt her.

But Will was detemined. 'Why not, Juliet? *You shagged him.*' His hurt was loud, causing the people in the café to look up from the papers and lazy Sunday afternoon conversations to glance at the couple in the corner.

As they did, Juliet felt an unexpected blast of anger. Who the hell did Will think he was? She was sorry but she wasn't a slag. And she wasn't going to just sit there and let him speak to her as if she was one. 'OK, Will, if you want to know, I'll tell you why. But first you tell me why you stood me up on Valentine's Day.'

'Christ, is this what it's all about?'

'No, it's not just about that night,' she snapped, cutting him dead. OK so she'd made one hell of a big mistake, but he wasn't without fault. Far from it. 'Or the night of the ball, or all the nights you fell asleep on the sofa, or the weekends I didn't see you because you were working. It's not about how detached you were, how you used to ignore me and take me for granted.' Her voice shook, but now she'd started she wasn't going to stop. This had been building for a long time. 'The rut was so big you didn't even notice I was there half the time, I was just your flatmate, the person who tidied up around you, who changed the sheets you slept in, washed the towels you dried yourself on, washed the plates you ate from. Who picked your fucking dirty underpants off the bathroom floor every bloody night.'

Shocked by the outburst, Will had gone pale. 'You weren't so perfect, believe me,' he lashed out. 'What happened to the girl who used to be a laugh? Who didn't obsess about car accounts and promotions and her career? Who lived for going out on a Friday night and getting drunk on vodka and cranberrys and who wouldn't have given a shit about some stupid work's ball?'

'She grew up, Will.'

There was a heavy pause.

Juliet's voice softened. 'Look, I'm not trying to make excuses, I'm just trying to make you understand . . .' She hesitated. Oh what the hell. 'Sykes made me feel special. He made me feel sexy and exciting, and alive.'

'Oh Christ, spare me the cliché,' Will spat scornfully.

'No, you asked, so I'm going to tell you.' She was determined. 'I wish to God it had never happened, that I could turn the clock back and make it all go away, but I can't. It has happened. And you can think it's a cliché, and it probably was, but that didn't stop it from feeling exciting and romantic and fun.' There. She'd said it. At least now he knew.

'If it was so much fun why did you finish it? Or don't tell me, he finished with you.' Will smiled cruelly. There was no comfort in his words but he wanted to try and hurt her any way he could.

Juliet didn't retaliate. 'I finished it because I realized how much I loved you.' She looked down at her hands, at the ring that glowed softly on her finger. 'I realized how much I was in love with you. How much I am in love with you,' she murmured softly.

'Wasn't that a bit late?' Will's scorn was an impenetrable shield around his heart.

'Love's not about perfect timing.'

As she spoke she looked up and met his eyes and it was as if the war was finally over. Nobody had won, but the rawness and anger and hurt had gone and all that was left was a weary sadness. Turning away, Will sighed. 'I had no idea. I think that's why it hit so hard . . .' He spoke as if he was thinking aloud. 'I didn't see it coming.'

'You weren't looking,' murmured Juliet to herself.

* * *

Neither of them was aware of how long they remained sitting silently together at that table, until they were interrupted by a couple hovering behind them with coffees wanting to know if they were leaving. Juliet could have quite happily murdered them, but Will only nodded and told them they'd be a few minutes.

A few minutes. Is that all they had left? thought Juliet sadly. She looked across at the man in the big black jumper and the messy blond hair, and the bit he'd missed shaving, trying to memorize every little detail as he moved from her future into part of her past. She wanted to always remember. 'Can't you forgive me?' she asked quietly.

He shook his head. 'Who am I, some kind of God? All I have to do is forgive you and everything's OK again? That's just bollocks.' Will stared into the pale brown irises of Juliet's eyes, but the anger had gone. Only sadness remained like a stain. 'Of course I forgive you, Jules.' His voice broke as he called her Jules. He hadn't done since that night. 'I'd forgive you *anything*.'

A flicker of hope.

'I just can't forget.'

Snuffed out.

Juliet watched as he began wriggling his arms into his coat, checking to make sure he had his mobile, putting his wallet in his pocket. As he did, it struck him that neither of them had bought coffee. 'Look, I'm going to go and stay with my parents this weekend. I thought it would probably be easier if I'm not around when you move your stuff out.'

She nodded. God, the awful practicalities.

'And then if you just put the keys through the letterbox . . .'

'Yeah, sure.' He'd obviously thought of everything.

Except he hadn't.

Closing her fingertips around the ring she slipped it off her finger and held it out to him. She didn't say anything. If she did she was afraid she might start crying again.

'Is that what happens in cases like this?' Will didn't take it from her. Instead he hid his hands away in his pockets.

Is that what they were now? A case? It sounded so cold and clinical. Juliet shrugged. 'I don't know.'

He shook his head sadly. 'I don't want the ring back. It's yours. I chose it for you.' Will's mind flicked back to that day with Amber, finding the little antique shop, his joy and happiness as he'd discovered the ring tucked in the far corner underneath the glass counter. The warm glow inside as he'd known instantly it was the one. 'You can do what you want with it, throw it away, sell it, I don't care.' He shook his head. 'It's probably worthless anyway, it came out of a cracker, remember?' Smiling weakly he stood up. If he didn't he was afraid he might never leave.

'Goodbye, Juliet.'

She remained seated as he walked across the café, weaving through the tables, the throngs of people closing up behind him as with each step he moved further and further away. Picking up the ring from the coffee-stained Formica table she curled her fingers over the delicate gold band. A perfect circle. And holding it tightly in the palm of her hand Juliet watched as Will disappeared.

Just. Like. That.

Chapter Forty-five

In a small back garden in West London, a big furry bumble bee was performing a brilliant acrobatics display, swooping and diving over a carpet of purple clematis, cascading honeysuckle and flower-filled terracotta plant pots. Fastening his silver cufflinks, Will leaned out of his open sash window to watch it buzzing happily in the hot August sunshine, marvelling as it trampolined from one marigold to another.

Lost in his daydreams, Will could have happily stayed there for hours but today was one day he couldn't afford to be late, so reluctantly turning away he began straightening his waistcoat, pulling on the dove grey jacket of his morning suit, checking his reflection in the wardrobe mirror. Not bad, although he did say it himself. Except . . . Looking outside, his eye fell on a cluster of bright purple flowers on the windowledge and leaning out he picked one. So much better than that boring old carnation, he mused, removing his buttonhole and replacing it with the single flower. Now he was ready.

Until now Will had been remarkably calm, but at the thought of what lay ahead of him he was suddenly engulfed in a whirling pit of nerves. He glanced at his watch. And freaked. Shit, where the hell did the time go? Grabbing his top hat, not forgetting his tobacco and Rizlas, he ran, coat-tails flapping, into the hallway and yanked open the front door. It wouldn't do to stand up the bride, now, would it?

* * *

Wearing a delicate jade green dress that showed off her golden tan, Juliet stepped barefoot onto a small wrought iron balcony. The sunshine felt warm on her skin and hair, still damp from the shower. Stretching out like a cat, she smiled to herself. What a perfect day. Closing her eyes, she lifted her face to the freshly laundered blue sky and breathed in a delicious lungful of summer air. What a perfect day to be getting married.

She'd just returned from two weeks in Rome filming the MAXI sportscar commercial. After a fortnight of extensive reshooting, entertaining clients and refereeing explosive arguments between the fiery-tempered Italian crew, her creative team and the Britpack actors, they'd finally wrapped and she was feeling exhausted but happy. A whole world happier than she'd felt on that cold Sunday afternoon when she'd sat at that small plastic insignificant-looking table and silently watched Will walk out of her life.

It was five months ago now, but Juliet could still remember it as if it was yesterday. Could never forget how she'd felt packing her life into cardboard boxes, shutting the front door for the last time, tearfully saying goodbye to Violet who'd stood on her doorstep, shaking her head sadly, a finger of ash hanging from her cigarette. But slowly and gradually, bit by bit, day by day, week by week she'd put herself back together again.

The sound of a car alarm in the street below roused Juliet from her thoughts, and she stepped back inside. After the brightness, the living room was dark and she paused for a moment, trying to focus on her surroundings. She'd got her own place now. Trudy had generously offered her the sofa for as long as she'd wanted, but after a couple of weeks of waking up every morning surrounded by the chaos of takeout cartons, laundry, washing-up and more stilettos than Harrods' shoe hall, she'd saved their friendship and her sanity by signing a lease on a flat. It wasn't luxurious by any means, it was in a grotty part of Hammersmith, poky and astronomically expensive. But it had one saving grace. A gorgeous little balcony.

Juliet's balcony.

The irony had been the only thing to make Juliet smile during those first miserable weeks, sitting out there on her old corduroy beanbag until late at night, wrapped up in her sheepskin coat, drinking more wine than she knew was good for her. But it had been therapeutic. After everything that had happened she needed space, silence, sanctuary. To lick her wounds, sort her head out, *to get over it*. Four words. It sounded so simple.

If only.

Work had felt like a consolation prize. With Gabby now gone, she'd taken over her office, un-feng-shuiing it with the help of rolls of brightly coloured sari material Neesha had brought back from a family wedding in Delhi. Along with a new husband, Sanjeev, a musician who played sitar in a hugely successful bhangra band, much to the horror of her parents, who'd been praying she'd meet and fall in love with one of the eligible guests, a nice lawyer or doctor perhaps. And not the wedding singer.

Neesha wasn't the only one with a man in her life. Juliet had been at the hospital with Trudy when she'd had her twenty-week scan, both watching this grainy image swirling around on the TV screen as the nurse informed her she was expecting a little girl. Until the 'little girl' had suddenly proved them wrong by proudly waving a tiny willy around. 'Men and their penises,' Trudy had grinned, and immediately named her son Jimmy, after Choo.

'Well it could have been Manolo,' she'd later remarked to Magnus as the three of them had perched on stools at a sushi restaurant, grabbing plates of food from a conveyor belt and ogling the fuzzy ultrasound print-out.

'Or Birkenstock,' he'd guffawed into his sashimi.

'Honey, take it from me, it could never have been Birkenstock,' she'd drawled in a *faux* Southern accent, lifting a fishnet leg to show off her five-inch spike-heeled boots from Prada. Pregnant or not, Trudy did not *do* sensible footwear. She did, however, *do* Magnus, who'd become a firm friend after hearing about her soon-to-be single mum status, taking her out for dinner, converting her to yoga, buying her lots of presents – the last one being a pot of organic hemp cream that prevented stretchmarks. Of course it was all terribly platonic. Of course Magnus was desperately in love.

It had been that same night Juliet had bumped into Sykes. Literally. She'd been leaving the restaurant, he'd been arriving with a group of friends and they'd collided. It had been weird. Dressed in jeans and a black shirt that was unbuttoned to reveal the bare olive skin in the hollow of his throat, he'd looked as gorgeous as ever. They'd exchanged a couple of awkward hellos, a bit of gossip – he was commuting between Verona and London, Gabby had left her husband for the MD, no he wasn't back with Gina.

'And how are things with you? Did you ever find your Romeo?' he'd smirked.

'Yeah,' she'd quipped. 'And then I lost him.'

Her flippancy had been a cover. Juliet might have put her life back together, but that didn't mean there wasn't still a gaping hole where Will had been. She'd just become used to walking around the edge and not falling down it any more.

Deftly slipping his hand around her waist, Sykes had kissed her goodbye on the cheek. 'Well, if you ever need any company, you've got my numbers,' he'd murmured in her ear, before joining his friends inside.

Juliet had felt nothing. For a few seconds she'd watched him walk across the restaurant, sit down next to the prettiest blonde, and slip his hand onto her knee. Before turning away. There wasn't just the one conveyor belt in that restaurant.

Her hair was dry now. Fastening a scattering of diamanté clips into the messy waves, she wriggled her glittery toes into a pair of strappy sandals and pulled on a tiny embroidered jacket. As she did she noticed the palms of her hands were sweating. It was nerves, not the heat. Late last night she'd got back from the airport to find a handwritten envelope on her doormat. It had been redirected all over London, and opening it she'd pulled out a small white card embossed with gold lettering. It was a wedding invitation.

Deep inside she'd felt a pang of regret. Heard a murmur of 'what if?' But blocking them out, she'd slowly opened the card, curiously smoothing back the gold cord and transparent paper inside to read, *Errol William Bartholomew and Violet Edna Crowther invite you to celebrate with them their marriage on the 25 August 2001*. Juliet's delight had been immediate – oh my God, Violet's found herself a real-life romantic hero – but it had been swiftly followed by panic. Oh my God, *Will*.

Juliet hadn't seen or heard from him since that day five months ago. So many times she'd picked up the phone, but had never been brave enough, *or drunk enough*, to dial his number. And then on 12 June – she could remember the date exactly – Trudy had gently informed her that she'd seen Will. 'Where? What did he look like? Who was he with?' Demanding the truth, she'd got it. He'd been jogging through Holland Park, he'd been wearing a dinky pair of shorts, and he'd been with a blonde. Jogging? A dinky pair of shorts? Juliet would have laughed if she hadn't been so gutted. *A blonde*. From that moment onwards she'd never picked up the phone again. They were over. And they weren't getting back together. She had to get on with her life, just as Will had.

Outside the church, crowds of guests were gathering. Drunk on sunshine and giddy with wedding fever, they were basking in the 80-degree heat, squeezing in a last few minutes before they entered the cool shade of St Stephen's. As was traditional, all the women had gone completely over the top. Using the excuse of the wedding to shun their normal workday attire, they'd dived head first into the girly dressing-up box, gaily pulling out hats of all shapes and sizes, strings of pearls, white gloves, God knows how many sequined handbags from Accessorize, and enough lilac two-pieces to stretch cuff to cuff around Greater London.

But the fun didn't stop there. After kitting themselves out as latter-day New Romantics, they were taking even more delight in telling each other where they'd found each and every item they were wearing, how much it cost, and whether or not it could be washed at 40 degrees. Conversely, the men had embraced an old-fashioned masculinity, shuffling around awkwardly in Dickensian-style morning suits, cravats, top hats and anything that was a shade of grey, pressed and formal, and were quickly forming little packs where they hung about smoking cigarettes and telling each other mother-in-law jokes.

Standing on the edges searching the crowds, Juliet finally spotted a heavily pregnant blonde in an antique silk dress the colour of raspberries, a feather boa, and a pair of stilettos held on by two wires that wound up around her calves like corkscrews. Fortunately, unlike most, this pregnant woman wasn't suffering from water retention. Which meant that instead of her legs looking like two flumps, they just looked fantastic.

It could only be Trudy.

'You look great,' gasped Juliet, walking over to her.

Trudy pulled a face. 'I look like Vanessa Feltz,' she grumbled, fiddling with her new highlights.

Juliet smiled and ignored her. She'd had to use all her powers of persuasion to convince Trudy to accompany her to Violet's wedding as her guest. Knowing Will would be invited she was desperate for moral support. All Trudy was desperate for was a size eight body. Although she loved the idea of being pregnant, this was a woman who decided on whether she was having a good day or a bad day depending whether or not she fitted into her Earl jeans. For the last five months Trudy had been having a lot of bad days.

'Do you wanna go inside and sit down, my legs are killing me,' she grumbled, wishing she'd opted for the Gina wedges.

'Yeah, sure,' replied Juliet, furtively scanning the mingling guests for any sign of Will. She caught sight of a couple that looked like Rolf and Amber. Actually, it *was* Rolf and Amber. Juliet was taken aback. They were barely recognizable. Rolf looked as if he'd lost ten stone, whereas Amber had piled it on. If she didn't know better she'd have thought she was pregnant.

Her eyes passed over them, flitting over faces, backs of heads, side profiles. If Rolf and Amber were here, Will had to be. They'd met Violet once or twice when Will had decided they should throw a couple of dinner parties at the flat, but they wouldn't have come to her wedding if Will wasn't going to be here. Would they? Fast losing hope, Juliet's eyes zigzagged across the churchyard. Will was still nowhere to be seen. She felt a mixture of relief and disappointment.

Holding her bump as if she was carrying a grocery bag, Trudy began making her way across the paving stones towards the entrance, but after only a couple of steps, her face contorted with pain. 'Ouch.'

'What's wrong?' Juliet felt a stab of worry as visions of waters breaking, ambulances, premature babies whizzed through her mind.

'Oh jeez, it's this new bikini wax I've just had done,' gasped Trudy. Being American she was obsessed with depilation. Shrieking she grabbed her crotch, as if she was a white, female, pregnant version of Michael Jackson. 'Forget Brazilian, this is the Tiffany.'

'A Tiffany?'

'Yeah, they shave it into a square, dye it blue, they even bleach in a little bow.' Trudy smiled as she leaned against a tree, her legs not-so-delicately splayed. 'Well, I thought I'd start getting myself prepared for the birth.'

'But it's not for a couple of months,' protested Juliet, perching next to her on a gatepost and taking the opportunity to have another look for Will.

'It's best to be prepared,' nodded Trudy sagely. Taking this opportunity to redo her make-up, she pulled out her new lipgloss and began smearing her lips with the wand applicator. 'Jimmy could decide to say hi at any time. And anyway – ' she continued, rubbing her lips together – 'how many men do you know who can say they came out of a Tiffany box?'

Cracking up with hoots of laughter, they were interrupted by a loud voice. 'Well, howdy-doody.' Turning around Juliet came face to paunch with a white caftan. It was Magnus, who'd just 'happened to be in the area'. A suspicious statement in itself, even without the fact that he was carrying a lavishly wrapped wedding present. Kissing Juliet on both cheeks he beamed at Trudy and slipped his arm protectively around her non-existent waist. 'Well isn't this wicked.'

Wicked wasn't the word Juliet would have chosen. Romantic, joyful, *nerve-wracking*. Most of the guests had gone inside now, but she still couldn't help surreptitiously glancing around for Will. But nothing. Obviously he wasn't coming. She felt relieved.

And disappointed.

'Oh look, here comes the bride,' hooted Magnus jovially, as a Silver Ghost Rolls-Royce glided around the corner. There was a collective sigh from the few people remaining outside. Violet's wedding fulfilled every romantic fantasy. Getting married again at eighty-three years old, being swept off her feet by a dark handsome stranger, proving that love can strike at any time. And Violet hadn't done things by halves. She'd wanted the whole fairytale, and she'd got it.

Juliet watched the car sailing down the street, its white satin ribbon fluttering. Just as her stomach did as the car pulled up in front of the church, the door opened and a man stepped out, squinting into the sunshine and self-consciously squashing his top hat onto his messy sandy blond hair.

Will.

Juliet was totally unprepared for her reaction. After five months she'd hoped her feelings would have dulled, faded, *changed* – but nothing had changed. Her whole body seemed to hold its breath for those few seconds it took for Will to hold out his hand and help the bride out of the car. She watched him smile and offer words of encouragement as Violet emerged in a cream satin jacket and tunic dress, a new pair of silver spectacles and her hair swept and sprayed into an elegant chignon. Holding a posy of African violets and Will's hand, she was every inch the blushing bride.

'How do I look, William?' Pausing for a moment by the bridal car, Violet anxiously began checking that her petticoat wasn't showing and patting her hairdo. Despite smoking two fags in the Roller and taking a swig from the chauffeur's hip flask, she was still a mass of nerves.

'Beautiful,' grinned Will, holding out his arm for her to cling onto. 'Errol's a lucky man.'

Giggling happily, Violet wrapped her bony fingers around his sleeve as she tottered gingerly in her new Hush Puppies.

'In fact, are you sure you don't fancy leaving him at the altar and running off with me instead?' winked

Will as they took their first fairy steps towards the church.

'You should be running off with Julie,' rebuked Violet, who'd been dismayed when she'd heard the news that they were breaking up. William had told her why, but to Violet, with a whole lifetime of living behind her, it seemed such a waste. To throw everything away over a silly mistake. 'And now's your chance. Look, she's over there.'

Taken aback, Will looked up, his eyes focusing on the entrance to the church, on the few guests lingering outside, some wearing sunglasses, others shielding their eyes from the sunshine. Trudy and some bloke in white who looked as if he was trying to outdo the bride, Rolf who, proudly showing off his new figure, had his arm around Amber who was proudly showing off her new pregnancy.

And Juliet.

'Go on, tell her you love her,' broke in Violet. 'I've seen you these past months William, and you've been a right miserable old so-and-so. Go on, swallow your pride, lad.'

But Will ignored her. Looking hastily away he tried to focus on getting Violet to the church, but it was impossible to concentrate. The image of Juliet was printed on his mind, in the same way as if he'd just looked at the sun. Long tendrils of messy hair falling over her bare tanned shoulders, her pale green dress fluttering in the breeze.

Violet's voice was providing the backing track: '. . . You've only got one life, lad, and it goes faster than you can imagine. If you love someone, whatever's happened, you can always work it out . . .'

He interrupted. 'Now, are we going to get you up this aisle or not?' he cajoled, forcing a smile.

Falling silent, Violet smiled sheepishly. 'I hope so,' she nodded, squeezing his arm tightly, before continuing, 'I know you think I'm a daft old bugger . . .'

Will opened his mouth to protest but she shushed him. She hadn't finished yet.

'But I want you to think on. Love's precious. It doesn't always happen twice, you know.' She looked serious for a moment, before melting into a rueful grin. 'I've just been a lucky bugger.'

Chapter Forty-six

There wasn't a dry eye during the service. Even Trudy, who swore vehemently that it was an allergic reaction to her new lash-lengthening mascara, broke out blubbing as Errol proudly kissed his new wife tenderly on the lips and the gospel choir, made up mostly from his family who'd flown over from southern Carolina, broke into a rendition of 'Oh Happy Day'.

Singing along, Juliet sniffed away her tears. It was a strange dichotomy. While it felt like the happiest day, it also felt like one of the saddest. Only a few feet away, sitting in the front pew, was Will. She couldn't take her eyes off him. Studying his grey-suited back, the shape of his shoulders, the tuft of hair at the crown of his head that would never lie flat. Continually forcing herself to look away. But when she wasn't concentrating her eyes kept wandering back to him. Wanting him to turn around. Wishing he'd turn around.

He didn't.

He never looked back. Not once.

'What kind of reception is it? A buffet or a sit-down do?' stage-whispered Magnus as they were filing out of the church. Ever hungry, his stomach had been making weird and wonderful noises throughout the entire ceremony.

'It's bangers and mash at the pub across the road,' answered Juliet, quoting the wedding invitation verbatim. Knowing Will was going to be there, she'd read it a dozen times. 'And snowballs all round.'

'Oh splendid.' Magnus's face lit up. Although he professed to be a teetotal, vegetarian Buddhist, he had been known to lapse. Most days.

Stepping out into the sunshine, Trudy glanced across at Juliet. By her pensive expression, it was pretty obvious that it didn't sound such a splendid idea to her. Trudy sighed. She knew what a rough few months Juliet had gone through, but recently she'd hoped she was getting back on her feet. Getting over it. Getting over Will. But then today, when Juliet hadn't known she was looking, she'd watched her gazing sadly at Will during the marriage vows and it had been pretty obvious she wasn't getting over anything. 'Are you gonna come, Jules?' Showing a rare moment of affection, she squeezed Juliet's hand supportively.

Smiling appreciatively, Juliet shook her head. 'No, I think I'll make a move.' She didn't want to risk bumping into Will at the reception, having to make awkward smalltalk.

'Are you sure? I mean if you don't fancy pub grub, perhaps we could all go for a pizza or something . . .' Magnus's voice tailed off as Trudy speared his big toe with her stiletto heel and gave him 'that look'. 'Though obviously if you'd rather be by yourself,' he added, attempting to make amends.

'I'm fine,' lied Juliet, forcing a grin. 'You both go ahead. Have a snowball for me.' Not wanting a fuss she quickly kissed them both goodbye and, leaving them standing on the steps, began to weave her way through the guests who were emerging from the church and converging by the entrance with cameras and confetti.

Escaping into the street Juliet paused for a moment and leaned against the wall that ran around the side of the churchyard. On a sweltering Saturday in August, London had deserted to the coast and instead of swarming with shoppers and tourists, the side street was quiet and empty. Checking that no-one was around, Juliet wriggled off her shoes. They might be lovely to look at but they were hell to walk in. She thought about Violet and her Hush Puppies. That had to be one good thing about getting old. Comfy shoes.

The pavement felt warm beneath the soles of her feet and, as Juliet began padding slowly along the kerb, she was reminded of her childhood. Playing silly games with the pavement as she walked home from school on a hot summer's day, her black plimsolls in her hands. Smiling as she remembered, she tried balancing along the edge of the kerb, holding out a shoe in each hand as if she was a trapeze artist. It seemed a lot harder than when she'd been eight years old, she thought to herself, wobbling precariously.

Juliet was so absorbed with concentrating on keeping her footing she barely noticed she was walking past the Silver Ghost Rolls-Royce and its red-faced chauffeur who'd zonked out on the back seat, or the gnarled, twisted old oak tree that had burst its way through the stone wall at the corner of the churchyard.

But she noticed the top hat.

Juliet paused to stare. It was lying upturned on the dusty pavement and, as she neared it, she could see its oyster white silk lining. She could even see the Moss Bros label. Curious, she continued walking towards it. Curving around the corner, her vision began to pan out, revealing more than just a top hat. There was a coat tail, a grey-suited arm, a hand, a cloud of cigarette smoke . . .

Will looked up.

Walking towards him was a woman wearing a pale green dress. Tanned and barefoot, she was staring at the pavement, her face hidden by waves of honey hair. Even so, he recognized her immediately. *Juliet.* His insides knotted sharply. Despite seeing her earlier outside the church, he was totally unprepared for his flood of feelings. He dragged hard on his baggy roll-up, trying to prepare himself for their inevitable meeting.

He had a few seconds. Juliet hadn't yet seen him and for a brief moment he watched her. Until, with the smallest movement, her head tilted upwards and, shielding her eyes from the bright sunshine, she stared straight at him.

Nothing could have prepared him. He stared back and before straightening up he gave an awkward wave, although they were standing only feet apart. 'Hi.'

Taken by surprise, Juliet froze. After all this time Will was standing there, *right in front of her*. For an instant she was almost tempted to reach out and touch him, to check if he was real. To make sure this was really happening. Instead she concentrated on struggling to regain her composure. Breathe. Swallow. Smile. 'Hi.'

Stuffing his hands into his pockets, Will looked self-conscious as he grappled around for the right thing to say. Was there a right thing to say? Looking at Juliet his mind went blank and he heard himself dumbly asking, 'How are you?' He groaned inwardly. Talk about inspired.

'Fine.' Juliet nodded nervously. After everything that had happened between them, the banality of the conversation was surreal. 'You look well.' She played along, fearful that if she didn't she'd break down, say something stupid, inappropriate. Tell him how she really felt.

Will smiled ruefully, patting his perfectly flat waistcoated stomach. 'It's my new trainer, Trisha. Makes me run around in the park, throws sticks for me, that kind of thing.' He laughed nervously, wondering what on earth had possessed him to start telling terrible jokes.

Juliet watched him, her mind slowly digesting the information. He had a trainer? She was a woman?

Called Trisha? 'Is she blond?' she asked before she could stop herself.

Her question caught Will by surprise. 'Er, yeah . . . she is, actually. Why? Do you know her?'

Juliet felt a ridiculous rush of relief. 'No, no I don't,' she smiled, shaking her head.

'Oh . . . right.' Will was puzzled. Never had he seen anyone look so pleased not to know somebody.

Juliet fiddled nervously with strands of her hair. She'd imagined this scenario a thousand times in her head, running through what she'd say while in the bath, on the tube, lying in her bed. Now it was for real, she couldn't remember a single one of those cool one-liners she'd rehearsed.

A space opened up. One of those yawning pauses when nobody speaks. A moment when it isn't easy to tell if conversation is over. Juliet assumed it was, and was about to say goodbye, walk away and spare them both any more awkward embarrassment when Will spoke quietly.

'You look great.'

Her stomach flipped. She caught herself quickly. He was just being polite. 'Oh this old thing,' she shrugged nonchalantly. This old thing being something she'd paid a fortune for in Rome 24 hours ago.

'You look beautiful in that old thing.'

The ache deep inside Juliet swelled. 'Oh . . . thanks,' she smiled unsurely.

Will immediately regretted the compliment. It was obviously the wrong thing to say. Too personal. He tried making amends by talking about work. 'I heard you got the MAXI account.'

She nodded. 'Yeah, we just shot the commercial in Rome.'

'That's great.' He tried to look suitably enthusiastic. 'It's what you really wanted, isn't it?'

No, you're what I always wanted, she thought sadly, desperately wanting to say it out loud. But she didn't.

She didn't say anything as she gazed at Will. He might have lost a few pounds but he still looked the same. Same blue eyes with flecks of grey around the edges, messy sandy blond hair that needed cutting, small chickenpox scar on his right cheek. Oh God, Juliet, why are you doing this to yourself. Just go. Make your excuses and go. Don't make it worse than it already is.

Except she couldn't. Painful or not, she couldn't leave. Not yet.

In the distance she could hear the whoops of delight and glancing behind her she saw a crowd of brightly dressed people milling around outside the church, taking photographs of the happy couple. *The happy couple*. The irony stung.

'What happened to us, Jules?'

Will's voice read her thoughts. Or were they his thoughts too? Turning, she saw he was gazing sadly at her. Finally, the polite pretence was over.

'I fucked up,' she replied simply. 'I believed the hype.'

He shook his head in disagreement. 'No, I fucked up.' Averting his eyes, he sighed. It was the sigh of a man who'd thought about this every single day for five months. It felt like for ever before he eventually looked up. Meeting her gaze he spoke, his voice almost inaudible against the sound of the distant traffic. 'I never stopped joking around long enough to realize you weren't laughing any more.'

Brushing a strand of hair behind her ear, Juliet smiled regretfully. 'Neither were you.'

He acquiesced. 'Do you think we can ever go back to what we were?'

Juliet hesitated. For so long that's all she'd wanted to hear Will say, believed that's all she wanted, but now, unexpectedly, she knew that wasn't what she wanted at all. She shook her head decisively. 'I don't want to go back.'

And she meant it.

It wasn't about the past any more. It was about the future. Their future. She didn't want to go back, she wanted to go forwards. *She wanted to go forwards with Will*. Anxiously she waited for him to say something. Willing him to say something.

But he didn't utter a single word.

His silence said it all. 'Goodbye, Will.' Her smile was resigned and, putting on her sunglasses to hide the tears she could feel beginning to well up, she turned and began walking away. One foot in front of the other. The bare soles of her feet making not the slightest sound on the pavement.

A peal of church bells began chiming as standing there, alone in the middle of the pavement, Will watched Juliet leave. Noticing how the sun was shining through her dress, making the material almost transparent. Tracing the silhouette of her body with his eyes. Thinking about the way her hair rippled when she walked, the way those little jewels in her hair sparkled, the way he knew that if he let her walk away from him now he would regret it for the rest of his life.

'Where are you going?'

Juliet stopped walking. Standing motionless while inside she felt as if she was one of those kites on Hampstead Heath. Soaring, swooping, fluttering. Struggling to remain calm, she turned to face him. 'It's such a lovely day I was thinking of escaping down to the coast,' she gabbled nervously, '. . . going for a walk by the sea . . . finding some little B&B somewhere . . .'

'Do you want any company?'

They gazed at each other. It said more than any words.

'Are you any good at directions?' Juliet eyed him challengingly.

Puzzled, he wrinkled up his forehead. 'Me? Directions? Oh, I'm the best,' he nodded, watching as she began fishing around in her tiny shimmery bag. Pulling out a set of keys she pressed the black keyring. The shiny red convertible across the street flashed its lights.

'Is that . . . ?' Will's voice tailed off in amazement.

'The new MAXI?' answered Juliet, padding quickly over the hot tarmac and pulling open the car door. 'Yep.' Looking back she laughed at Will's expression, which had moved from amazement to shocked delight. 'A present from the clients.'

Throwing her high heels onto the back seat she jumped into the soft cream leather interior, leaned across the passenger seat and released the lock. The car door swung wide open.

Momentarily Will stared at it, then scooping up his top hat, he half ran, half jogged across the street and climbed in next to her.

Juliet turned the key in the ignition. As the engine growled into life she put the car into automatic drive and deftly pulled out of the parking space. Ahead of them was the small sandstone church, and as they slowed down by the entrance they were engulfed in loud cheers as Errol and Violet's very last wedding photograph was taken. A photograph that would later be carefully glued into a white and gold embossed album, shrouded by tracing paper, and would capture the utter delight of the bride's smile. The girlish laughter on her face as she threw her posy of African violets into the air, and the startled expression of one of the guests, a pregnant American in a raspberry silk dress who flung out her arms as if she was in a baseball match and caught it.

People were throwing confetti and out of nowhere a gust of wind caught those tiny paper petals and blew them towards the red sportscar, enveloping the two passengers in a flurry of tiny coloured snowflakes. Juliet looked up. Watching it swirling around their heads, she felt as if she was in one of those snowglobes. Driving off into the sunset . . .

Suddenly aware she was getting carried away,

she stopped herself and glanced across at Will. He was gazing down at her hand, at the ruby glowing softly in its gold band, and without saying a word he gently, lovingly, completely interlaced his fingers through hers.

'Which way?' she asked quietly.

He looked up at her, a king-sized grin breaking onto his face. 'Forwards.'

For a moment they just gazed at each other, Will and Jules, before, staring straight ahead, Juliet slammed her foot down. And, as they accelerated away from the church, into their future, she was hit by a surge of exhilaration, hope, *happy ever after*.

And smiling to herself, she surrendered to it.

What the hell, once a romantic, always a romantic.

THE END